D0403249

Murder
TAKE TWO

Murder
TAKE TWO

Charlene Weir

St. Martin's Press
New York

Library of Congress Cataloging-in-Publication Data

Weir, Charlene.
    Murder take two/Charlene Weir.—1st ed.
        p.   cm.
    "A Thomas Dunne book."
    ISBN 0-312-18136-1
    I. Title.
PS3573.E39744M8   1998
813'.54—dc21   97-40421
                                                                CIP

First edition

10   9   8   7   6   5   4   3   2   1

Heartfelt thanks to Jane Paul for reading the manuscript; to my daughter, Leslie Weir, without whose help, etc., and who went above and beyond; to Leila Laurence Dobscha for many things (in all my books—it's about time I thanked her), including the color of the carpet; to Kullikki Kay Steen, MD, for medical advice; and to Detective David Pires of the Daly City, California Police Department and Alexander Kump of the Kansas City, Kansas Police Department, who answered questions about police procedure from a frantic unknown author. These busy people patiently and graciously answered all my questions. Any errors are mine, either because I didn't ask enough questions or didn't understand the answers.

To Patty and John Westley

1

—

*Y*ancy wished they'd get to the murder. He shifted his belt—
gun, ammo clips, handcuffs, radio, baton, and flashlight—aware
of the sweat it left around his uniform shirt. Slapping at the buzz
of flies by his face, he leaned a shoulder against the inside barn
wall. Anything to break up the boredom, and him being a cop it
wouldn't have to be more than mildly interesting. He stood well
out of the way, by the small door at the side of the barn, a big old
limestone place, the uneven stone floor littered with coils of
cable—cable, cable everywhere—cameras, lights, mikes, and
people constantly moving in a hurry. The huge lights on tripods
were off right now, so the far corners dipped into dim shadows.

"Clem, for God's sake, what's the problem? We're ready."
Hayden Fifer, big Hollywood director, stood on a raised platform
with camera and cameraman. His voice thundered through the
more than three-story height of stone, rattling rafters and rais-
ing dust. Livestock were long gone, but the effluvia lingered and
seemed to rise up with the dust and hang in the air to be caught
on the rays of sunlight rushing through the big open doorway.

Clem was Clem Jones, a skinny kid, female, with spiked pink
hair and an attitude. Yancy didn't much care for Clem. They

stared fish-eyed at each other. With her weird hair, far-out clothes, and air of serious intent, he found her slightly ridiculous. The feeling was probably mutual. She was Fifer's assistant, and, Yancy thought, not responsible for shepherding actors onto the set, but Fifer yelled at her anyway. He yelled at Clem a lot. She muttered into a handheld radio, and Yancy barely heard her words through the static. "She won't come out of her trailer."

"Tell them to get her in here! What do you think I pay you for?"

Clem jammed the radio in the pocket of the ankle-length, prison-striped smock she wore and scuttled over cables, around cameras and mikes, through clumps of crew, and out the big doorway into the fierce sunshine.

For two weeks Yancy'd been hanging with the movie crowd, doing nothing, just being there: handy, making sure they weren't bothered, had everything they needed, turning up whenever one of them hollered. Some assignment, right? Shit. It didn't take more than two days before he was brain-dead. Nothing ever happened. Nothing. Ever. Happened. Near as he could figure, movies were made by herds of people milling around for hours until the director called, "Action." Cameras rolled for sixty seconds, or ground away for hours to get sixty seconds of usable film.

If he'd ever had any inkling of running away to became an actor, this would cure it, one giant yawn giving him nothing but slow time that let his mind tick over. Which he didn't want. He should do something, but he didn't know what. And if he did, ten to one, it'd be wrong. What about simply running away? Now there was a thought.

From Mac, one of the teamsters he'd been idling away time with—teamsters hauled in all the trucks necessary for the making of a movie and chauffeured around the stars—Yancy had gotten the hot tip about the murder on the call sheet today. So far that was just as unreal as everything else.

He had no idea what the movie was about, except it was a thriller. *Lethal Promise.* He knew that much because every vehicle had a placard on the dash with the name printed on it. Filming wasn't done in any sequence that allowed perception of a story.

Movies weren't a cushy way to go, long hours and hard work. Today, they'd started at six A.M., which meant *he'd* started at six A.M. It was now after one, temperature ninety, humidity ninety, and the hot wind that blew in was more irritating than welcome. It was so hot he wondered they didn't all pop off of heat stroke. Being from California, maybe they could survive anything. He smacked the fly feasting on the back of his neck as his mind played through who he might get to swap duty time with. Could he get away with that? It might nettle the chief, she wasn't exactly all sunshine these days.

"Officer?"

Startled, Yancy turned. He hadn't heard her slip through the small door behind him. Laura Edwards. Big-time actress. The Star. "Uh—" Oh, yeah. One cool cop. *There she was.* Remote fantasy from the movie screen standing right beside him. In the flesh. Spectacular flesh. Up to now, he'd only seen her at a distance, on the set, or disappearing into her town car. She was beautiful. Small, maybe five two with hair of pale gold that dazzled like sunlight on new snow, and blue eyes, the soft warm blue of a Kansas sky on a spring morning, a body that only Hollywood could dream up—taut and tawny and ripe.

He clasped his hands behind his back, lest they stray of their own accord toward all that female lushness. "They're looking for you," he said.

"They can look."

Director Fifer, still on the raised platform, bellowed for the harried Clem who was nowhere to be seen. "Will you, for God's sake, tell them to get her up here?"

They'd been using the platform to shoot a bad-guy-menaces-heroine scene in the hayloft. Villain had caught the beautiful Laura and had her bent backward over the railing, whether to send her falling to her death or choke the life out of her hadn't been clear. Since she was the heroine, the murder most likely wasn't of her.

3

Before lunch, hours had been spent setting up lights with a photo double hanging head down over the railing. Fifer, up on the platform peering at a monitor, issued instructions that resulted in minute changes in the position of lights, or cameras, or various appendages of the hapless female upside down over the railing, and ditto the villain, primarily his hands around her throat.

After achieving whatever effect he was striving for, Fifer had called for Laura Edwards to drape her beautiful form exactly as the stand-in had been. Therein followed more minute moving of appendages. Hours later all was perfection.

"Roll cameras."

"Speed."

"Scene twenty-four, take one."

"Action."

Before anything much happened, a young female with a clipboard trotted onto the set. Fifer called, "Cut!"

An argument ensued. Fifer got irate, the female stayed implacable.

"Now what?" Yancy asked his teamster buddy.

Mac grinned. "It's been six hours."

"Only six?"

"Contract. A break after six hours or the pay goes up at thirty-minute intervals. Meal penalty. Fifer's way over budget already. He can't afford more."

Polaroid pictures were taken of Laura and the villain from every conceivable angle and then Fifer called a lunch break. The barn couldn't have emptied out faster if he'd shouted, "Fire!"

After the break they all trooped back, except Ms. Laura Edwards. She was not on the rail and Fifer was royally pissed.

Now she was standing right by Yancy. She put an index finger, featherlight, on his forearm and looked up at him long and intensely. "I'd like you to do me a favor." Her voice was low with promise, the spot beneath her finger was warm as a downy duck.

What might she want from him? She smelled like fresh air and wildflowers. In her tight black pants and scoop-necked white blouse, she looked ready for a romp in the hayloft, but not with the likes of him; we're talking light-years away. So what's with all this luminous intensity? Obviously, she wanted something from him. The question was, what? He'd been with this bunch since they'd rolled into town, and she'd ignored him so far. She hadn't gotten a speeding or parking ticket she wanted him to take care of, hadn't caused any riots or broken any laws. Unless maybe after filming shut down and he'd gone home? Naw. He'd have heard about it. The guys at the department were using all kinds of heavy-handed humor, they wouldn't let anything like that go by. So what did she want from him? "Yes, ma'am," he said.

She inched closer. "Come to my trailer after the shot," she whispered. "It's very important."

Is it now? You have intrigued me, lady. "Yes, ma'am." She was so compelling he found himself whispering back.

"Clem!" Fifer bellowed.

That much put-upon young woman materialized at the foot of the platform and yelled up at him. "The designer said Laura won't come out of her trailer because the blouse looks like a potato sack."

Fifer held a muttered conversation with the stunt coordinator who was agitating to block out moves. "Enough assing around," he said. "Kay!"

A shadow angled through the open doorway and paused. Kay Bender, the stunt double, backlit by bright sunshine, dressed identically and wearing a gold wig, was the image of Laura Edwards without the passion: a doppelgänger.

Laura glanced at her and shivered. "Please," she pleaded and floated away through the small door.

The apparition in the wide doorway and the appeal in Laura's single word made the hairs stand up on his neck. Don't be a goofus, he told himself. This is the land of make-believe.

The stunt double clambered up wooden rungs to the loft.

During the lull the bad guy had been up there lounging against the hay bales. Instantly, he put on a murderous expression. Kay draped herself with her back over the railing, head hanging down, hair trailing. So far as Yancy knew, haylofts didn't have railings, but what the heck, this was Hollywood. The villain grabbed Kay by the throat.

The stunt coordinator gave instructions.

Fifer gave instructions. Cameras rolled.

Then everything seemed to happen in slow motion that took up a fraction of an instant.

There was a splintering crack. The railing gave way. Kay plummeted.

"Cut!"

Kay seemed to gather herself into a ball in midair. She landed hard on her back on a layer of straw, jerked convulsively, then lay still.

"No!" Fifer yelled. "Wrong! What's the matter with you people?"

Looked pretty good to Yancy, except maybe that athletic pulling together on the way down. And she didn't scream. Surely Hollywood would want a scream, but that maybe got put in later. He moved closer to where he could see a little better over equipment and people. Not much blood; he was surprised by the small amount, almost none. He would have figured these folks to ladle on lots of artistic blood, made with Karo syrup and sugar and red coloring so it wouldn't poison the actor who had to let it dribble from the corner of his mouth as he died.

He watched Clem scurry across snarled tangles of cable. Fingers at her throat, she knelt and peered nearsightedly at the stuntwoman, touched an arm and sprang back. She covered her mouth and made a strangled squeal.

Yancy moved without thinking, a cop's conditioned response. Standing in front of Clem, he put a hand on each shoulder and stared in her face. She was sobbing and gagging.

He pivoted her to one side just in time for her to spew all over the straw. He anchored her by the waist. When she straightened, she clung against him, gasping and shuddering. He patted her back, made soothing sounds, and looked over her head to see what set her off.

No genius was needed to figure it. Clem lived in the world of make-believe, where nothing was what it seemed. Phony horror was dished out all the time; broken and maimed bodies strewed the landscape, features distorted into death masks.

Only this one wasn't make-believe. Kay lay motionless with the tines of a pitchfork through her chest.

2

—

*P*ornography." Mrs. Oliver, on the other end of the phone line, spat out the word as though it tasted bad. "Filth."

"Yes, ma'am." The sun glaring through the window slats left stripes on the desk that made Susan squint. She swiveled a half turn, putting her back to them. A fly circled and landed on the wall at knee level. She kicked at it; it flew to the ceiling.

"I was the one who had to scrub it off. And let me tell you, that was no easy job. It took hours. Hours, do you understand? Getting rid of that smut. I expect you to do something about this."

Mrs. Oliver hung up before Susan could utter another "Yes, ma'am." She swiveled around and replaced the receiver. The phone rang again immediately. Another art critic?

"It's the mayor," Hazel, the dispatcher, said. "You want to talk with him?"

She did not. "Put him through."

"Chief Wren," Bakover said.

"Mr. Mayor."

"What is going on with this vandalism?"

Well, let's see. Vandals will be vandals? Vandals for the sake of vandalism? Vandals unite? The fly landed on a stack of papers on the desk. From another stack, she rolled up a report and smacked the damn thing. With an irritated buzz, it took off. "We're looking into it."

"Not good enough. It's upsetting people."

Some people. Pornography being more or less in the eye of the beholder, there were those that were upset and those that were amused and those that felt honored to be chosen and those that said sometimes a garbage can was just a garbage can.

"You are perfectly aware these Hollywood people are in town. We don't want anything like this to offend them."

She trapped a laugh in her throat by coughing around it. Hollywood? Offended by nudes? Oh, boy, it was this weather. Who was it who said this was the kind of weather when wives sharpened their knives and eyed their husbands' necks?

"Put a stop to this," he said and hung up.

She replaced the receiver, rolled the report tighter, and chased the fly around the office, swinging wildly. It took shelter behind the blinds at the top of the window, buzzed angrily. Yeah, well, you think you got troubles.

She tilted the slats to get rid of the glare, then shifted folders until she got to today's *Hampstead Herald* and spread it open. Page two. Headline: MAD PAINTER'S LATEST RAID. There was a picture of a garbage can with a female nude tastefully draped in plastic grocery bags so as not to upset the delicate sensibilities of those who saw porn in the unclad human form. The mad painter—a reporter had come up with that one—hit only garbage cans, and left a nude figure—either male or female—equal opportunity salaciousness—and disappeared into the air.

Chase Reardon, San Francisco police captain and Susan's former boss, had drilled his maxim into her: *Evidence is always at the scene of the crime. If you didn't find it, you didn't search enough.* They'd better go more carefully through the garbage.

She picked up the phone and told Hazel she was going out to look at the scene of the crime.

The pickup's fuel gauge hovered around empty. Not wanting to find herself without gas while hotly pursuing the mad painter (if she learned who he was and he ran) she U-turned into Pickett's service station. Kevin Murphy came from one of the service bays, wiping his hands on a greasy rag.

"Ma'am?" He shook black hair from his face, stuffed the rag in a rear pocket, and tucked in the brown shirt with PICKETT'S stitched on the back. Sullen kid, high school football star, fire inside, so far no trouble.

He squeegeed her windshield, she paid for the gas and was headed for Ohio Street when the muttering radio caught her attention. She picked up the mike. "Wren."

"Osey, Chief." O. C. Pickett, her country boy detective, the youngest son of the service station owner, sounded hesitant and apologetic. "I'm at Josiah's barn. I thought you'd better know there's been an accident. A stuntwoman's dead."

"Oh, shit."

She didn't know she'd spoken aloud until he said, "Yes, ma'am."

The sky, vast and blue and empty, stretched forever over the low hills. The midday sun of early June blazed relentlessly on the field of high grasses and goldenrod, struck sparks on boulders, and created shimmering heat illusions in the distance. Occasional hot gusts of wind whirled dust devils on the dirt road.

She kept the pickup at a moderate speed, no lights, no siren, not that it would make a difference. News traveled with the speed of lightning in a small town, and there would already be a crowd. Movies and actors always drew them, especially when the actors were in the megabucks category, as these were. Nick Logan and Laura Edwards.

When word had come that Hollywood was coming to Hampstead, Susan was the only person in town who wasn't thrilled. Her experience was—from directors and actors on down to cameramen, lighting techs, and grips—the whole bunch and their moviemaking was a gigantic pain in the butt. They moved in, took whatever they wanted, broke it, altered it, mangled it, and dropped it when they were finished. They pulled out and left the place trashed, like picnickers who left litter and breakage in their wake.

San Francisco—oh, yes, summer fog, cool ocean breezes— she leaned forward and plucked at the white blouse sticking to her back—was the site of many a movie. They'd even managed to close down the Golden Gate Bridge on one occasion she knew about. Irate drivers trying to get into or out of the city were not thrilled to be watching a movie in the making.

They did spread money around like syrup over pancakes. Which was, of course, why they were given the red carpet treatment and why the mayor was so ecstatic. He'd informed her that as police chief she was to make sure they felt welcome and to give them everything they wanted.

She rolled past the field where they'd parked their trucks and trailers, vans and cars, and drove on another quarter mile to old Josiah's barn. Good Lord, thinking like a native, referring to a piece of property by the name of a long-dead owner.

Josiah Hampstead, an early settler before Kansas was a state, made himself wealthy in land, cattle, and oil, got a town named after him, and late in his life donated some of that land for a college. The house was long gone, but the barn remained, a large weathered stone structure. Off to one side was a power and light truck—the generator that ran all those huge lights. Cables, taped to the ground, snaked inside the barn.

An empty squad car, overheads blinking, was parked parallel to the wide-open door. An ambulance, rear doors open and waiting, was pulled up behind. A dozen or so people stood in what shade the two tall cottonwood trees provided. Susan's arrival separated the media from the spectators and they rushed at her with mikes and questions.

She edged the pickup in beside the ambulance and slid out. Heat came up to greet her as though she'd opened an oven door. When she'd dressed that morning, she'd tried to strike a compromise between dignified businesslike and what she could survive in given the heat. Tailored white blouse and beige cotton pants was the best she could do. Linen jacket, if the occasion demanded. The pants were wrinkled and sweaty where her legs had rested on the driver's seat. She left the jacket on the passenger side. Hot wind caught her full-face and lifted her dark hair, blowing it straight back.

"Can you tell us what happened?"

"What's the name of the person killed?"

"Was this an accident or do you suspect foul play?"

"Is this going to affect the movie?"

"How long will the filming be stopped?"

"What happens when a death occurs in—?"

"I just got here," she said. "I don't know anything yet."

Just inside the big sliding door, two paramedics in navy blue jumpsuits leaned against the wall, arms crossed. One glanced at her and gave a brief shake of his head. No need for urgency.

Despite the wide doorway, the interior was gloomy. The barn was cavernous, easily over three stories high: hayloft overhead in the rear, above that a steep-pitched ceiling with rough-hewn beams. On the ground, box stalls ran the length of one side, on the other were open stalls. Actors and crew were contained inside these with White and Demarco riding herd. Cameras, lights, snarls of cable, and dollies cluttered the large open area in the center. Just below the loft, on a layer of straw, the dead woman lay on her back, the tines of a pitchfork jutting through her chest.

Susan picked her way closer, careful to stay back from Osey Pickett taking photographs. Dr. Fisher waited patiently for him to finish. She studied the victim. Young, no more than twenty, she judged. Cascade of blond hair, one errant strand across her still lips, eyes slitted, but not enough to tell color. Alive, she would have the attractiveness of youth, health, and fitness. All that had been taken by death and now she was gray and flat. The heavy theatrical makeup seemed a mockery. She wore tight black pants, a white knit shirt with a scooped neck, and black ankle boots with fringe up the back.

When Osey finished snapping pictures, Dr. Fisher drew on

latex gloves and knelt for a close look at the body. Susan took out her notebook and made a rough sketch even though Osey would be doing the same. Habits from her years on the San Francisco force stuck with her.

She backed carefully away and left them to it. Yancy was waiting for her at the edge of the cleared area. "Ma'am," he said quietly. His tentative tone made it clear he was wondering whether an ass chewing was coming his way.

She'd like to chew somebody's. This would come down like an avalanche on her and her department. The movie crowd might make trouble, the mayor would be furious and worried. More media would turn up. She was beginning to understand why the brass was so quick to jump on someone. Sheer frustration.

"What happened?"

"Her name is Kay Bender," Yancy said. "The stunt double for this film."

Oh, my. Film, not movie. He'd been infected with showbiz.

"She did all the risky stuff for Ms. Edwards."

If there was anything to be thankful for about this, she could be thankful Laura Edwards wasn't lying dead with a pitchfork through her chest. A stuntwoman would rate a paragraph in the back pages of the newspapers, maybe a brief mention on television news. Only *Hollywood Reporter* would care. The media would still come, anything touching Laura Edwards was news, but they might not descend like locusts as they would if she'd been the one killed.

Susan made quick notes while Yancy gave a clear, concise account of what had occurred, ending with Ms. Edwards asking him to her trailer. "When Kay fell, I had Mac call nine-one-one."

"Mac?"

"Laura Edwards's driver. I prevented anybody from going over there and secured the scene. I wouldn't let them move her. That meant they had to stop filming. Fifer, the director, got furious. I got a cold whisper that I had no idea what I was costing him." Yancy paused, giving her the opportunity to yell, if she was so inclined.

14

"Go on."

"I think he wanted to shove the body aside and get on with the movie. I told them all to move over into those stalls along the side there." Yancy nodded. "I figured that's the best I could do. Everybody's been in and out of them all day anyway, and at least I could keep an eye out till backup arrived. Fifer refused, said he'd be in his trailer. Short of cuffing him to a manger, there was nothing I could do."

"Was there any reason to make you think this was more than an accident?"

"No." He hesitated. "The director kept yelling it was a tragic accident and I was being an asshole." Yancy took a slow breath. "Damned if I can figure what this movie is about. Laura Edwards was supposed to be thrown backward across that railing"—he nodded up at the loft—"with the bad guy choking the life out of her. Then Kay Bender, the stuntwoman, would take over. The rail breaks and down she goes."

He shifted his weight to his other foot. "Down below they would have it set up such that when she fell she wouldn't get hurt. Except, Ms. Edwards wouldn't leave her trailer."

The star having a fit, Susan thought. Not a rare occurrence.

"The stunt coordinator then insisted he wanted to work something out and the director agreed. The railing broke. There wasn't supposed to be a pitchfork under it." He shrugged. "I didn't want to take any chances."

"Laura Edwards wanted you to come to her trailer. Why?"

"No idea."

"Cop business or because you're tall, dark, and handsome?"

Yancy smiled. "Much as I'd like to think it might have been the latter, I doubt it."

Yancy was tall all right and dark-haired; handsome didn't say it. He was soft-spoken, with soft brown eyes, and a smile as sweet and soothing as a summer night. Trim and fit in his blues, he was dynamite. She could see even Ms. Big Hollywood Star being interested.

"I assume you asked her what she wanted."

15

"Yes, ma'am. She said she'd tell me later."

"Where is she now?"

"In her trailer. At the base camp. I went to check."

More movie talk. Base camp was the place where all the trailers, cars, trucks, et cetera were set up. In this case, the field a quarter mile back.

"You go baby-sit. I'll be right there. I want a word with Dr. Fisher. Oh, and Yancy, have somebody move the newspeople back."

Owen Fisher, a man of solid bulk, wasn't able to tell her any more than she already knew. He brushed straw from his dark trousers and peeled latex gloves from his hands. Those hands always fascinated her; they were perfectly shaped, delicate, and long-fingered, a total mismatch with the rest of him, which was thick and bearlike.

"Well?" she said.

He peered at her from under dark heavy eyebrows, a sharp contrast with his white hair. "Yep, she's dead all right."

"Anything else?" she asked dryly.

"Just what you can see. Newly dead. Body temp not even lowered yet. Course it is hot in here. Lividity just beginning. Mucous membranes just beginning to dry." He bent over and snapped his instrument bag shut. "Something might show up when I get her on the table."

Susan clambered up the wooden rungs to the loft and found Osey on his hand and knees sifting through straw. Needle in a haystack. When she stepped off onto the loft, Osey unfolded his tall, thin body in a series of jerks. Hair the color of the straw he was fingering through, guileless blue eyes that were deceptively naive, hands and feet that seemed to get in his way, brown pants and white shirt with the sleeves rolled up, tie askew. The impression—harmless country boy, not too bright. Reality—mind like a gin trap.

"Anything of interest?"

"Naw." He whacked at his pants legs. Dust filled the air and

16

sunlight slanting through the small window under the peaked roof sparkled on the motes. "Not yet anyway. People all over the place. Up here, down there. Now that railing there. That's maybe a mite interesting. I'm going to have to get both pieces together and see. They got a rail that's rigged to break. It's part of the action. But this one was supposed to be solid. Was solid right before they all took off for lunch. Now it looks like it was cut most of the way. Then with weight on it, it just gave." He showed her the spot where the rail gave way.

Damn, Susan thought. Murder? Accident would have been bad enough. And who was the intended victim? Stunt double Kay Bender? Actress Laura Edwards? Any hint of an attempt on Laura Edwards's life and the media would be all over it.

"Where's Parkhurst?" she asked. Ben Parkhurst was her most experienced officer. She used him to sound out data and surmise, he pointed out the difference. They made a good team. At least, they had until personal stuff started leaking over into cop stuff.

"On his way. He was up in Topeka dropping off some water samples at the lab, from the Sackly well."

"When he shows, I'm at Ms. Edwards's trailer."

Pale green. Laura my beloved. The universe is pale green. The spirits are worried. I know you're in there. I know you're not hurt. I saw you go in. You're afraid. I can feel your fear. Don't be afraid. Everything's going to be wonderful. I'm here. Near. My love, my light. The light of truth. Sweet and lovely. I'll watch. I'll wait.

He watched the tall, black-haired policewoman knock on the trailer door. He didn't see Her inside, but he sent love.

Yancy opened the trailer door at Susan's tap and she walked into welcome coolness. The only sound was the hum of the air-conditioning unit. The kitchen area had sink, cabinets, and a table with a green padded bench. The living-room area, carpeted in pale blue, had two blue-tweed couches at a right angle to each other with a large round coffee table in the bend, two end tables, large television set, and a VCR. Watercolors hung on the walls, flowers done with intricate detail.

The woman sitting on a couch brought a split instant of surprise before Susan's mind caught up. A stunt double would of necessity be made to look like the star. Laura Edwards wore the same form-hugging black pants, white knit scoop-necked shirt, and black ankle boots with fringe.

She sat perfectly still, legs crossed, hands palm up in her lap with the fingers loosely curled, staring blankly ahead. She took no notice of Susan.

Even frozen in shock, Laura Edwards was stunning. A thick tangle of hair the color of pale gold curled away from a smooth forehead and high cheekbones, it fell in loose swirls along her neck and shoulders. Long dark lashes over blue eyes that tilted up slightly. Perfectly shaped nose, generous mouth.

"She won't say anything," Yancy said. "Hasn't even moved. She didn't answer when I knocked. I'm not even sure she knows I'm here."

Uh-huh. This stricken beauty had aroused protective instincts in Yancy the cop. Susan could understand it, even she felt a tug to protect the vulnerable maiden. Laura Edwards was as still as a stone sculpture.

Let us not forget here, the woman is an actress.

"Ms. Edwards?"

No response, not even a focus in Susan's direction. Kneeling in front of her, Susan took one of her hands. Cold and limp. "Laura."

No reaction. Susan put the hand back in Laura's lap and rose. "We'd better get a doctor in."

There was a tap on the door. Yancy opened it and Parkhurst stepped inside. He nodded curtly to Yancy and said to Susan, "You wanted to see me?"

Laura blinked her beautiful blue eyes, shiny with unshed tears. "Ben?" Her voice, low and husky, caught on a sob.

18

Parkhurst's face went hard. Laura hurled herself at him, wrapped herself around him, and nestled her face against his neck.

Yancy's jaw dropped. Susan's eyebrows shot up.

3

Laura's muffled sobs and the hum of the air-conditioning blended together for a stretched-out moment. Parkhurst, arms around the actress, held himself board stiff, a muscle ticked away in the corner of his jaw the way it did when he was angry. Susan, startled by the woman's actions, was even more startled to discover tiny seeds of jealousy. What's all this?

Confusion. She'd known Parkhurst a little over two years. They'd gone from suspicious dogs snarling at each other to grudging mutual respect to just recently something else that she didn't want to admit to but had attraction thrown in and would, if not stomped, lead to trouble. So why was she getting all prickly around the edges because Ms. Movie Star was sobbing all over Parkhurst's chest, and acted like she'd done that very thing before?

Why Parkhurst? If Susan were the flinging type, given the choice between Yancy and Parkhurst, she'd choose Yancy every time; any limpet would. Yancy had a gentle look, with "pliable" and "kind" thrown in. Parkhurst looked dangerous. Everything about him was hard, from his dark eyes to his tight back, and when he lowered his voice it wasn't soft, it was menacing. So what the hell?

She eyed Yancy and gestured with a thumb. He slipped out the door without protest. His curiosity was probably as high as hers, but she was the boss. Parkhurst peeled Laura's arms from his neck and held both her hands in one of his. He put an arm around her and edged her to the couch. She dropped, not at all gracefully, and clutched his hand tight when he tried to pull it loose. Short of a clip to the jaw, his only choice was to perch at an angle beside her and allow her to keep the hand. Which she did, clasping it to her bosom.

Every male's fantasy. Parkhurst's? She never could tell what he was thinking; he had a great ability at self-concealment. Thick dark hair, medium height, mid-thirties, he was self-assured, self-contained, intelligent, and a good cop. Just lately, she'd learned that stuck back there behind the air of reined-in violence was a sense of humor.

Laura kept her eyes fastened on him, as though he might disappear if she so much as blinked. Tears glistened and left smeary trails through the heavy makeup. This did not detract one whit from her beauty, if anything it made her more attractive by throwing in vulnerability and an appeal for help. Susan poked around in the tiny pale-rose bathroom and found a box of tissues. She plunked it on the coffee table and backed over to the padded bench in the kitchen area, out of Laura's line of vision but able to watch her.

Laura snatched a tissue, then another, wadded them together, and rubbed at her eyes. Susan reminded herself again that this woman was an actress. Yet the crying was real, red eyes, splotched face, and runny nose. Even Susan wanted to help; any red-blooded male would grab his lance, leap on his horse, and gallop to her defense. Susan caught Parkhurst's eye and gave him a short nod. His show. She pulled out her notebook.

"It's good to see you, Ben," Laura said. "You look great."

Parkhurst knew Laura Edwards. That was a little like the sun rising in the west. The whole Hollywood circus had been in town almost a week and he never mentioned he'd known the famous Laura Edwards.

Susan wished she could read him better. Whatever was going on inside, he had it under control—face set, eyes flat—but he had to work at it. His jaw muscles were so tight, she wondered if he'd ever be able to speak again.

He worked his hand free. "Likewise."

They were mouthing platitudes, Susan thought, while they fought off the emotions of the underlying situation. She noted the pulse beat in his throat and judged his heart was banging around inside his chest.

Laura smiled. "You haven't changed, have you?"

"No," he said, "and right now I need to ask you some questions."

"Still the cop. You have a title?"

"Lieutenant."

"Really? I expected by now you'd be chief, or commissioner, or whatever is at the top."

A tiny bit of hostility oozed through here.

Parkhurst responded with raised hackles. "Don't tell me you've forgotten my personality. It always did get in my way."

"All right, Ben, ask your questions." Tears overflowed again and Laura grabbed another handful of tissues. "I know you have to. I just didn't want to think about it."

"How well did you know the dead girl?"

"I've worked with her several times. She looks a little like me. Basically same height and weight. Not that it really matters. The camera takes great care to protect the deception. You know, dreams of shimmering illusions."

This seemed to refer to something Parkhurst knew about. "Cut the crap, Laura. It doesn't have to be me. If you'd rather talk to somebody else—"

"No." For a moment she looked panicked, then as though she wanted to challenge his getting down to business, then she dropped it and sighed. She drooped. "Oh, Ben, unbend a little. I'm nervous. Aren't you?"

It was a direct appeal and Susan could see Parkhurst try to ease up on his tight emotional hold. "I know this is awkward, Laurie, but—"

Laurie?

"Would you ask her to leave?"

He tucked up the corners of his mouth in a wry smile. "She's the boss."

Laura's eyes widened in a parody of surprise and her mouth rounded into an O as she looked around at Susan, then flattened into a tiny smile.

It was quick, but Susan caught it. I don't know what you're working here, lady, but there's a plan rolling around in your mind.

The smile vanished and was replaced by bewildered sadness as she turned back to Parkhurst.

"Tell me about Kay Bender." His voice was quiet with underlying anger.

They stared at each other, squaring off for battle. "Still hostile," she said.

"It's what I do best."

"You're an insensitive prick!"

"Good. Now. How old was the stuntwoman?"

Laura took in a breath; tears filled her eyes; she scrubbed at them with balled-up tissues. "I don't know. Twenty. Twenty-one. Around there."

"How well did you know her?"

Laura hesitated, either to collect her thoughts or to sort through and pick and choose. "Not very. When I try to think I guess I really don't know anything at all." Look of remorseful sorrow.

"What about her family?"

"She's from San Diego, I think. I guess she has a family. I don't recall her ever saying anything about them."

"Boyfriend?"

Susan studied the woman's hands, small and shapely with tapering fingers, they were in constant motion twisting and untwisting the tissues, crumpling them into a ball, smoothing them out—nervous movements that didn't seem a deliberate way of stalling or evading answers, but a try at controlling the shock, and maybe grief, that sat waiting just beyond the mind's focus.

"Boyfriend," Laura repeated. "Yes, I think so."

"Name?"

She shot him an angry look. "For God's sake, Ben, soften up a little. I'm trying to think— I don't— You're treating me like a suspect. There are always romances on a shoot, especially on location. It happens. It's like not real time, you know? Away from home, temporary, and the place doesn't seem real either. It's like it doesn't count. It's aside from life, part of the make-believe. Kay is—was a professional. She did the job. It's a risky job. No matter how careful, stunt people get hurt. Accidents—"

A horrified expression came over her face. "It was an accident," she said very carefully with more statement in her voice than question, as though by sounding positive she could make the answer come out the way she wanted it to.

Parkhurst, as far as Susan could see, didn't respond with so much as a flicker of an eyelid, but what little color there was behind the makeup on Laura's face drained away. Susan was afraid she'd drop over in a dead faint. Parkhurst apparently thought so too. Before Susan could move, he had Laura's head down around her knees.

Seconds passed, then she started making muffled mewling noises and he released her. The heavy smeared makeup was still the only color in her face. Susan retrieved a glass from the cabinet in the kitchen area, filled it from the tap, and handed it to Parkhurst.

He did a surveillance of Laura's face as he placed the glass in her hand.

"It should have been me," she whispered.

"Why do you say that?"

"I was supposed to be up there—on the railing—when—"

"Why weren't you?" Parkhurst asked, but he'd lost her; her attention was caught on something in her mind. Probably the fall. Her skin got a little green; her eyes went unfocused.

Putting his hands on her shoulders, he said quietly, "Talk to me, Laura. Concentrate. That's right. Now, where were you when you were supposed to be in the loft?"

"Somebody killed her? Why?"

"We need to find out the answer to both those questions. Who would want to kill her?"

Laura simply looked at him, then shook her head. "Accidents happen, you know. Even when everyone's being very careful. They just do. They—"

"Laura—"

"Deliberate?"

"Maybe. How long have you known Kay Bender?"

"I don't know. Two years. Maybe longer. What does it matter?"

"Did she have any conflict with anybody, anybody dislike her?"

"I don't know. I don't think so." Laura's head swiveled around to look at Susan.

Parkhurst turned her back, held his hands on both sides of her face like blinders. "Never mind her, Laura. You're bright enough to know that if Kay wasn't the target, you were. You in any trouble?"

"What kind of trouble?"

"You tell me. If someone tried to kill you, or hurt you, there must be a reason."

"No. I don't know. Something is wrong on this film."

"What do you mean wrong?"

"I don't know. It's not anything I can point to. It's a feeling. Something going on underneath the surface."

Under whose surface? Susan wondered cynically.

"Always, or just since you came here?"

Laura hesitated. "I'm not sure. But it's certainly been stronger since we got here."

"Have you made anybody angry? The director?"

"Fifer would never try to harm me. That'd mean his movie wouldn't get finished. You've no idea how much money would be lost."

But there would be insurance, Susan thought. A possibility? Director kills, or seriously injures, star to collect? She made a note to check into the financial situation of this movie.

"Your co-star?" Parkhurst asked.

"Nick? Why would he try to hurt me?"

"That's what I'm trying to find out. Maybe you eat garlic right before the love scenes and he's tired of it. Maybe a lover's spat, true love not running smooth."

"Okay, so we have our moments. We're both professionals. It doesn't affect our work."

He stared at her. She lowered her head, shiny gold hair obscured her face. Her breathing got quick and shallow. Parkhurst was getting to her, Susan thought, but damned if she knew what was going on here.

"All right, Laurie," he said. "You're smart, even observant when you want to be."

She raised her head, tried to look him in the eye, but her gaze slid away and her face flushed a soft pink.

"You're not being straight with me, Laurie. You're holding back. That's of great concern."

"Damn you, Ben. I'm not holding anything back."

Susan heard the almost imperceptible catch in her throat.

"You care about finding out what happened to this girl?"

"Of course I do. I honestly don't know anything that could help."

Parkhurst let a couple beats tick past while he pinned her with his eyes. This time she held up to it without flinching. "I don't know anything. Honestly, I don't. Don't you think I'd tell you if I did?"

"Laura, something doesn't feel right here. What are you hiding?"

"Nothing. I've told you. Nothing. Jesus, you haven't changed a bit. Get your teeth into something and you shake it to death. For God's sake, why would I hide something?"

"I don't know. That's what I'm trying to get to. Where were you when she fell?"

"What?" He'd jumped too fast and left Laura a step behind.

"You were supposed to be on the railing when it broke. Why weren't you?"

"Oh. I was on my way back here after talking with that very nice officer."

"Why were you talking with him?"

"I wanted to ask him if he would do something for me."

"I'm sure, Laurie," Parkhurst said tightly, "if you asked him and it was remotely within his power, he certainly would. Now, stop playing coy and tell me what you wanted from him. I assume it wasn't simply his hard, lean body."

"Don't be crude, Ben." Her blue eyes lost the glazed look and flashed anger. "I wanted him to ask you to come see me."

"Why?"

An impish smile played around her mouth. "You can't think of any reason? None at all?"

"Can it."

Laura's eyes teared again. "It's hard to explain. It's like smoke, when I try to catch hold of it, there's nothing there."

"What's like smoke?"

"Something brooding and ugly. It worried me."

"Threatening? Directed at you?"

Susan didn't know what to make of this under-the-surface ugliness story. There was way too much emotion here. Too damn much drama. She'd been a cop a long time; her ears were tuned to pick up false notes, and there was something false here.

"What did you want from me?" Parkhurst asked.

"I wanted to ask you to help. I knew you'd want to do all you could for your wife."

4

$\mathcal{I}$ wanna know!"

Exactly, Susan thought, but while the words were hers, the voice wasn't. It was male, loud, and came from outside.

Parkhurst at her elbow, his eyes guarded, she opened the trailer door to see what was going on. A tall young man, red hair, both fists clenched at his sides, was demanding to see the cop in charge.

Fiery eyes shifted to her. "Who are you?"

"This is Robin McCormack." Yancy put a restraining hand on the young man's arm, a hand that looked casual but was firm enough to make McCormack wince.

"It's okay," she said to Yancy. "I'll talk to him. And would you get Ellis over here?"

Feet planted, hands loose by his side, Parkhurst stood ready for any aggressive moves from McCormack.

Cast and crew were all staying at the Sunflower Hotel. They were transported back and forth to base camp or set by vans. Superstars like Laura Edwards had their own personal town cars with drivers, muscular guys who could respond as bodyguards if needed.

Susan told Officer Ellis, another big muscular guy, a weight lifter and boxer, to stick on Ms. Edwards's tail like a burr. Anything happened to her and his ass was on the line. When the actress was tucked in and rolling away with Ellis in a squad car on the bumper, Susan asked Yancy to find Nick Logan and bring him around, then turned her attention to Robin McCormack.

He thrust out his jaw. A rangy young man in cutoff jeans and a T-shirt with the sleeves ripped out, he looked sullen and every inch belligerent, from his longish hair, closely trimmed red beard, and turquoise earring right on down to once-white Nikes now coming apart at the seams.

She invited him inside the trailer. Parkhurst stayed on his heels, avoiding her glance.

McCormack shot her a confused look and demanded of Parkhurst, "What the hell happened?" His fists were still clenched at his sides and he seemed to bounce on tight springs.

"Have a seat, please." Parkhurst aimed an index finger at the couch.

After a moment of internal struggle—which she thought he would lose and end up taking a swing at Parkhurst—McCormack did sit. Barely. Feet planted, ready to leap up, fists on his knees.

"What's your job?" she asked quietly. She'd do the questioning on this one. With this kid's attitude, Parkhurst's manner would strike sparks. The matter of a marriage they'd go into later.

"Your job?" she repeated to get his attention.

He looked at her. "Props. I want to know what happened to Kay."

"How long have you known Ms. Bender?"

"Two years, a little more." Short words, clipped.

"You were friends?"

"Yeah, friends. Now will you tell me?"

"Close friends? Lovers?"

"So what?"

"We're trying to find out what happened, Mr. McCormack. It seems to have been an accident."

"The hell it was! Kay was an athlete. Physically fit. She didn't

30

have *accidents*. She was careful. She always checked everything. Always."

She undoubtedly did, Susan thought, but stunt people got injured, it went with the job, and Kay wasn't expecting to go through a railing, or to hit a pitchfork when she landed. "Have there been problems in making this movie, Mr. McCormack?"

Parkhurst, once he decided the kid was going to keep his fists to himself, drifted to the kitchen area and slid onto the padded bench at the table.

McCormack made a sound somewhere between a grunt and a snort. "There are always problems. Actors get moods. Weather doesn't cooperate. Directors have fits. Things break. Props get lost. Doors don't open."

"Was Kay blamed for any of these things?"

"No."

"Who didn't like her?"

Robin glared with such fury she could see Parkhurst set himself to intervene. "Nobody. Kay was a stunt double. They can't afford anybody not liking them. They don't have tantrums. No matter how bad it gets, they just do the job."

"Other boyfriends? Someone she rejected?"

"Who left a pitchfork lying around? No!"

"It wasn't lying around, it was below the railing hidden under straw."

He winced.

"Where did it come from?"

"The prop cart." That probably played over and over in his mind.

"It was yours." Accusation in her voice.

"It was a prop, yeah. Used in a scene this morning. When we broke for lunch, I left it on the cart for a scene coming up this afternoon."

"Did you notice it missing after lunch?"

"Yeah."

"Why didn't you look for it?"

"I did." He rubbed a hand, hard, over his face. "Fifer told

31

me to stay out of the way and shut up, he was filming." He pressed thumb and forefinger against his eyes. "She wasn't supposed to fall."

"If Kay wouldn't have an accident and nobody would want to hurt her, what do you think happened here?"

He took in air to prevent an explosion. "Laura Edwards."

"What about her?"

"She was supposed to be there, wasn't she?"

"You're suggesting someone wanted to harm Laura Edwards?"

"I'm not suggesting anything. She was supposed to be there. Kay wasn't. Laura's important. Kay isn't."

"Who would want to hurt Laura?"

"How the hell should I know."

"Was she mean? Nasty? Selfish? Did she trample on somebody?"

With a thumbnail, he scratched at a cut on his forefinger. "You better ask Nick."

"What did she do to Nick Logan?"

Robin looked at Susan as though she were two beats slower than the rhythm. "Huh. They're this great Hollywood success story. Great romance. Making a great movie."

She dearly wanted to glance at Parkhurst and get his reaction to this, but she kept her eyes fixed on Robin McCormack. With Parkhurst's ability at concealment, he probably wasn't reacting anyway. "Not true?"

"No," Robin said, but his eyes looked through her.

She'd lost him again; he'd tuned back into the tape playing through his mind. The one that was edited so the ending turned out differently. "Which part isn't true?" she said. "The love story? Or the great movie?"

His clenched fists tightened until the knuckles stood out white. There was much anger in this young man. He might react in violence if told by Kay she didn't want to see him anymore. "What's wrong with the movie?"

"Nothing," he said definitely. "It's coming good. The dailies—" He glanced at her to see if she knew what dailies were. She nodded.

"They're good. Fifer gets all lit up after seeing them. We're running over budget and we're running out of time. He'd be all silent and tight like he'd set himself for the chop going in and then he'd come out with a face like there was gold in the mining pan."

"So he was pleased with Laura's performance? Was he ever angry at her?"

"Never. Not her. He only sometimes got quiet and cold. Scary. He yells at everybody else, especially Clem . . ."

Clem? Oh, yes, Fifer's assistant.

". . . but not at Nick and never at Laura. With the dailies so great I think he didn't want to risk an upset of a good thing."

"Laura's a good actress?"

"Yeah," he said as though anyone with half a brain would know that.

"So if there is nothing wrong with the movie, then it must be the great romance that's in trouble."

"You might say that."

"Have Laura and Nick been fighting?"

Robin looked undecided, then said, "Yeah."

"Screaming at each other? Throwing things? Hitting each other? What?"

"Some of that." He shrugged. "The screaming part. Mostly just charged-up attitudes. Never being in the same place. Not seeing each other if they were."

Charged-up attitudes. Uh-huh. How much do we place on that, coming from a kid who didn't seem quick to pick up nuances? "How long has this been going on?"

"From the start."

"Why were they fighting?"

Robin propped an ankle on the opposite knee and held on to it with both hands. "Sheri, I guess. Sheri with-an-I Lloyd."

33

"Who is she?"

"Another actor. There was a rumor going she thought she had a shot at the role."

"The role Laura's playing."

"Yeah. Laura had something else going and wasn't available. Then all of a sudden, she was available. Sheri gets offered a nothing part. 'Supporting role,' " he stated in a passing good imitation of Fifer's clipped, staccato enthusiasm. " 'Very important. Pivotal. Only you can do it justice.' "

"Mr. Fifer wanted Ms. Edwards for the starring role?"

"Damn straight. Fifer wants a hit. Better get one. His last two bombed. He's counting on Laura to pull him out of the toilet. Sheri sure couldn't do it. Your name doesn't last long if you have a couple of losers under it. Especially multimillion-dollar losers."

"How does Sheri feel about this?"

"What do you think? She's not real smart or she'd never of believed she'd had a chance in the first place."

"What does that have to do with Nick Logan?"

"Well, the great romance wasn't so great after he started snuggling with Sheri."

So what have we got here? Kay Bender dead, maybe in mistake for Laura Edwards. So far—and we've only just begun—no known reason for anyone wanting to harm Kay Bender. Laura Edwards, on the other hand, seemed to bring out motives. Another actress who'd hoped to snag the role. Nick Logan, co-star, finding love and romance, not with the star but with the starlet.

This was beginning to sound like a soap opera. Did Sheri try to kill Laura to obtain the starring role? (Would that happen if Laura were gone?) Was Nick Logan, handsome, sexy co-star, tired of Laura? Was Laura not letting go and needed to be gotten rid of? Tune in tomorrow. Maybe somebody's evil twin will show up. Susan looked at Parkhurst to see if he had a question, a comment, an expression. He looked impassively back in true Parkhurst style. She told Robin McCormack she had no further questions at this time.

He lit out, but before she could get to Parkhurst about this wife business, Yancy had Nick Logan coming in. The actor stood in the living-room area of the trailer, taking up too much space, smelling of expensive aftershave and cigarette smoke. And somehow, she didn't know quite how, he brought with him an air of California. Maybe it was the suntan, or the sun-streaked light hair. Whatever, it made her homesick. For San Francisco, that is. This man—denim shirt unbuttoned halfway, gold chain with some kind of medal hidden in chest hair, denim pants, thongs on his feet—was strictly Los Angeles and never the twain shall meet. But still, California is California.

Rugged in appearance rather than handsome. Coarse features, questing hazel eyes that examined her, moved on to Parkhurst, and stayed there taking in some inventory. Logan then quirked a famous eyebrow and waited. Despite her preset notion that he was going to be a self-centered, arrogant pain in the butt, she found she liked him.

"Please, sit down, Mr. Logan." She indicated the couch and he flip-flopped over to it, waited until she seated herself on the other couch, then settled in with an elbow crooked along the back, a hand on his thigh. There were fine lines around his eyes and down a path from nose to mouth. Early forties, she thought.

"Call me Nick." Low gravelly voice, but not grating to the ear. He twisted his head and looked at Parkhurst sitting unobtrusively in the kitchen area. "Don't I know you from someplace?"

"I doubt it," Parkhurst said.

Nick looked unconvinced.

"We're investigating the fatality that happened this afternoon," Susan said.

Nick nodded. "Making a film seems frivolous in this context, doesn't it?"

"You were in the barn this morning. Is that correct? Scenes were filmed."

"Right." He stuck thumb and forefinger into his shirt pocket and pulled out a pack of cigarettes. "May I?"

"I don't mind. Laura Edwards might. It's her trailer."

Nick stretched out a leg, stuck his hand in his pants pocket, and fished out a lighter. He flicked it and inhaled deeply, tipped back his head and blew smoke at the ceiling.

Susan took a deep lungful of secondhand smoke and wondered why she'd quit. She got up and found a saucer in the kitchen that she handed to Nick in lieu of an ashtray.

"You don't care," she said as she sat back down, "if Ms. Edwards gets upset, or are you deliberately trying to annoy her?"

Nick smiled and Susan realized the smile came from somewhere deep inside; he'd switched something on and the muscles around his eyes created a smile that gave out warmth. It had made him famous, also made him a megabucks star and she could see why; he exuded sensitivity and understanding and, being big and strong, gave the impression he could take care of any threatening dangers.

"She won't mind," he said with a touch of malice, suggesting Ms. Edwards would mind very much.

The first lie, she thought. "Where were you during the lunch break?"

"In my trailer."

"The entire time?"

"Most of the time."

"When you weren't in your trailer, where were you?"

With a thumb, he flicked the end of the cigarette to get rid of ashes. "Uh—the caterer's truck, wandering around to work the kinks out. Uh—I don't know. Around."

"How well did you know Kay Bender?"

"Not at all."

"She worked on this movie."

"Yes, but we did no—socializing."

"Did you ever talk with her?"

"Maybe."

"What did you talk about?"

He didn't have his mind on Susan or her questions, or even on his answers; he kept craning his head to flick glances at Parkhurst. Parkhurst made a lot of people nervous, especially if he was behind them just out of their range of vision, but Nick didn't seem nervous.

"You know," he said after a moment's thought. "I don't believe I ever did talk with her."

"Tell me what you know about her."

He puffed on the cigarette. "Nothing. I didn't know anything about her." There was surprise and sadness in his voice. "Who said no man is an island?"

"Who went into the barn during the lunch break?"

"Oh, hell, I don't know. People might have been in and out. They're always in and out."

"You?"

"No."

"Who wanted to hurt Kay?"

Nick again focused attention on Susan. "I thought the fall was an accident."

Lie number two. She'd questioned too many suspects to miss the slight rise of shoulder muscles. "That's what we're trying to determine. Who had problems with her?"

"Nobody that I know of. You have to understand, I really had nothing to do with the girl. She did her work, doubling for Laura, and that was it. I mean, she must have been around, but—" He shrugged. "Sorry. We have dividing lines here just like every place else."

"Were you aware a pitchfork was on the set?"

"Sure."

"When did you last see it?"

"This morning. I used it in one of those cutesy bits where city slicker male ineptly spreads around straw." Engaging self-deprecating smile.

"What happened to it then?"

"I don't know, the prop man would take it."

"And do what with it?"

"Put it in the prop truck, most likely."

This was said with such offhand sincerity that Susan didn't know whether it was lie or truth.

37

She glanced at Parkhurst over Nick's shoulder and gave him a nod. Let's see how Nick Logan responded to Parkhurst. Moving fluidly, like one of the big cats, Parkhurst slid from the padded bench and came around where Nick could see him, then took a step closer, forcing Nick to look up at him.

"What's the conflict between you and Laura Edwards?"

Nick stubbed out his cigarette. "Conflict?"

"Love gone sour?"

Nick paused. "What does that have to do with Kay?"

"What do you know about her death?"

"Nothing."

"You didn't find her attractive?"

Nick answered that with a look of "come on, you can do better than that."

"You only interested in actresses?"

"What does that mean?"

"Sheri Lloyd."

"I see you've been picking up the on-site gossip."

"You're sleeping with Ms. Lloyd. How does Ms. Edwards feel about that?"

Susan wondered what Parkhurst felt about this whole tangle of lovers and ex-lovers. His face gave nothing away, it was cold and hard.

"That," Nick said, "is none of your business."

"Wrong, Mr. Logan." Parkhurst backed off and slid a haunch on an end table. "A young woman was killed. That makes it our business."

"The two aren't connected."

"Ms. Edwards was supposed to be on the railing when it went down. Figure it out, Mr. Logan."

He already had, Susan thought.

"You accusing me of trying to kill Laura?" There was something wrong about the way he said that. No explosive anger, the way an innocent man would normally respond.

"Why would you harm Ms. Edwards?"

Parkhurst's questioning differed greatly from Susan's soft-

38

voiced, "Let's find out what happened here." He dripped disbelief and made suspects so angry they got tangled up in explanations and said things they didn't mean to.

There was none of the laid-back California slouch about Nick Logan now, he was paying close attention, but if he was angry he was keeping a lid on it.

"I wouldn't harm a hair on her head."

"Who wants her dead?"

"No one that I know of." Nick swallowed.

The third lie. A suspect often swallows when he lies.

"Guess. Give me names."

"Laura's a beautiful woman," Nick began.

Parkhurst waited, the panther in the brush patiently waiting for the right moment.

"She raises passions . . ."

"Names." Parkhurst waited a little less patiently, the panther flicking the tip of his tail.

"I don't have names," Nick said. "You have to understand a lot of emotions run around on location. It comes from being so close together and being focused on the film. I don't know of any anger or hatred toward Laura, but that doesn't mean there isn't any. The costumer because Laura always slumps during fittings? The script writer because she transposes two words of his dialogue? None of that means anything and it's all forgotten when the director calls a wrap."

"What part do you play?"

"What?"

"Part," Parkhurst said slowly and distinctly, "as in role. In the movie."

"The hero," Nick said dryly. "I play a cop."

"Uh-huh. That's all for now, Mr. Logan. You're free to go."

Nick remained seated, took a breath, opened his mouth to ask a question, then changed his mind and got to his feet. He nodded and strode firmly—even in thongs—out. Hero exits trailer.

"Got a little carried away, didn't you?" Susan rose, stood behind Parkhurst in the doorway, and watched Nick Logan's back.

"He was using me."

"Using you?"

"Research for his role. I thought I'd show him how a hick cop conducts an interrogation." Parkhurst smiled, the panther seeing the antelope stumble. "Before I'm done, I may show him a thing or two he's never seen before."

5

Where the hell was Clem Jones? Yancy was worried about her. He hadn't seen the director's assistant since she'd upchucked on the barn floor. She didn't have sense enough to take care of herself, he'd known smarter geese. With her pink hair she wasn't easy to miss, so how come he hadn't spotted her anywhere, in his sheepdog missions to separate one individual and herd him along to the Edwards trailer? The director, Hayden Fifer, took some nipping at the heels to keep moving.

"This is wasting time," Fifer said.

He wasn't a large man, but he had a large voice. It must come from all that commanding of actors, the power went to his head. It sure didn't go to his heart, that was black like his hair. Black hair threaded with gray, gray beard and eyes the color of slate. Or flint maybe, the state of his heart. He had a good line in scowls, one of which he was using on Yancy. Yancy ignored it. You wouldn't pick him out of a crowd as the great Hollywood director. No jodhpurs, no beret, no long cigarette holder. Plain jeans— they did have somebody's fancy name on them, but jeans nevertheless—and a plain white T-shirt. Not even a smart-ass message. His forehead was sunburned and so were his arms.

Just as they reached the trailer, Nick Logan opened the door. Fifer barely waited for his male star to clear the doorway before he barreled in. Logan took a side jump off the trailer steps and raised a puff of dust and pollen from the dried grass. With a mock salute to Parkhurst, he strode off.

"How long are you going to hold me up?" Yancy heard Fifer say as the trailer door closed.

"I'm sorry to keep you waiting," Susan said. And she was, too.

Hayden Fifer was tightly wrapped, either worry about his movie or maybe just plain irritation that someone else was calling the shots. "Please sit down, Mr. Fifer. We'll try not to keep you long." No longer than necessary and she intended to pour deferential regard all over him, soothe his ego, and anything else that needed doing so he wouldn't get in her way while she did her job.

"I can't sit around wasting time."

"Just a few questions," Susan said.

Fifer slid onto one of the couches, sat with his hands on his knees, ready to get this nonsense over and get back to the important substance of life.

"Disruption and waiting are inevitable after an unexplained death, I'm afraid." Susan used her best cool voice, the one that stood her in good stead in numerous situations: with irate superiors, malcontent subordinates, drunks, belligerents, and just plain when she didn't know what the hell was going on. A voice that allowed her to skate around on potential thin ice with the best of them.

"It was an accident."

"If the pitchfork hadn't been where it was, Ms. Bender would probably be alive. We'll need to speak separately with everybody who was present, and we'll try to do that without causing undue inconvenience."

The fingers on Fifer's left hand danced against his knee. His eyes clicked left and then right, he nodded. "Sure, sure. How long?"

"We won't be certain of the cause of death until after an autopsy."

Fifer's eyes fixed on her face, the fingers became still. "She fell."

"Yes, sir. There will also be some lab investigations and that will take time. We'll try to take care of everything as quickly as possible."

The fingers resumed dancing. "It isn't that I'm not affected by the girl's death."

"I understand, sir. We will need a list of all the people employed by you, and it would be helpful if you could give us their room numbers at the hotel."

"Clem can do that," he said.

There was still no sign of Clem Jones as Yancy tromped around in search of Sheri Lloyd. These fields used to be pastureland. Way off in the northeast corner was a small stock pond, scrub pines grew here and there. Knee-high weeds and grasses had been mowed down in one section to accommodate the vehicles. Trailers for superstars and director. Trailers divided into cubicles called honey wagon rooms for lesser actors, photo doubles, stand-ins, and stunt people. Trailers for wardrobe, makeup, and props. Caterer's truck—Better Than Home Cookin'—from Los Angeles. Ha. Probably afraid we didn't have calamari and garlic ice cream out here on the prairie. A tent staked out for serving hot meals from behind a row of steam trays, long tables and folding chairs for eating. Semis and vans and town cars, flatbed trucks and an electrician's truck and a grip's truck. Bicycles. Did these California people know it rained here? One solid Kansas gullywasher and that's it, Joe. No movin' anything except the bicycles.

Sheri Lloyd was in her own cubicle with her name on the door, but she didn't care to come with him. After some convincing, she got up and followed along, high-heeled sandals tottering over taped cables on the uneven ground. She made her displeasure apparent when he then asked her to wait, standing right out there under the cottonwood, in the heat if not the sun. "It's too damn hot," she repeated many times. He had to admit she had a point there.

"Where's Ms. Jones?" he asked.

"I have no idea. You said they wanted to see me." Sheri twitched her shoulders, raised a hand, and flicked long bronze hair over her shoulder.

"Yes, ma'am. It'll be only a moment." He wanted her all lined up to go as soon as they were finished with the director. With Lieutenant Parkhurst looking like a storm about to happen, Yancy didn't want to give him any aggravation. You couldn't tell so much with the chief. She just always looked poised and classy, kind of haughty with her blue eyes and dark hair, but he didn't think she was any too cool either. She hadn't wanted the movie here from the start, back when everybody else thought it was more exciting than Fourth of July fireworks.

"Well—" Sheri smiled at him. She had the prettiest, whitest, straightest teeth he'd ever seen, dazzling bright in her tanned face. Everything about her dazzled. Well-toned muscles. Surfing probably. Wasn't that what they did in southern California? When they weren't in aerobics classes.

She surely did not like to be kept waiting. She pointed that out to him over and over. Not that he blamed her. It *was* hot; little beads of sweat stood out on her smooth forehead. She constantly tugged at the ends of her skimpy white top thing. No bra. He admired the flexibility of the red shorts that were just a little bit too short—exposing small half-moons of her buttocks, also tanned, he noted—and the shapely length of thigh and curve of calf.

"How come they want me? I wasn't even in there when she fell."

"I wouldn't know, ma'am."

Delicately, she patted fingertips at the hollow of her throat. "Is it always this hot here?"

44

"No, ma'am. Only half the time, the other half you're freezing your butt off. Being from California, I figure you must like heat."

"I don't like it here, I can tell you that. I can't wait to get out of this place."

Yancy nodded. Hollywood go home. He could go back to being a cop. But this accident that smelled like homicide sure beat all to hell whatever story they were trying to film.

"If you want to know the truth," Sheri said, "I'm not terribly terribly surprised this happened. Laura's been hyper-uptight from the beginning, you know?" She stopped for a second, then added, "Like just waiting to mess up super bad," in case he wasn't following along with his dim countrified brain.

"If you want to know the truth," she said again, "Fifer knows it too. You can be sure he isn't telling it like it is in there. You can be *sure* of that. He needs a great success artistically and financially and I'm afraid—" She shook her head sadly.

"I understood this movie was going well."

"Oh, that's what they *say*, but Laura—well, she was quite good in her day. With a certain type of part, one that didn't require—how shall I put it—a quality of vulnerability—she was okay. She has no subtleties. Just a certain hard—ah—brittle, you might say, archness. It's all just so—so—TV miniseries."

"Isn't Ms. Edwards supposed to be a great actress?"

"*Pa-leese.*" Sheri laid a hand on her chest, fingers fanned out over a breast. "I have nothing but the greatest respect for her as a performer, but I'd have to admit, since you force me, that her—talents are limited. And this film—she was killing it."

Why was she wasting all this stuff on him? In her view, he could only be a gofer, sent to fetch and carry. Rehearsal maybe? "Fifer isn't pleased with Ms. Edwards's performance?"

Sheri lifted her hair off her neck, making her nipples poke against the halter top. "You have to know the kind of man he is. In control, very circumspect, on the outside, but inside—inside he's really—screaming. And I know—only because I know him

45

so well—I know he realizes he made a mistake with Laura. As a matter of fact . . ." She leaned closer, stroked a long curl of hair, and twirled it around her finger.

He knew he was supposed to be spellbound here, lost in all her sexy shimmering. He smelled her musky perfume, got a glimpse of those incredible boobs.

"I just happened to overhear—and I wouldn't want you to think I was eavesdropping—I mean, I wouldn't *stoop*—but he was on the phone and there was this despair in his voice and he was saying"—she lowered her voice—" 'I know something has to be done.' And then there was this pause, like the other person was speaking, you know? And then Fifer got this really cold—I mean actually frightening, it was so cold—look on his face and he said, 'I'll take care of her. She won't be a problem.' " Sheri widened her eyes at the enormous implications.

"You believe he was talking about—?"

"Laura." A little impatience here. She caught it right away. "Laura forced him to take her on. I personally know he didn't want her. She has some kind of"—Sheri searched her mind for a word of enough devastation— "*something* she's holding over his head." Sheri nodded sagely. "That's the only reason she's in. And she's destroying this movie."

"Who was Fifer talking with?"

"Well, one of the investors, of course." She was a wee bit exasperated he was wasting time on the nonessentials. She moved constantly while she talked; her hands fluttered and her hair swayed and her butt jiggled and her boobs bounced. No wonder she was sweating, all that action had to be exhausting.

She was putting on quite a performance. He had to give her flawless skin, mouth-drying shapeliness, hair asking for fingers to get tangled in, and certainly gorgeous teeth, but she wasn't lighting any fires. He'd never, at work or at play, found contempt a turn-on. All right, she probably didn't have much experience with homicide. Maybe this was her way of coping, handling fear, shock, anxiety, grief even—anything's possible. Or maybe she was just a cold, emotionally stunted, selfish little bitch. Or maybe she had a hand in the fall and there was some purpose behind this titillating display.

"Oh, pay no attention—" She laid her fingers on his arm. "It's just—oh, I just—everything is too much. There's a curse on this movie. Something more, something very bad—" Tears glistened in her eyes.

Now Yancy was impressed. When the emotion got turned on, he'd have expected heaving bosom and muffled sobs.

"Yes, ma'am," he said.

Suddenly she stopped all the jiggling and bouncing and stood stock-still. A breath caught going in. He turned to see what got her attention. Ambulance out on the road. Slow and silent. The very stuff of which movies were made. Endless blue sky. Not a cloud. The tortured scream of a jet plane and then a thin white jet stream. Ambulance rolled by leaving a cloud of dust in its wake.

She paled. He took her elbow. "Ms. Lloyd?"

She swayed. He eased her around so she couldn't see the road. She shivered. The ambulance, swaying and bouncing, moved on.

"Listen," she said. "I can't wait around here all day. I can't help any way. So—"

The trailer door popped open and the director shot out.

"Fifer?" She put out her hand to stop him.

"Later, baby." He patted her arm. "I'm busy now."

With a little pout, she watched him stride off. Lieutenant Parkhurst got her attention and invited her inside. She turned on the smile and the jiggle and bounce and tripped up the steps, managing to slide very close to Parkhurst as she went by. Hey now, must be some kind of performance she was planning for the lieutenant.

"Yancy," Parkhurst said, "round up Clem Jones. Tell White he can turn the rest of them loose. Make sure he has names, local and permanent addresses, and phone numbers ditto."

Yancy nodded and headed for the caterer's tent where White was keeping two dozen or so people corralled. They sat in folding chairs at long tables, or stood around in clumps, yakking with each other. Soft drink cans, glasses, cups, and plates with various snacks were all over the place. Nobody was pounding a fist and demanding to be let go. These people were used to hanging around waiting. He did notice all eyes shift to him when he passed along the message to White. Clem Jones wasn't with them. He asked if anyone had seen her.

"Here somewhere."

"Around."

"Every time you move, you trip over her."

But nobody could tell him where she was now and the last time anyone remembered seeing her was in the barn after Kay Bender fell.

Had she slipped through in all the confusion? Gone back to the hotel? He was getting all tense about her. He hoped nothing had happened to the silly little twit.

Tapping at Nick Logan's trailer got him Nick, but no Clem Jones.

"You mind if I talk with you for a bit?" Nick asked.

"I'm looking to find Ms. Jones. Any ideas?"

"I'll help you." Nick stubbed out a cigarette and shoved his feet into thongs.

"You work with that guy in there?" Nick gave a hitch to his jeans and fell into step beside Yancy.

"The lieutenant? Sure."

"What's his name, Parkhurst? How is he to work for?"

No way Yancy was going to reach into that funny little can of worms. Sometimes the lieutenant was a volcano about to go off, and sometimes he wasn't. You didn't know. You paid attention. "He gets the job done," Yancy said, sidestepping the obligation to be specific.

With a mocking expression in his eyes, Nick acknowledged the diplomacy. "You been a cop long?"

"Six years."

"Like it?"

"Sometimes."

"Tell me about being a cop."

"What do you want to know?"

"Why a cop?"

Yancy shrugged. That was simple; he'd needed a job. If he had a father somewhere he'd never met the guy. His mother didn't live in the same world as everybody else. Sweet, yes, and beautiful, but loony as owl shit.

When he was a little kid he'd come home from school hoping there'd be something to eat in the house. Like as not, his mother would hug him fiercely, grab his hand, and race with him to the woods. She'd point out butterflies and wildflowers, touch a petal with a fingertip as gentle as a puff of spring breeze. She'd sing in a soft clear voice, eerie haunting songs about blood and murder and revenge and unrequited love. He'd have made a pact with the devil for one peanut butter sandwich, would even have shared it with his sister who used to fantasize about food until he yelled at her to shut up.

"It's a job," Yancy said. He'd wanted to be fireman. Saving children from burning buildings, rescuing kittens from treetops. A hero. God help him, he was his mother's son. She'd marked him with all her fairy stories without him even knowing it. The fire department wasn't hiring, but the police department was.

At the makeup trailer, a man told him Clem wasn't there, he didn't know where she was.

"What kind of man is he?" Nick asked.

"Who?" Yancy's mind was still running along the track that read what to do about his mother. By this time it was worn into a deep rut. For a moment he thought Nick was asking an oblique question about Yancy himself. And it startled him. Not only because he didn't know the answer, but also because it seemed to hold echoes of his sister's accusatory voice.

"This Parkhurst guy."

"What are you getting at?"

Nick smiled, shrugged. "Oh, hell, I don't know. I got the impression a whole lot of hostility was coming my way. Made me wonder why. Does he not like outsiders? Is that it? Or is it me in

49

particular he doesn't like?" Nick hooked his thumbs over his belt and loosened his knees. "All right, stranger." Good John Wayne imitation. "This town isn't big enough for both of us."

Yancy smiled. For a big movie star type, Nick was an okay guy, they'd even gotten friendly over a beer or two. "The lieutenant's a good cop."

"Yeah? Good enough he won't be swayed by trying to solve this immediately? Just to get it cleaned up?"

"What are you getting at?" Nobody answered his tap at the wardrobe trailer. With Nick at his heels, he went inside. Clothing on racks filled it until there was barely room to walk the length of it. Stacked washer and dryer at one end, worktable for sewing, mending, et cetera by the door.

"Hell if I know," Nick said as Yancy closed the door behind them. "I'm just concerned. Kay was an okay kid. I didn't know her well, but she was a part of this game and if it was more than an accident—somebody has to look out for her. She can't do it herself."

"What does that mean?"

Nick hunched his shoulders and shoved his hands in his pockets. "Oh, hell, justice, I guess. If that doesn't sound too high-principled."

Yancy stopped and looked at the actor. "Are you asking me if the lieutenant has the smarts to recognize a clue if he trips over one? What are you going to do? Step in and clear the case? Real movie stuff. The cops are so stupid they don't know what they're doing. But, by God, you're going to track down the killer. See justice is done for this woman, because she can't do it for herself and she's one of your own."

"Something like that, yeah."

"You've been seeing too many movies, Nick."

The actor gave him a smile. "Yeah, I guess." After a moment he sketched a wave and started to flap off in his thongs. Not the best footwear for the terrain, his feet and ankles would likely be covered with chiggers by the time he got back to his trailer. For half a second Yancy wondered what that was all about—with

50

these people you never could tell what was real and what was made-up—then he went back to worrying about Clem Jones. She was always around, looking at him with withering scorn, mouthing at him. She chewed bubble gum, for God's sake, and had pink hair.

"Oh, Yancy?"

He turned. "Yeah?"

"You might try the barn," Nick said. "Clem's a morbid little thing. She might be there."

Yancy headed for the barn. The yellow tape was down, that meant Osey had finished taking prints and picking through straw for evidence. The chief really was moving this along as fast as possible. He looked inside. Body gone, no Clem, no people, but everything else still there, tangles of cable, cameras, booms, mikes. Just as he turned away he heard noises, muffled sounds from the loft, then a high thin keening that stirred the hair on the back of his neck.

He clambered up the ladder, halted when he got to eye level, and cautiously peered into the huge shadowy space. It took a moment to spot her; the ankle-length prison-striped smock sort of fit in with the dimness. Pink hair didn't. She sat at the edge of the drop just where the railing had broken, knees drawn up, arms around them. She froze when she saw him.

"Ms. Jones?"

Like a wild thing, she scrabbled away, ended up against the rough wall, eyes wide with panic, mouth open for air.

"Hey now," he said softly. "Take it easy."

She was a mess; black eye makeup smeared all over her face, nose running, pink hair all every which way.

Recognition slowly seeped into her eyes. They were an odd tan color and a shaft of sunlight angling through the small window at the peak of the roof picked out gold flecks. Tears spilled.

"I killed her," she whispered.

51

6

Slowly, Yancy levered himself up into the loft. Go easy here, Clem didn't look too well wired together. A sudden move on his part and he'd have her exploding, then there'd be raw nerve ends dangling all over the place. He edged along to a spot where he was between her and the broken rail, then squatted, facing her.

"It's all right," he said. "Nobody's going to hurt you." He kept his voice loose and slow.

She brought an elbow up over her eyes, gulped, and sniffled on a ghost of a sob. "Yancy, you got a sweet voice, but you're full of shit."

Her flip, so quick from damp misery to attack, surprised him. Relieved him too. As long as she was mouthing off she wasn't likely to throw herself over the edge. She looked like a homeless cat, scared and spitting at everybody.

He'd better treat her like a stray, she seemed better able to handle that. This brought up thoughts about her life he didn't have time to go into at the moment. He stood up, took four strides, sat beside her with his back against the rough wall, and rested his forearms on his bent knees. "What are you doing up here?"

She pinned him with a gaze like rifle barrels. Leaning forward, he pulled a handkerchief from his back pocket and held it out to her.

She looked at it like she'd never seen such a thing before, then she scrunched it and scrubbed it over her face, mixing tears and black mascara and blue eye shadow and white makeup into one big muddy mask. She blew her nose. "Go away, Yancy. I hate men."

"You said you killed her." He waited. "What did that mean?"

"Life is all one big gigantic joke. Nothing but banana peels and pratfalls. A fart in a cathedral. It was my fault."

"What was?"

"Take your questions and your busy little mind and your dithyrambic little self and get away from me."

Dithyrambic? He better get himself a dictionary. "Why was it your fault?"

"If I'd gotten Laura up here like I was supposed to, Kay wouldn't have fallen."

"Then it might be Ms. Edwards who'd be dead."

Clem grimaced. "I'm slaying dragons."

"I've slain a dragon or two in my life. Maybe I could help."

"Are you deaf? Get lost."

"Sorry. I didn't just wander up for a straw to pick my teeth with. I was sent to get you."

"Good boy. You did what you were told."

"Yes, ma'am, I usually do."

"Your mother must be very proud."

"As is yours, I'm sure."

"I don't have a mother. Go away."

"You don't have a hope of making me go away. You will come with me, docilely and mutely, or I will cuff you and drag you."

Clem looked at him seriously for a long minute. "Can you really do that?"

"No. So I'd appreciate it if you'd just haul ass out of here and come with me."

She let a beat go by, then another, then tossed off, "Okay."

Yancy attempted to help her down the ladder and got a kick for his attentions.

"Where are you taking me?" she asked when they passed from the dimness of the barn out into bright sunlight.

"Laura Edwards's trailer to answer some questions by the higher-ups."

"That guy that looks like a grizzly about to attack? What's his name?"

"The lieutenant, that who you're talking about? Parkhurst."

"He's a cop," she said, getting everything clear.

"Yeah."

"I don't want to talk to him."

"They just want to find out what happened."

"I saw him before."

"Before what?" Yancy asked, sitting hard on exasperation.

"He was hanging around the barn during the lunch break, when nobody else was here."

Yancy delivered her at the trailer and wondered if that crack about the lieutenant had any truth in it.

Susan pulled her blouse untucked as she opened the door of the pickup. The sky was taking on the hue of cobalt blue. The air was finally cooling down a little—it damn well should at almost seven-thirty—but the pickup, having baked all afternoon, was like an oven. She pushed on the air-conditioning, then pushed it off and cranked down the windows. With the truck in motion, a little air passed through and it smelled of coming dusk and recently cut grasses and lilacs. Cicadas hummed somewhere. Her mind replayed the session with Clem Jones. Susan couldn't get a clear fix on Clem. One minute she was world-weary, the next smart-ass, the next lost and bewildered. Parkhurst was surprisingly easy on her. Susan wondered why.

Parkhurst and Laura Edwards. Talk about surprise. Wife, for God's sake.

Lately, her interest in Parkhurst had just as much to do with hormones as business. She'd listed all the reasons why it wasn't a good idea, why she'd be a damn fool. And then this famous actress comes along, wraps herself around him, and Susan is as green-eyed as any teenager. Jesus. What a mess.

Focus on the dead woman and how she got that way. Get over to the Sunflower Hotel and go through Kay Bender's room. Find out next of kin and notify. Go through all the statements of cast and crew and see what doesn't fit. Find out when Owen Fisher had scheduled the autopsy and be there. Probably early tomorrow morning. Attending autopsies, while not her favorite activity, sometimes turned up important information that got to her quicker than if she'd waited for the formal report.

Okay? That enough to keep your mind in check? It still wandered back to Parkhurst and Laura Edwards.

Get a grip.

She drove along Main Street, a street paved with red bricks and lined with tall maples, and thought as she had many times before that Hampstead was actually a pretty little town. In the gathering dusk, the old-fashioned lantern-shaped streetlights glowed softly throwing out pools of gold. The buildings, many of them made of native limestone, were old and impressive with fancy cornices and parapets. At Seventh Street, she turned left past the courthouse, a Gothic-style type with a clock tower; the stone had mellowed over the years to a warm cream color. It had been built in 1906, the year of the San Francisco earthquake.

San Francisco. Maybe now was the time to go back where she belonged.

Can't. Work to do.

She pulled into the lot behind the police department, a relatively new building, red brick with white trim, and nosed in beside Parkhurst's Bronco. Sliding from the truck, she glanced up at the communications tower to make sure the owl was still standing sentry. Birds tended to roost there and interfere with transmitting and receiving, sometimes to the point of reducing everything to fuzz. The stuffed owl was to keep them away. Detective Osey Pickett's idea. He'd also been the one to scale the tower. Good kid, Osey. Chock-full of local lore.

Inside, she took the corridor covered with indoor-outdoor carpeting in an icky brown color and paused at the doorway of Osey and Parkhurst's office. Osey wasn't in. Parkhurst stood by his desk, back toward her, and turned before she could speak. The room was dim, not dark, but murky enough that she couldn't see his eyes clearly. His face was carefully blank.

"Right," he said. "I'm on my way." *To your office* was unspoken.

Well, at least they were still a team, no need for dialogue. Her office had glass halfway down across the front. She flicked the light switch—more light, more clarity, right?—and adjusted the blinds to half-mast. During her first year the natives had stared at her like she was a strange and wondrous fish. She was from San Francisco. We know what that's like. Freaks and perverts. The fishbowl effect still made her self-conscious. The carpet here was dark blue, not much better in quality, but at least better in color. The desk was gray metal, standard government issue, also the chair, swivel with green vinyl. The visitor's chair was a wooden relic with arms. She hung her shoulder bag over the coat tree in the corner.

She'd started as acting chief, temporary. The mayor didn't like her; the townspeople didn't like her and didn't want an outsider, especially a woman, in the job. Members of the department agreed with both. There was no danger of permanence. Well, the acting recently got dropped. Now she was the real thing, and the mayor still didn't like her, the townspeople still didn't want her, and some of her officers still agreed with both.

Parkhurst came in with two soft drink cans—a delaying tactic, she assumed—and handed her one. She bent up the tab and took a sip. He looked at her, paced to the window, held down a slat, and looked out at the street where streetlights were coming on.

"Wife?" She'd meant to be a little more smooth, work up to it with some finesse, for Christ's sake, but the word just popped

57

out. She put her feet on the desk, legs crossed at the ankles. Why had she given up smoking? This was a cigarette moment, if ever she saw one.

With a knee, Parkhurst nudged the wooden armchair closer, sat low on his spine, and stretched his legs out. "Once upon a time," he said. "Long long ago. Not now."

"You were married to Laura Edwards."

He made a sound, half laugh, half snort. "She was just plain Laura Edwards back then."

He tipped the can, took a long drink, and rested it on his chest. "It was twelve years ago. We were a couple of kids. She thought I needed my horizons expanded. I thought she needed taking care of." He gazed at the can, rubbed a thumb through the condensation, and took a quick swig. "It turned out we were both wrong."

His voice was flat: don't push it, this is as far as I intend to go. If it had been only personal, Susan would have dropped it, but a death had occurred. She couldn't simply let it hang there. "It seems like you might have made at least a mention of the fact that you were married."

"Oh, hell, it was an awkward *fact* to just drop into conversation. Lovely weather we're having. Oh, by the way, I used to be married to Laura Edwards."

Yes, actually, any normal person would have done just that. Especially when news got around that Laura Edwards was coming to town. Susan hadn't known he'd ever been married at all, let alone to an actress of Edwards's note.

Parkhurst sat quietly, his hard gaze playing over her face. She had no idea what thoughts were behind the silence that stretched out. This case was going to be a bitch no matter which way she turned it.

"Have you kept in touch with her over the years?"

"No." He looked perfectly relaxed, except for the little knot of muscle at the corner of his jaw.

"God damn it. I know this is awkward, but we have an investigation going on. You're involved, simply by your relation-

58

ship to what may be the intended victim. At this point I don't even know which side of the fence you're on. It doesn't help any when you answer emotionally loaded questions with yes or no. I can see there's all kinds of stuff here you'd rather not go into. I'd like to respect your wishes"—the hell, she would—"but that's not possible. You will talk to me or I will put you on suspension until this case is cleared." She kept her voice calm and low with no hint of challenge. Challenge would set him off like a rocket.

"You're the boss."

Yes, and she didn't like to hear that response. It meant he wasn't going to cooperate, he was going to be combative, and that made her angry.

He continued to look at her, then to her great surprise, he smiled. A quick, apologetic "you're right and life's a pie in the face" smile that disappeared fast, but nevertheless a smile. That was such a rare occurrence she immediately got nervous.

"I'm sorry," he said. "You don't know what I'd give for this film company to be shooting their damn movie somewhere else."

She could make a good guess. "You didn't leave town."

He gave her a sour look. "The thought crossed my mind. It seemed cowardly. Besides, they're probably going to be here too long. And she had no idea where I was. With a little care, there was no reason our paths should cross."

"Sometimes life is interesting that way."

"Oh, yeah." He studied the cola can as though he were memorizing it. "We were from different worlds. Me, slums and street gangs. She lived in a nice middle-class house with a nice middle-class family. Her father was an accountant. He used numbers and pencils. My father used curses and fists."

"How did you meet?" If the question wasn't strictly pertinent, it was one she wanted answered.

"It was a dark and stormy night." He took a drink. "She was on the highway with a flat, drenched to the bone. I changed the tire."

Susan waited for him to go on. He didn't, but she could imagine how it went. Laura damply grateful, intrigued by this dark man in uniform. It probably started with coffee somewhere first, moved up to a drink, and then dinner. From there everything took off.

"I courted her," Parkhurst said with mocking humor. "Flowers and chocolates. Very traditional. Very unoriginal. We were married two months later. Her father gave her away in the family church while her mother wept and her brother looked manly."

"Do you feel any bitterness?" Susan emptied her can and set it silently on the desk.

"After twelve years?" He tipped up his can, drained it, and sailed it to the wastebasket with a little more spin than he intended. He picked up Susan's—held it easy. Lots of other stuff maybe, but no bitterness. It clinked when it hit.

Laura had been swept away by the idea of marrying a cop, especially a hard-ass like him. She'd never known anybody like him, he smelled of danger and violence, she could pretend to dance close to the edge. He was crazy in love with her. Laura was all that was good and kind and warm and clean; everything he wanted and assumed he'd never have.

She was a drama student, going to be a star someday. And so were all her friends. They liked classes, they liked each other, they liked to party. They didn't like him. They thought he was a dead brain and they couldn't understand why she had saddled herself with him. He was a rookie then, finding it difficult to play all night and function on the job. He kept going with it until the drugs finally tore it. Her friends, used to him, got more and more open about what they were smoking, shooting, or snorting. Finally, they got so blatant, he couldn't turn his head anymore. His job put him on the other side of the fence. One evening he lost patience and dragged her out of there. They slung words at each other that ricocheted around the enclosed car.

That night he came close to hitting her, close enough it scared the shit out of him. He had a temper, legacy from a drunk, abusive father, about the only inheritance he got. And at that exact moment he knew he was losing her. Anger and frustration grew in his belly and built a hot rage so fierce it roared through his head. His mind flashed on the old man, face red, fist raised. He lit out and walked for miles, then walked some more, solemnly promising himself it would never happen again. Never would he get that close, never would he become his father.

He and Laura had stayed together a few more months, shouting at each other, inflicting pain, but he didn't ever come near to hurting her with his hands. Feelings ran high between them. They rolled around in bed with a hot passion, then lay dripping and spent, not speaking a word. Through it all, he had the sense she was standing to one side and observing: this is the way tragic, doomed love is played.

"Another dark and stormy night," he said to Susan, "she had enough of my mundane character, my repressed personality, my provincial thinking, and my exceptionally closed mind. She took off for California."

"You have any unfinished business?"

"No." Before today he'd have bet his life on it. He shouldn't be so careless with his life.

"Anything else you need to tell me?"

"What do you want to know?"

"Whether you have any reason, real or imagined, old or new, for trying to harm Laura Edwards."

"No." Embarrassment. He'd known when he heard she was rolling into town that someday she'd land him in a shitload of embarrassment. And she came through like the trouper she was.

"No conflicts? No, she took your collection of baseball cards and you vowed to get them back?"

"No." Laura took her dancing and dazzling and curious and exciting self and left him sad and ashamed and failed and relieved. "We didn't have anything except our clothes. She took hers and left mine."

Susan let her feet drop to the floor and leaned forward. "As

I see it, we have two paths to explore. Someone tried to kill Laura Edwards and we need to prevent another attempt and find out who."

She picked up a pencil and threaded it through her fingers, tapped eraser end and sharpened end alternately. "Or Kay Bender was the intended victim. In which case the perp could be Laura Edwards. She didn't show up when she was supposed to. Who better than Laura could manage that?"

Parkhurst took a breath, let it out. "Yeah," he said, "I realize that."

"You realize that because of your relationship with Laura Edwards I have to consider you a suspect?"

7
—

$\mathscr{I}$t was after eight, with only an hour or so of daylight left, by the time Yancy turned in the squad car and got into his own vehicle. Rolling his shoulders to work out the knots left by the fourteen-hour day, he cranked the windows down to let the hot air inside mingle with the tepid air outside and fired up the Cherokee. It idled rough. He needed to take care of that.

Shoving the gear in reverse, he backed out and took Eleventh Street for a block, then swung right on Vermont to get out of town. He was late. Beyond the city limits, he accelerated past barbed-wire fenced fields of buffalo grass and wild flowers, a few dark green cedars dotted over the hills.

What should he do about the little nugget Clem Jones had tossed him? Ask the lieutenant? Yeah, right. With all due respect, sir, what were you doing at the barn just before the stuntwoman got killed? Forget about questioning Clem. She'd tell him whatever suited her fancy at the moment, with no relationship to the truth.

Drop it on the chief's desk? Bad idea. Ratting out a superior was never a good idea. Anyway, he liked the lieutenant, would trust his life to the man. And Clem was some kind of nutcase.

Okay, then what? Ask questions? See what turned up. If Parkhurst was there, somebody else might have seen him. Maybe Yancy's teamster buddy Mac would know something. A crow sat on the mailbox, and as Yancy made a left, it fixed him with a bright malicious eye, uttered a jeering "caw," and took flight.

"You're probably right," Yancy muttered as he jounced toward the house. A white wood frame, in this kind of light, it didn't need paint so bad. Small, one-story, it had a quiet pitch to the roof, wide windows all around, and a porch that extended the whole length of the front. Trees reached up behind, flowers—snapdragons, bluebonnets, poppies, hollyhocks, and God knew what else—ran unchecked front and back. Tall structures like birdhouses sprouted here and there, looking like they'd simply grown taller than the other plant life.

He backed up the drive and parked the car ass end against the garage door. As late as he was, it couldn't hurt to have a fast getaway in the making. Joke.

"Finally decided to show up?"

Startled, he turned. The hammock strung between two walnut trees sagged under the solid weight of Dallas Walsh, all spiffed up in suit and tie. A suit and tie kind of guy he wasn't.

"Hi, Dallas. Sorry I'm late."

With a polished shoe tip, Dallas shoved at the ground and swung the hammock. "Tell it to your sister, buddy. Last I saw her she was crying at the kitchen table."

"I had to work."

Dallas waved a beefy hand. "Take it to Serena."

Yancy found his sister sitting at the table in the graying daylight taking lemons, one by one, from the blue pottery bowl in the center and carefully placing them in a circle around it. He flicked on the ceiling light. She squinted at him. She wasn't crying, but she had been, eyes red and watery.

"Serena—" He sat across from her and took both her hands, they had a strong citrusy smell. "I'm sorry."

"You might have called." She jerked her hands away and went back to lemons.

64

"I didn't have a chance. I'm sorry."

"Sorry won't do it. I've been looking forward to this evening for weeks. Dallas and I had plans. It was all arranged. I bought a new dress, for heaven's sake." She touched the high neck of the green dress and stood to shake the folds from the flared skirt, a pretty green that matched her eyes and set to advantage her auburn hair.

"You look fantastic."

"Frankly, Peter, it wasn't you I was trying to impress." She tip-tapped across the wood floor to the stove in the center. With its copper hood, it was the only modern touch in the old-fashioned room. Open shelves packed with supplies lined two walls above the counters, and glass-fronted cabinets took up the third.

She clicked on the burner under the teakettle, then went to the window, turned to face him, and crossed her arms. "This can't go on."

"Why didn't you go to your party? You knew I'd get here as soon as I could."

"Haven't you heard anything I've said?"

"Serena—"

"She's your mother too, and right now I'm feeling like you don't fully appreciate that, because if you did you'd give some consideration to the fact that I'm still living here. I've been doing it for a long time now and I haven't voiced many complaints."

She stared at the three glass flycatchers on the counter, ran a fingertip over the middle one. "I'm trapped here, Peter. And I'd like to move out. Dallas and I—we want to move in together."

"That's great."

Serena spun around. "She set herself on fire today."

"What!"

"Sit down. She's okay. She's asleep."

"What happened?"

"I was a little late getting home and she decided she would fix supper. She was making an omelet and her sleeve caught on fire."

"You're sure she's all right?"

"Yes, Peter, she's all right. This time. Fortunately, I came home and managed to get it out before she got burned. Since the stroke, she's just not—"

A stroke didn't seem right, not at forty-six.

"She can't be left alone, Peter. When I came to fix her lunch today and make sure she was okay, she wasn't here. I was frantic."

"Where was she?"

"I have no idea. I drove around looking for her as long as I could. I had to get back. I called and called and kept calling. Finally, she answered the phone."

"Where had she been?"

"Who knows. She couldn't remember."

Scooting the chair to a slant, he stretched out his legs and rested one arm on the table. "What do you suggest we do?"

"You know perfectly well what we have to do. I can't be here every minute. I have a job. And don't tell me to quit. Maybe it's your turn to quit." She glared at him. Tears ruined it; you can't glare effectively through weepy eyes.

He went to her and folded his arms around her, rested his chin on the top of her head. He couldn't quit, even if he wanted to. While his salary wasn't diamonds and caviar, it beat hers by a country mile, and they needed the money.

"This can't go on," she said.

"I know," he murmured. "I'll think of something, I promise."

"Oh, Peter." Hands flat against his chest, she gave him a push, went to the towel holder next to the sink, and yanked off a paper towel. She ripped it in half and blew her nose. "Thinking won't do it. There's only one solution and you know it. We have to find a place for her to live."

"This is her home."

Serena started crying again. "I know."

"Okay." He smoothed her hair back. "I'll look into it. We can't do anything tonight. Why don't you and Dallas go—"

"Peter!"

"I know it's too late. Isn't there something? I don't have to be back till six in the morning. I could stay here tonight."

"It won't do. You can't make atonement by staying one lousy night. You might ease your conscience, you won't solve anything."

He kept his voice low. "I only want to do what's right."

"That's what we all want. The problem is what's right for one isn't right for all. Right depends on viewpoint. What do you think is right? She stays here and everything goes back to the way it used to be? That's not going to happen. She had a stroke, Peter. She's not ever going to be like she used to be, and all your wishing and ignoring the facts isn't going to make it so."

Eyes closed, he rubbed a hand down his jaw. Fighting with Serena made him feel small and beady-eyed. They'd always stuck together. Growing up as they did, it was the only way to survive. "What do you want to do?"

She sighed, part sadness, part irritation. "You know what we have to do."

"She's afraid of that very thing."

"Damn it, Peter, you think I want this?" Serena blew her nose on the other half of the paper towel. "You think I don't ache for her? Wish she was all right?" A high giggle popped out. Yancy smiled.

All right didn't fit with their mother. She'd always had a flexible attitude toward reality.

"That's not the only option," he said. "We could find somebody to stay with her."

"Twenty-four hours a day?"

"I could move back, be here at night."

"That's great. And what will you do when you have to work nights? And how will you pay for it?"

"I don't know. I'll work something out." He didn't suggest Dallas move in here. In her more lucid moments—as lucid as she ever was or could be—their mother liked Dallas fine. Other times she got him confused with the villains in the grimmer

Celtic tales. Besides, Dallas had a larger, more livable place of his own. "And the money for some kind of home?"

"The house."

Yancy suddenly felt bone-tired; sadness—the kind that clings after grief ebbs—oozed over him like an oil slick. "What about Elmo?"

"I don't know about Elmo. I just don't know."

"*Peter?*" Their mother's voice came from the other room. "Is that you?"

"You mind if I see her?"

"Stop that!" Serena slapped the cabinet with the palm of one hand, the sound was like the crack of a circus whip. "I won't be the bad guy here."

"No. I'm sorry." His hands cupped her head so she couldn't look away. "I don't know what to do. That makes me mean."

"*Peter—?*"

Serena poked him in the chest with an index finger. "Go. You always make her happy."

The house was basically four rooms, kitchen and living room in front, two bedrooms behind, bathroom tucked in between. Their mother's bedroom was on the right of the hallway, Serena's on the left. Until he was eight and Serena ten, they'd shared it. For his eighth birthday, he got to move into the garage. A little nippy in the winter, but all his.

On the floor in the corner, Elmo, the giant schnauzer his mother had rescued from the pound, inched himself up to a sitting position, gave Yancy a swipe with a soft tongue, and inched himself, toenails clicking, back down. Time to trim those nails again. His mother sat in the white wicker rocking chair tucked into bright yellow cushions. Outside the window, a fiery sun was slipping behind the hills, the dark blue sky was smeared with violet and pink and purple. Jasmine scented the night air.

A small fan purred on the table beside her gently lifting the ends of her dark hair. When he was a little kid, he'd thought she looked like Snow White, fairest in the land. At forty-six, Raina Yancy was still lovely, white skin, oval face, brown eyes, air of innocence and wonder. She brought to mind fireflies and moon-light and silvery wind chimes.

She sang quietly to herself in a clear voice, a song about blood and murder as she worked on a quilt square.

". . . Then he cut off her head
from her lily breast bone
and he hung't up in the kitchen
it made a' the ha shine."

Before the stroke, her fingers would dart like hummingbirds over the bright colors; now they were slow and awkward.

"Peter." A smile lit up her face. She dropped the square of cloth in her lap and held out both hands.

"How are you, Mom?" Squatting beside her, he took her hands and kissed her soft cheek.

"No longer very skillful." She nodded at the square.

"It's perfect." He backed up and sat on the edge of the bed. It was covered in a quilt she'd made of white squares with stars of every color and a blue and yellow border.

"I'm so glad you're here."

He reached past her and switched on the lamp sitting on the bookcase. "This might help."

Light pooled on a white pitcher with blue flowers and a framed photo of himself in uniform brought out the cheery yellow of the striped wallpaper and paler yellow in the tied-back curtains.

"I've been watching the bats leave," she said.

Other people had birdhouses in their yards; his mother had bat houses, way back before bats were popular. Little differences like this had made his childhood difficult.

"It's just that they're ugly," she said. "They suffer from bad press. And they do so much good. Think of the thousands of mosquitoes they eat."

Elmo, supercilious expression, bushy eyebrows, and muttonchop whiskers, stretched his forepaws out in front of him and raised his rear end in the air, then righted himself, moseyed over and butted his head up under Yancy's hand. Yancy obliged. The *Herald* daily ran a picture of a cute puppy or kitten needing a home. Why they chose Elmo, he couldn't guess, but his mother had taken one look and raced right out to save the beast. Elmo hadn't strayed from her side since. He knew lady bountiful when he saw her. After bestowing a lick of appreciation on Yancy, he swung his large head into her lap and looked up at her with eternal love and loyalty.

She stroked his pointy ears. "Tell me about your day, Peter. What happened to make you so late? Serena's upset."

"I'm sorry."

"I know, dear. I told her to go ahead. What kind of trouble could I get into sitting right here?"

"She didn't want you to get hurt."

"I'm not a child, Peter."

"No, you're not, but sometimes you get—confused."

She laughed. "I hate to be the one to tell you this, but I've been confused all my life."

"Well—" He smiled. "Maybe different." Nobody else's mother put fairy tales and Bible stories in the same bin. He grew up with a steady diet of things in the world that needed doing, missions to accomplish, wrongs to correct, causes to champion. "And what have you been up to?"

"Watching movies."

"Yeah? What did you see?"

She frowned in thought. "Somebody was trying to kill her. The weapon was hidden in the basket. It broke and fell."

"What fell?"

"I'm not sure. Remember Lucy Locket?"

"I don't think so, Mom."

"Of course, you do. She had two eyes on a platter."

"Oh."

"Obsession." She examined his face. "You look tired, love. Are you getting enough sleep?"

"Sure, Mom. It's just been a long day."

"You know, Peter, I've lived here all my life." Her voice was soft. "Elmo and I like to sit out there under the ash tree." Her voice grew softer. "Are you going to make me leave?"

"No, Mom. No, I won't."

8

$\mathcal{S}$usan managed to be at the hotel, the lobby dim and deserted, by ten o'clock. Howard Gilbert, the assistant manager, handed her the stuntwoman's room key—an actual key, not a coded plastic card.

"This is the first time since I've been here," he said, "that we've had a guest die."

He didn't look over twenty-five, round face more suited to smiling than somberness.

"Tell me about Kay Bender," she said.

"Quiet. Tell you the truth, I hardly remember what she looked like. Never any trouble. Not like some of them."

"Who caused trouble?"

"All of them," he said darkly. "They're worse than fraternity boys on a weekend drunk. They play football in the hallways, pull down chandeliers. I think they swing on them. Once they took lobby furniture and jammed it all in the elevators. And you wouldn't believe the state of the bathrooms. One maid out-and-out quit, said I couldn't pay her enough."

"That's showbiz," Susan said. "Did Kay make any calls? Receive any?"

"Not that got charged for. Maybe local or room to room."

"Are you sorry this whole bunch is here?"

He grinned. "I'm not and that's a fact. It's the only period in my time that we've turned away guests."

"Is everybody staying here connected with the movie?"

"All except for two or three. And I have to say they're really something."

"Who?"

"You know. From California. Making the movie. Laura Edwards. I mean, right here. I'm an extra," he added proudly.

She congratulated him.

On the third floor, she slipped the key in the lock, opened the door, and flicked the switch. A ceiling fixture with four tulip-shaped globes bloomed into light. She'd never been in one of the rooms. It was pretty much standard hotel room of the past type, which was, she assumed, what the decorator had in mind. Brass bed with floral spread, small tables on each side, two easy chairs with a table between, a low chest with a television set—a bow to modern times—alcove with mirror and vanity table, and a bathroom with the usual fixtures, albeit of a bygone era.

Everything was neat and tidy. The stuntwoman had left before six in the morning and never come back. The maid had been in around nine. There was no way to be sure, but the room seemed undisturbed by any unauthorized individual; certainly no one had sneaked in and tossed the place.

She checked the bathroom, making sure an ax murderer wasn't skulking behind the shower curtain—she'd actually encountered that once—then pulled on latex gloves and began a methodical search. She missed Parkhurst's help, but all things considered, it was better that he had no more connection with this case.

Osey could be doing this search, and he was a little miffed that he wasn't, holding unspoken resentment that she didn't believe him capable. It wasn't that; he was a good cop with a quick mind and thorough in his work, but this situation was a potential bag of trouble, and she was the most experienced investigator the HPD had, including Parkhurst. Though he came from a fair-sized city, with all the mess and pain and horror and inhumanity that cities have, her background was more extensive. She wanted this death cleared in record time, before anything happened to Laura Edwards, before the media got wind of a threat—if there was one—and got into a feeding frenzy.

Kay Bender had been a neat young lady; nothing was left on tabletops, not even a note or paperback book. T-shirts, shorts, and underwear lay folded in drawers; three dresses hung in the closet—two casual, one for a more fancy occasion; shoes were lined on the floor, two pairs of white Reeboks, one pair of black pumps with medium heels. The bathroom counter held a toothbrush and toothpaste; a neat row of cosmetics, only a few, sat on the vanity table.

One of the drawers turned up a scrapbook and Susan paged through it. Pictures and newspaper articles of Kay Bender in high school. An accomplished gymnast, she'd won competitions and awards, had even been an alternate for the Olympic team. Toward the end of the book were articles and stills about the movies she'd been in, stunts she'd done, pictures of her with the actresses she'd doubled for, both smiling into the camera. She'd been very focused, this young woman, and devoted her entire life to gymnastics, and then movie stunts. Nothing frivolous or frothy. Twenty-one years of life, Susan thought as she laid the scrapbook on the bed. She hoped Kay's dedication had brought her fulfillment, satisfaction, happiness, whatever was most important to her.

The room revealed no more surprises than had Kay Bender's body. Susan hadn't expected it would, but she searched thoroughly. She checked under the bed, between mattress and springs, in the toilet tank, under the lamps, through all pockets and in the toes of shoes. She emptied all the drawers, pulled them out, and checked the bottoms. She'd never found anything taped to the bottom of a drawer, but there was always a first. No cryptic messages, hidden treasures, or meaningful items. It all added up to a picture of a young woman caught in somebody else's hatred. She hoped she wasn't dismissing Kay Bender too blithely.

Peeling off the gloves, she took one last look around before she left, making sure the door locked behind her. She headed for the elevator and poked the button.

The doors slid open, and Sheri Lloyd stepped off. A denim-clad Nick Logan gazed above head level with polite indifference. When he realized who she was, he smiled. "Working late?"

And there she was getting into the elevator with one of the rich and famous. "It's in the job description."

"Time off for dinner? You pick the place, I'll buy."

Now, there was a bang-up idea. "Another time. Murder investigation."

"Murder?"

Watch your mouth, Susan. "Or accident. We're working on it."

The doors slid silently shut leaving her in a small confined space with a man who took up too much of it. Something about him was so big and so vivid and so directed, it drew you in.

He pulled on an intent look of idiocy. "If you could tell me," he said as Inspector Clouseau, "where you wear. 'Wear?' Yes yes, wear. 'A pin-striped suit, a white shirt and gold cuff links.' No, you idiot. Not the cluths you had on. Where you wear at the time of the murder."

She smiled. Talented man, Nick Logan. How about that dinner invitation? She could file it under suspect, interrogation of.

"I thought you always worked in pairs," he said. "Where's your partner?"

A casualness in the question brought her mind back to a sharp point. "Was there anything you wanted to say to him?"

Nick shook his head. The elevator glided to a stop at the fourth floor and the doors opened. "Good hunting," he said.

With her thumb on a button to keep the elevator in place,

she watched him stride along the corridor and knock at Laura Edwards's suite.

Laura wriggled out of her pants and stepped into the shower. She felt hot and sick and worried. Seeing Ben after all these years brought emotions and memories and regrets and desires like a tidal wave. There she was standing on the beach and this twenty-foot wave rose up and flattened her. She hadn't expected it. She was only curious to see him, and she wanted to talk to him. The thing about Ben was, she could trust him. There was nobody else she could say that about.

Turning off the water, she groped for the towel and rubbed herself dry, then slipped into a white silk robe. Was somebody actually trying to kill her? She'd worked hard to get where she was. That didn't happen in a vacuum. Had she offended somebody along the way?

Well, maybe. Okay, probably. But that was just the business. She'd never schemed and manipulated in any underhanded manner. Never deliberately tripped up anybody. Never stabbed anybody in the back. Never pushed anybody down the stairs. Never lied—well, of course, she'd *lied*, but nothing vicious. Like she could speak Spanish when her Spanish was two words, like she could ride horseback when she never got on anything that didn't have wheels. Never slept with anybody either. Not for gain. Except her first agent and she'd married him. He didn't have murderous thoughts about her. Did he? Of course not. It hadn't been very long into the marriage when she discovered he was unfaithful, and they'd parted with no hurt feelings, except hers, maybe. She'd been heartbroken. The betrayal had left her devastated. Anyway, he was in L.A.

She'd had love affairs, two serious. They'd ended the same way. With the guy betraying her. No man had ever been faithful, except Ben.

There she was all set to believe Nick was the one. He'd been

77

married twice, so had she. She was madly in love, so was he. They were supposed to live happily ever after. Yes, well, it just goes to show. She pulled a tissue from the box on the counter and blew her nose. Along came Ms. Overdeveloped Spider and sat down beside him. Instead of being frightened away, he hustled her into bed. Laura never could stand spiders.

She didn't know how she felt about Nick now. Only once, he'd sworn. Well, maybe. She didn't know if she believed him or not, and even if she did, once was too many. She didn't know what to believe anymore. She felt alone and afraid. Could he want to kill her? Impossible. Why would he? Because he didn't love her anymore? Well then, why wouldn't he just say so? Afraid she would make a scene?

She slid her feet into high-heeled white slippers. Well, of course, she'd make a scene. Was that any reason to kill her?

What about Sheri? Little Ms. Sex Object. Sheri wanted Nick and also wanted Laura's role. Was she so dumb she thought she could get it if anything happened? Nobody's that dumb. But she was a vengeful spider. What about that? If Nick really did say he wasn't interested, she might think getting rid of me would change his mind.

And that would also get back at Hayden Fifer. What about him? He have any reason to harm his star actress? No, he loved her. He'd wanted her for this movie. Of all the directors she'd ever worked with, he was the one she liked the best. He'd never harm a hair on her head.

The knock made her heart skip a beat. She edged to the door. "Who is it?"

"It's me."

Nick. Come to finish what he'd failed at earlier? Her heart kicked in so fast it threatened to choke her. Then she took herself in hand. Everything is not a movie, Laura May. And Nick does not want to slaughter you. Open this door.

When he tried to kiss her, she stepped back. "What do you want?"

"What kind of line is that, coming from my beloved?" He

sprawled on the Victorian sofa and gazed up at the crystal chandelier.

"You gave up any rights to being beloved when you took up with the Lloyd person." She flipped on the chandelier; a zillion teardrops blazed into light.

Nick blinked, rubbed his eyes, and hauled himself up straight. "I just saw the police."

"What police?"

He gave her a look. "The woman police chief."

"So?"

"They're looking at the stunt double's death as a murder."

She backed up to a wing chair and sat, crossed her legs. "How do you know?"

"Who'd want to kill her? All she ever did was work out, or work on stunts. That's all she ever thought about. Nothing else was ever on her mind. How could any of that turn into a reason for murder?"

"What are you saying?"

"I'm saying, I'm worried."

"You suggesting someone wants to kill me?"

"Laura," he said, "the world is full of nuts."

She recrossed her legs. "You're not being very comforting. Why aren't you holding my hand and saying, 'There, there'?"

"I would, if I was sure you wouldn't spit in my eye."

"What's that supposed to mean?"

"Love scenes between us lately have been only on the set." He reached for a low vase on the table behind and eased a cigarette pack from his shirt pocket, then stretched out a leg to get his lighter from his pants pocket.

"What do you expect, you bastard? And if you're going to smoke that, go to your own suite."

He smiled. "That's my girl. I'm glad to see a little fire. It means you still care."

"I care about the air I breathe and the company I keep."

"Well, let's talk about that for a minute. What company have you been keeping lately?"

79

"What does that mean?"

"That small town cop?"

"Don't be ridiculous. After your antics, you can't in all good conscience expect to play the jealous suitor."

"Come on, Laura. Stop playing to the camera."

It was true, everything was a scene for her. Well, she had to have some way to get through the pain. They weren't even married yet, and he couldn't keep his pants zipped.

"I told you the thing with Sheri just happened."

She jumped up; the shiny robe swished as she paced. "You couldn't help yourselves. Love like yours couldn't be denied."

"Oh, hell, no. She's a beautiful and determined lady. I had just enough to drink that it seemed like a good idea. I'm sorry."

"Sorry it happened? Or sorry that now she's got her sticky fingers clutching at you?"

"Don't be snide, Laura. You don't do snide convincingly."

She stopped in front of him and crossed her arms. "I'm a damn sight more convincing than your girlfriend. She's a lousy actress."

"She's not that bad."

"She's wood. And just barely managing to get by without cue cards."

"My darling Laura, I've told you I'm sorry. I've groveled at your feet. What more do you want?"

An ugly bust sat on the table at the end of the sofa. She considered hurling it at him. Better not. She might miss and break it. Or not miss and break his nose. Fifer would never forgive her.

Nick was watching, waiting to see what she'd do. She turned, swirling the skirt of her robe, and tossed herself in the chair.

"One thing I could always count on, Laura," he said.

He didn't go on. The bastard was going to make her ask. "What?"

"Your honesty. Behind all your emoting, you've always been straight. With yourself, with me, with everybody."

"Well, thank you very much. What has that got to do with your betrayal?"

"Betrayal, is it? My self-esteem just went up a notch. If you're betrayed, I'm important."

"Not anymore, you slime."

He stretched both arms along the back of the sofa and crossed his ankles on the coffee table. "Have you ever done anything you regretted?"

She eyed him warily. "Yes." Probably lots if she made a list. "So?"

"This is one of those things, Laura. It was a mistake. It was stupid. I regretted it from the moment it happened."

"Ooohh. All this regret doesn't keep you from letting her hang on to your arm."

"Yes, it does."

"Oh, really. I suppose it wasn't her in your trailer this morning. Who was that? Somebody selling Girl Scout cookies?"

"You're beginning to piss me off, Laura. I came to do a little more apologizing, a little more groveling, but there's a limit. I told her there was nothing between us."

"Maybe you should try words of one syllable."

He leaned forward so abruptly he scared her. Her heart started doing that thing again. "Aw, Laura, come on now. Was there ever somebody in your life like that? Who got a scenario in his mind that wasn't anywhere near reality and wouldn't give it up?"

There was, actually. A man who swore undying love. Wanted to marry her. That he was already married never fazed him. He wouldn't give it up, he even left his wife so they could be together. She eased one slipper off and let it dangle from her toes.

"All clear? Enough groveling? Can we have dinner now?"

"I'm tired, Nick. And there's something I need to take care of."

"Yeah? With a cowboy cop? What is it? Unfinished business? Sweet nostalgia? A thing for a man in uniform?"

"He doesn't wear a uniform."

"He does in that photo you have of him. I knew I'd seen him before. Maybe we should talk about that."

"Talk about an old photo?" She sighed, weary, stagy. "I can't deal with this, Nick. Just leave."

"That the best you can do? No storming fit? Flashing eyes and flaring nostrils?"

She smiled, then pointed to the door. "Out."

He got up and left without a backward glance. She was considering being outraged. At least he could have put up more protest.

The phone tore through the fog wrapped around his mind, collected a fistful of nerves, and jerked him awake. He grabbed the receiver to shut off the noise. "Yeah."

"Oh, Ben, I'm so sorry. I woke you."

He cleared his throat and tried to do the same with his mind. "Ben?"

"Yeah, Laura. What is it?"

"I need you."

"I'm no longer working the Bender case."

"Please."

"What's the problem?"

"Just come."

"Where are you?"

"My hotel room." The dial tone hummed in his ear.

He swung his legs over the edge of the bed and stared at the floor under his bare feet. My ex-wife, who is now a Hollywood sex goddess, has just invited me to her hotel room in the middle of the night. He replaced the receiver. It couldn't get any better than that.

He got into the shower with the idea of clearing his mind and stayed only long enough to sluice the sweat off his body. What Laura wanted teased at him while he brushed his teeth, zipped up his jeans, and rolled up his shirtsleeves. In ten minutes he had the Bronco headed for the Sunflower.

Laura wrapped her arms around his neck and hung on as if she were drowning. She kissed him; the kiss was slightly aggressive.

His arms went around her automatically, his hands felt the muscles of her back under her silky robe. Her perfume filled his mind with memories. The physical responses were still there; maybe they were always there between old lovers.

She tilted her head and smiled up at him. "Oh, God, Ben, you don't know how much I've missed you."

"You got me here in the middle of the night to tell me that?"

"It isn't the middle of the night. It's only eleven. Did you ever think about me after I left?"

"Never."

She laughed: light, pleased. "Liar."

He smiled. "I read about you now and then, after you got famous. You did good, kid." He let his arms drop, felt awkward, like he'd stumbled onto a movie set. Fancy hotel, subdued light, beautiful woman in slinky attire, and a rube who didn't know what the hell he was doing here.

She stepped back and tightened the belt on her robe, then took his hand and led him to the sofa. He sat; she perched beside him, hands together on her knees, and leaned slightly toward him. A small lamp on the end table created a halo effect around her platinum hair, picking out gold highlights.

"Regrets?" she asked softly.

"Laura, what are you doing? We made a mistake a long time ago. After all the hurt, and the scraped pride and ruffled feathers, there was sadness, and then there was relief."

"I had regrets. Lots of them. Still have sometimes."

That tugged at desire. Irritation came along. Well well, just like old times.

"Don't, Ben." She barely touched his jaw. "This muscle always jumps when you get mad. Please don't. I'm scared. I need you. I don't have anyone else I can trust."

"What are you afraid of?"

"Don't be a cop!" Her hands clenched. "Jesus, why can't you just be human?"

"I was under the impression you wanted a cop. Did I get that wrong?"

Her blue eyes glistened. "I wanted a friend."

Which made him feel like a total shit. This too was just like old times. He wondered if she was as snared in the undersurface nuances as he was. "To help, I have to ask questions. The only way I know how is as a cop. What's the problem?"

"All business. No drinking a cup of kindness for auld lang syne."

"What do you want from me, Laura?"

The tears filled her eyes and trailed down her face.

Oh, shit. He slid over, put his arms around her, and held her close. The cynic that he was pointed out that histrionics were her forte. The mind might twist situations with complications, or worry at them to find the hidden meanings, but the body cut to the chase, and his body responded to hers just as it always had.

He still didn't know what she wanted from him; he still didn't know how much he was willing to give. He didn't know what Susan would do either, about him being here since she'd told him to keep clear.

"Laurie." Putting both hands on her shoulders, he looked at her. With a thumb, he rubbed tears from her cheek. "Just talk to me. Okay?"

She stared back, blue eyes, wide and full of emotions he couldn't guess at. After a second that stretched thin, she nodded. In confusion, she looked around, then went into the bedroom and came back with a handful of tissues.

"This is hard for me too." She stood in front of him.

"Yeah."

"What would you like to drink? Wine? I don't know what kind they might have. Scotch? You still drink that?"

He got up, took her elbow, and steered her to the chairs at a small round table. "Sit," he said.

Somewhat to his surprise, she did so without comment, protest, or struggle. He sat opposite her. "Now," he said.

"Maybe somebody does want to kill me." Her voice was low but matter-of-fact, with no overtones of great drama.

"Who?"

84

She got up, went to the bedroom again, and returned with a burgundy briefcase that she placed on the table, snapped open, and took out two newspapers.

With a raised eyebrow, he picked up the top one. It was a copy of the *Hampstead Herald*, dated two weeks ago. Page one had a photo of her getting out of a limo in front of the hotel. With a red ballpoint pen somebody had circled her name in the caption. The second paper also had her photo on the front page, but this time the focus was on Nick Logan, sitting at a picnic table near the old barn where they were shooting. Laura's back was toward the camera. In the same red ink, a circle had been drawn on her back.

"How long have you had these?"

"The dates are on them. The first one the day after I arrived. The second one a few days later."

"You handled them?"

"Of course I handled them. I looked through to see if there was anything else in them."

"Was there?"

"No."

"Where did you get them?"

"I always get the local paper on location. I told the person at the desk when I got here. He said it would be at my door every evening. I didn't know whether I should be worried or not when I saw the first one. I mean it could be a fan. I do have fans, you know."

"Yes."

"And then the second one and it's not exactly—I mean, it's creepy."

"Who have you told about this?"

"I don't know. Nick. I guess my hairdresser. The makeup girl. Mostly it's letters, you know? This kind of thing, it's part of the game. I guess any celebrity—some are nice and some are not so nice. This feels threatening. Then—" She took a white envelope from the briefcase and slid it across the table.

He handled it carefully. Plain white, drugstore variety; Laura's name and room number. Inside a piece of cheap typing paper with a crudely sketched gun and, in block letters, BANG.

"When did you get this?"

"This evening."

"Anything else?"

"No. And now after Kay—" Laura shivered, crossed her arms, and clutched her elbows. "What can you do?"

"They aren't clearly threats." He watched her like a snake after a rabbit. She could be doing it herself, the papers, the note. Like the chief said, Laura could have arranged the accident that killed the stuntwoman. Laura should have been on the railing, Laura wasn't. Kay Bender was. This might be reinforcement. But he didn't know why she would.

"Ben, you're not going to do anything?" She grabbed at his arm. "You do believe—"

"Calm down. I'm going to take care of this." He took her hands and looked at her steadily. "I need to ask some questions. They're going to sound like cop questions because they are cop questions. Understand? Just the facts, ma'am."

She nodded.

"Have you hurt anybody?" He forestalled her protests. "I don't mean minor hurt feelings. I'm talking about serious injury. The kind that could destroy someone's life."

"Oh, God, I hope not. Hurt feelings and irritations and that kind of thing. You know, the sort of 'I hate her' thing. There must be lots of those. I've had my share of both sides."

"Not minor grievances, people who are just pissed. Normal people get over it after a while. The exception is a nutcase. Some guy you wouldn't go out with, or an actor who feels he didn't get a part because you didn't like him. This type can put in three, four years plotting out revenge."

"How could I know if it was something like that?"

"They don't usually keep it to themselves. They send hate mail, make threatening phone calls."

"Nothing but this. It feels threatening."

Yes, it did.

She started to put her hand on the papers and he stopped her. "Don't touch it."

Startled, she jerked her hand back. "It's so scary out there. You know? All those people and some of them—you never know what they are. You never know what's coming or who's going to jump out at you with acid or a knife."

Yeah. A stalker who'd fastened on her. He hoped not. The thought of a psycho who mixed fantasy and reality and fed both through a sick mind scared the shit out of him. "They usually send mail too. Or try to see you." And often the creeps believed the victim had a romantic interest in them.

"Anybody who always shows up when you're filming? Tries to get close? Tries to talk to you? Touch you? Get past barriers? Anything like that?"

"I don't know. I don't pay close attention to the crowds. I need to focus on what's coming up, otherwise my performance would be—on a level with that of Ms. Lloyd."

Laura wasn't so frightened that she could pass up an opportunity to throw a dig at the other actress. "Why didn't you mention this stuff this afternoon?"

She looked at him, then got up and stalked to the bedroom. When she came back, she smacked the box of tissues on the table. "It knocked me out, if you must know. The accident—Kay and—and then seeing you and—I just—I didn't expect it to hit me so hard and there was that other police person."

"Yancy?"

"No. The woman."

"The chief."

"Anyway, you were so hard. Like you always were when you were mad. I mean, you came in angry."

With a sour smile, he acknowledged the truth of her assessment. Old memories and old responses had come over him. He'd felt she was going to shove him into the stew pot.

"And I wanted to talk to you without all those other people.

Just you." She rested her forearms on the table and clasped her hands together. She fell silent, looking at him with wonder, then tilted her head. "We were so young."

"Yes."

"Oh, Ben, I've missed you."

"Don't get carried away," he said dryly.

She laughed. The laugh roused memories; it was the same delighted, life-is-so-interesting laugh she'd had when they were married. For reasons he couldn't figure, it made him sad. Lost youth maybe, lost promises, lost chances.

It also said that underneath all the Hollywood glitz was the girl he'd married. Pretty little girl who looked up at him with curiosity and interest, made him feel like maybe he was worth something after all.

Suddenly he was aware of exactly where they were. Hotel suite. Just through that doorway was a bed.

Laura, eyes alight with impish malice, said in a velvet voice. "For old times' sake?"

9

Serena, sitting at the table, busily dunked a tea bag in a cup of hot water and barely gave Yancy a glance when he came in. "Well, you certainly took care of that, didn't you?"

"What do you expect?"

"Right. You're the only one with feelings." She threw the tea bag at him. He ducked and it landed with a splat on the floor.

"You think I want to toss my crazy sick mother out of her home?"

"Serena—"

She shoved the chair back, got up for the tea bag, and dropped it in the trash, then wiped up the floor with a paper towel. "You want something serious to happen? Maybe even fatal?" She plopped herself back in the chair. "How would you feel then?"

"She doesn't want to leave here."

"You keep refusing to look at the point. She needs to be safe, Peter. Sometimes she's perfectly all right. Sometimes she isn't. I don't know about you, but it scares me silly to come home and find her on fire. What if I'd been fifteen minutes later? Or an hour?"

To get away from her demanding gaze, he went to the refrigerator and reached in for the carton of orange juice. He shook it, then poured a glass and took a sip. "I told you, I'll think of something."

"You'd better hurry because time's running out."

"Oh, hell, Serena. She doesn't want to leave here. It'd be different if she was totally out of it, didn't recognize us, didn't know what was going on. She loves this place. She loves the flowers. She loves the trees. She loves—"

"Maybe we can find a place with flowers and trees."

"And a place that will let her have Elmo?"

"That's something else we'll have to do something about."

He gave her a startled look. "You want to do away with Elmo?"

"No, you jerk. One of us will need to keep him."

Yancy's beeper went off, saving him from having to respond. This beeper was something that came with his assignment to the movie bunch. If they needed anything, wanted anything, got bored, lonely, or wanted another hand for poker, he got beeped.

"Don't answer it," Serena said.

He didn't much want to; a fourteen-hour day ought to be enough. He downed the orange juice and set the glass on the counter. "I have to." She might not like his job, but it was the only one he had and he wanted to keep it.

He'd be the one in trouble if he didn't respond, and if he got fired, they'd really be in the shit. Who'd pay for the old folk's home then? He rubbed his face. Damn it, damn it.

In the living room, he dropped into the old green easy chair by the front window. A rectangle of light spilled in from the kitchen. Night had closed in while he'd been talking with Serena. Fireflies blinked on and off in the soft black air. After a second, he picked up the receiver and punched in the number.

"Hi, buddy. How's it going?" It was Mac, his Hollywood teamster friend. "I have a mind to get something to munch on.

How about you and me go out and find us some barbecued ribs? You folks know how to barbecue ribs around here?"

"Yes, sir, we do. If you'll give me"—he held up his arm to catch the light from the kitchen and squinted at his watch— "twenty minutes, I'll take you to a place with barbecue sauce hot enough to blow off the top of your head."

"That a promise?"

"No, sir, that's a threat."

Mac chuckled and hung up.

Yancy leaned back and closed his eyes. His mother often sat here in the dark. She watched the moon rise and the small animals come out with the night, the foxes and possums and skunks, the occasional coyote. Sometimes she talked to them. No big deal.

Sometimes they talked back. That was a little different. She listened.

He didn't feel like being with movie people anymore today. Aw hell, Mac wasn't really movie people. If Yancy wanted to ask about the lieutenant being near the barn around noon, now was the time to start.

Get a move on then.

Serena was still drinking tea. He rested a hand on the table and leaned down to look into her face. "I've got to go."

"You always do."

"We'll talk about this later." He kissed her forehead and left, told Dallas, still in the hammock, that maybe Serena needed him, and got in the Cherokee.

The stars lost some of their brilliance as he got into town. He drove through on Fifteenth Street, took Crescent Road past campus, and then turned west on Mississippi. In the driveway at the side of the old Victorian house, he parked under the maple tree and fished keys from his pocket. Alice Blakeley, the owner, divorced and struggling to keep afloat, lived downstairs. In addition to tutoring students in math, she gave piano lessons and rented the upper half of the house to Yancy.

Outside stairs went up to the second story. Stephanie, his

landlady's daughter, sat on the bottom step. At thirteen, mother and daughter didn't always see eye to eye.

"Hey, Steph, what are you up to?"

"Writing."

"Isn't it a little dark?"

"I'm just making notes. Have you solved the murder yet?" He sat beside her. "Not yet."

"Would you like a clue?"

"Do you have one?"

"You're just like my mother, you treat me like a child."

"I'm sorry." This was his evening for apologizing to irate females.

"No, you're not. You just say that. I'm making character studies. You're one of them," she added darkly.

That was a little daunting. "How come you never let me read what you write?"

"Maybe I will sometime."

"Tell me your clue."

"Those eyes the greenest of things blue,
The bluest of things gray."

"What does that mean?"

"Nothing, but it sounds great, doesn't it?"

"Yeah." He patted her knee and took the stairs two at a time to prove he wasn't tired. Just as he stuck the key in the lock the phone rang. He rushed in and grabbed the phone.

A breathy voice cooed in his ear. If he didn't know females didn't go in for that kind of thing, he'd have thought he had a heavy breather.

"Hello, Officer Yancy."

"Ms. Lloyd. What can I do for you?"

"You recognized my voice."

"Couldn't miss it." Nobody else he knew sounded like a seduction scene.

"So businesslike," she pouted. Even over the phone he could

hear the pout. "And here I was trying to work up the courage to ask you a favor."

A favor, is it? And what might that be? "Yes, ma'am." Her usual disdain wasn't apparent, but the promise of good things to come was a shade overdone.

"If you'll come over here, I'll explain. I might even tell you a few things you don't know."

Oh, yes, lady, I'm sure you could. He bent his chin to his chest, squeezed the back of his neck, then stretched his head backward as far as it would go. He had a little dilemma here. He was due to pick up Mac in a few minutes. Within the confines of his edict—take care of these show biz folks—actors probably beat out drivers any old day.

What was clear was, he should tell Mac he couldn't make it and hie himself over to Ms. Sheri's hotel room.

He hauled in a breath on the wings of fatigue. Hotel room. Breathy coo. He wasn't important enough to warrant the usual attention that would suggest. In her opinion, he was just some clown hired to guard doorways, so what was the favor she wanted? Anything pertinent she'd lay on a higher-up. If she wanted information . . . Now there was a thought. She'd think he'd spill it. With the right lure. "How'd you get this number?"

"I went to a lot of trouble." Sexy and cute.

Howie, he thought. His old friend Howie Gilbert, assistant manager at the hotel. If Sheri did her song and dance for him Howie'd give out state secrets, let alone a little thing like Yancy's home number. Yancy wished he wasn't so tired, he could think better if his brains weren't mashed potatoes. He was curious about what she wanted, but too tired to trot into her room, the mouse accepting the cat's invitation.

"Well, ma'am. I sure am sorry but I'm on my way to pick up Mac."

"Who's Mac?"

"Ms. Edwards's driver. Hey, I've got an idea. Why don't you join us? We're going to get a bite to eat." Boy, would she be a hit. "You like barbecue?"

"It doesn't sound like my kind of place." Her voice was losing some of its warmth. "Call this Mac and tell him you can't come."

"Well, yeah, that's an idea all right, but he's nowhere I can reach him. How 'bout I come right over to the hotel as soon as I can."

"That'll be too late."

Too late for what? "Oh, gee, yeah, it will be getting late. Tell you what. I'll see you first thing in the morning."

There was a frosty silence, then she said in a tart, irritated, dealing-with-the-help voice, "You just made a mistake."

He probably did at that. And he probably wouldn't get another chance either. He stripped off his uniform and got in the shower. If this favor had to be granted right now, it most likely couldn't be about the investigation. Mac would have been routinely questioned, but Yancy wanted to get at questions that Mac probably hadn't been asked. Like had he seen the lieutenant near the barn.

Toweling dry as he went, he padded to the bedroom and pulled on jeans and a blue knit shirt long enough and loose enough to cover his gun. Hot as hell up here. The ficus plant his sister had given him was dropping yellow leaves in the corner.

This old Victorian was a great place to live: lots of space—bedroom, kitchen, living room, everything sparse and barren, the way he liked it. Hardwood floors, bookshelves in the bedroom floor-to-ceiling that he'd put up himself. Gray couch and chair in the living room, round table to rest his feet on when he watched television. Built-in desk. Walls papered in gray stripes with dark gray and dark rose trim around the top. No pictures, no knickknacks.

He thought about getting up at five in the morning and wondered how late barbecued ribs with Mac would run. How did actors do it? The hours alone would kill him.

He shoved keys, change, and wallet in his pockets and headed out. Moths were flying around the light intent on suicide, and a couple of june bugs dive-bombed the door. He accidentally stepped on one and it made a loud crunch. He hated the things, big and lumbering.

Mac was pacing up and down the walkway in front of the hotel. When he saw Yancy's Cherokee, he stepped into the street. Late forties, big belly and flat butt, dark hair receding up his forehead and hanging long around his ears. He wrenched open the door and slid in.

"Hey, buddy." With a friendly fist, he punched Yancy's shoulder. In the interests of projecting male bonding and macho toughness, Yancy did not flinch.

Rose. Laura my beloved. The universe is rose. He stood under the trees and watched the taillights, red eyes of the evil spirits, retreat down the street. He was careful not to get directly in their path. If he did, they'd see into his soul and scramble his plans. He must never allow that. They were forming, falling into place. The universe had told him the most humane way was a gun. Now it told him he had to kill that cop and take his.

This close to eleven, the Blind Pig wasn't overflowing with business. Red padded booths ran along two sides, tables in the middle. Western flair for decoration—ten-gallon hats, spurs, tack on the walls. Tex Ritter sang in the background.

"I should warn you," Mac said as he slid into a booth, "I take barbecue sauce very seriously."

The waitress brought menus and a basket of hush puppies. Yancy looked the place over.

"Cops always do that?" Mac asked.

"Do what?"

"Check the place out. Like you're looking for felons, or escape routes."

"Yeah." He wondered what kind of a cop he was. Now that he was here, he figured he probably made the wrong call and should have gone with Sheri Lloyd.

Mac ordered the ribs with the picture of a red-horned devil holding a pitchfork beside it. Yancy went for a milder version.

"Tell me about this movie," he said, slyly working up to his questions.

Mac took a slug of beer, leaned beefy shoulders against the seat back, and raised his eyebrows. "What, kid? You all of a sudden getting star struck?"

"I'd like to know what your thoughts are about this bunch."

"One thing you gotta understand. There are the top cats and there are the rest of us. Except for what's strictly necessary, like driving all their crap out on location and driving them around, we don't have anything to do with each other."

"Well, thanks. That's a big help."

"You gonna ask me if somebody was jealous of the big cheese, wanted her out of the way, was itchin' for the part. Hell yes."

"Who?"

Mac laughed. "That's what I'm telling you. Jealousy, fighting back and forth, spreading dirt—it goes with the territory. It's a given. Just the same as cameras and mikes and clapboards. As to specifics—" He shrugged. "There I can't help you. The fat cats don't hobnob with the rest of us."

The waitress plunked steaming platters of ribs in front of them, refilled Yancy's iced tea, and brought Mac another beer. Mac pushed up his sleeves, gave Yancy a look of this-better-be-good good, and grabbed a rib dripping sauce. He chomped down and chewed. Tears sprang to his eyes. He swallowed, grabbed his beer, and took a long drink.

"Not bad," he allowed. He pulled off another rib and worked his jaws.

Yancy did likewise with his sissified version. "Who had it in for Ms. Edwards?"

Mouth full, eyes streaming, Mac shook his head.

"Anybody feuding with anybody?"

"Well, I'm not one to be sensitive about atmosphere and pretentious crap like that, but I gotta admit these clones didn't give out like happy campers." Mac wiped his greasy fingers on the oversized napkin. "All covered up and hidden away poison was coming through somebody's pores."

"Whose?"

"Don't know. I'm just a driver. I go where I'm told. It's all these other folks with sensitive souls that'll have to tell you about that. I know Fifer had a sling-out fight with his big box office star."

"Ms. Edwards?"

"Naw. The other one. Nick Logan."

"When was this?"

"Right after we got here."

"Where?"

"Out there in that barn. Everybody else had split. The director asked his big moneymaker to hang back a minute. And then told him to get his ducks in order."

"Meaning?"

"Oh, hell, how do I know? I walked in in the middle of it. The director was saying it took more than reputation to carry a career."

"What did that mean?"

"My big guess would be Fifer wasn't real ecstatic with Nick's performance."

"What did Nick say?"

"Laughed a not funny laugh and said, 'Go careful. It wouldn't be much of a movie if you lost your star.' That's when I blundered in with my big feet and they both turned around to look at me. I got out of there."

Yancy hadn't picked up anywhere that Fifer was dissatisfied with Nick's performance. On the contrary, he was under the impression both stars were doing great and the director was dancing around hugging himself. "What were you doing there?"

"Laura sent me in to tell Nick she'd be at the hotel."

"Is she hard to work for?"

"At her level, they're all hard to work for."

"You ever have any trouble with her?"

Mac, greasy rib between thumbs and forefingers, looked at

him. "What are you getting at?" Everything changed: voice, eyes, posture. He went from good ol' boy to steel-jawed driver/bodyguard.

Yancy wouldn't care to tangle with him, he could see how Mac would be good at this job. "What did you do, make a pass at her?"

Mac snorted. "That'd get me killed. No, I was late picking her up. The car wouldn't start. A kid from a service station came out and replaced the battery. It took him a while. She threw a hissy. Wanted to fire me."

"You're still here."

"Yeah, well, she cooled off and threatened, 'Once more and you're gone.' "

"Why'd she do that?"

"It gave her an edge."

"Edge?"

"Something to hold over my head."

Artfully, Yancy changed direction. "Around noon, were you anywhere near the barn?"

"Yep. Well, part of the time. You gonna ask me next if I smuggled a saw in there and cut through that railing?"

"No smuggling was required. The saw was already there. I was going to ask if you saw anybody."

"Like who?"

Like the lieutenant. "Anybody."

"Naw. I didn't see anybody sneak into the barn, but back at base camp Nick was in and out of his trailer, Laura Edwards too. And Clem Jones, our director's assistant with the personality plus." Mac cleaned the meat off the last rib, then picked through the bones making sure he hadn't missed anything.

"Nobody else?"

"Who you getting at?"

Yancy shook his head. "Just wanting to know."

"Well, you gotta remember I wasn't exactly standing there with my eyeballs glued to the barn door."

So much for checking up on the lieutenant.

98

Mac finished up with apple pie and ice cream.

By the time Yancy dropped off Mac in front of the hotel and started off for home he was so tired his eyes were beginning to cross. Five A.M. wakeup. Ah, the glamorous life of moviemaking. His mouth opened with a wide jaw-creaking yawn that nearly unhinged it. Side vision caught a dark shape staggering in front of the headlights. He stood on the brakes.

There was a thud.

"Oh, shit."

10

$\mathcal{Y}$ancy hit the street. Oh, Jesus, the man wasn't moving. Crouching, Yancy shined his flashlight in the guy's face. It was Robin McCormack, the stunt girl's boyfriend. He ran the light over Robin's T-shirt and cutoff jeans.

Robin stirred, put an elbow over his eyes, and muttered, "The moon in June is goddamn soon."

"Don't move." No blood, arms and legs seemed to work all right the way he was thrashing around trying to get up.

"Stay where you are," Yancy said. Alcohol fumes rolled over him like fog.

"Can't."

"Can't what?" Yancy felt eyes staring at him from the darkness. A quick glance didn't spot anybody.

"Can't stay. Have to find the bastard pushed me."

"Somebody pushed you?"

"Didn't fall over . . . er . . . er."

"You hurt anywhere?" Yancy couldn't see any injuries, just grime from the street.

Robin made swimming motions trying to get up; Yancy held him down. "Did you hit your head?"

"Quit helpin' me, man. I can do it." His arms flailed and he tried to roll.

Christ, if he was injured, this was making it worse. "Robin?"

It took him a long time to respond, processing through a thick soup of alcohol. When he did answer, his voice was slow and sleepy.

"Yesss . . . sss . . . sss?"

"Robin? I want you to lie still. You understand?"

"Yes. Fine . . . ine . . . ine."

"Robin, don't try to get up."

"What?"

"Stay where you are."

"No," he said. "I have to go . . . go . . . go." He tried to crawl.

"Robin—"

"Stop calling me Robin!"

"It's your name." Yancy shined the flashlight in Robin's face. "Look at me!"

"Fuck off!"

He grabbed Robin's chin and held his head still. Pupils reacted sluggishly, not surprising as smoked as he was.

"Knock it off." Robin closed his eyes. "Tired."

"I can see you are. What day is this?"

"Today."

"What is the date?"

"Monday. It's the Monday of June."

"Robin, where are you?"

"Never been here. Kay. Never Kansas."

The poor bastard was just soused out of his mind, Yancy thought, but that left him in a little bit of a quandary. He had no radio on him, none in the Cherokee. He didn't think this guy was hurt, but he wasn't a doctor. Concussion. Spinal injury. Fracture. To get Robin to stay lying down, he'd have to sit on him. If he left Robin to go into the hotel and ask somebody to call an ambulance, Robin would get up and stagger around, further aggravating any possible injuries. Loading him in the Cherokee could do the same, plus Yancy might have a fight on his hands. Or if

Robin passed out on the way, there was nothing Yancy could do. Or any way to stop him if he got it into his head to get out of the moving vehicle.

Lights inside the hotel shone brightly over the entrance, but not a soul was visible.

Yancy stopped trying to hold Robin down and helped him up. Draping one of Robin's arms over his shoulder, Yancy put his own arm around Robin's waist and aimed them both for the door.

"Where we goin'?"

"Inside." And we're hoping like hell there's no spinal injury.

"Over there in the anywhere and Kay in the nowhere." Robin sobbed; his whole body shook.

Yancy steered them to the entrance and was wondering how to get them both through the door when Howie came dashing up and held it open. Yancy needed to talk to Howie, sometime friend and assistant manager, about giving out cops' phone numbers to sexy actresses.

"What happened? Is he hurt? Oh, my God." Howie held the door, stood back, and peered anxiously at Robin.

"I seriously hope not. Would you get an ambulance?"

"Sure. Yes. Right away." He loped off to the desk.

Blue. Laura my beloved. The universe is blue. He didn't know why he'd pushed that drunk. He was just there and it seemed right. Maybe it was out of sequence. The cop got out of his car and was bending over him. If he'd obtained a knife or a hammer, he could have done it right then. Killed the cop, and taken the gun. He should have thought ahead. He could have bought a knife. Damn. Was this a test? Did he fail?

He had to have the cop's gun. That was the most humane way. Shoving and cutting through railings was wrong. The spirits had been against it.

An ambulance drove up, lights flashing, but no siren. Two guys jumped out and opened the rear doors. They got a stretcher and wheeled it up to the entrance. A minute or two later, they wheeled it back with the drunk strapped on. The cop got in his car and followed.

One good thing, Yancy thought, this late on a Monday—he glanced at his watch—one-thirty—early on a Tuesday morning— the emergency room wasn't stacked three deep. They were all home resting up from the weekend. He trotted up the ramp to the admitting area where the ambulance attendants were unloading Robin. The glass doors slid open and they trundled him through and along to a treatment room.

Mary Mason—he'd gone to high school with her—was on duty tonight. "What have you brought us this time, Peter?"

"Just a drunk, I hope." He explained what had happened. "Since he's one of the movie people, give him every test you've got."

"Sure. We do that anyway, you know. Go sit down. It'll be a while."

For a few minutes he sat in the waiting area, but all that unneeded adrenaline was jazzing through his bloodstream. He told Mary he'd be outside.

It was still hot, probably seventy-five degrees. They could use some rain, cool things off some. Not a cloud in the black starry sky.

He made his way to the courtyard on the side of the building. Light poles with round globes lit the area of shrubs and flower beds and wooden benches. In the center was a three-tiered fountain and water spilled endlessly down.

"What is it about moving water?"

Startled, Yancy turned and saw a woman sitting on a bench, middle-aged and plump with short gray hair. She wasn't crying but her face was slack and dull as though she was long finished and there was no emotion left.

"It's just there." Yancy sat on a bench at a right angle to her. "It's soothing."

She gave him a ragged smile. "I wish I smoked. Then I'd have an excuse."

"You need an excuse?"

"My husband is dying."

Yancy had assumed as much, a relative or someone she loved. "I'm very sorry," he said.

"I stay in the room until I can't stand it, and I have to leave. But I feel so guilty when I'm not there I have to go back. I sit and listen to him breathe. Awful strangled breath, then nothing. I pray, 'Oh, God, please let him take another breath.' "

She wasn't talking to Yancy, she wasn't talking to anybody really. Her mind was so full of darkness, she had to let some spill, like the water trickling over the fountain edges.

"And he does," she said. "Another awful strangled breath. And I pray, 'Oh, God, please let him go. Give him peace.' I feel so ashamed because I want him to die."

She rubbed the heel of her palm up and down her cheek, a gesture of rubbing away guilt. "I'm so afraid he'll go when I'm not there. I'm terrified he'll go when I am there."

The fountain trickled water down its tiers, crickets chirred in the grass, the moon shone full, and the air smelled of jasmine.

After a long silence, she said, "Someone you love is here?"

"No. A minor accident. I don't think he's hurt."

After another long silence, she stood and dusted off the back of her skirt. "It was a pleasure meeting you," she said. "I guess it's time to get back."

Yancy silently wished her the best, whatever that might be.

Later, Mary came looking for him. "There you are," she said. "You can come get your boy. He's been poked, jabbed, X-rayed, lab tested, and, aside from some bruises, pronounced suffering from the excesses of alcohol."

Yancy let go of a long breath he'd been storing up. He had no idea what kind of trouble he was in, but he knew one thing: running over one of the movie people was not permissible. He loaded Robin into the Cherokee and drove as carefully as if he were delivering unboxed eggs.

He went with Robin into his hotel room, placed the key on a chest, and switched on the lamps on both sides of the bed. Robin slumped on the edge of the bed with his head drooping. He managed to prop it on his fists. He wasn't as way-out drunk now, but he wasn't sober either, and he looked thoroughly miserable.

"You need to get some sleep," Yancy said.

"No," Robin mumbled, tipping his head back and forth. "I need to see Sheri."

"Why?"

"She did it."

"Did what?"

"Knows—she knows—"

"Ms. Lloyd knows who hurt Kay?"

"Nobody wanted to hurt Kay. Laura."

Yancy leaned back against the door. He thought if he sat down, he might fall asleep.

"Had a fight." Robin's eyelids were at half-mast.

"Sheri and Kay?"

"Nick."

"Nick and Kay?"

"No." Robin's eyes closed. He forced them open and settled for slits. "Nick and Sheri."

"What about?"

"Not gonna throw everything over for her."

Yancy wondered if it was worth trying to follow this drunken rambling. The lieutenant would have retrieved whatever was to be had from Sheri, and Yancy was overstepping his duties. A dull headache was developing just behind his temples, the result of long hours and hanging with these California people.

"Oh, God." Robin took a deep breath, shoved himself up, and stumbled into the bathroom. Yancy heard water running. Robin came back drying his face and hair.

"We were getting married. After this shoot." He twisted the

106

towel. "You want to hear something funny? She liked working with Laura. Ain't that a kick? Twenty-one." He glared at Yancy. "Twenty-one goddamn years old."

Robin wasn't much older, Yancy thought. Twenty-three or four.

"She lived in Van Nuys. You know? Family. Normal people. Two older brothers. Daddy a history teacher. Mother works for some business, secretary. I called them. I had to tell them—" Robin clamped his teeth and swallowed rapidly. His fingers dug into the towel until the knuckles whitened.

"She got along with Ms. Edwards?"

"Sure. Who knows what Laura thought. But stars don't suffer in silence. If she didn't like Kay, you can bet your bottom dollar she'd have said so."

"What do you want with Ms. Lloyd?"

A crafty look came over Robin's face, then it turned blankly innocent.

Oh, Christ. He's got it in his head to find out who killed Kay Bender. Be an avenger? Slay the slayer? What the hell was the matter with this Hollywood bunch? Couldn't any one of them tell reality from a movie? Yancy sighed. Actually, they couldn't.

He took a deep breath instead of yelling at Robin. He didn't go over and slap him around either. Partly because that wasn't the done thing, partly because Robin had just toppled over and started snoring. After removing Robin's shoes and shoving a pillow under his head, Yancy left him to it.

He debated with himself all the way to the elevator. Any information should go to Osey. The trouble was, he didn't have anything concrete. Drunken ramblings, facial expressions. The hallway was discreetly lit. Yancy felt hairs prickle on the back of his neck. He jabbed the button and looked around. A door seemed to be just closing. Optical illusion. Or somebody was watching him wait for the elevator. A little creepy music and he could turn this into a slasher flick.

When the elevator arrived, the room door opened quickly and a male in his thirties came out. Brown and brown, five ten, hundred eighty, brown pants, white shirt. Small brown back-pack. Yancy ran down the description like he was eyeing a sus-pect. Careful, boy. You don't watch it, you'll be as nutsy as the movie folks.

Inside the elevator, a kid from room service, holding a tray with covered dishes, balanced the tray on one hand and wrapped the other hand around the edge of the door to prevent its closing. Yancy got in. The hotel guest veered off toward the stairway. Two floors up, Yancy tapped softly at room three-eighteen. It wouldn't do to wake Ms. Lloyd; she most likely wouldn't take that too kindly.

The door was yanked open so fast it startled him. For a frac-tion of a second Sheri Lloyd smiled in welcome, then anger flushed her face. She was wearing something pale pink and flow-ing, semi see-through. Obviously, she had been expecting some-body. He wondered who.

"What are you doing here?" She didn't invite him in. Behind her, an ice bucket and two glasses sat on a small table.

He came in by dint of simply stepping forward and forcing her to move back. He closed the door and leaned against it.

She poured something in a glass and tossed it down. "Well, what do you want?"

"You invited me." He crossed his arms. "You said you had something for me."

"It's too late." Sharp. Sexy coo nowhere in sight. Back came the usual disdain.

"What were you going to tell me?"

"Nothing."

"Who were you expecting?"

"None of your business."

Yancy was tired, his head ached, he wanted to go home, he wanted to go to bed. He did not want to be looked at like yes-terday's dinner. "Ms. Lloyd, you could find yourself under arrest for withholding information in the matter of the death of Kay Bender." He sounded like such a pompous ass, he expected her to laugh.

She topped up her glass and slugged it down.

"We don't have to talk here. I can take you in. Book you. Take your prints, and your picture. It would be in the paper, but hey, you know what they say about publicity."

"Are you trying to scare me?"

"No, ma'am. I'm just explaining what could happen in the event that you did not cooperate."

"You are a low-life shit."

"Yes, ma'am."

"You know—" Her voice got husky, breathless. She glided toward him, one hand extended in invitation. "If you'd be nice to me I could be very nice to you."

"Let me make it perfectly clear here, Ms. Lloyd. Whatever the game is you're playing, you don't have to be so nice you need to sleep with a cop. Just answer a question or two and I'll get out of here. All right?"

She dropped her hand, flounced to a chair, and threw herself down in it. "Ask."

"Who were you expecting just now?"

"Nick." Very clipped. The lady didn't want to talk with him. Fine. What he wanted to do was go home. He also wanted to know why Robin McCormack thought this woman either knew something or was guilty. He sat in an easy chair that was so comfortable, he was tempted to close his eyes. Just for a few minutes. He fixed her with a steely-eyed stare, projecting authority and low-life shittiness. "Go on."

"He's been cool toward me ever since we got here. It's because *she's* been giving him a hard time."

"She being—?"

"Laura! Nick is just too sensitive for his own good. And he doesn't want to do anything that might have repercussions on the film. He's a professional that way. She's just barely carrying it off anyway. This role is way beyond her. Nick has asked me to be patient. *Begged* me to understand."

"Patient?"

"Of course, I told him I'd be patient, I did understand. But there's a limit." She smiled, like the evil stepsister. "So I asked him to drop by."

"And he agreed?"

"Oh, yes. He said he would try. And I could hear in his voice how much he was longing to be with me."

"You think he no longer loves Ms. Edwards?"

She glared at him. "He wanted me. On a permanent basis."

"Marriage?"

"Yes."

"What time was he going to do this dropping by?"

She flashed him a look of irritation. "Nine-thirty," she snapped.

"Have I got this straight? You wanted me here at nine-thirty and Nick here at nine-thirty. Wasn't that going to be a little crowded?"

"He is a man who could be spurred by jealousy."

Yancy thought maybe he ought to be flattered here, if she felt Nick would be jealous of such as he.

"We are exactly suited for each other," she said. "I know it and he knows it. He's a brilliant, highly successful actor and I— well, I like to think I have my own brilliance even though I'm not quite as established as he is. We can help each other. We're both concerned with social issues. We both have intellectual pursuits. A little jealousy—well I must admit, it's exciting. Just the beginnings, you understand. It makes him very *attentive.*"

"You think he loves you?"

"Of course, he loves me."

"Then why isn't he here?"

Her face hardened to porcelain and her eyes took on the intent focus of a raptor spotting a rabbit. "I saw him," she said. "This morning. He stayed behind in the barn when everyone else left for lunch."

So much for true love.

Going to the elevator, Yancy got the same prickly feeling of being watched. He stopped and looked around. Nothing. If he didn't get some sleep, he was going to be just as out of touch as these film folk. He poked the button, heard something behind him, and spun around. Guest. Same one he'd seen earlier.

The man held himself stiffly and rocked slightly forward on his toes. He fiddled with his backpack and never looked Yancy in the eye.

To Yancy's surprise, when the elevator door opened, there stood the lieutenant. Muttering something about forgetting something, the guest went off down the corridor.

"Yancy," Parkhurst said with a curt nod.

"Sir," Yancy replied. What was the lieutenant doing here? He wasn't working this case anymore. Oh, Lord, will this day never end?

11

$\mathcal{L}$aura twisted the lock after Ben left. She hadn't really expected him to stay; she hadn't expected to be quite so disappointed either when he said he didn't think that was a good idea. Odd, all those years since she'd seen him and there it was, the same old excitement, the same old rush of hormones.

One thing about him, he made her feel safe. He couldn't let anything happen to her. He had some kind of code that wouldn't let him. She could trust him to find who was sending weird pictures and notes. Someone trying to kill her? It didn't seem actually real, yet she knew it was a possibility. They all lived with it. Stand out there in the open and you catch attention. The world was full of crazies. If you let it get to you, you'd never go anywhere.

They lived in different worlds, she and Ben. Yet here he was in the very place she was sent out on location. Karma?

She'd been restless lately, twitchy, unlike herself, unhappy, feeling like something was missing in her life, who knows. Nick playing footsie with that no-talent nitwit hadn't helped. Maybe maybe maybe a few changes would come along. Would that be interesting?

There you go plotting again, Laura May. Remember what your mother always used to say. You're never satisfied with what you've got, you always have to be planning and plotting for something else. Well, all that planning and plotting got her where she was.

The muscles across her back, just below the shoulders, were pulled up tight. She shrugged and moved one shoulder forward and one back, then the other way, to ease them. It was all very well to tell yourself there might be some idiot out there tracking you, but that's the way it is and just carry on. The body had its own responses.

An aromatic bath was what she needed.

In the bathroom, she turned on the taps in the old-fashioned tub with claw feet and let it fill to the brim. She dug out the chart given to her by her aromatherapist. Bergamot for tension, worry, and anxiety. Agitating the water, she carefully allowed two drops to fall. Two drops of lavender to balance the emotional extremes of stress, shock, worry, impatience.

Interesting impatience was included. By all means include lavender, she was getting impatient.

Patchouli, she noted, was an aphrodisiac. Lure Ben over and push him in the tub. Except it wasn't a physical thing that stopped him. It was that personal code again. Anything to do with that woman cop?

Two drops of vetiver for anxiety and tension ought to do it.

Slipping off her robe, she stepped in, slid down until water rose to her chin, and let her skin absorb the essential oils. A little guilt was always a useful thing. Maybe something could be done along those lines.

Silver. Laura my beloved. The universe is silver. In the world of magnificent palaces we will love each other in a new life. He stared up at the window, all he could see was light behind the curtains. He couldn't even see her move around, the curtains were too heavy. But in his mind he could see his beloved. Her beauty surpasses all others. She is the princess of the universe, the angel of all that is caring, the countess of all that is good. My soul mate. Hand in hand we will walk through a meadow of buttercups. We will spend eternity together.

This day seemed to last an eternity. Clem stepped from the shower, grabbed a towel, and wrapped it around herself. She was totally wrung out. With a hand towel, she made one swipe over the steam on the mirror and looked at her reflection. What a mess everything was, including herself. Fifer walking around like God creating the world with his very hands. Laura and Nick at each other's throats. Big surprise the film wasn't run out of Eden. A snake handing out apples right and left. Fifer should direct a new film. *The Snake That Ate His Career.* He was so uptight all the time it made everybody jittery. His butt was on the line here, and the accident—

She pulled on an oversized pajama top patterned with zebras, then tried to call room service for some ginseng tea. It was after midnight, room service was closed. She knew that. No room service after midnight. Her mind wasn't working right. She padded barefoot around the room, touching the table, the chair, the chest, the lamp. How could she go to sleep without ginseng tea? Her mother always brought it to her.

Pulling back the curtain, she peered up at the night sky. The moon was full. A cloud like a wispy piece of gauze floated across the face of it. The Patio below, with chairs and tables, lights strung through trees like fairyland, was deserted. Except someone stood on the very edge looking up. There was something creepy about him. He blended into the shadows and she couldn't tell who it was.

Creepy, quivery, bump in the night, bad will. Even before the accident, astral influences were stacked against this film.

She shivered, let the curtain fall back, and rubbed her arms. Go to bed, get some sleep. Business as usual in the morning. Oh, Laura's scenes might be postponed, the dangerous ones, but not in acknowledgment of Kay's death, only because the new stunt double wasn't due until afternoon.

The bed was tall, high off the floor, a good place to leave a body under if you had one lying around. The phone rang, sending her three inches into the air.

"Hello?" she whispered.

"Oh, did I wake you?"

"Not really."

"I'm sorry. I didn't realize how late it was. Listen, I'll let you go back to sleep. Tomorrow I need to talk with you. I think you can do something for me."

"What?"

"You shouldn't have any trouble with it."

Climbing up the outside stairway, Yancy had trouble lifting his feet high enough to clear the risers. They tended to catch on the soles and pitch him forward. His landlady had turned the light off again. He'd explained to Mrs. Blakeley more than once that the best way to discourage prowlers and burglars was to keep lights on after dark. She always nodded, then turned them off anyway, worried about the cost. With the full moon shining down he could see well enough, but the stairs stretched twice as high as normal. At the top, he shoved his key in the lock, then raised his head. Noise. The concrete driveway below was empty, silver in the moonlight. The Cherokee, parked by the storage shed, cast a black shadow.

The house next door was dark. At one-thirty, they would be in bed and long asleep. As he should be. The yard behind the neighbor's house was shadowy with trees and shrubs. Occasionally, a shadow moved, nudged by a warm breeze.

He rubbed his eyes and squinted. He couldn't see around to the rear of the house. Honeysuckle was soft in the air. Night sounds came on the wind, of birds nesting in the trees, frogs conversing with each other, and crickets sawing away.

As he turned the key, he heard the whisper of a shoe on damp grass. Fatigue cut so heavy through his mind, he wasn't sure he could trust his senses. A metallic clink sounded, silenced almost immediately.

Wishing he had a flashlight, he ran down the stairs and hugged the house as he inched toward the back. A footstep came from the driveway. He stopped, looked behind him. Nothing. He imagined it. Or somebody had melted into the dark below the stairs.

Three-quarters of the way to the rear of the house, he tangled with Stephanie's bicycle. It clattered onto the driveway as he sprawled across it, banging a kneecap and scraping a hand. Oh, Lord, little cat feet.

He pushed himself up and dashed to the Cherokee for a flashlight. When the dome light went on he ducked low—even though he didn't think precautions were necessary at this point, unless the prowler was deaf and blind he was long gone—and snatched the flash from the glove box.

In the backyard, all was quiet. Holding the flash at arm's length, he clicked it on. He was still a pretty good target if the prowler was so inclined.

Whoever had been here had hightailed it over the fence disturbing the lilacs and spreading their scent through the night air.

The mad painter had struck again. Somebody with an artistic soul or a keen sense of the absurd started creeping around painting nudes on garbage cans when people were away on vacation, then when they were out for an evening. Lately, he—or she—had gotten even bolder. But to come here, with a cop in residence, was downright insolent.

Yancy checked all ground-floor doors and windows, then went back and studied the artist's rendering. Mrs. Blakely now had a garbage can with a female nude on it. He wasn't sure what they'd charge the guy with, if they ever caught him. Defacing private property? The garbage cans actually looked better. Lewd and lascivious?

The bicycle belonged in the shed. Stephanie was thirteen, an age when things didn't always get where they belonged. He put it away and limped up the stairs. Sufficient unto the day.

What a day this has been, what a rare mood I'm in, Susan thought sourly as she let herself into the house. She checked the messages on her machine. There was only one, from her father. It could wait. Upstairs, she took a quick, tepid shower to wash away the sweat, dirt, and irritation of the day. In the bedroom she dug a white T-shirt from a drawer and slipped it over her head. It hit her about midthigh. Her husband had been a tall man. He'd been dead now about a year and a half, sometimes it seemed only days, sometimes it seemed forever.

She reversed the cassette in the portable player and pushed play. Soft sounds of Boccherini floated around her. She shoved the window all the way up and invited in any breezes. They came, but they were hot. San Francisco nights—most days also, but especially nights—were cool. A soft puff of air, like a baby breathing, touched her cheek. The silver moon shone full, crickets sang, fireflies blinked. They intrigued her, those fireflies.

Perissa, the Siamese kitten, squeezed her furry little self between Susan and the window screen. Perissa gave it a chance and when she was still ignored, she jumped from the sill to the floor and bit Susan's ankle. The cat had been an unwelcome gift from Sophie, a nutty old woman with a passion for cats and snooping. Susan didn't know much about these cat creatures, but this one seemed to sense when her thoughts were far away; if she was reading the cat would spread itself across the book; if she was staring thoughtfully into space it would climb up and pat her face. Weird creatures, cats. She rubbed Perissa's chocolate brown head and thought about Kay Bender. Dead at twenty-one, almost certainly killed because she was in the wrong place. A stunt double for Laura Edwards at dangerous moments, and a double for her murder.

A shadow of cloud passed across the moon, leaving a dark

blotch on the dark lawn. An owl called, then some other night bird.

She hadn't yet come up with much of a motive for anyone to ice Ms. Edwards. That she didn't need to show motive didn't matter, she wanted one. That it had been only about twelve hours since the death didn't matter either, those were crucial hours. She got impatient when nothing showed. She needed movement on a case or she got irritated. Not enough was happening here.

She had Sheri Lloyd, jealous of Laura Edwards and wanting the starring role. Ms. Lloyd was not superbright, but could she really believe she'd get the part of the star if the star was out of the way? Maybe. Some people simply couldn't see beyond their own wants.

Nick Logan. Susan liked him. That didn't mean anything, she had known charming killers before. He was easy in himself, not handsome, but had rugged good looks, and that flavor of southern California. Large, talented, charismatic, a man whose very presence commanded attention. He'd had an affair with Ms. Lloyd, was supposed to be madly in love with Ms. Edwards. Would he kill Laura to be with Sheri? This was sounding like a soap opera again. Someone in a coma ought to show up here pretty soon. It just wouldn't fly. Why not simply walk away from Laura? It was done all the time, and these two weren't even married.

She listened to the cello concerto on the tape and felt homesick. Her mother played cello for the San Francisco symphony. When Susan was a child, she could remember lying in bed at night hearing her mother practice.

Fifer, the director. His motive seemed even weaker. Get rid of Laura and collect the whopping great insurance he had on her. The movie was in financial trouble, it was true. It was way over budget. But everybody except Sheri Lloyd—and that was maybe jealousy—said Fifer was ecstatic about how it was going, fully confident that when it was released he'd have the hit he needed.

Parkhurst. No motive at all. True, spouses and ex-spouses headed the list of suspects, but she wouldn't believe it. However, as her former boss used to say, what she believed didn't cut any cake.

Laura Edwards herself. Which meant Kay Bender was the intended victim. No motive at all that showed so far. Early days, early days.

Sheri Lloyd, Nick Logan, and Hayden Fifer, all with weak motives for doing in Laura Edwards. Laura Edwards with no motive at all for doing in Kay Bender. None of them had an alibi worth looking at. Okay, making great progress here. Damn it, she missed Parkhurst. Much of a homicide investigation had to do with theories. She tossed them out. Parkhurst said, that stinks, that's asinine, or maybe you've got something here.

She looked at the clock by the bed. Almost one, nearly eleven in San Francisco. Her father would still be up. Did she want to deal with him tonight? When she was a child she felt she always had to fight or her life would be his. As an adult, she still sometimes felt that way. It was ridiculous at thirty-five to be still rebelling against a dynamic father who loved her very much, but she could only deal with him when she felt she had the necessary strength. Tired or drained, forget it. He'd swoop down and engulf her. Oh, hell, wasn't it time she grew up?

"What do you think, cat? Time to make my own decisions? Uncolored by choices made because they're the opposite of what he wants?"

Perissa stared back, unblinking.

"It's probably why we're still here, instead of back in San Francisco where I belong. Unless the power has gone to my head. Chief of police, impressive, yes?"

Perissa washed a paw.

"That impressed, I see." She stretched out on the bed and reached for the phone. It rang before she could pick it up, startling her.

She sat up. "Hello."

"Parkhurst."

Unsaid things growing like vines filled the silence.

"Sorry to call so late. I just drove past the house and saw the light." Parkhurst also lived on Walnut Street, but way on the other end. He told her about his visit with his ex-wife.

"That likely means," he finished, "we have a stalker in our midst."

"You're off the case."

"Yes," he said. "I'll turn all this over to Osey."

"And stay away from Laura Edwards until this is cleared."

"Yes," he said.

She hung up a little harder than was necessary, a mixture of emotions bubbling around: jealousy—of a woman Parkhurst had been married to before she even knew him. Yes, but this woman was beautiful and famous.

Worry about this new information and keeping Laura Edwards safe. Irritation that he'd disobeyed her orders. What was she going to do about that? Let it ride for tonight.

Oh, hell, call your father. That'll take your mind off things. She picked up the phone again and punched in the number. "Hi, Dad."

"Hello, baby. What are you doing up so late?"

His rich resonant voice sounded tired. Her father never got tired. "Is everything all right?"

"Sure, except my only child is way off in the middle of some unreachable, forsaken jungle contracting rare swamp fevers instead of by my side where she belongs."

That was better. "I had the measles, Dad."

"You okay now?"

"Fine."

"Spots?"

"All gone."

"You got running water yet?"

"Downhill. We also got California." She told him about the movie being made.

He snorted. "That's not California."

She smiled. North and south never quite got along; periodically there was commotion about splitting into two states.

"I just read something about that," he said. "Nick Logan had to turn down fifteen million and a role he wanted because of the commitment to this one."

Oh, really? "Where'd you read that?"

"The *Chronicle.*"

She asked him what the weather was like there, that led him into a soliloquy on the beauty and desirableness of coastal fog and a comparison with heat, humidity, and general awfulness. She fended questions about when she was coming to visit, then talked with her mother.

When she hung up, she propped pillows behind her head and stared at the ceiling. Nick Logan had just moved from no motive to a fifteen-million-dollar one. She spent at least sixty-five seconds in serious thought before sleep took over.

12

The tennis court wasn't the only thing sizzling. Laura Edwards and Nick Logan dashed around zinging the ball back and forth, with the tension hot enough to strike sparks. Yancy kept his eye on the ball.

According to Mac, Ms. Edwards's driver and Yancy's buddy, this was the time of the second murder attempt. Yancy never did figure out who the first victim was, but the tennis game was supposed to be a tense moment in the movie. Some kind of explosive was inside the ball. There was a lot of close-up stuff of the ball flying to a racquet, the racquet making a big slow arc. The *thwock* and the ball flying. Yancy followed the ball like a myopic puppy. It wasn't going to explode. That's what he'd been told and he'd looked at every tennis ball around. Still, he clenched at each smack. Another accident, this time with Laura Edwards scattered in pieces all over the court . . . Stupid way to try to kill someone. It would have to explode when the intended victim was near. How could anyone make sure of that? He wanted this piece of filming finished.

The aging Lockett mansion had been given a face lift. It was a large rectangular place with two-story white pillars across the front. Sparkling white paint, gray-blue shutters, double doors replaced at the entrance, windows repaired and replaced, and spanking clean. Shrubbery had been planted, thick green grass rolled out, and pots of purple, yellow, pink, and red flowers set across the porch. That was the front of the place. The north side looked fantastic too, but the back and south sides were left in their faded and peeling paint, boarded-over doors and windows. The maple trees were real though, tall and green against the cloudless blue sky.

The mansion, used as the main set for *Lethal Promise*, had everything a mansion should have. It had been built for the new wife William Lockett was importing from the east. Nothing was too good for Lucy. Marble bathrooms, stone fireplaces, kitchen appliances big enough to handle restaurant crowds, tennis court, swimming pool, small lake stocked with fish, and stables.

Poor Lucy never saw it. The private plane William had sent to fetch her had gone down in a storm, killing all on board. Shortly thereafter, the oil business fell on hard times and William lost buckets. He put the house up for sale and went off to Texas. There were lots of lookers, but no buyers. Mostly people were just curious, they just wanted to see the inside of the place, but even those who might want to buy couldn't afford it.

The place sat empty, except kids breaking in for parties or homegrown vandalism, until Hollywood came along. They cleared out the rats and the spiders and the old beer cans and the used condoms, and painted and fancied up all the rooms they wanted to use in the film.

Yancy stood on a pathway under the shade of the maple trees, almost kissing the fence around the tennis court, sweat trickled down between his shoulder blades. Whenever a camera operator yelled he was in frame, he moved back a grudging inch.

A dozen or so onlookers—boring as this was, he'd expect them to get tired of it, but they were always around—were behind a roped-off area back of the trees. He kept an eye on them too. Some he was beginning to recognize, like the guy with the backpack.

The temperature once again approached the mid-nineties and the humidity topped that, too damn hot for early June, and too hot for Fifer's artistic demands. Periodically, Fifer stopped the action and a team moved in to mop up his stars. Apparently, stars weren't allowed to sweat. For all Yancy knew this was supposedly taking place in the dead of winter. That made as much sense as anything else. People with umbrellas and battery-operated fans would swarm out, makeup and hair people, people carrying bottles of water with straws. Actors couldn't just grab a bottle and chug it down, that smeared the makeup.

It must be torture out there. Yancy could barely tolerate the heat and he was standing still. These Californians were tough, you had to give them that.

In the far corner of the court, Sheri Lloyd waited, with somebody holding an umbrella over her, for the director's call. Robin McCormack, the dead woman's boyfriend, looked pale and sweaty. In shorts and sleeveless T-shirt, even the snake tattoo on one bare arm looked subdued. He wore dark glasses and moved carefully, obviously protecting a pounding head. Yancy saw him speak to Sheri. She turned away. He grabbed her arm. In her snotty way, she tossed her hair and took a step back, distancing herself.

At Fifer's word, the swarms cleared and the actors went back out in the sun and smacked the ball back and forth. Yancy pulled tight on all his muscles and clamped down on his back teeth. Nothing could happen. This ball was just an ordinary ball, the exploding one was locked in a safe under the eye of the special effects man, and wouldn't be used until Fifer called for it. Then the new stunt double would be on the court.

Fifer was beginning to look like a candidate for sun stroke, his face taking on the color of rare steak. Khaki shorts and white T-shirt left a lot of skin exposed to the sun and all of it was turning brick red. Nick seemed to know how to play tennis and moved with the sureness of an athlete. Laura could hold the ball up there and place an okay serve, even make the right moves, but she wasn't quick with it. She looked beautiful though. Periodically, a man behind a wind machine would turn it on making her gold hair flutter.

"She had lessons in preproduction."

Yancy looked around and found Clem Jones, narrow face looking pinched, coming up behind him, eyes fixed on Laura. Envy of all that beauty and perfection? Clem would be better off without the black mascara, white makeup, and pink hair. The men's black swimming trunks and huge shapeless orange shirt didn't help much either. Maybe she was also just hoping nothing would go wrong.

Fifer called, "Cut. Beautiful, children. Just beautiful." He granted everybody a twenty-minute break.

Pink. Laura my beloved. The universe is pink. He watched Laura, his lovely Laura, go into the mansion surrounded by cast and crew. The cop went in too. Soon, my beloved. Do not get discouraged. Soon we will be together in a land of beauty throughout eternity. He needed the gun. Always, too many people around. The gun was his. I'm coming my princess. It will be fast and painless. We'll be together. He edged up to the barrel of trash that held the water bottle and straw she'd used. He grabbed the straw and walked off. Away from the court he put the straw in his mouth, moved it slowly back and forth, sucking gently. It tasted of the sweetness of her lips, the purity of her soul.

Both Nick and Laura, along with a herd of people whose job it was to soothe and succor, trailed up to the mansion. Yancy followed. On the way, he snagged a doughnut and bottle of foreign water from craft service. Inside, the stars climbed the big staircase side by side, without touching, without looking at each other. At the top, they split and Nick went into one room, Laura into another, with Mac on her heels, Officer White on his.

Yancy plopped in a love seat in the hallway and downed the water. Knowing Laura's minders were on her tail—and beautiful as it was—he zeroed in on Sheri Lloyd's petulant face as she chugged up the stairs. He let her get settled, then barged into a room that had obviously been meant as a child's bedroom. The switch plate was a train with a smiley face, the wallpaper had trains, trucks, and hot air balloons. William Lockett had been planning a male heir.

The two females patting Sheri's cheeks, forehead, and the nape of her neck with damp cloths looked at him with astonishment. He pointed, they stomped out, he closed the door.

The room had a bed, two chairs, a bar stool, and two carousel horses. Why carousel horses? Sheri had, naturally, arranged herself on the bed with pillows propped around her in such a way as to show off her body. "It's so terribly hot. I feel ill. I can't talk with you."

He pulled a blue bottle of water from the six-pack on the table next to the bed, twisted off the cap, and handed it to her. "Sit up and drink it. You'll feel better."

She took it and glared. Apparently, he wasn't being sensitive.

Hard-faced, he pulled one of the chairs close to the bed and sat on it. Ms. Sheri Lloyd would be apt to misinterpret anything else, so in the interests of intimidation and the pursuit of information, he sat rigid, eyes flinty.

Automatically she wiggled herself around on the pillows so that her tits were thrust forward in maximum position for distraction.

"What were you talking about with Robin McCormack?"

"I don't believe that's any of your business, but if you must know I was extending my sympathies."

Miss Sheri was not one to drop sympathy around where it wouldn't do her any good, and it had been Robin who'd approached her. "Ms. Lloyd, I told you before the consequences of withholding information in a murder investigation."

"When two old friends make a date to get together, it hardly constitutes *withholding evidence.*"

"You and Robin are old friends?"

"Of course."

127

"When are you getting together?"

She studied the veins in the back of her hand as though they were a road map. "There's nothing definite."

Yancy wondered if maybe Sheri Lloyd was one of those people who simply lied all the time.

"Now, if you don't mind, I really need to regather my strength." She flipped on her side and mashed another pillow under her head.

He left her to the ministering women and went in search of Robin. In the condition Robin was in, it wouldn't need thumb screws; a loud voice ought to do.

Six or seven crew members were schmoozing in the kitchen, Robin sat glugging down a Coke.

"Talk to you a minute?"

"What about?"

Yancy looked at the other guys. "Maybe we could step into the pantry."

Yancy could see him want to refuse, but in the end it was just too much trouble. He drained the can, crushed it, tossed it in a trash container, and grabbed another.

The pantry hadn't been spruced up, it remained in its cob-webbed seedy condition. Robin propped himself against a wall of empty shelves. "What is it?"

"How you feeling?"

"I been better."

"Remember last night?"

Robin gave him a rueful grin, and rubbed a hand along the back of his head. "Not crystal clear. Didn't you run over me?"

"You said somebody pushed you."

"Did I?"

"Who?" Yancy slouched against the door frame and crossed his arms.

Robin popped open the Coke and took a long drink, giving himself time to think, or because he was thirsty. "I don't know."

"You see anybody?"

He started to shake his head, grimaced, and thought better of it. "I wasn't exactly in top condition."

"Why would anybody push you in front of my Jeep?"

"Nice guy like me?" Robin shrugged. "I can't imagine."

Yancy was getting a little irritated. "You loved Kay Bender, right? If you had anything to help, you'd give it to me, right?" Yancy paused. "Who'd you see?"

"Could you, maybe, not talk quite so loud? I don't know." He tipped up the can and swallowed. "A kid, I think. And—oh, yeah, another guy."

"The kid, male or female?"

"Male."

"What do you mean by kid? Ten, twelve?"

"Seventeen, eighteen."

"What'd he look like?"

"I don't know."

"The other guy, it was a guy? Male?"

"Yeah."

"What'd he look like?"

Robin closed his eyes, kept them closed so long Yancy wondered if he'd gone to sleep. "Somebody who came out of the hotel."

"Describe him."

"You're asking an awful lot, man. Medium. Medium everything. Not tall, not short. Kinda stocky, maybe. That's it. You think I was studying him?"

That description would fit any number of males, including his old friend, Howie. "Age?"

"Youngish. My age or so."

"Who else?"

"Only you."

"Why do you think Sheri killed Kay?"

"I don't."

"You wanted to talk to her last night. Just a few minutes ago, you did talk to her. Why?"

"I need to get back to work," Robin said.

"Not until you lay it out for me."

"It's nothing, okay? It's only a feeling. You ever heard the expression the cat who ate the cream? That's the way she looked, Sheri. Like she knew something and she was going to use it to her advantage. Okay? That anything you want?"

"You're reading an awful lot into an expression."

"I told you."

"What else?"

Robin hauled in half the air in the room. "She was singing. 'Take what comes and use it your way.' "

"That's a song?"

"Yeah, man. A line from the theme song for this movie. I gotta go."

From the bedroom window, Sheri looked out at the tennis court and watched Laura hit the ball back to Nick. It should be her out there. She'd be much better. And she could play tennis, for God's sake. None of this holding the ball up and serving and then cutting in the stunt double. Laura was hot and sweaty and not at all sexy. Sheri hoped she'd drop over from the heat. Sheri patted at moisture on her own forehead. It was so hot. Even when they managed to get the air-conditioning going, it kept breaking down. Fifer would yell and they'd fix it again.

Maybe this might have been some house when it was new, but now it was a dump, falling down and moldy. Even if it was all remodeled it wasn't practical. She was nothing if not practical. She knew what was important, like the right script, the right money, a limo and driver. She should have a trailer of her own. Not that little crummy cubby she was stuck with. She'd tell her agent, her own trailer from now on.

She liked things to be right. If they weren't, she would make them so. Like her name. She'd been born Martha Gutlet in Newark, New Jersey. As soon as she got to California, she knew immediately that wouldn't do. Gutlet was impossible and Martha was a plain, obedient kind of name. The whole name just didn't have a euphonious—her high school English teacher would be surprised at the use of that word—ring to it.

The way she found her name, she was taking the bus home to this shitty apartment that she shared with another girl and somebody'd left a paperback book with this handsome guy on the cover. It turned out to be this really sweet story about this girl who fell in love and the guy loved her too only she didn't know it and the girl's name was Sheri Lloyd. Then and there she knew that was her name. Her best friend from high school laughed and said it was just like her to choose such a dumb name. Well, she got the last laugh. She made it. And her best friend wasn't her best friend anymore, she was a housewife. Sheri knew the name was right. She knew a lot of things. It was just a matter of figuring out how to use them. She wasn't as dumb as people thought.

She frowned, then consciously smoothed her face. Frowning caused wrinkles.

And she was not only fulfilled as an actress, she was a right-thinking member of society, advocated the right causes. She was against pollution and offshore drilling and oil spills. And for endangered species, saving trees, and AIDS research. Women who wore fur coats deserved to have red paint thrown over them. People who picketed abortion clinics should be dragged away and shot. Except, of course, that would be capital punishment and she was against that.

And then there was religion. Religion was all right, even though it was the opiate of the masses—see, Miss Strickler, I was paying attention—and everybody had the right to worship in his or her own way, but the God squad wasn't satisfied with choosing for themselves, they wanted to ram their choice down everybody else's throats. You couldn't even talk to them, because they wouldn't hear and you might as well be talking to a brick wall, or they made you feel like the biggest sinner since Pontius Pilate. Or they wanted to pray for you. She hated it when they wanted to pray for you.

And that time on the *Tonight Show* when she said she was for abortions. Of course, she didn't mean that. She meant for choice. Picketers followed her around for days. Good Lord, you'd think she'd recommended slaughtering whole nurseries full of babies. Most people didn't have the scope to transcend their own narrow horizons.

She swung the crystal on the gold chain around her neck. Wasn't it ever anything but hot and sticky in this godforsaken place? Even at night, it was hot. Dreadful place. She watched Nick out on the tennis court smack a ball that Laura missed completely. She wasn't even graceful about it. Not that it mattered, the finished film would only show what Fifer wanted, the stretch and the hit and the bouncy flouncy. Sheri studied Nick and wondered how she was going to get him in bed again. And get him she would. It was only a matter of working it out.

Laura ought to understand. Good God, they weren't even married, and these things happened. Sheri knew Nick was much more suited to her than to Laura. Look at how they were fighting all the time. If that romance wasn't already dead, Nick wouldn't have been interested in the first place.

Out on the tennis court, Fifer called a break. Everybody rushed like commuters to the mansion. If Laura's fans could see her now they wouldn't think she was so sexy. Her face was red and she was sweating like a pig.

"People!" Fifer called after them.

Sometimes Sheri thought Fifer didn't appreciate her. She'd mentioned it once, tried to bring it right out in the open like you're supposed to do for good relationships, but somehow they'd ended up talking about team playing and the good of *Lethal Promise*.

"I want everybody in the ballroom," Fifer said. "That means everybody."

13

$\mathcal{S}$heri took tiny sips at her drink. The moment of silence was turning into a cocktail party. It had started out all quiet with everybody in the ballroom and kind of avoiding looking at each other, and Fifer making that sweet speech about the stuntwoman. How Kay Bender was one of us. What a tragedy it was. How sorry we all were. How good she was at her job. How much we'd all miss her. How we were a family and what happened to one affected us all. Everybody had shuffled their feet and looked at the floor, but Sheri thought it was touching. After he finished, alcohol was poured. Ice cubes tinkled and glasses clinked, hors d'oeuvres on a long table were being perused and eaten. Sheri liked cocktail parties. People tended to drink too much and say things.

The sound level rose. Eighty people in one room with alcohol and food and you had a party. Sheri was drinking rum and Coke. So what if it was sneered at? She liked it. She usually tried to limit herself to one drink unless she felt really comfortable and knew what was going on. She didn't know what was going on here but something was. There was a really bad aura, and she kept feeling somebody was watching her. She couldn't catch anybody, just people standing around wondering how soon they could leave. It was tense in here. Really tense. She was sensitive to these things.

She didn't know why Fifer picked this room. It wasn't like it was nice or anything. Just this one huge empty room, nothing in it but the folding table brought in by the caterers. There wasn't even anyplace to sit down or anything. It was scummy, cobwebs on the ceiling and patches of wallpaper missing.

That Yancy police person stood by the wall looking like he was watching everybody. Laura was holding court in the middle of the room like the Queen of Sheba. Sheri tipped a teensy bit more rum in her Coke and plopped in another ice cube. Nick was standing by the fireplace. Kind of a nice fireplace. Stone, sort of massive, all the way to the ceiling. She weaved around through people, wedged herself between Clem and a makeup girl, and slipped her arm through Nick's. He gave her a smile and tried to step sideways. She stayed with him.

Laura glared at her. Sheri smiled. Stupid bitch. When would she realize Nick and I are meant for each other?

"Excuse me, darling." Nick tugged his arm loose and set off for Laura.

"You shouldn't do that." Clem fingered the locket at her throat.

"Do what?"

"Upset Laura like that."

"Poor Laura. She just won't admit it's over between her and Nick." Sheri turned to make her way to the snack table and found Robin McCormack standing beside her.

"I'm so sorry about Kay." Sheri put her fingertips on his forearm so he'd know she really meant it. She was sorry she'd been so short with him earlier. After all, he'd suffered a Loss.

"Yeah? Then help me."

"Help?" What did that mean? Of course, she would make allowances because of his grief, but what did he want? No way would she sleep with him if that was what he was working up to. That's usually what they wanted, starting with her stepfather. "What?" she asked in a voice that slipped a little from sympathy.

"What do you know about Kay's death?"

"Oh." She was relieved. "I told you earlier, I don't know anything."

"I'm not in the mood for coy." His voice was awfully cold for somebody who was grieving.

Her hand closed around her crystal. Too many bad feelings were coming from all around. This movie just had bad karma. She needed to meditate, to get herself centered. And call her astrologer. Her astrologer would tell her what to do. Sheri concentrated on putting out good thoughts. "I don't know anything."

"It's not smart to play games with me."

"Really, it's true. If I did, I'd tell that police person. He's supposed to help if we need anything. Although when I asked him for one teensy favor he said he was too busy."

"Things happen," he said menacingly.

"What's that supposed to mean?"

"It means"—he spoke very slowly like she was an idiot or something—"that you could find yourself in a situation your conniving little mind won't be able to get you out of."

"Are you threatening me?"

"Just a warning."

How dare he talk to her like that? She left the snack table and went all the way across the room. With her back toward the wall, she peered around for Nick. He was over there with Laura. Sheri elbowed through to him and stood on his other side. Her arm slid through his, just where it belonged.

"Fifer seems to be trying to get your attention," Laura said with sweet poison.

Sheri, fingering the crystal dangling between her breasts, glanced over at the director.

"I doubt that will help you any, darling," Laura said.

What was she talking about? All of a sudden it seemed everybody was talking from pink pages that she didn't get. "If you have the idea—"

"Sheri, darling, in all the time I've known you I don't believe you've had a single new idea. Or a single old one either."

"Now just listen here—"

Nick detached her arm and gave it a little pat. "See what Fifer wants, sweetheart."

"Sheri." Fifer beckoned with one finger. She couldn't believe it. Like she was some kind of underling. Oh, this had to be straightened out. Hayden Fifer didn't appreciate her at all. Dialoguing was the only way to clear this up. She had to work really hard and make sure he listened to her this time. Well, of course, she was all for team playing and the good of the film, but there was such a thing as making her own needs known.

He just walked out like she'd follow and didn't even look back to see if she was. People parted for him as if he were Moses at the Red Sea. Or whoever it was, she couldn't remember. By that big wide stairway, he studied her and said, real quietlike, "My hotel room. Eight o'clock."

Then he left, just like that. Back inside the ballroom, she searched out Clem and caught her arm. "What does Fifer want with me?"

"I'm not always in his mind, but I'd say he wants you to stop getting our star all ruffled by trying to steal her boyfriend."

"But that's just silly. Nobody steals anybody. He wouldn't be interested if he still loved her. I didn't do anything. It just happened."

"Great line."

Sheri looked at her, puzzled. "Maybe I should talk to Laura. I mean, just explain that Nick loves me and we need to be together."

"You really believe that's going to happen?" Clem asked curiously.

"Of course. It has to."

"Why does it have to?"

"Because that's what my astrologer said. I shall win out over my enemy."

"Well," Clem said, "if I were you I wouldn't mention that to Laura."

"It's always better to dialogue and get everything out in the open."

"Right." Clem snorted and made her way over to the drinks table.

Clem was a really odd person, Sheri thought. Into her self too much. Did she ever have a boyfriend? The way she looked what could she expect? That awful makeup and those awful clothes. Maybe she had one once who gave her that locket and that's why she always wore it. There were times when Sheri really didn't think Clem liked her. Sheri would show Christian charity. Clem's life was hitting too many wrong planes. Sheri had offered the name of her astrologer, but Clem had refused. What more could she do?

She slid the crystal back and forth on its chain. The bad auras were making her jumpy. Of course, Nick loved her. He was going to marry her. Hadn't her astrologer said her true love would return that love twofold? Besides, she was twenty-two. Laura was old.

Sheri leaned over the bathroom cabinet and frowned at her image in the mirror. There wasn't enough light. This really wasn't a nice hotel. Compared to the Four Seasons, it was just crummy. Why was everybody so thrilled with old?

She examined her makeup. It was perfect, but her eyes were a little puffy. Nobody had dared leave the mansion until Fifer said they could, and then she'd come straight to her hotel room and taken a nap. It was so hot and awful, she'd felt just really drained, and she'd slept too long.

Now she didn't even have time to get anything to eat. Hayden Fifer didn't like it if anybody was late. She turned her head a little to one side and then a little to the other. She took a step back. She couldn't even see her whole self in the dinky mirror, only the top half. Although she had to admit that part looked pretty good. The white blouse with a wide neck looked great against her tan. The skimpy skirt, green to show up her green eyes, hugged her hips. Slipping her feet into high-heeled sandals, she grabbed her room key.

Fifer had a suite, of course. He answered her knock, motioned toward a couch, and went into the bedroom. He swung the door shut, but it didn't quite latch. She sat down, crossed her legs, smoothed the skirt, and waited.

She recrossed her legs. What was taking him so long? If she'd known he was going to make her wait, she could have picked up something to eat. The snacks at Kay Bender's moment of silence hadn't really appealed. From a carafe on the old-fashioned desk thing she poured herself a glass of red wine and took a sip. She grimaced. She never could understand what people saw in wine. The murmur of Fifer's end of the phone conversation drifted in from the bedroom. She tiptoed to the door and put her ear to the crack.

". . . not any trouble . . . I keep telling you."

Silence a moment, then he said, "Yeah, yeah. Don't worry about it . . . if there's trouble, I'll take care of it."

Silence.

"Just leave it to me . . . I told you . . . little setback . . . can be fixed . . ."

Silence.

She was caught taking a giant tiptoe toward the couch. He grabbed her wrist so tight she couldn't even twist it.

"Interested in other people's phone conversations?" He released her with a little push and she landed on her butt on the edge of the couch and slid to the floor. She got up, eased onto the couch, and rubbed her wrist. What was the matter with him? He didn't usually push people around, he just yelled, or got creepy quiet. That's when he was scariest.

He went back into the bedroom and she heard him say, "I'll

get back to you." When he came out again, he poured himself a glass of wine. "Refill?" His voice was dangerous.

Since she had a glass she'd only taken two sips from, she shook her head.

"Want to know what that call was about?"

She shook her head again.

He gave a little laugh that wasn't really a laugh, drank off the wine, and poured another glass. He started to pace. "The money people. They hear rumors. They get twitchy and make noises about pulling the plug. That makes me nervous. I don't like getting nervous. Understand?"

She nodded.

He stopped in front of her, leaned over too close, and stared in her face. "Who's the most disliked person on the set?"

She shrank back.

"The director." He straightened and continued pacing. "You want to know why? I'll tell you why. He makes people act. He doesn't allow them to get away with what they think is acting. He makes them be things they never thought they could. They might think the actions are stupid, or wrong for the situation, but he insists. He demands too much and ignores their carefully considered suggestions. He's never satisfied and makes them work their butts off. He has no understanding of the sensitive artist, sets impossible goals, and doesn't make allowances for weather or technical problems. He demands the impossible and yells when he doesn't get it."

He sat on the arm of an overstuffed chair. "Why is that, Sheri?"

She stared at him.

"He has a vision. A vision of what he's working toward. The final product. He feels each section, has an overall sense as the work progresses, even if it gets changed along the way. He has to fight to create that vision. You understand? Sympathy on the set isn't possible, or tolerance for individual foibles. That would create chaos, turn out a project with no focus. A cause without a leader."

His voice got even scarier. "I'm not a person who yells a lot. I've found it's more effective to speak softly. I believe in *Lethal Promise*. I want to see it finished. I'll fight to make that happen."

Her heart was beating fast. She shivered. Her fingers found her crystal.

He waved toward the bedroom. "They heard about Kay's accident. They heard about the possibility it was an attack on Laura. I'm running the line that any publicity is good publicity. By the time *Lethal Promise* hits distribution, the public will be clamoring to see it. An attack on Laura will bring them charging in."

He pinned her with his eyes. "What is not good is your upsetting Laura. I don't care about your hormones. I care about this movie. Drop all your sexy little plays for Nick. Don't give Laura even a smell of anything to complain about. Understand? Or I will be forced to take care of you."

He stood up, took away her almost full glass of wine, set it on the table, and opened the door.

As if hypnotized, she got up and walked out. She didn't get mad until she was in the elevator going down. How dare he talk to her like that? He couldn't tell her what to do. When the doors opened at the lobby, she was momentarily confused, then realized she'd pushed the wrong button.

She stomped out, then stopped and drew in a deep breath. Calm. Ease the anger. Deep breath in. Let it out slowly. Release all the tension. Deep breath in. Out slowly. For a moment she wasn't certain what to do. But only for a moment. That pathetic man at the counter, assistant manager or whatever he was, was watching her and pretending not to. With a smile on her face, she walked to the desk.

"Hi," she said with a throaty purr. At least he appreciated her. Hadn't he been so kind as to give her that Yancy person's phone number? It wouldn't hurt to be nice to him. She might want something else, you never knew.

Howie, who had been acutely aware of her from the instant she got off the elevator, looked up from the papers he was pretending to work on. "Hey, Ms. Lloyd. Is everything all right?"

"I'm going out there." She pointed. "Could you have someone get me a drink?"

"I'll send someone right out."

"Thank you so much." She glided across the lobby, then marched down the corridor and out through glass doors to the Patio. She paused and blinked to let her eyes adjust to the dimness.

The area was glass-enclosed. Shrubs, growing in big pots and draped with strings of tiny white lights, sat on the uneven flagstone floor. Little round tables with two or three chairs placed here and there. Most were unoccupied. A ring of large trees outside screened the area from the rest of the grounds.

She waited for somebody to notice her. A hicksville kid, sitting in the corner where it was almost pitch-black, couldn't take gawping eyes off her. And a local nobody in a white dress. She'd been gazing out at the stars or something. A big black dog lay at her feet. Dogs shouldn't be allowed. She intended to complain. Laura and Nick were at a table with their heads together. They pretended like they didn't see her, but she knew better. Clem and Robin were over there with a makeup girl and somebody from wardrobe.

With her chin up, Sheri tip-tapped across the flagstones, high heels on the uneven floor making her stumble a little. "Okay if I join you?" Without waiting for an answer, she pulled a chair from a nearby table and joined Nick and Laura.

A waiter was at her elbow the moment she sat. She gave him a captivating smile and asked for a rum and Coke, then turned the smile onto her companions. Laura glared daggers. Somebody really ought to tell her how unattractive she was when she did that. It made her look haggard. Caused wrinkles too. At her age, she needed to be careful. Nick didn't seem really happy to see her either. That frightened her. She needed to get him alone so she could fix everything. It was Laura, sitting there sending out hateful auras, who made him act that way. Sheri felt very discomposed. She really did.

When the waiter came back with her rum and Coke, she took

a tiny sip, tipped her head, and looked out at the moon, full or almost full, like she was enjoying its beauty. This was an awful place, she hated it here, she'd be so glad when they left.

With a scrape, Laura shoved her chair back and stood up. "You don't realize who you're playing with." She smiled and stalked away.

"Good," Sheri said. "She's gone." She scooted her chair closer to Nick and laid her head on his shoulder. "I wanted to be alone with you."

He sighed and dropped his chin to his chest, then looked at her and shook his head. Without a word he got up and started to leave.

"Nick—?"

With one hand, he made a gesture like he was brushing her away. It brought tears to her eyes. She concentrated hard on not crying and sipped her drink like she wasn't in pain, like the moon really was beautiful and she was enjoying gazing at it. Aware that everybody was leaving, she didn't even look around. Put out confidence and confidence would be there.

When the woman in the white dress started over to her—actually, more like floated, the long white skirt and tuniclike blouse shimmered around her—Sheri felt tired at what fame brought. At least, this woman's aura was peace and serenity.

She sat at Sheri's table. "I'm Raina Yancy," she said. Her dark eyes were odd, kind of luminous and—she was scary somehow. Like crazy. The big black dog paced by her side and flopped at her feet.

Sheri drew away. Big dogs frightened her, but she smiled, even if the smile was maybe a little bit strained. Always smile at the fans. "Sheri Lloyd," she said, just as though she was an ordinary person. She always did that, even though the other person obviously knew who she was. It made them feel like she wasn't setting herself above them. And she didn't want to do anything to upset this woman. You never knew what might set them off.

" 'The moping owl does to the moon complain,' " Raina said.

Sheri looked around. Everybody was gone, even the kid in the corner.

"Is there anything I can do to help?" Raina said.

"How very kind of you, but I have to go now." Sheri smiled and shoved back her chair.

The noise made the dog leap to its feet and she shrank back.

"Don't mope, child. Sometimes you can't have what you want; that doesn't mean there aren't other things you can have. That are just as good."

"Excuse me." Sheri walked slowly and deliberately away. They were like dogs, the mad ones. If you didn't stare them in the eye and didn't run, maybe you could get away.

Sheri didn't look around until she had reached the door into the hallway. The woman didn't come after her. With a deep cleansing breath, Sheri let her shoulders relax, and went to complain about the vicious dog and the crazy woman. Howie—that was his name—said he'd take care of it right away. Because she felt so unnerved, she chatted with him awhile. He was really kind of sweet, in a short, stocky kind of way.

She couldn't stay long. She needed her beauty sleep. Fluttering her fingers at him, she went to the elevator that took an age to get there. It always did. One more thing about this crummy place.

On the third floor, she stuck the key in the lock and turned it. Just as she stepped inside, she felt a sharp pain in her back. She stumbled forward, and fell. Rough pile carpeting pressed against her cheek. Brown and beige. Ugly.

The door shut behind her.

Her tanned hand, nails painted red, crawled on its fingertips toward the crystal around her neck. The fingers went still, the hand fell flat and soft against the ugly carpet.

14

*Y*ancy, transferring keys and change from his pockets to the chest, let the phone ring. God damn it, it's ten o'clock. I put in sixteen hours. He counted twelve rings, then with a sigh of exasperation, irritation, and downright annoyance, picked up the receiver.

"Hey, Pete."

"Hey, Howie," Yancy said. "This better be important or I'm cutting you from my will."

"Sorry. Your mother's here."

"Where?"

"The hotel."

Oh, hell. With thumb and forefinger, he squeezed the bridge of his nose. "How'd she get there?"

"How do I know?"

"Trouble?"

"No. You know I like your mother, but I had complaints about the dog."

"Elmo's there too?"

"She really did complain and, actually, dogs aren't allowed, you know."

"I'm on the way."

Yancy put keys and change back in his pockets, turned on the outside light over the stairway, and trotted down.

When Yancy came into the lobby, Howie said, "On the Patio."

With a wave of thanks, Yancy turned down the corridor and went through the doors to the glass-enclosed area at the back of the hotel. No one there. The small white lights threaded through potted shrubs twinkled on empty tables; chairs sat at angles, crumpled napkins lay on the cobblestones. Oh, Lord, she'd gone.

Back in the lobby, he said to Howie, "She's not there. You see her leave?"

"I'd have told you. Is the dog gone too? Elmo's a big dog, he can look scary."

"Who complained?"

"What difference does it make? Dogs aren't supposed to be in there."

"Come on, Howie. Who was it?"

"Don't get so short. One of the actresses—"

"Howie, I'm tired and I'm not in a very good mood and I want to be home in bed. Don't hold back on me."

"What's with you? Okay, okay. Don't get so worked up. It was Sheri Lloyd."

"She coos at you and you drop all your bones at her feet." Yancy pointed a finger. "Watch it, Howie. Haven't you heard about bad women from the big city?"

"Yeah. What I'd like is a little firsthand experience."

"You could ask the lady out."

"I did. Hey, nothing like that. I only asked her to dinner. She said no."

"Did you tell her you owned a chain of hotels and you had so much spare money lying around you were thinking of investing in a movie?"

"Of course not. It's not true."

"No wonder she turned you down. How could my mother and a big black dog get out of here without you seeing them?"

"I don't just stand here, you know. I have work to do. I have an office to do it in."

Hours for assistant hotel managers seemed even worse than hours for cops baby-sitting movie people.

"Anyway, I may have been gone for a second or two. Hey, sometimes things need to be seen to. Like seeing if everything's all right in the bar. And sending someone out to take care of drinks for the people on the Patio." Howie flushed bright pink.

Yancy hadn't seen him do that since high school when a girl looked at him. "You sent a waiter? Missed opportunity, Howie."

"Go to hell."

Before Yancy could think of a clever but no doubt equally juvenile reply, his beeper went off. He tipped it so he could see the number and asked if he could use a phone. Without waiting for a reply, he eased around the counter and picked up the one on the desk.

"Peter," his sister said, "Mother's not here."

"Calm down. She's all right."

"How do you know?"

"What time did you last see her?"

"About seven-thirty when she went to bed. I was reading for a couple of hours and just now when I checked on her she was gone. I've looked everywhere. She's gone, Peter."

"She came to the Sunflower."

"Oh, God, is she all right? How on earth did she get there? You'll bring her home?"

"Well—she's not actually here right now."

Silence on the other end of the line. "You mean you don't know where she is."

"I'll find her. Don't worry. I'll bring her home."

"Don't worry," Serena said flatly and hung up.

Guilt reared up again. He punched in a number and told the dispatcher he'd appreciate it if the patrols would keep an eye out for his mother.

"Affirmative."

He got in his Cherokee and cruised. With the big dog at her

side, she shouldn't be hard to spot. After an hour of no sign, he was getting seriously alarmed. Nothing like a shot of adrenaline to clear ideas of sleep from your mind. He widened his circles, stopped what few people were out and about at eleven o'clock at night. Nobody had seen her. Damn. By this time, a patrol should have spotted her.

When his beeper went off, he grabbed it. Serena's number. At the pay phone outside the library, he called her.

"She's back," Serena said.

Thank God. "She okay?"

"Seems to be. But, Peter—"

"I'll be right out."

"Maybe now you'll start to understand what I've been telling you," Serena said when he walked in the kitchen door. She stood by the sink with her arms crossed, a hard crust of anger under her quiet words.

"I'm tired, Serena. I need to get up early."

"You're the only one?"

"No." He gave her a one-armed hug and kissed her forehead. "But I don't want you mad at me tonight. Okay?"

She shoved him. "If I didn't love you so much, I'd yell at you. Listen, I've been trying to tell you—"

"Peter?" his mother called from her bedroom.

"Can we talk about this later?"

"Will you listen?"

"Peter—?"

"Go ahead. She thinks the moon and stars rise and set by you. See if you can find out what she did."

His mother, pillows propped against the headboard, closed the book she was reading and held out both hands. "Peter, darling. What a lovely surprise."

Elmo bumped his big head against Yancy's knee. Yancy gave him a pat, sat on the edge of the bed, and took his mother's hands. He kissed her cheek.

"Where were you, Mom?"

Elmo rested his head on the bed and she stroked it. "We went for a walk. It was a beautiful night."

"You were at the Sunflower." The book she'd been reading was *How to Recover from a Stroke*.

She smiled, slightly embarrassed. "I hoped to see an actor. I know that sounds silly, but how often are famous people in Hampstead? I saw Nick Logan. Such a handsome man. And Laura Edwards. She's very beautiful. And there was one other. What's her name? Oh, what was it? I can't think."

"Sheri Lloyd?"

"That's the one."

"How did you get there?"

"Taxi. I asked for Eddy. You know Eddy. His wife has arthritis so bad. He's the only one who doesn't fuss about Elmo."

"How'd you get home?"

"It was such a nice night I thought we'd walk. It's cooler now. It won't be so hot tomorrow. I just can't walk like I used to. I'm afraid I pooped out before we were even halfway."

"Then what?"

"Somebody gave me a ride." She seemed to shake a bag of suppressed memories. "Who was it?"

"I don't know, Mom."

"Sure you do, Peter. We went up by the ridge to see if we could spot bald eagles."

"At night?"

"Oh, I don't think so." She noticed his uniform. "Why are you dressed like that?"

"I've been working."

She smiled fondly and squeezed his hand. "You still want to be a policeman?"

"I am a policeman, Mom. I've been one for five years. What did you do at the hotel?"

She sang so softly he could barely hear her.

> *"And it is thou art come, childe Orm,*
> *My youngest son so dear?*
> *And is it gold, or silver plate,*
> *Or coin, thou seekest here?"*

The stroke hadn't affected her voice; it was pure and clear, but she had slipped away into whatever part of her brain waited in the shadows. He gave her a kiss, removed a couple of pillows, and said, "Good night, Mom."

Serena was still standing in the kitchen, arms crossed, hands cupping her elbows. He knew a battle stance when he saw one. "I can't throw my mother out of her home," he said.

"Peter, I've been trying to tell you. When she got home— she had blood on her hands."

15

$\mathscr{M}$ain Street jumped with activity. Everybody wants to be in the movies, Susan thought. More people packed the sidewalks than would turn out for an end-of-the-world sale. College students in herds, Sophie the cat lady, Bob Haskel from heating and plumbing, Ab Perley from the hardware store. Her friend Fran Weymore from the travel agency. Kevin Murphy, high school football star and part-time gas pump jockey. Howie Gilbert, assistant hotel manager. Teens and preteens.

The director was intending to film a parade. If he didn't get it moving, his parade was going to get rained on. He stood on a camera truck speaking into a walkie-talkie, checking the status of every section along his route. Bright and sunny now, there were clouds on the horizon that might bring in thunder and lightning. One thing about Kansas, it knew how to stage a thunderstorm.

By eight, Fifer judged everything ready and a skeletally thin AD—assistant director to those who weren't in on movie lingo—alerted the crowd to put parade excitement on their faces and cheer at everything.

Fifer shouted, "Action." The cheers began. With Yancy at her side, Susan watched from the steps of city hall. The high school band played loudly, scout troops marched smartly, street clowns and jugglers did their thing. Horses stepped along, decorated flatbed trucks rolled, with drama students, tumblers, and choral groups. Hampstead could be proud.

Fifer stopped and started his parade so many times she lost count, and reshot every sequence a zillion times. The extras weren't having fun anymore. The first AD worked harder and harder getting cheers. Movie-trained horses, she noted, knew the meaning of action and cut as well as the rest of the actors.

At two, when Fifer finally finished filming his parade, the AD asked all the extras to gather by the river. Lyrics from a song? Something about gathering by the river.

"You get to gather with them," she told Yancy.

He smiled. "I thought I might get to do that very thing."

Through the milling crowd, she crossed the street to the police department. She hoped to get the work done that she'd neglected by watching the parade.

Gather, they did. For a picnic. Yancy wondered who might give him a copy of the script. So far nothing made any sense.

By now the extras were definitely not having fun and needed to be coaxed and jollied by the first AD. They milled around picnic tables brought in by the crew. Barbecue pits, also brought in, blazed and settled to low flames. Howie looked dubiously up at the sky. The AD clapped him encouragingly on a shoulder and bellowed through his megaphone, "The food is edible. Please do not eat the food unless the cameras are rolling. The food is edible. Please do not eat the food unless the cameras are rolling."

The river—sometimes slow and lazy, sometimes fast and angry after heavy rains, like now—swept by at a good clip, rippling through the reflections of trees. The building clouds overhead lent a dark ominous look to it. Yancy rested against a tree trunk on the edge of the buzzing activity. Working in the movie industry belonged to people with stamina. Nobody moved at less than a trot. He stifled a yawn. Before Hollywood came to town, he couldn't remember ever being this tired and this bored for this long. He swiped at a cloud of gnats and hoped Fifer knew rain might start pissing down anytime. Around all these trees wasn't the best place to be with lightning forking from heaven to earth.

The shouting back and forth between Fifer on dry land and two guys in a motorboat stopped; one guy in the boat inflated a raft and tossed it in the river. It darted from side to side behind the motorboat like an eager puppy. More shouting, and the guy jumped into the raft to test its seaworthiness, then clambered back into the motorboat. Much peering into cameras on the motorboat and into those planted along the river's edge.

Rescue teams set up a station, ready to race out and save anybody who fell in. Even extras and spectators? Probably not, not spectators anyway. Which left that duty to him. Promises to protect and serve, after all. He was a good strong swimmer, but more than one sinker would be a problem. With the humidity matching the temperature, the air was approaching liquid. Anybody out here for an ersatz picnic wasn't right in the head.

Although, he might be wrong about that. Laura Edwards appeared in the prow of the motorboat with a drenched T-shirt clinging to her superb body.

To be heard over the noise of the river, Fifer had to yell at Clem. Yancy could tell the director was on the thin edge of his patience.

So was Clem.

"She's not here," Clem yelled back.

"Find her."

"It's not my job."

"I need her now."

"Where's the second second?" Clem demanded. "It's her job. Why isn't she finding Sheri?"

"Get Sheri here!"

On a shoot the director was dictator and everybody did what he said, especially the director's assistant. With a look of mutiny, Clem fished keys from the large pocket of her purple tentlike thing and stomped toward the rental car parked behind all the vans used to transport cast and crew from the hotel to base camp or set. Stars had town cars—each one had hired his or her own for personal use—and the rest went by van, all piled together.

Sheri Lloyd's honey wagon room at base camp wasn't much bigger than an overgrown closet with a bench to sit on, a rod overhead to hang clothes on, a bathroom you could get into if you weren't overweight, and a mirror with lights. No Sheri. Clem knew that she wouldn't be here; Sheri wasn't big enough to throw a temper tantrum and get away with it. Be on the set and do what you're told or there are five hundred just like you to replace you.

At the Sunflower, she called Sheri's room from the lobby and let the phone ring twelve times, then she took the elevator to the third floor and banged on the door of three-eighteen.

Heart ticking away like mad, she tried the knob. It turned under her fingers. The room was dark. Holding her breath, she hit the light switch.

She choked on the air in her throat.

Sheri lay on the floor. Knife in her back. Blood. Looked different from the fake stuff. Dark, and sort of thin and black around the edges. It puddled out—the smell—

Oh, God. Nausea tickled her throat. She gagged, coughed. She backed against the door, swallowing hard.

Hand against her mouth, she turned and hurried down the hallway. Oh, God, let me get to my room. Please let me make it to the bathroom. Fumbling for her key, she shoved the door open and reached the toilet just in time.

Cupping her hand under the tap, she rinsed her mouth, then pawed through the bottles on the counter until she found mouthwash. She swirled it around and spit it out.

Stiff-kneed, teeth chattering, she went to the bedside table and picked up the phone.

Red. Laura my beloved. The universe is red. You belong to me. We are as one. It's his fault. I need the gun. I missed the opportunity. Your destiny is mine. The way will be shown to me. The universe will be dark. We'll be together. The knife is here. The silver blade is ready. The spirits are getting tired of waiting.

He needed another opportunity. When it came, he needed to be ready. Before the universe turned black. If that happened, Laura would choke on evil spirits and suffer a painful death.

Go deeper into the trees.

He looked at the boat that held Laura and heard it again. Go deeper into the trees.

He understood.

Lure the cop into the woods and then— His fingers curled around the knife in his pocket.

Yancy, propped against the leaning trunk, one knee bent, thought if he took up whittling that would lend a certain bucolic note of local color. He could do bats. That would be fitting and his mother would be thrilled.

The AD rushed toward him and Yancy straightened. Linsel had to be the skinniest human being still breathing; his black T-shirt that hung from chicken-bone shoulders and black shorts with wide legs didn't help. The poor guy's personality bordered on the average houseplant.

"Problem?"

"There's somebody too far back in the trees." One skeletal arm pointed. "Fifer wants you to get rid of him, so he doesn't bumble into the shoot."

Yancy tromped through layers of rotting leaves covered with tangled new vines and low-growing plants. Earthy smells of dead vegetation mingled with the sharp tangy scent of new growth. Sunlight, filtering through leafy branches overhead, dappled the brown and green footing and provided good protective coloring for snakes.

A guy thrashed around ahead, setting off a flutter of small birds from the cottonwood.

"Hey!" Yancy loped after him, tripped over a thick vine, and pitched forward. Uh-huh. He was right up there with all those other heroes. Rambo. The Terminator. Daffy Duck. Scrambling to his feet, he looked for the guy. Gone. He slapped leaves and dirt from his pants.

"Sir?" It was quiet under the trees; river sounds were muted, breezes whispered through branches. A woodpecker went to work somewhere giving him a start.

He wandered along, weaving around tree trunks. "Sir? You need to stay clear of the filming."

What the hell? This wasn't a jungle. This was a grove of trees and broad daylight. Where was the guy? Captured by aliens? Maybe it was the guy who was the alien. Beam me up.

The woodpecker stopped. An oriole sang three shrill notes. Hairs stirred on the back of his neck. He stood still and listened. On a branch overhead, a squirrel chittered, flicked its tail with irritation, and scampered away. Something had set off the squirrel. Could the guy be hiding? Waiting to ambush him? That ash over there, when Yancy went by, would the guy spring out?

Leaves and vines rustled beneath his feet. He eased one foot over a fallen limb, lifted the other—

His beeper went off.

Oh, Jesus. Heart going a mile a minute, he hauled in a barrel of air and checked the number.

"Sir," he called out, just in case the guy was hiding behind that tree and not on Mars, "this isn't a good place to be. Copperheads inhabit the area." He added, "Don't pick up any sticks until you know they won't move."

Back at the river's side, nothing had changed that he could see. Fifer still paced; cameramen still fiddled with cameras and peered through lenses. Robin hurried by at a ground-eating trot on his way to get something from the prop truck parked on the road.

"You got a phone?" Yancy yelled at him. Robin shook his head.

"Excuse me, sir." He stepped in front of Fifer midpace.

The director focused on him blankly, and had to shift through mental gears to remember who he was.

"Borrow your phone?"

Fifer made come-here motions with his fingers without even looking around. A female, obviously attuned to his every twitch, handed Yancy a flip phone. He backed off and punched the number.

On the other end of the line the phone was picked up immediately. Nobody spoke.

"Yancy," he said.

"Oh, God, what took you so long?"

"Ms. Jones?"

"Please get over here right away," Clem Jones said.

"Are you all right?"

"No! Get—"

"Calm down. What's the problem?"

"Oh, God—"

"Where are you?"

"The hotel. Please—"

"I'll be right there. Where in the hotel?"

"Room three-oh-seven."

He flipped the phone shut and returned it, then hiked the three-quarters of a mile to the road where a line of vehicles, including his squad car, were parked along the shoulder.

At the hotel, he knocked gently at Clem's door. It opened a crack and one hazel eye, black makeup smeared around it, peered out at him. The door opened wider and a hand fastened itself to his arm and hauled him in. Inside, Clem Jones fastened herself to his chest.

He patted her back. "What happened?"

"Sheri's dead and—a knife. There's blood—it's all over and—she looks so flat."

"Where is she?"

"Her room—" Clem waved awkwardly, either indicating direction or bursting with horror.

157

"Room number?"

"Three . . . I don't know. Three-eighteen. Three-eighteen."

"Stay right here."

"You think I'm going someplace?"

Eleven doors along the corridor, he tapped at 318, waited a moment, then eased the door open. Careful to avoid stepping in blood, he went to the body, knelt, and pressed his fingertips just below the point of her jaw. He knew he wouldn't find a pulse. She felt cold and clammy; her cheek, where it rested against the carpet, was dark; her neck and jaw muscles were tight with rigor.

When he got back to Clem Jones he found her sitting on the edge of a chair almost as frozen as the body.

"Fifer sent me to get her. It's not my job. It's the second second's. I didn't want to. He yelled, she was holding things up. Get her."

"Did you touch her? Move her?"

"Are you crazy?"

Putting a hand on each shoulder, he got in her face, made her look at him. "Did you touch anything?"

"No. Yes. The doorknob."

"Then what?"

"I came back here."

"Then what?"

"I called you. You're supposed to be a cop. Don't you know what to do?"

"Just relax." Using her phone, he called in and asked for the chief. She had just left; since Parkhurst was out of this one, he asked for Detective Osey Pickett.

16

Food, Susan thought. Something good. She didn't have to wonder if there was any in the house, and claiming too hot to cook wouldn't do it. She didn't cook even when it wasn't hot; she heated in the microwave. Or gave custom to Erle's Market. The deli had wonderful things, pasta salads, fruit salads, baked chicken, barbecued—

The radio, which had been mumbling to itself, caught her attention. She responded.

"Osey, Chief. We have us another one of those movie people dead."

No, God damn it, no. She made a U-turn. The big puffy clouds that had been piling up all day so far hadn't come to anything, but heat lightning flickered way off to the north and there seemed an increase in humidity, if that was possible; any more and they'd be swimming through the air.

Behind sawhorses and spilling into the parking lot, the media were waiting. Television crews were fixing up lights to film their correspondents' reports, print journalists shot questions at the nearest officers, and photographers waited with their cameras ready to snap pictures of anybody who might be connected with the death. When she walked up to the Sunflower, they surged around her. Was this death a homicide? Were there any suspects? Was this homicide connected to the death of the stuntwoman? Was Laura Edwards in danger? What did Chief Wren have to say about the suggestion this movie was jinxed? That Hayden Fifer was jinxed? Susan's response was, "No comment."

The lobby was empty except for the assistant manager who seemed just this side of wringing his hands, and Officer Ellis who was guarding the door. "Elevator to the third floor, ma'am, then right. Osey asked that nobody use the stairs until he can look at them."

When she got off at three, Officer White was waiting to escort her to the victim's room.

Heavy beige drapes were pulled across the windows. Overhead, a small chandelier dripped crystal tears and four flame-shaped bulbs shined dully on the congealed blood. A large brass lamp on the bedside table was also on, suggesting the attack had taken place sometime last night.

Sheri Lloyd's body lay facedown, her darkened cheek rested on pale tweed carpet, one arm was tucked under her, the other stretched ahead as though reaching for something. Long chestnut hair fell away from her face; her legs in a tight skirt were slightly bent at the knees. A bone-handled knife with an eagle emblem skewered a bright blue tank top to her back. Blood, puddled in the hollow of her spine, had run down her rib cage and soaked into the carpet.

Susan let her eyes take in the room. The bedspread, brown and beige, was crumpled and the pillows crushed; Ms. Lloyd had lain on the bed without pulling back the spread. A white skirt and a knit shirt were crumpled on the floor. Drawers were partly open with clothes spilling out, tote bag on top of the chest bulging with contents Susan couldn't see from where she stood. A pair of high-heeled sandals and a pristine pair of white Reeboks were thrown in a corner. The armchair had clothes draped over it. Not compulsively neat, Ms. Lloyd.

"She's been dead twelve to eighteen hours," Osey said. "She's cold, rigor still present, the blood's pretty much coagulated."

"You notified Dr. Fisher?"

"He's on the way."

Owen Fisher, even if he were just sitting down to dinner, would cheerfully leap up and gallop over. He was a man who deemed his profession his great good fortune; he probably sprang out of bed while it was still dark so he could get a head start on the day.

"Where's Yancy?"

"With Clem Jones in three-oh-seven."

"She found the body?"

Before he could answer, Dr. Fisher lumbered along the corridor toward them. "Another one?"

"Afraid so."

He peered at the body and told her solemnly, "My definite opinion upon superficial examination is we can almost certainly rule out accident this time."

Pathologists have a weird sense of humor. "I'll be in room three-oh-seven," she said to Osey. "Have somebody take care of these people lining the hallway. Do you have somebody going room to room on this floor?"

"Yes, ma'am."

Yancy opened the door to 307. Clem Jones sat hunched over in a padded peach chair with wooden arms. She eyed Susan warily like a frightened child on Halloween. Her pink hair stood up in spikes; the white makeup smeared with black eye shadow made it impossible to judge accurately any degree of pallor. She held herself completely still, as though if she didn't move none of this would be real.

Susan swung a chair around and sat in front of her. "Ms. Jones, would you like some water, or maybe coffee?"

"Yeah." Clem sniffled and rubbed her nose with the back of her hand. "Coffee."

"Cream? Sugar?"

Clem cleared her throat. "Yeah." A little louder this time.

Good. At least some life was returning to her face. A slack face and a weirded-out mind didn't produce answers, and Susan wanted answers. She glanced at Yancy. He nodded and left.

To start Clem talking, to keep her mind from the horror and let it ease back to functioning, Susan asked personal questions. How old was Clem? Twenty-six. Where did she live? Los Angeles. Has she always lived there? All her life. Did she go to school at UCLA? USC. How did she happen to get interested in the movie industry? Her father was an art director, she'd grown up in the business. Did she have a boyfriend? Not really. How many movies had she worked on? Shrug, lots. Did she ever work on the same movie with her father? Small shake of her head. Was her father working on this one? Another shake of her head.

After a soft tap on the door, Yancy came in bearing a tray, with coffeepot, cream, and sugar. Bless him, he'd brought two cups. It might be a long time before she could get around to food; a little caffeine would help.

Taking the tray, she set it on a table and poured two cups. "Tell me about this afternoon." She added sugar and cream to one and handed it to Clem.

Clem held the cup against her chest with one hand under it, as though it were a puppy that might wriggle away. "She was on the floor when I went in," she whispered.

"What time was that?" Susan sat back down, keeping herself where Clem would focus on her.

"I don't know." Clem gulped hot coffee.

"Give me a guess."

"She was supposed to be on the set." Clem started breathing hard.

"Take it easy," Susan said. "Just take your time."

Clem took smaller sips. "Fifer had the second second doing something, so he yelled at me."

"Second second?"

"Second second assistant director. I called Sheri's room and she didn't answer so I went out to base camp and checked her honey wagon room, even though I knew she wouldn't be there."

"How did you know?"

"Fifer was getting ready to chop off heads. Oooh." Clem turned slightly green, clapped a hand over her mouth, and rushed to the bathroom. Sounds of retching could be clearly heard. The toilet flushed, water ran, and Clem came back patting her face with a towel.

"Sit down," Susan said. "Take it easy."

Clem sat and breathed quickly and shallowly for a few moments. "And I came back here. Something was wrong or she'd be on the set. I mean, if she wasn't there, she'd be having a tantrum and we'd hear about it. She wouldn't just—she'd be screaming to everybody and—I knocked on her door and—"

"Was the door locked?"

Clem shook her head.

"Was the light on?"

"I don't know. Yeah. No."

"Which?"

"On."

"You're sure?"

"Yeah. It gleamed on the blood—like a one K—"

"One K?"

"Light. Like a scene—kinda like from *Lethal Promise?*" Clem rubbed her face with the towel, removing much of the mess of white makeup and black mascara and further smearing around the rest. "Except the blood wasn't red enough. I thought—I thought Fifer's gonna yell about this and make them do it over. It doesn't look at all realistic. I had no idea."

"No idea about what?"

"They were so flat. Dead people. Flat—like, like—I don't know."

"What did you do yesterday evening?"

Clem pressed the towel hard against her cheeks, pulling them down and distorting her eyes. She looked like a sad clown. "What?"

"Where were you yesterday evening?"

"After wrap, you mean? Here, I think. Dinner in the coffee

shop. A drink out there on that, that—" She waved her hand.

"Where was Sheri?"

Clem shrugged. "In her room. I don't know. Later she came out. She was miffed at Fifer. Saying something about she'd show him. She's not really all that swift. I didn't listen."

"What about her family?"

"We weren't buddies. I don't know anything."

"Who else was out there last night?"

Clem squeezed her eyes shut. "Robin." A tear seeped under a closed eyelid and trickled down her face.

Susan pressed a tissue in her hand. Clem took it and blew her nose.

"Who else?"

"I don't know. Some guy. Oh, and a woman."

"Describe them for me."

"The guy was medium. I don't know. He was kind of on the edge."

"What do you mean?"

"I don't know. Creepy."

"What did he look like?"

Clem's mouth turned up in a quirky smile. "Oh, wow, you're asking an awful lot." She shifted from side to side, and leaned her elbows on the chair arms. "Just a guy. Thirties? Maybe brown hair."

"Tall? Short? Fat? Thin? Skin color? Eye color? Distinguishing marks?"

Clem tugged on a tuft of pink hair. "You ever think of being a script supervisor?"

Susan smiled. "Not my field. Come through for me."

"He important?"

Probably not. Likely, he was just a guest who had a drink, then went innocently to his room. Unless he followed Sheri Lloyd and drove a knife in her back. Reason? Susan couldn't guess. A stalker, if they had one, was obsessed with a single individual. Assuming the person was Laura Edwards, why attack Sheri? He felt, somehow, she stood in his way?

Clem curled her fingers over the ends of the chair arms. "He was medium height, maybe a little stocky. That's the best I can do. Oh. He had a backpack. A little one, it was on the floor right by his feet. The only reason I noticed was he patted it now and again."

"Was anybody with him?"

"I don't think so. He was just sitting there."

"What about the woman?"

"Maybe fifty or something. Pretty. I mean for her age. She wore this long kind of skirt, white. There was something about her—I liked her and I didn't even know her."

Without looking at him, Susan was aware that Yancy, standing behind Clem near the door, tightened up like a bird dog spotting a quail.

Susan refilled both coffee cups and waited while Clem added cream and sugar. "Did Sheri mention that anyone was bothering her? That she was getting phone calls? Maybe notes or flowers?"

"Like Laura, you mean?"

"You know about that?"

"Sure. Everybody does. There are no secrets on location. Anyway, Sheri doesn't—didn't keep quiet about things. She would have gibbered on to everybody."

"What about you? Anybody annoying you?"

Clem looked startled, then shrugged. "Why would anybody send me flowers? I'm a nobody."

Not in Hampstead, she wasn't, not with that hair. Susan refilled her own cup, set the pot down, and leaned back in the chair. Clem, with one forefinger made tiny rubbing movements on the chair arm, as if she were feeling for grains of sand.

"Is there anything else you can tell me?" Susan asked.

Clem shook her head.

"Who shall I have stay with you?"

Clem propped her head on one hand and tipped it sideways to look up at Yancy. "Him."

Susan smiled. Sweet, handsome Yancy with his soft brown eyes and soft voice. "Sorry. I need him."

Clem took a breath. "I'm okay."

"Are you sure?"

"Yeah."

Susan left her feeling for imaginary grains of sand. When they had gone partway along the corridor, Susan turned and faced Yancy, "Who was the woman?" That sounded like the lead-in to a tired joke.

He gave her a wry smile. "My mother."

That was unexpected. "She's involved?"

"No."

Stated in a nice firm tone. "Then why are you worried?"

"She was here last night, on the Patio. Howie—the assistant manager—called me to come get her."

"She was causing trouble?"

"The dog was with her."

"Clem didn't mention a dog."

"I don't know why, he's a big dog."

"Vicious?"

"Very friendly. Sheri Lloyd complained." He stood squarely, feet planted at a wide stance.

"You think your mother stabbed Sheri Lloyd because Ms. Lloyd complained about her dog?"

"No, ma'am." This wasn't said with quite the same conviction.

"Then what is it?"

He hesitated. "She had blood on her hands when she got home." He spoke easily, but it came hard; ethics played hell sometimes.

"You realize I'll have to talk with her."

"Yes, ma'am."

"You wouldn't happen to know who the guy is, would you? The guy who's medium all the way around?"

"As a matter of fact, I think I might."

Brown. Laura my beloved. The universe is brown. From the edge of the parking lot, he watched them roll the stretcher toward the ambulance. The body was all wrapped up in a black bag, like a package. They lifted the stretcher, shoved it in, and drove away. It could have been you, Laura, my darling. Don't worry. I'm coming soon. Nothing will get in the way. Until then you can be assured. She won't bother you anymore. She was a snoop, not worthy of attention. She couldn't compete with your beauty. Soon, my beloved, soon.

"His name might be Delmar Cayliff," Yancy said.

Well now. She liked Yancy; he was easy to have around, young enough to be handy for college student problems, if necessary, and it looked like he might be coming along to being a good cop. "How do you know this?"

"A man of his description waited for the elevator with me one evening. He had a backpack that he handled like it had the combination to the safe. It had a luggage tag with his name on it."

"Do you know anything about him?"

"No, ma'am. Except he's been around watching the filming."

"Any reason why you noticed him?"

"No. Just a face I saw a lot."

They searched out Howard Gilbert in his office. When they came in he stood up from his desk and grimaced. "Don't tell me there's something else."

"I need a piece of information," Susan said.

"Oh, boy, this really isn't good for the hotel. The manager's not happy. This really isn't good. What information?"

"Have you got a Delmar Cayliff staying here?"

"I can't tell you that."

"Sure you can."

"No." Howie looked between her and Yancy and gazed somewhere in the distance. "There's privacy and confidentiality and—"

"Don't be an ass," Yancy said. "Tell her."

"Oh, God. Why do you want to know?"

"Only to talk with him," Susan said.

Howie shook his head back and forth in another "oh, boy, this isn't good for the hotel" gesture, then without sitting down tapped keys on the computer. "We have a Delmar Cayliff staying here."

"Room number?"

He sighed extravagantly. "One-oh-three."

Yancy leaned over the desk and patted Howie's cheek. Howie didn't think it was funny.

In the corridor, she asked, "Have you known him long?"

"Ever since elementary school. He's a sort-of friend."

"What kind of friend is a sort-of friend?"

Yancy smiled his enchanting smile. "The kind your mother tells you to be friends with because he's a weird kid and nobody likes him and he never gets chosen for the team and he's lonely."

Susan would have picked Howie for that kind of kid, she'd guess as an adult he was a loner. When her knock at 103 went unanswered, she tapped again. "Mr. Cayliff?" No response.

Before she could get back to check on Osey's progress, Officer Ellis said Robin McCormack wanted to see her.

17

"I heard Sheri Lloyd was stabbed." Robin McCormack, standing at the steps to the prop truck, which was actually a long trailer, jammed his fists into shorts and directed the question at Yancy.

Susan replied in the affirmative and waited to see where this was going. The sun was riding low over the hills and mosquitoes were venturing out for the night's victims. One buzzed past her ear and she slapped at it. The ever-present wind was blowing in warm breezes.

"And the knife has a silver eagle on the handle?"

"It might be an eagle, yes."

"I think it's mine." He slapped his bare thigh leaving a bloody smear where a mosquito had landed for dinner. "I just checked. One's gone."

"Where was it kept?"

Robin, a hand raking reddish hair back, took the four steps into the trailer with two jumps.

A narrow open space ran the entire length. Tall wooden chests lined both sides, their tops covered with plastic bins and cardboard boxes, all labeled—wedding rings, eyeglasses, police hardware, earwigs, license plate screws (wherever the story was supposed to be had to have the correct license plates). "You never know what the director might call for," he said as she read labels.

He shoved a plastic basket of umbrellas closer to a phone booth and stacked a box of handbags on top of a hotel-type ice machine, handed Yancy a box of briefcases, and removed the padlock on the solid piece of metal running up the length of a stack of drawers. In the bottom drawer, knives of all shapes and sizes—curved blade, curved handle, rope handle, with silver, with turquoise, with lapis, jeweled—were wrapped in bubble packing.

"One's missing. Steel blade, bone handle with a silver eagle inset."

"These are all real?"

He nodded. "Except the gems. They're as fake as you get. But the blades are steel and I keep them sharp."

"You always keep them locked up?"

"Not always, but the truck doors are locked unless I'm here."

"You never leave without locking the door?"

"No."

"Then how did the knife get itself missing?"

"If I was going to be gone for just a second—only a second or two—I might not take the time."

"When was it taken?"

"No idea. It was there Friday morning because we used one."

"This one?"

"No." He unwrapped a black-handled knife with a six-inch blade. "But the eagle-handled knife was here then."

"How do you keep track of things?"

He looked around the solidly packed truck. "You'd be surprised how good I am at it. It's my business."

"Do you have any guns?" If a gun or two were also missing, there'd be additional worry. To use a knife, the assailant had to get close to the intended victim. With a gun that wasn't necessary.

"Yeah."

"Where are they?"

170

"The safe."

At the other end, surrounded by boxes, sat a tall black safe. "Who has the combination?"

"I do."

"Anybody else?"

"No."

"Blanks?"

"Yeah."

"No live bullets?"

Robin shook his head. "They're never used."

"After it's been gone over for prints, I'll have somebody show you the knife to be certain," she said. "I need to ask you a few questions."

"This hasn't been questions?"

She smiled. "A few more." She nodded at the caterer's tent. "Let's go over there."

At eight in the evening the long tables were empty. She indicated to Robin that he should sit at one and she sat across from him. Yancy stood behind him and the sunlight that angled in sketched his shadow long.

"What time did you see Sheri on the Patio?" she asked.

"I don't know. It felt late, but it probably wasn't. Putting in a long day makes you cash in early."

"Sheri was still there when you left? Who else?"

He leaned back in the folding chair and slid his feet under the table. "Some guy. Who knows."

"Have you seen him before?"

He shrugged. "Maybe."

"Where?"

"The hotel, I guess."

"What does he look like?"

He straightened, shifted from side to side, leaned forward with his elbows on the table. "Just a guy. Thirties, maybe brown hair. He was just sitting there with a glass in front of him. I was drinking club soda, that I can tell you. Nick and Laura were head to head over a table spitting at each other."

"What about?"

Robin slumped back. "You mean, this time? Who knows. They've been fighting ever since we got here. Sheri sat down with them and they both froze up with politeness." For the first time there was emotion in his voice, it was black.

"Why did you dislike Ms. Lloyd?"

"She was a pain in the butt. The only thing she had going was looks and she didn't waste them on being easy to work with. She was so dumb she couldn't cross the street by herself."

"Who killed her?"

"Hey, that's not my job, man. If you're through, I'd like to get out of here."

She let him go, stuck her notebook in her shoulder bag, and poked the pen in beside it.

"Let's go see your mother," she said to Yancy.

He was obviously uncomfortable, but he kept his eyes on the road and flicking across the mirrors, hands competent on the wheel. It was an odd situation and not one she had ever experienced before—driving your superior out to interview your mother. She knew Raina Yancy had suffered a stroke about a year ago and wasn't showing much sign of improvement. Hazel Riis, dispatcher and keeper of the flock with clucks and coos, had told her.

"She may or may not be lucid," he said.

"What is it you're worried about?"

"Uh—you mention blood and she's apt to wander off into some ballad. She knows a lot of those that deal with blood."

"You're afraid I won't be able to tell fact from fiction?"

"Uh—no, ma'am."

"Relax. I've been a cop a long time. I've even been known, once in a while, to separate fact from fancy."

"Yes, ma'am," he said, still tight as a tick.

They drove past fields of growing things, she had no idea what. Due to all the heavy rain in early spring, everywhere was lush and green. The greens were different here than in California. She didn't know exactly how—deeper, denser, richer some-how. Small hills stretched away under the endless sky, clouds, big and puffy, lazily broke apart and drifted south.

He turned down a gravel drive. Sprouting up here and there in the middle of a field of flowers were tall poles with what looked like birdhouses on top.

"Bats," Yancy said, either because he guessed her thoughts or he was accustomed to explaining. He pulled up to the garage and cut the engine. She slid from the car. Locusts were sawing away, ubiquitous sound of a Kansas summer, like the hot winds always blowing. The air smelled of honeysuckle. Yancy was looking a lit-tle apprehensive.

The screen door opened and a woman said, "Peter? Is any-thing wrong?" Raina Yancy, Susan assumed. A big black dog rushed out, tongue lolling.

"Nothing, Mom." He patted the dog's shoulder and then it nudged its big head up under Susan's hand.

On the porch, Yancy held the edge of the screen for Susan to enter. In the kitchen, she was introduced to his sister, Serena, slender in jeans and T-shirt, who held some sort of nonverbal communication with her brother and then excused herself, say-ing she'd be in her room if she was needed.

"This is my boss, Mom. Chief Wren."

Raina Yancy slid her arm through her son's, hugged it tight, and held out a hand. "I'm pleased to meet you, Ms. Wren. Let's go into the other room."

"This is fine, Mom. Sit down. She just wants to talk."

"I'll put the coffee on."

"I'll do it." Yancy steered his mother to the table.

The dog squeezed underneath and flopped down with a big sigh.

Raina smiled and Susan knew where Yancy got his sweet smile. "They don't like me using the stove," Raina said. "They think I'll set myself up in flames."

"It's happened," he said.

"Unfortunately, that's true," she admitted to Susan. "What is it you want to talk about?"

With an apologetic glance at Susan, Yancy brought two cups to the table. From the refrigerator, he took a carton of milk and poured some into a small pitcher, snatched the sugar bowl and put both on the table.

She studied Raina Yancy. Late forties, she judged. Perfect oval face, dark hair to just below the jawline. Dark eyes, clear and luminous. She was beautiful now; as a young woman she must have been stunning. Susan wondered about Yancy's father. Who was he and what happened to him?

"Mrs. Yancy—"

"Please call me Raina."

"Raina, you were at the Sunflower Hotel last night."

"Was I?" She looked at her son for the answer. "Come and sit down, love." She patted the chair to her right. "You look tired. Have you been getting enough sleep?"

"I'm fine, Mom."

"Go ahead," Susan said when he hesitated.

He pulled out the chair and sat sideways in it, then picked up his mother's hand. "What did you do at the hotel last night?"

"You think I'm nutty."

"Mom, you've always been nutty. Think about last night."

"He's right, you know," she confided to Susan.

"You were sitting out on the Patio at the hotel," he said.

"Was I?"

"Yes, you were, Mom."

"Oh dear, I don't recall—" She looked frightened.

"It's okay," Susan said. "What did you do yesterday evening?"

"I watched a movie."

"On television? What movie?"

"I usually only watch lighthearted fluff movies. This one wasn't. A woman got stabbed."

Susan felt Yancy tense. "What was the name of the movie?" she asked.

174

"Oh, I can't seem to remember—"

"In the movie, who did the stabbing?"

"A woman. I remember she had long blond hair."

Susan tried to get details, about the movie, about the stabber, about the victim, but got nothing. "What else did you do yesterday evening?"

"We went for a walk. Elmo and I."

The dog, under the table, hearing his name, thumped what he had for a tail.

"He likes to go out after the sun goes down, when it cools off. It's cooler today, did you notice? Much more like it should be this time of year. The heat wave's over."

Susan hoped so. Mrs. Baker had called her again today to repeat that the heat wave was because of the wicked movie people. It wouldn't cool down until they left. "Where did you go on your walk?"

"I did," Raina said as though suddenly remembering. "I went to the hotel. I sat out there on the Patio and had something to drink. Oh, what was it—?" She kept her eyes on her son as he got up to pour coffee.

"Who was there?"

"Laura Edwards and Nick Logan. Right here in Hampstead. Isn't that a hoot? Another one—I can't think of her name." She looked to Yancy for help as he set a cup in front of her. "Hair like a winter fox. Pouty expression."

"Sheri Lloyd?" Susan said.

"Yes. She didn't like Elmo. Poor Elmo, there was a man there who didn't like him either. A girl with pink hair—" Raina's voice faded out as she thought, then she said, "I talked with her."

"What about?"

"Movies, I'm sure. People who worked in the movie business." She thought, mind searching. "Clem Jones."

"Then what did you do?"

"I guess I must have come home." She sang in a clear soft voice.

175

> *"God give you joy, you two true lovers,*
> *In Brides-bed fast asleep;*
> *Lo I am going to my green grass grave,*
> *And am in my winding sheet."*

Susan felt goose bumps on her arms. Yancy patted his mother's hand and said, "Come back, Mom. Last night. How'd you get home?"

"We walked—no, only started. I pooped out before we got even halfway."

Susan wasn't surprised. It must be ten miles or more.

"That boy—what's his name—oh, you know, the one who works at the service station?" She looked to Yancy. "Oh, you know the one I mean."

"Kevin Murphy?"

"Yes." She turned back to Susan. "Kevin gave me a ride. He didn't mind Elmo in his car."

"How did you get blood on your hands?"

She looked at her palms, then at the backs. "Blood?

> *"And first came out the thick, thick blood,*
> *And syne came out the thin,*
> *And syne came out the bonny heart's blood;*
> *There was nae mair within."*

Raina either didn't know she'd had blood on her hands and therefore couldn't know how it had gotten there or she was deliberately sinking into vagueness. What a handy excuse, if you had something to hide. Susan drank the coffee, thanked Raina, and stood up.

"Peter—?"

"I gotta go back to work, Mom."

"Ohh, I hoped you could stay awhile."

"I'll be in the squad car," Susan said.

A minute later Yancy came out and slid under the wheel.

"Sorry," he said. He backed out and headed into town.

"Your mother is lovely," Susan said. "Does she stay by herself?"

"She shouldn't, according to my sister."

He didn't volunteer any more and she dropped it. None of her business. "Where does she get the movies she watches?"

"You're not thinking she saw Sheri Lloyd stabbed?"

"Isn't it a possibility?"

"No," he said. "You saw how she is, she's hardly coherent."

"Calm down. She's coherent. She simply can't remember things. It's unlikely. It needs to be followed up. We have a long blond-haired woman with something that could be construed as a motive."

"Laura Edwards? But—"

"I said it's unlikely. I'll put in extremely if that makes it better. Now, where does she get the movies? She owns them? Television? Video rentals?"

"My sister keeps her supplied with videos. That way, Serena hopes she'll be occupied. Look, it's not as bad as it sounds. A friend comes by in the morning and in the afternoon."

Guilt was leaking into his voice. "Yancy, I'm not making judgments here, I'm conducting an investigation."

"Yes, ma'am."

"Is Pickett's garage open this late?"

He looked at his watch. "Just barely."

"Head over there."

On Fourth Street, he pulled up to the open door of the bay at the end of the garage. At a gas pump, Kevin Murphy was checking oil for a customer. Susan and Yancy got out of the squad car and waited. Kevin slammed the hood, cleaned the windshield, and collected money, paying no attention to them beyond a sideways glance. After he'd made change and the customer drove away, he started back into the repair area. Susan called to him.

"Ma'am?" He was not quite sneering. Seventeen, high school football star, an athlete who moved with the lightness of a cat. Broad-shouldered, narrow-hipped, straight dark hair that fell into resentful dark eyes. A narrow face that would have been handsome except for the insolence that was barely hidden. A young man full of resentment, not especially of cops, or apparently even of authority, but for the entire adult world. How Charlie Pickett put up with him, she didn't know. Except that Charlie knew boys. He had five of his own, four worked with him at the garage. Osey was the youngest and a damn good detective.

"Talk to you a minute?" she said.

"Certainly, ma'am." His politeness was almost mockery.

"When did you last see Raina Yancy?"

Kevin looked at Yancy and then he looked a long time at her. He had no problem making eye contact. His self-assurance held challenge and mockery and hatred. He was not a young man any mother would like to see with her daughter.

"I saw her yesterday evening." The clear precise way he spoke was guaranteed to ruffle adult feathers, but there was nothing overt that could be pointed at, so adults were left with unfocused irritation.

"Where?"

"Mrs. Yancy and the dog were proceeding south on Massachusetts Street, approaching the city limits."

"What time?"

"Just after eleven."

No hesitation or qualifying sounds. "You seem very sure."

"Absolutely, ma'am."

"How can you be so positive?"

"The vehicle contains a digital clock."

Yancy, beside her, was getting pissed. So was she, which was, of course, Kevin's goal. She hoped Yancy kept a lid on it.

"Who owns the vehicle?"

"My father, ma'am." The guy climbing the tower with a rifle slung over his shoulder probably had the same expression. It made her pay attention.

"Did Mrs. Yancy ask you for a ride?"

"No, ma'am."

"How did it come about that you transported Mrs. Yancy and

her dog in your father's vehicle?" Tiresome as he was being, she tried not to let a trace of irritation seep into her voice.

The flicker of pleasure in his dark eyes said she hadn't been successful. "She looked tired. I asked her if she'd like a ride."

"Where were you going when you saw her?"

"To see a friend."

"The friend's name?"

"He wasn't expecting me, and I decided it was too late anyway."

"Mrs. Yancy got in the car, the dog got in the car, you drove her home. Is that correct?"

"Absolutely, ma'am."

"Did you notice blood on her hands?"

For the first time, there was a hair's hesitation before he answered. She took note, but had no idea what it meant. "I had a nosebleed. She made me stop and she held a handkerchief against it."

"How'd that happen?"

"I ran into a door."

A lie. What did she have here? *Go with your instincts until you can back them up with facts.* The voice belonged to Captain Reardon, her boss in San Francisco. She took Kevin tediously through question and answer of picking up Raina Yancy, what they talked about, what time they reached her house, where he went then, what time he got home. Nothing resulted except a waste of time. Not once did his demeanor slip over into disrespect, but it always teetered right there on the edge. She had known repeat felons with less control.

"What were you doing at the Sunflower Hotel last night?"

The switch in subject didn't catch him off guard. "Who says I was there?"

"Never mind who says so, why were you there?"

"Anybody can go to a hotel. It's meant for the public."

"I see. That doesn't tell me what you were doing there."

"Do you have any reason for asking?"

He had her there. The only reason was something was going

on here that she didn't understand and she wanted to find out what it was. "I'm looking for information," she said.

Mockery danced in his dark eyes. "I was working yesterday evening." He waved a hand at the garage. "I was sent over there to take care of a dead battery."

"Who had a dead battery?"

"A driver of a van used to take crew to the set."

"What time was this?"

"Eight when I left here. Eight-thirty when I returned."

A customer drove up to the gas pumps and Susan let him go. As Yancy was driving back to the hotel, she asked what he knew about Kevin Murphy.

"The Murphys moved to Hampstead last year. Kevin is the best quarterback the high school has ever had. They made state championship, and after seldom even winning a game, that's close to miraculous. The father is retired military. I heard he was a navy test pilot, and had a crash that smashed him up pretty bad."

"Mother?"

"I only know there is one."

"Why'd they come here?"

"Because this is such a great place?"

"Right."

When he parked in the hotel lot, she said, "Ask your sort-of friend Howie if Kevin's been around the hotel. Ask your movie pals if they've seen him hanging around watching."

"He's been around a lot. He was hired as an extra."

It must be because of his looks; it couldn't be his charm. "Let's go see if Delmar Cayliff, the ordinary man, is in his room."

18

$\mathcal{S}$usan knocked. The room door opened.

"Yes?" Delmar Cayliff was not an ordinary man, Susan thought. Brown pants, brown shirt, medium height, medium brown hair medium length, mid-thirties, slightly stocky. All that was ordinary enough. But there was something here that set off little alarm bells. He smelled strongly of cloves—not ordinary, but not alarming. He wouldn't look her in the eye, but stared off in the distance between her and Yancy.

"Chief Wren, Mr. Cayliff." She held out her ID. "This is Officer Yancy. We'd like to ask you a few questions." She stepped forward as she spoke and he automatically moved back.

"Sure, I guess so. Is it about the actress who was killed?" His eyes strayed to the small brown backpack on the bed. The roll of clove Life Savers beside it explained the odor of cloves.

"You know about that?"

"People have been talking."

"You mind if we sit down?" Without waiting for a response, she took a chair at the small round table near the window. Yancy stood by the door.

Cayliff backed up and sat on the edge of the bed; he let one arm rest on the backpack. Those little alarm bells kept pinging. On the surface he was clean, neat, probably not wildly successful from the cut and quality of his clothes, but not unsuccessful or he couldn't afford to stay here.

"Where are you from, Mr. Cayliff?"

"Irvine. Oh, Irvine, California. You've probably never heard of it."

"You're here on vacation?"

"I suppose you could say that. A working vacation anyway. I teach history. American history. You interested in history?" Even when he asked a question, he couldn't look at her. "Fascinating. I don't understand why everybody isn't gripped like I am." A smile flicked on and off. "I've got students who actually fall asleep in class. Ha ha. Cattle trails are my interest. Every summer I pick one and go there, study the area around and the exact trail. I follow it all the way, taking note of—Well, as you can see, it's not only my occupation, it's my hobby."

"You teach at UC Irvine?"

"Yes. Did you know the Santa Fe Trail runs right near Hampstead? It goes all the way from Independence, Missouri—that's where I started—and I'm following it to the end. You know where that is?"

She was afraid she didn't.

"Santa Fe, New Mexico. William Becknell—he was a trader—opened it in 1821. They did have some trouble right around here. About 1864 Indians started attacking. The wagons would get into a circle just like you see in the movies. You'd be surprised how many things the movies get wrong."

No, she wouldn't.

"Daniel Boone, for instance, never wore a coonskin cap. But circled wagons is one thing they got right."

"Are you interested in movies, Mr. Cayliff?"

His fingers tightened on the backpack. "Only in the general way that I see one sometimes." The smile flickered on and off again.

"You've been watching the filming." She made it an accusation.

He didn't respond to her tone, simply said, "Somewhat to my surprise I'm finding it interesting."

"Sheri Lloyd, have you watched her?"

"If she's what's being filmed."

"Did you think she was pretty?"

His fingers relaxed. "Pretty, yes, very pretty."

"And Laura Edwards, is she pretty?"

"Beautiful. You have a reason for asking me these questions?"

She wondered if he had some sexual fantasy about beautiful women or thought they were evil or needed punishing. He didn't respond in any extraordinary way to the two beautiful women she'd mentioned, except he still wouldn't meet her eyes, his glance slid right past and landed somewhere over her shoulder. She wanted Parkhurst's opinion of this man. Damn it, she needed Parkhurst's help.

"You saw Ms. Lloyd last night," she said. "On the Patio. What happened there?"

Much abbreviated, he gave her the same story she'd gotten from Clem Jones and Robin McCormack. When he mentioned the dog, his breathing grew short and fast. "I don't care much for dogs."

"What else can you tell me?"

"A young person was there."

Nobody else had mentioned a young person. "Male or female?"

He shook his head. "The—uh—person was sitting way back at one side. I didn't really pay attention."

"How young?"

"Oh—teenage, I suppose."

"What was this teenager wearing?"

"I'm sorry, I simply didn't notice. I wasn't paying attention, you see."

"How did you know it was a teenager?"

He thought about that. "He had on—maybe she—shorts like

they all wear, and a T-shirt. It had Wolverines in big letters and a picture of the animal."

The Wolverines were the high school football team.

"Hair color?"

"He was wearing a baseball cap. I guess that's why I thought it was a boy, but girls wear them too. Anyway, this person was writing in a notebook. Does that help?"

Susan thanked him and slung her bag over her shoulder.

"Somebody followed her out," he said as she was leaving.

"Followed who out? Ms. Lloyd?"

He nodded. "A man."

"Describe him."

"Tall. Red hair."

"Robin McCormack?" Yancy said as they waited for the elevator.

"That's the only tall, red-haired man we know of who was there last night," Susan said. "Have you any idea who this young person might be?"

"Kevin maybe? Could Cayliff be lying?"

"Anything's possible. To what end?"

Yancy's beeper sounded. She could see he wasn't enamored of the technological advancements of the telephone company.

That was simply awful, Laura thought, when she left Nick's suite and trailed Mac down the hallway to her own rooms. The food hadn't been fit to eat, she couldn't even remember what it was supposed to be, they'd sniped at each other, or sat there in charged silence. He kept smoking until she thought she would choke, and drinking that ridiculous beer he always had flown in wherever he was. Dinner with Nick in the hotel had seemed better than alone in her suite. Going out was impossible. She couldn't remember the last time she'd been able to do that, people gaping at her and whispering to each other behind their hands.

Come on, Laura May. They're what make you famous. Ah,

the price you pay. If you can't appreciate your fans you better get out of the business.

Yeah, right. If it just wasn't all the time.

Nick would start to talk, then she'd start to talk and it was stops and starts and stilted and careful so neither would upset the other. It wasn't like her to be concerned about upsetting anybody, but there you are, she could be nice sometimes.

Neither mentioned Sheri, and her murder was the only thing on their minds. They should have talked about her, poor little cow. How much was Nick affected? Everything was a mess. When she'd left, he'd given her a kiss with all the warmth and excitement of leftover oatmeal.

While the bodyguard checked the place, she wondered if that was an apt turn of phrase.

"Everything clear," he said. "This was slipped under the door." He held up a small white envelope. "You want me to give it to your assistant?"

"Never mind. Thank you, Mac. You can go."

Dropping it on the small writing desk, she sat down to read the little pile of letters already waiting there. "I've seen all your movies." "I think you're wonderful." "It's so exciting that you're actually here."

She smiled, carefully folded each letter, after she read it, and stuck it back in its envelope. Her assistant would write personal replies to each and every one. Laura never got tired of them. They made her feel good all over. Okay, so she was vain and shallow, insecure even when she felt her work was good. She was never sure until it was confirmed by fans and critics. Fans liked you or they didn't. You never knew about critics. Sometimes she wondered if their reviews had anything at all to do with the movie.

She slit open the envelope Mac had handed her and unfolded the paper.

YOU WON'T GET STABBED.

Her breath caught, her heart skipped around. It took sheer force not to crumple the loathsome thing and burn it.

Okay. Calm down. Do what Ben said. Don't touch it, call the police.

The hell with that.

She picked up the receiver and punched in Ben's number. It rang and rang. Damn it, answer. She paced back and forth in half circles as far as the cord would allow. Ridiculous there wasn't a cordless phone here. She banged down the receiver and went to the little refrigerator for the bottle of white wine. She poured herself a glass.

Take a deep breath and calm down.

She tried Ben's number again, still no answer.

Okay, Laura May, what now? Be calm, be brave. She found the beeper number for that cop who was supposed to take care of things for her and punched it.

Only a minute or two went by before there was a tap on her door.

"Who is it?"

Yancy looked at Susan; she nodded.

"Police, ma'am. Officer Yancy."

The lock clicked and the door opened cautiously. Laura Edwards, a little wild-eyed, shifted her glance to Susan and her expression froze; for just an instant she looked irritated. The lady is not pleased to see me, Susan thought. She was expecting only Yancy, young and male and maybe in her mind malleable. Peter Yancy, Susan was learning, was not as malleable as he appeared.

For all Laura Edwards's look of distress she hadn't let her appearance be affected—hair artfully tousled, makeup discreet but perfect. Gold silk pants and white silk blouse with gold splashes swayed loosely but managed to cling in all the right places.

"I've been trying to call Ben," she said. "Get him for me, please."

"Is there a problem?" Susan asked.

Laura bristled, then took hold of herself and smoothed herself out. "There." She pointed to the note on the writing desk.

Susan walked over and looked at it. "When did you get this?"

"Just now. It was slipped under the door."

186

"Please sit down," Susan said.

Reluctantly, Laura sat on the love seat. "I want you to get Ben, please."

She surely did, she could barely stay seated. Simply to have him around? Because she thinks she can lie to him and be believed? Or could it be the lady simply doesn't like me?

"I'm sure you would, Ms. Edwards, but this is a homicide and what you've got is me. I need to ask questions."

She watched Laura consider: throw a fit, have hysterics, refuse to say a word until Parkhurst arrived? She decided on cooperation. Why, Susan couldn't guess. Fear? Playing the good citizen?

The Q and A session covered all her movements from the moment she came into the hotel this evening. Nothing startling resulted, and not because Susan didn't work at it. Laura had showered and changed and had dinner with Nick Logan in his suite, they'd ordered from room service. She'd been out of her room from seven until she came back just now.

"Mr. Logan was there the whole time?"

"Except for when he went out to get ice."

"He got his own ice?"

"Sometimes he likes to show how unaffected he is." A hint of sarcasm seeped through.

Susan went back to yesterday evening and questioned her about being on the Patio, and her encounter with Sheri. Nothing new came from that either. While answering with no hesitation, Laura Edwards was getting tired of questions and her cooperation was running a little thin.

This made Susan push harder; Laura stuck with her script, whatever it was. There was no relaxing of her guard even when Susan stood up, carefully collected the note in a plastic evidence bag, and made noises about leaving. Perhaps the lady is telling the truth. Even an actress can have a genuine emotion now and then. The lock clicked solidly behind them.

"Did you believe her?" she asked Yancy as they headed toward the end of the corridor.

"I think she's worried," he said slowly, "but she could have printed that line on the paper to reel in the lieutenant."

He wasn't Parkhurst, but he wasn't stupid.

She knocked at Nick Logan's suite. He looked a man tired after working all day, relaxing in jeans, the sleeves of his white shirt rolled up. There was no irritation on his face at seeing them, only a certain interest.

"Come on in." He gave Yancy a friendly slap on the shoulder. "Have a seat. What can I get you?"

"Nothing, thanks." She sat on the love seat opposite a flowered sofa and took in a deep breath of secondhand smoke. Ah yes.

"You mind if I have a beer?"

"Go right ahead," she said.

"Pete?"

Yancy, standing with his back to the door, shook his head. Nick in stockinged feet, a hole in one toe, padded off and returned with a bottle of Chimay and a glass. "Are you sure? It's made by Trappist monks in Belgium."

She declined again, but did wonder what the stuff tasted like.

He took a swallow and sat on the arm of the sofa. "I figured you'd be around. Fifer's got to be grateful you didn't interrupt the filming."

"Tell me what you did this evening."

He shot her a shrewd look. "Has something else happened?"

"Answer the question, please."

His story fit with Laura's except for one omission. "What reason would you have to lie, Mr. Logan?"

He flared up like a match. "You calling me a liar?"

"Are you?"

"Dinner with Laura?" Righteous indignation. "What is there to lie about?"

Dealing with these actors was exhausting. Who could tell what was real and what was acting? "You said you were here the entire time. Why didn't you mention going to get ice?"

Deep laugh rumbled. "No attempt at concealment, I assure you." He retrieved another bottle of Chimay from the small refrigerator. "I forgot," he said when he came back. "How long was I gone? Two minutes? Three? What happened this evening?"

"It's odd you get your own ice. I'd expect you would have sent a lackey or called room service. Weren't you concerned about fans?"

"The only people around are cast and crew."

That wasn't exactly true, but maybe he didn't know.

"They don't get excited on seeing me."

"Let's go back to yesterday evening."

He took a long swallow, then gave her the same story she'd heard from everybody else. Sheri was angry. When she joined them Laura got pissed. Nick himself was irritated. He mentioned Clem Jones and Robin McCormack, and Raina Yancy and Delmar Cayliff, although he hadn't known either of their names.

"I've heard Sheri Lloyd wasn't a great actress," Susan said. "So why was she hired?"

"Fifer wanted her. What the director wants, he gets. A director of his standing anyway."

"Why did he want her?"

Nick gave her a dry smile. "I'm sure you've guessed."

"He wanted to sleep with her."

"There's a Sheri in every one of his movies."

"You also had an affair with her."

"Not exactly, and to my regret."

"Enough regret to kill her when she wouldn't let it go?"

"No." Quietly said.

"How did Fifer feel about your sleeping with her?"

"He was—no longer interested." Nick chipped at the bottle label with his thumbnail. "She got ideas in her head that weren't real and—" He tipped the bottle over the glass. "She could be exasperating."

"Because she wanted love and got only sex?"

"You don't pull your punches, do you?"

"She was murdered. What kind of ideas? Marriage? She's no longer alive to be exasperating. Does that make things easier for you? Your relationship with Laura Edwards will be mended?"

189

He started to raise his glass, then stopped. "I didn't kill her. I felt sorry for her."

"Uh-huh. How could Fifer get away with hiring a bad actress?"

"She was okay in the right role."

"And that was—?"

"Herself. A bimbo. Not real smart. Vulnerable. Somebody you ultimately feel sorry for."

"Somebody didn't feel sorry for her. Somebody shoved a knife in her back."

"Yeah," he said softly.

Right. Couldn't be put any clearer than that. "Tell me who was on the Patio last night."

He mentioned everyone except Cayliff's young person.

"You forget anyone?"

He thought a moment, then shook his head.

"Teenager," Susan said. "Way off in the corner."

He turned his head and scratched the side of his jaw. "I didn't notice any teenager. One could have been there. I try not to look at people. That way they're not as apt to come over for an autograph."

She thanked him for his help.

In the elevator, she asked Yancy, "What do you think of Nick Logan?"

Yancy hesitated. "I like him. Except for that Trappist monk beer, which I never heard of, he seems like just an ordinary guy. Had a hole in his sock, for God's sake. He's not even that handsome. I don't know why he's supposed to be such a great actor."

"He's great enough that he gets paid even if this movie never gets made. And if it's washed up soon enough maybe there's still time to get the role he had to turn down. That one pays fifteen million."

"I'm in the wrong business," Yancy said.

"Indeed."

They took the elevator down and tracked Howie Gilbert to

190

his office behind the registration desk. The assistant manager was looking distinctly gray around the edges.

"Who did you give Ms. Edwards's suite number to?"

"What?" He shot up. "What happened to her?"

"Nothing. She's fine."

He deflated slowly. "You know, I think I'll be glad when they all leave. It seemed such a—so exciting, and good for the hotel, but all this—"

"Ms. Edwards's suite number?"

"Room numbers are not given out," he recited primly. "And that goes for suites. Especially suites. Never."

Of course, just about anybody on the staff would know: housekeeping, room service, security, registration. How many spouses and friends would they have told?

After reminding Yancy to keep his mouth shut with the media, she told him to take himself home.

The media pack launched an attack on her when she came out. What kind of sentence would she get for backing them off by firing a round or two?

Gray. Laura my beloved. The universe is gray. The spirits are getting impatient. When you know, you'll understand. If I don't get the gun, the spirits will be angry. They'll turn against us. I'll follow him until the opportunity comes. When the time is mine, I'll get it. He won't escape. I'll be there. When the world is dark.

19

*I*n the pickup, Susan made a note to have Osey question hotel staff, ask if any unauthorized individual was seen, if anyone had been asked to slip a note under Ms. Edwards's door. Media people had been known to pay for information, but if a large amount of money passed hands, it was very unlikely anybody would admit to anything.

She stopped at the McDonald's drive-thru and got a burger, fries, and a Coke. Popping fries in her mouth, she drove back to the department, entered by the rear door, and took the hallway to her office. The place was quiet this time of night. She flipped the light, hung her shoulder bag on the coat tree, and dropped her very late dinner on the desk. Mouth open, burger halfway there, she was aware of someone in the doorway.

"Hazel, what are you doing here? You should have left hours ago."

"Marilee's having baby-sitting problems. I said I'd cover until she found somebody." Hazel looked pointedly at the hamburger.

"One word and I'll fire you," Susan said.

Along with being dispatcher, Hazel was mother hen of the department, affectionately and behind her back called Rhode Island Red. Susan always assumed it was because Hazel had auburn hair; only recently had Osey told her a Rhode Island Red was a chicken.

"Idle threats," Hazel said airily. She ticked off on her fingers. "Cholesterol, fat, salt, caffeine—"

"The phone is ringing," Susan said. She bit off a chunk of cholesterol and fat and washed it down with a slug of caffeine. While she chewed, she searched out a pen under the folders and message slips, then she flipped pages in her notebook. To her list of suspects, she added Kevin Murphy, high school football star and summertime mechanic, and teenager, with a question mark— as in, could he be Cayliff's young person?

She tore off another chunk of the burger. He had a lot of anger packed away in a well-muscled body. Put him, for just a minute, in the shoes of a stalker. Would they fit?

They might. Sixteen, unbalanced by hormones like all teenagers. He excelled at football, a violent game and violence can spill over into the rest of life.

She leaned back and tried to remember what she knew about stalkers. Not much. She'd never worked a case with one. They were mentally or emotionally disturbed—paranoia, manic depression, schizophrenia. Did this fit Kevin? They often deluded themselves that the victim had a romantic interest in them. They were socially isolated. A football star? Possibly. Withdrawn, a loner. Again, possibly. She also thought they were usually unattractive. This didn't fit Kevin. He was very good-looking. That impenetrable air of control that she found so hair-raising would attract teenage females.

She didn't know enough about him, and made a note to ask Osey to check into Kevin Murphy.

What about Sheri Lloyd's murder? With a knife in the back, there was no question of accident. How was it connected with the death of the stuntwoman? How how how? Sheri Lloyd stood in the way of the stalker getting to his victim? Not that Susan could see, but she couldn't see into the mind of a psychotic. Could they have a killer and a stalker? Two crimes, two separate perps? An imported killer and a homegrown stalker? She read her list of suspects for Kay Bender's death. Assuming that the intended victim was not Laura, but Kay, why ice Sheri Lloyd?

Fifer: killed Sheri because she was causing trouble with his superstar Laura and/or Nick. He had to save his movie and Sheri was a thorn that could burst his expensive bubble.

Laura: jealous because Sheri was getting it on with Nick.

Nick: Sheri was causing trouble with true love Laura.

Robin: prop master, the knife came from the prop truck, thought for whatever reason Sheri killed Kay. This would tie it up. Sheri killed Kay (reason unknown) and then Robin killed Sheri in revenge. Dust off your hands, inform the media, and go home.

Bah. Susan tossed her pen on the desk, leaned back, and sipped the Coke.

Raina: out of the mists in her mind she was confused about being in some murderous old ballad. Very weak, and Susan hoped it was as weak as it sounded for Yancy's sake.

Then we have the unknown stranger brought to town by the lure and glamour of the movie being filmed here. A stalker, a psycho, a serial killer.

She was going round and round and getting nowhere and it was making her furious. She had the same suspects for Sheri Lloyd's murder that she had with the stuntwoman's death. All she'd done was mix around motives and throw in unknown variables.

She needed a break here. Why couldn't she see one? Damn it, she wanted to discuss this with Parkhurst.

As though she'd conjured him up, he appeared in the doorway. Angry, he looked dark and dangerous; eyes cold, small muscle ticking in his jaw.

"Hi," she said.

Back straight, he sat in the wooden armchair in front of her desk. In normal circumstances, he paced until she got nuts and told him to sit, whereupon he slid low on his spine with his legs under the desk. Not since she'd first arrived had he been so still and controlled.

"There are two points of view," he said. "It's an abomination or an honor, depending on your background, education, religious leanings, and/or sense of humor."

She looked at him blankly. "What are you talking about?"

"The mad painter."

There was an edge to his voice that she didn't like. It was challenging and she didn't want to pick it up. This bit of garbage-can nonsense didn't stack up against murder. She knew it and he knew it. He was pointing out that ability and experience were being wasted here.

She grimaced and rubbed her forehead. "Have you got anywhere?"

He took out his notebook, flipped it open, and recited in a flat voice. "So far there have been eight female nudes and six male. One fish. Opinions differ as to whether the fish is supposed to be a carp or a salmon . . ."

She broke out laughing.

"Comach Meer, however, says that art is not merely representational . . ." He laid a folded newspaper on her desk.

Comach Meer, owner of a local art gallery, had gotten his picture in the *Hampstead Herald*. Kneeling, finger extended, he was quoted as saying, "There is talent here, but undisciplined." He went on to list flaws in the latest garbage-can art.

She tossed the paper to one side. "Do you know who it is?"

"Not yet. But I'm closing in. I deduce that it has to be somebody with paint on his hands."

"All right," she said. "We still have to find him."

"Yes, ma'am. I've been trying to spot a pattern. In the areas he hits, the days of the week, the length of time between hits. Nothing's showing. I escorted Professor Black of the Emerson art department out to take a look, to see if the latest painted can brought to mind the style of a particular student."

"And?"

"The work is vaguely reminiscent of Matisse. He agreed with Meer. Some talent, undisciplined. No student came to mind."

"So what are you suggesting?"

"We're not going to catch this guy except by accident. Not by fancy footwork. Unless you want to mount a gigantic stake-out."

She looked at him.

Parkhurst unbent a little. "He'll get tired and quit. He'll pick the wrong garbage can at the wrong time and get shot. We'll stumble across him on the way to something else."

Parkhurst was right, but when citizens call and make complaints, when the mayor calls and makes threats, the chief of police makes a show of being on top of the situation.

"Your point is?"

"I talked with Laura last night."

This was what she'd been expecting. The chair squeaked as she leaned forward. "And?"

"She wants my help."

"Two bodyguards and the Hampstead PD aren't enough for her?"

He said evenly, "I'm obliged to help."

"What is it you want from me?"

"You can put me on suspension. Or I can resign."

"Would Laura want that? Your throwing out your career?"

A dry smile crossed his mouth. "She wouldn't see it that way." He pushed himself up. "You want me to quit?"

Captain Reardon had once told her, "I stand behind my men."

"What about women?" she'd asked. "In case you haven't noticed, I'm a—"

"Yeah, yeah. Her too. Unless that's sexual harassment. In which case I wouldn't."

Stand behind your men. She hadn't been chief here long, a year and a half roughly, but long enough to feel Parkhurst wouldn't kill or try to kill his ex-wife, and to believe he wouldn't cover up a killing by somebody else.

"Would you give me a week to clear this?"

He took so long in answering she began to get queasy.

"Three days."

That might not be enough. "Parkhurst," she said as he was leaving, "were you at the Sunflower last night?"

Anger flashed through his dark eyes, gone immediately leaving them flat and blank.

"Don't," she said sharply.

"Ma'am?"

"React like a suspect. Just tell me."

"I was not at the hotel last night." His words were evenly spaced and clipped off at the ends.

Oh, bloody hell, she shouldn't have asked. She didn't know if she believed him.

20

The sun, a great red ball, rose over the horizon, streaks of pale light shot through the dark, birds rustled and twittered in the trees. A silent figure in a long coat kept to the shadows as he wound through the woods. A searching stream of light struck silver from something in his hand. On a rise above, a rider on horseback sat motionless, black against the pink and lavender light of the rising sun.

"Cut," Fifer said. "Beautiful, ladies and gentlemen, just beautiful."

Good thing, Yancy thought. Even Fifer couldn't get the sun to come up over and over until he was satisfied. Though, he might have tromped everybody out here day after day until he got what he wanted.

"Yucky, yucky," Clem mumbled to herself.

"What?" Yancy said. The scene had looked very artistic to him.

Fifer, the cameras and crew—strange shapes moving around in the dark—had set up, stumbling and cursing and had all been waiting for Fifer to get the moment when the sun came over the hill.

"Hokey," Clem said, far enough away that Fifer couldn't hear. Her bib overalls hung sacklike over a red tank top so tight Yancy wondered how she could breathe.

He'd thought there would be some acknowledgment of Sheri Lloyd's murder, but Clem had used her best face of scorn when he'd mentioned it.

"What will Fifer do about her role?" he asked.

"Fortunately, most of her scenes were already shot," she said. "For what's left he'll cut in footage of earlier pieces, use long shots, and improvise. You know, somebody else, just hands, shoulder, back of the head, that kind of thing. Same hair, same clothing. Just no close-ups on the face."

Without a word, Fifer took off through the field toward the road about a half mile away where his town car waited to take him to the Lockett mansion. Clem was left with the crew that had to hassle equipment half a mile to the vehicles. With a lot of swearing and grousing, they managed.

"You look like shit," Clem said when they were inside the mansion.

"Little sleep."

"Take a nap."

"What, and miss all the excitement?" The story line still eluded him, but he'd figured out the layout. Laura Edwards's character lived in the mansion that had belonged to her father; he had been killed in such a way that it looked like an accident— broken his neck in a fall from a horse. Josiah's barn was part of the property and it was all adjacent to the river. She had come back for the funeral. Nick Logan's character was a local cop she'd gone to for help because the bad guys were trying to kill her. Why wasn't made clear. Local cop was the only one, of all the people she talked to, who believed her. Or maybe he didn't believe her, only wanted to get next to her.

Currently, they were filming an indoor scene, or interior to be correct. Hero (Nick Logan) and heroine (Laura Edwards) were in the kitchen. It was late at night—this was apparent from the black duvetyn tacked over the windows—and she was fixing a snack. The kitchen had been repaired until it looked shiny bright and contained nothing but the newest and best—ovens, refrigerator, stove top, and fancy wood cabinets. One wall had been removed to accommodate the film equipment.

All the hot lights and all the people made for a room with no air flow and no oxygen. It was unbelievably stuffy. Fans or air-conditioning weren't possible, they made noise. The temperature was a hundred twenty degrees. Everybody, including Yancy, was dripping sweat. Hell couldn't be worse.

"I can't make sense of this movie," he said to Clem. Trying to track the plot was something to use the center of his mind for while the edges all around worried whether his mother had stumbled into a homicide.

"It doesn't need to, it's about Laura wiggling her ass."

God had been more successful with the sunrise than Fifer was with this scene. Take after take went wrong. Laura flubbed her lines, then Nick came in late on a pickup. Then it was going great and one of the crew dropped a hammer that made Laura jump. Then a camera jammed, then the sound was wrong and after that the lighting was off. Once everything was going perfectly until Laura sneezed. Everybody broke up.

"Cut," Fifer said. He spoke quietly to Laura, she nodded. He said something to Nick, then went back to his position behind the camera. "Let's try it again."

"Roll cameras."

"Speed."

The young woman with the slateboard said, "Scene ninety-two, take nine," and clapped it.

"Action."

The actors tried to figure out how to get through the night without getting killed. Take nine did it. Also take fifteen. At that point, Fifer called a lunch break; everybody split. In a hurry.

The caterer had set up in a room on the first floor, the original purpose of which Yancy couldn't figure. Library maybe, but there were no bookshelves.

A chicken sandwich and bottle of foreign water later, he

stayed on his feet by moving; if he stopped he'd be gone. It was very odd to see one room all fitted out with plush furniture, thick carpets, knickknacks, sculptures, pictures, and fresh flowers, and the next was bare with cracked plaster, spiderwebs, and dirt.

Up the staircase and at the end of a hallway, voices came from the corner room. Nick Logan and Fifer were inside. Only half the room had been completed; the far end had a highly polished wood floor, floor-to-ceiling bookshelves filled with books, burgundy leather chairs around a long wooden table, and a large, highly polished wooden desk. This was the office of the head honcho in a megabucks company. In his hand, Nick had pages of the latest script changes.

He scanned them, mumbling as he did so. He put in pauses and gestures, walked the length of the room, and leaned over the desk.

"Nick," Fifer said quietly, "this is a cop who's been framed for murder. They're tired of him bothering them, they want to get rid of him."

Nick nodded. He read the script again, then went through the scene speaking the lines carefully, using the pauses and gestures, shifting his weight and building anger. Then he did it again.

The concentration of effort showed. Yancy began to appreciate why Nick was considered a good actor.

In the afternoon when Fifer shot the scene, a rich powerful man sat behind the desk. Yancy leaning against a wall hoped he wouldn't drop over asleep and ruin the take. Nick went through the lines and moved step by step while the lighting was set up.

When Fifer got to the actual filming, Yancy felt he could do the scene himself. Nick's voice jolted Yancy wide awake. It carried such raw emotion that hairs stood up on Yancy's arms. As Nick stalked the man with white hair, every bit of him yelled *killer*; no matter how furiously he cried, "Frame up!"

The menace in his face sent the CEO cowering back. At the scene's finish, the room was absolutely silent.

Two ticks went by and then Fifer said, "Beautiful, Nick."

Beautiful, Yancy echoed in his mind and was left with the feeling Nick Logan was capable of murder if the stakes were high enough.

Blue. Dark blue. Laura my beloved. The universe is dark blue. I'm coming. Just be patient. I'm following him. The universe will provide the right moment. I'll be ready. The gun belongs to me.

The next day was taken up by love scenes with Nick and Laura, both half naked, tumbling around in bed. Yancy wondered how two lovers felt portraying make-believe lovers with a roomful of people looking on. Or two ex-lovers who were feuding playing current lovers. It boggled the mind. These two did it with a lot of electricity.

By the time Fifer called wrap, it was nearly seven o'clock. Yancy was just as quick to speed off as the rest of them. A fourteen-hour day that started at five A.M. made quitting seem a fine idea.

With escape in mind, he put the squad car in reverse, had an arm over the seat back, and was looking out the rear window when he heard Clem Jones call him. Black gauze draped her from shoulders to ankles like a shawl, she was a costume who couldn't find a party.

"Hey." Both hands gripped the open window. "Would you do something for me?" A ragged note under her words didn't sound like the usual nasty Clem.

He didn't look at his watch. "If I can, certainly."

"Take me someplace for dinner. Someplace I won't be recognized."

With her appearance she'd be recognized everywhere. For a full second, he considered saying no. Then duty prevailed, it was his job, she looked right on the edge, and besides, he felt sorry for her. He tried to come up with a place that would be dark and empty.

"Please," she said, apparently thinking he was about to refuse, which with Serena waiting he'd certainly like to do. She wouldn't be happy when he was late again.

He got out of the car, went around, and opened the passenger door for her.

"I knew I could count on you. Gentleman to the core."

He sighed. "You know a whole hotel full of people. You could get any one of them to take you to dinner."

She slid in, he closed the door and went back to the driver's side. "What would you like to eat?"

"It doesn't matter. I'm not hungry."

Right. The Best Little Hare House in Kansas was loud and full of truckers. She'd probably start a riot. Poppy's Pizza? A student hangout. And she'd probably want something like kiwi and squid pizza so she could sneer when they didn't have it. The Blind Pig? He got it, Perfect Strings. He made a right, cut through town, and got on the Interstate.

"Everybody's looking at me," Clem said darkly when they walked in.

"Nah." Of course, she was right. Locals didn't see very many people with purple hair decked out in black gauze and white face paint. Nonlocals were media folks and they were on the lookout for somebody like her. This place had been a mistake.

A waitress with a long black skirt seated them in a booth and handed them each a menu.

"I need to make a phone call," he said.

"You need somebody's permission?"

"You need to change your attitude or I'll leave you right here."

"Sorry." She opened the menu and stuck her face in it.

She really was feeling low. Sorry wasn't in her vocabulary. He found the phone and called his sister.

"Let me guess," she said. "You're not coming. You have to work."

"I'll be a little later is all."

"Sure."

"I'll be there as soon as I can."

"Sure."

"Espresso," Clem said with disgust when he slid into the booth.

"What did you want? Moonshine?"

"Yeah. Local color."

"Wrong color. You're sixty years too late."

She asked the waitress for a glass of wine. He ordered iced tea.

"You don't even drink?" Clem sneered.

"Shove it."

"You aren't your usual sweet self. Phone call go badly? Who was it? Girlfriend?"

The drinks arrived and he took a gulp. "Why do you do that?"

"What?"

"Deliberately irritate people."

"Oh, that. It's just my personality. It goes with funny faces." She crossed her eyes and made her mouth go up and down like a retarded fish.

He smiled. "Good for a laugh, and it keeps people standing on one foot."

"What?"

"They never put the other one down to get a step closer."

"What are you? Some kind of closet psychiatrist?" She glared at him, started to make some smart remark, then just sat there with her priorities all confused.

"Want to try a little dinner talk? Did you go to California to get into the movie business?"

"We call it the industry. I'm an only child. My mother was a housewife. They don't make them much anymore. You know, at home baking cookies when you get there from school. Dad out in the big world earning a living."

When the waitress came for their order, Clem asked for another glass of wine.

"What do you want to eat?" he said. She looked on the way to getting drunk and he wanted to get food down her.

She picked up the menu. "I don't know. Anything."

"Bring her spaghetti and meatballs," he said.

"I'm a vegetarian."

"Bring me spaghetti and meatballs. Bring her spaghetti." He handed back the menus.

"What did your father do?" He eyed the media people. So far none had approached.

"Movies. What else?"

"Actor?"

"Art director."

Before she finished answering his question about what that was, big platters of spaghetti arrived with Clem's wine and a refill of iced tea.

"Did you ever want to be somebody else?" Clem poked a fork at her spaghetti.

"Like who?"

She shrugged. "I don't know. Anybody who seems to have it all in control." She broke off a chunk of bread and crumpled it on her plate. She sipped wine. "Life's a bitch and then you die." She started to laugh and it got caught somewhere.

"Were you a close friend of Sheri Lloyd's?"

"No. She had a hard time when she was growing up. I know that because she was always wanting to 'dialogue.' Get it out in the open. Huh. She was always trying to be somebody else, because her life was so yucky. She wasn't very smart."

Clem's eyes got blurry; she pressed the heels of her palms against them as though to hold back tears. "She probably didn't even know why."

Reporters at the next table were comparing information. One asked, "Did you get a picture of the hotel room?"

"No. Cops wouldn't let me in. I got an interview with a local though. She said the death was God's punishment. Have you ever noticed the people on God's side like lots of blood with His punishment?"

Clem placed her fork on her plate, folded her napkin carefully and placed it neatly beside her fork, and said in a very soft and careful voice, "I have to get out of here."

He took one look at her, beckoned the waitress, and mimed scribbling on his hand. When the check came, he threw money down, got up, and took her elbow. She held herself totally stiff, as though one misstep and she'd shatter like fine china. He steered her to the squad car and helped her in.

"To the hotel?"

"No. Drive."

With longing regrets for his spaghetti, he drove north and kept going. The sky was getting darker, stars were beginning to pop out and the moon, just past full, was covered by thin clouds. He took back roads, past barbed-wire-fenced fields of wheat and milo, over easy hills and down to the river at a spot three miles below where they'd been filming. He stopped and cut the motor.

For a second quiet took over, then sounds filtered in, the rush of water, the *tick-tick* of cooling metal, and the rustle of wind through the trees. The water, a dark slick endlessly moving, reflected a veiled moon, and minutes later a bright moon when clouds slid on. His mother always said this spot was magic, a place of healing. He didn't know about healing, but it did provide a spot to catch up and regroup, gather the wherewithal to carry on.

Clem sat motionless, looking down at the water. Abruptly she hit the door handle and jumped out. She moved so fast, he was left scrambling and cursing. If she fell, hurt herself—

She simply stood on the bank gazing up at the night sky. "She was just a joke to them, those reporters. They just—" Clem shook herself like Elmo after a bath. "I didn't even like her, but at least I knew her—" She looked at him and smiled, a crooked little smile of sadness.

In a second misery took over and she wrapped her arms around his neck, gulping and booing all over his uniform shirt. He let her sob, didn't say a word, didn't give encouraging pats on the shoulder. When she was done, she'd be mad at him, but right now she needed something to cling to and he obliged, holding

207

her tight to let her know she wasn't alone, but not intruding on the spasms of damp misery.

When it ended, she was quiet with her arms around his neck, face on his chest, leaning heavily against him, all energy spent. Occasionally a ghost of a hiccup escaped. The night sounds crept around them, tree leaves tossed as the wind picked up, the heedless river rippled on. There was an eerie cry of an owl, the whine of mosquitoes, and the rustle of small hunters in the low ground growth.

21

*W*ind blew in from the north pushing a bank of clouds and bringing the temperature down so fast Yancy could almost feel it drop. Rain was coming. He could smell it. Wind whipped through the Cherokee's windows as he goosed the accelerator to take the hill, trying to catch up for being two hours late. Lightning flickered behind the clouds, too far away to hear thunder, making the radio crackle.

As soon as the Cherokee's nose hit the driveway, Serena appeared in the doorway, a silhouette against the kitchen light. "I was afraid you wouldn't come."

"I told you I'd be here." Heavy lazy drops slapped down as he trotted to the house; they felt good on his face and arms. The rain wasn't ready yet; it would take its own good time.

"You've also been known to call and say you can't make it."

"I'm here. Go."

In the dark living room, his mother sat at the window with Elmo at her feet. When he bent down to kiss her cheek, the dog extended a friendly poke with his muzzle.

"Peter." Her fingertips gently ran down his cheek.

"Don't you want some light?"

"I suppose." The sudden light made her blink. "You look tired."

"It's been a long day." He jerked off his tie and unbuttoned the top button.

"You and Serena have had a lot to cope with over the years."

Dropping to the couch, he rested his head back. "What are you talking about?"

"I wasn't exactly a conventional mother."

"That's true."

She was silent for a long moment. "I've been thinking—trying to think. It's so hard when I can't concentrate. A few seconds and then my mind—skitters. Remember when you used to skip rocks on the pond? It's like that. Jumping around so I never get anyplace. Frustrating—"

He pulled himself forward and leaned his arms on his knees to study her face—tears glistened in her eyes. "Hey," he said softly. "What's wrong?"

"I'm sorry, Peter. All those years—when you were little, you and Serena. I'm sorry it was so hard for you. I was selfish. When you're young, you don't think. I never had any relatives. My parents died, and then I didn't have any family at all. I decided to make my own. I never thought how hard it would be for you and Serena."

Elmo, hearing the sad tinge in her voice, whimpered and put his head in her lap. She stroked his ears and eyebrows. "It's still hard for you."

"What are you talking about?"

"Your crazy mother, that's what I'm talking about. I don't know how I could have been so selfish."

"I've always been proud of my crazy mother." For the most part that was true.

She smiled. "Well, Serena hasn't."

"Girls are more delicate."

"Both of you put up with so much. Don't think I don't know."

"We had everything we needed." Except for food, he thought, and some way to fit in with other kids. That was hard, being different, being laughed at. It got him in a lot of fights, which she never could understand, but there were things he had that they didn't. Through her eyes, he was given magic. He had Shakespeare for breakfast, and flowers unfolding in the moonlight, saw birds and animals living lives of heroism.

"Will you take care of Elmo, Peter? I wouldn't want anything to happen to him."

"Nothing's going to happen to Elmo."

"Promise?"

"Yes." This mood worried him. She'd always been loony, but she was happy with it, not despairing like this. "Don't worry."

"Poor Peter. You always had to take care of things."

"Mom, what—?"

She dropped her hand over the arm of the chair and Elmo laid back down, planting himself just under her fingertips. "He's been restless this evening. I don't know what's bothering him. He keeps pacing around, and barking."

Her mood, Yancy thought.

"Tell me what happened in the movie business today," she said.

He gave her an account of his day, starting at five A.M. at the river.

"The actress who got killed—I can't remember her name. Who killed her?"

"No solution yet. The chief is walking around with fire in her eyes and ice in her voice."

"What's the name of the movie?"

"*Lethal Promise.* Don't ask what it's about because I don't really know."

"A promise that shouldn't be made? Which you should never do, by the way. I hereby absolve you of any promise which shouldn't have been made. Except the one about Elmo."

"I'll keep only promises that need keeping."

She smiled. "You're a good boy, Peter. You deserved better, you and Serena. I love you and your sister more than life itself. I didn't know— Only looking back do I realize—"

Her voice was so thin with sorrow he wondered if she were seeing a particular memory.

"Don't look so worried, Peter. I'm all right. Anyway, as all right as I ever get."

An echo of his own voice resonated in these words and he felt like he maybe shouldn't be so flippant.

She kissed him, squeezed his hands, and said she should get herself to bed. He kicked off his shoes and stretched out on the couch, trying to figure out what her regrets had been all about. An hour later something woke him.

He swung his feet to the floor and rubbed his grainy eyes. His teeth felt like green fuzz. Elmo barked. Yancy plodded into the kitchen where Elmo had his nose against the door. He barked again.

"I'm coming, I'm coming."

Head low, Elmo growled deep in his throat. Yancy fumbled with the lock, half-asleep.

The dog's toenails scrambled on the linoleum as the door opened. He shoved his muzzle through and took off, barking furiously.

Oh, Christ. What was the dumb dog after? He never learned about skunks. Yancy took off in stockinged feet, wincing and limping as gravel cut into them. The rain had fizzled to mist blown by the wind so that he had to turn his head to one side and blink as he peered into the darkness.

"Elmo!"

The dog skidded to a stop and looked uncertainly at Yancy. "Come!"

Elmo looked in the direction of his prey, looked at Yancy, seemed undecided, then galumped toward Yancy, leaped up, and tried to lick his face.

"What's the matter with you, you stupid mutt?" Yancy grabbed his collar. "Hey! Anybody there?"

No answer but the wind fanning mist in his face. Whoever or whatever it was had fled from the hound of hell who didn't want to be dragged back inside.

Yancy limped over to the couch and stripped off his damp socks. When Serena got home an hour later, Yancy shoved bare feet, horrible as that was, into his shoes and took himself off.

The mist, thinned to not much more than an occasional fat drop from wet trees, made muzzy halos around streetlights. As he pulled in at the old Victorian, movement flickered across the side mirror. Somebody had slipped down the driveway of the house across the street. The moon glowing behind clouds and the moisture in the air put him right into a spy movie. Except for a light over the front door, the house was dark. The owners were away and he'd been asked to keep an eye out. "If this mad painter should strike," Mr. Fandor had said with an impish smile, "let him finish the picture before you arrest him."

Yancy wasn't waiting for anything. He grabbed his flashlight and loped across the street. The shiny slick drive reflected the light. "Police! Come out with your hands up."

No response.

At the far end, he swung the beam in a wide arc through the rear yard. Nothing.

Behind him, he heard a shoe slide on wet concrete. Before he could turn, somebody barreled into him. Stumbling forward, he landed on one knee, lost his balance, and fell hard on his left side. His breath caught on the sharp pain.

Oh, shit.

He'd been stabbed. And if that wasn't enough, he'd fallen on the knife and forced it in farther.

2 2

*L*ightning split the sky. Thunder crashed. With his face against damp cement, Yancy stared at the fan of light from his flashlight a couple feet ahead where it had rolled when he'd dropped it. Whoever had stabbed him had taken his gun. He waited for a shot in the back. His heartbeat thudded in his ears.

He was clammy, shivering, but didn't seem to be lying in a pool of vital fluid. His breathing didn't crackle from blood in his lungs.

He heard a whisper, "Oh, God. Oh, God."

Heart banging nightmare time. A hulking form materialized above him, bent to pick up the flash, and ran the beam over him. He flinched; the pain made him clench his teeth.

"You got a knife in your side."

"Don't touch it!"

"No way, man. I'm not getting near it." The light lit up the lower half of Kevin Murphy's face.

"Why'd you do it?" Not coughing. Good sign, still no blood in his lungs.

"Uh-uh, not me."

"Bleeding?"

"Yeah."

"How much?"

"Your shirt soaked around the knife."

"Keys. Left pocket. Go up to my place. Call for help."

"Right." Kevin didn't move.

"Do it!"

"Right. Yeah. Okay." Gingerly, Kevin eased his hand in Yancy's pocket and, in sliding the keys out, jiggled Yancy slightly. Yancy clamped down on his back teeth.

"You got sweat all over your forehead," Kevin said.

"Phone."

"Yeah, I'm going." Kevin hesitated, then sprinted down the driveway.

Lightning split the sky, thunder rolled over it, and cold drops of rain pattered on Yancy's face.

Some minutes later—two? Five? Yancy couldn't judge time—Kevin sprinted back. "Okay," breathless, like he'd been running miles, rain dripping down his face. "They'll be right here. You all right? Oh, God, come on, man, don't die."

Somewhere in Yancy's mind there were words to respond, but they were far back. When he tried to reach them, they went farther back, until there was nothing but velvet blackness.

Overheads on the squad car bled red, blue, and red into the rain-slick street and across faces of neighbors clustered on porches. EMTs slipped an oxygen tube under Yancy's nose, started IV fluids, and kept checking his blood pressure. Parkhurst stood around like excess baggage, and kept out of the way while they strapped Yancy on a stretcher and loaded him into the ambulance. It took off with the siren competing with thunder.

"His sister."

Parkhurst turned.

Mrs. Blakeley, Yancy's landlady, held the ends of a scarf together around her chin. "Would you like me to call her?"

"I'll take care of it," he said. "Are you all right?" She looked a little wobbly. "I'll have somebody see you get back to the house."

"I'm fine. Just—" She breathed in. "Will he be all right?"

"I hope so."

The small group of neighbors, stunned by what had happened, hadn't seen or heard anything until they'd heard the ambulance. Parkhurst had Kevin Murphy taken in, then sent White and Ellis on a door-to-door. What were the chances some individual was home, knew something, and hadn't rushed out to check the action?

Windshield wipers humming back and forth, he drove ten miles south to Raina Yancy's home. Bringing bad news to a family was the worst of it. At least, the current duty wasn't bringing death. It was just past two A.M. when he got there. Using his flashlight to avoid puddles, he trotted through the rain to the rear porch.

Inside, the dog barked; outside, the light came on, and the kitchen door opened. Serena, white-faced, robe thrown over pajamas, had one hand on the dog's collar. "What happened?"

"May I come in, Serena?"

"Is he dead?"

"No, Serena. He's been hurt. He's at the emergency room."

Her knees loosened. Parkhurst grabbed for her and the dog came at him with all its teeth hanging out.

"Elmo!"

"Easy. Okay." Parkhurst released her and stepped back.

Serena caught the dog around its shoulders and let it slink under the table. "I'm sorry about that. He's been weird this evening. I don't know what's wrong with him. He's really a very sweet dog."

Sure he is. Parkhurst eyed the beast warily and guided Serena to a chair. "Your brother's been stabbed. We don't know yet what happened."

"How bad?"

"Until I get in and talk with the doctor, I don't know."

She shot up. "I have to go."

Toenails scrapping, the dog got out from under the table. Parkhurst remained sitting, not wanting to set him off again. "I'll take you. You might want to get dressed."

217

In confusion, she looked down at herself. "Yes. Oh, yes. Of course."

"Leaving you with me," he said to the dog.

Elmo padded over to him, placed his big head on Parkhurst's knee, and peered up at him through bushy eyebrows.

"Does this mean we're friends?"

Elmo wiggled his eyebrows. Parkhurst gave him a careful pat and the dog snuggled closer, squashing one foot with a large paw.

Five minutes later, Serena came back wearing jeans and a blue blouse, carrying a raincoat that she slipped on.

Parkhurst stood carefully. Elmo, now that they were friends and all, just seemed sorry to see him go. "What about your mother?"

"She's asleep. I'll leave her a note in case she wakes up. First I'll see how bad—how he is and if—if I need to I'll come back and get her."

With a hand on her elbow, Parkhurst guided her to the Bronco, turned it around, and headed back to town.

Eyes fixed on the silver strands of rain caught in the headlights, Serena said, "I've been nagging at him."

It was a confession in a voice laden with guilt and remorse. A common occurrence, from a family member or loved one. Regrets. People don't seem to live with love uppermost in their lives, or they don't remember it. They remember the anger and sharp words they can't take back.

When they got to the hospital, he parked in a loading zone, careful not to block entrances or emergency vehicles, and they went inside.

"Where is he?" she asked the emergency room nurse.

"Don't worry." The nurse, Mary Mason, gave her a reassuring smile. "He's fine. We're working on him. He's in the last room."

Working on him didn't sound so reassuring to Parkhurst. He shepherded Serena in the direction indicated.

"Hey," Mary said.

He turned.

"Peter's had a big shock to the body. He's also had morphine. He is not to be pestered with questions."

"Yes, ma'am. All right if I take a look at him?"

"No. You're not family. And I know you, you'll ask questions."

"The doctor? All right if I see him?"

"He's busy. You wait right over there and I'll let you know when he's free."

Parkhurst paced the waiting area until Dr. Sheffield appeared in scrub greens and booties.

"How is he?"

"Stable."

Parkhurst crossed his arms and said evenly, "This is me you're talking to. Tell me what's going on with that officer, or I'll shoot your foot off."

A smile crossed Sheffield's tired face. Padding to a yellow plastic chair, he plopped down. "He's fine. Young, fit, healthy. Barring complications, he'll be good as new in a day or two. He was lucky. The knife was rammed into his side approximately here." Sheffield bent his right elbow and placed a thumb against his side about halfway between waist and armpit. "The knife point hit a rib and went skating along the bone. It's cracked, either from the blow or from the force of his fall. But it didn't go straight in between ribs and puncture a lung."

Parkhurst felt his shoulders ease. "How much strength did it take? Was the assailant male?"

"I suppose a woman could have done it. He did most of the damage himself when he fell."

"I need to talk to him."

"Tomorrow."

Parkhurst stared.

"He's not Superman, for God's sake. He's a kid who's just had a hell of a traumatic insult to his body. He's not on the critical list, but that doesn't mean it's just a scratch. He's got a cracked rib and a stab wound. He's in pain, and in shock. He's also lost some blood. Give him time to rebound. This is my domain and

I'm telling you to stay away from him." Sheffield started to stride off.

"A couple of questions."

Sheffield threw up his hands. "Go. Just don't stress him out."

Shirt off, rib cage wrapped, Yancy lay on a bed, Serena at his side, and a young nurse making notes on a chart. Seeing Parkhurst, he tried to get up.

"Hey," the nurse said, "you want to fall?"

"They gave me something," Yancy said apologetically.

Parkhurst could see that they had. Yancy's eyes didn't quite focus. "What happened?"

Considering the drugs, Yancy related the incident clearly.

"What did you see?"

"Nothing. A shove. Next, I'm on the ground, waiting to meet my maker. He took my gun."

"He?"

"I don't even know that."

Parkhurst collected the bloody shirt, asked the nurse to date and initial the tag after he did. He told Serena he'd have somebody take her home when she was ready.

He went back to Baylor Street to make sure Osey was working the scene and find out what the neighbors might know. He told White to get back over to the hospital and look after Yancy's sister.

Rose. Laura my beloved. The universe is rose. He held the gun in his hand and tested the weight, looked down the sights and gently put a finger around the trigger. Beautiful. It won't be long, Laura, my sweet, my love. It won't be long. We'll be together. Forever.

It was three A.M. when Parkhurst called the chief. Her voice was clogged with sleep.

220

She'd been dreaming. Down jacket blowing around her, she was running along the beach, trying to catch the man ahead. Cold wind clawed her face and whipped her hair. Her bare feet made sucking hollows in the sand, waves rolled in and washed the sand clean as they rolled out. Seagulls wheeled overhead in a gray sky, their high plaintive mews grew shrill, then dissolved into the ringing of the telephone.

Snaking out a hand, she groped at the bedside table, turned over, and cleared her throat. Rain pattered against the roof like tears she had to grieve. "Wren."

"Parkhurst." He told her what had gone down.

Dregs of sleep wiped from her mind, she told him what little she knew about Kevin Murphy. An only child, his father a navy test pilot who'd smashed himself up in an accident, now retired and moved to Hampstead with his family. Then she said, "I'll be right down."

While he waited for her, Parkhurst watched Kevin through the one-way mirrored glass. From the kid's manners, Parkhurst could have guessed the military father. Years ago, Parkhurst knew a military brat. Parkhurst was twelve, Noah a couple years older. At fourteen Noah had that same outward respect of authority, posture straight, stance at attention with adults, and the same self-assurance a kid might get from living all over the world, being transplanted every couple years and asked to survive.

Noah knew four languages, and even in English he could talk rings around Parkhurst. He called everybody *sir*, even Parkhurst's drunken, abusive father. At fourteen, he'd lived places Parkhurst had never even heard of.

They'd met one hot summer day. Noah, flying down a hill on his skateboard, was heading right into an ambush. Four local kids had decided to take the skateboard. Noah—hair short, clothes clean, matchstick arms, expensive shoes—looked like easy fun. They shouldn't have been so confident. Like a dancer, he stepped off the board, picked it up, and smashed one kid across the face. A broken nose with gushing blood put him out of commission. The other three, with just enough brain power combined to know one heavy offensive would take him, came in a flying wedge.

Parkhurst lent a hand, or rather both fists, and his knowledge of street fighting. Even so it wasn't a walk over. All six were bloody and bruised before it was finished, but by God he and Noah won. They grinned at each other, chests filled with the pride of young males walking away from battle as victors.

Skateboard under one arm, Noah turned to him. "I suppose you think we're going to be friends."

Parkhurst, nonplussed, hadn't given it a thought. "Why not?" Even in preadolescence the battlefield made fast friends.

"I don't have friends," Noah said in that tight-assed way he had of showing he was better.

"How come?"

"Who needs them?" This was said with jaw firm, shoulders back. "Keep moving. No baggage."

Wow. A motto. Like the Three Musketeers, one for all and all for one. Noah didn't need anybody. Keep moving, no baggage.

Despite Noah's motto, the distances when he was off in some country Parkhurst couldn't even spell, and the time between Noah's visits to his grandmother, they did become friends.

Years later, in a bar, late one night with both of them slightly squiffed, Parkhurst asked why.

"You were the only person who ever came into a fight on my side," Noah said. "A new school every year. You walk into a classroom and every face stares at you. There's never time to make friends because you're always packing up and moving on. Next class, different faces stare at you, but they're the same damn faces. You learn to fight your own fights. You learn to live as a loner and you're lonely. Jesus God, are you lonely," he said to his vodka.

He drained the glass. "The only person in the entire world who ever came into a fight on my side." He swiveled the bar stool and punched Parkhurst's shoulder. "You, my friend, are the only reason I'm not in a nuthouse."

222

In those days Parkhurst was packed with gunpowder waiting to explode. He was always looking for a fight, any fight would do.

Susan came up beside him and they both looked at Kevin in the interview room, seated in a brown plastic chair at the long wooden table, face worried and young. They stood side by side for a minute or two. She'd obviously dressed in a hurry, but she looked as cool and poised as always. Without taking her eyes from Kevin, she said, "You take this on."

He didn't know what she'd based her decision on, but he was glad. He wanted a go at this kid. When he stepped into the room, Kevin's head whipped up with insolent, thin-lipped assurance and a reckless air of being ready to stand his ground, no matter the consequences.

"Why'd you stab him, Kevin?"

"Sir?"

The *sir*, drilled into him by his military father, had the same hard spin as fuck you. He had a calm self-confidence seldom seen in a seventeen-year-old kid. Forced into being a loner either created self-assurance or sent a kid straight down the tubes.

A natural athlete, with reactions the speed of a prairie rattler, this kid was a miracle for the high school Wolverines; it was the only time in the history of Hampstead High School that they had a team to be reckoned with. A lot of newspaper space got devoted to him at every game.

"You got a score to settle with Officer Yancy?" Parkhurst asked.

"Sir?"

Staring got no more than amused contempt. Of cops? All adults? Susan was probably right. He was at war with the adult world, and that made Parkhurst think. He just might know what made this kid tick. As a teenager, Parkhurst had zeroed his hatred in on cops, because he was constantly hassled. Back in the days before there was so much noise about illegal search and seizure, he'd be netted on the street during routine hauls and dragged in for questioning. Once in high school, between classes a plainclothes man had slammed him against his locker, crushed

223

a forearm against his throat, and said, "You're coming with me." No fooling around with Miranda, he was thrown in a lineup. He never knew what he was suspected of. The witness didn't come through with an ID and the cop grudgingly dropped him back at school. He'd swaggered into English class. Most likely, nothing like that had ever happened to this kid, not a kid who had a father who knew how to raise hell if it did.

"Why'd you do it?"

Kevin, back straight, both hands lying loosely on his lap, had no trouble looking Parkhurst in the eye. "You'll have to be more specific," he said.

"What'd you do with the gun?"

"I thought he was stabbed."

"Where'd you get the knife?"

"You don't hear very well. I said I didn't do it."

"You didn't, huh? Why you protecting the bastard who did?"

"I don't know anything about it."

Parkhurst walked around behind the kid, rested a shoulder against the door frame, and crossed his arms. "You were there." He spoke softly because he didn't want Susan, watching on the other side of that glass, to know how near he was at slamming this kid against the wall.

If Kevin had a nerve anywhere it was under control. He hadn't said anything about an attorney, or a parent. Parkhurst wondered why. "What were you doing there?"

"Passing by."

Parkhurst walked around and leaned forward, hands on the table. "You a pretty smart kid?"

"Genius range."

"What kind of grades you make in school?"

"C's and D's."

"What kind of genius gets C's and D's?"

"I know more than the teachers. They're so boring they could stop birds from singing."

"These poor grades, they annoy your father?"

Kevin grinned.

Now Parkhurst was getting someplace. "He ever hit you?"

"No."

Bingo. "Ever hit your mother?"

"Of course not."

He lied with conviction. "What interests you?"

"That have anything to do with the subject at hand?" Kevin said.

"What is the subject at hand?"

"This is your show, don't you know?"

Parkhurst smiled. Kevin didn't know it, but Parkhurst now knew a lot about him, could describe the home atmosphere and the despair he lived with. Parkhurst knew because he'd been there, the yelling, the backhanding, the fists. The misery was constant, unless the old man was gone; then the air was poisoned with dread of his return. "You trying to say you didn't stab that police officer and you don't know anything about who did?"

"You finally got it. Congratulations."

"Maybe you can tell me why I should believe you when you're a liar."

That got to him. Kevin stiffened, clenched his jaw, and made a fist of the hand in his pocket. "You don't know anything about me."

"I know more than you think."

"When did I lie?"

"You said your father never hit you, never hit your mother."

"He never laid a hand on either of us."

"Right. You were on the Fandors' driveway. What were you doing there?"

Good as this kid was at hiding whatever went on in his mind, he couldn't suppress a flicker across his eyes of I'm-so-smart-and-you're-so-dumb. It was an expression any cop knew well, the expression of somebody who thinks he's getting away with something. What was it that Parkhurst was missing here? He wondered if Susan knew.

"I thought I heard a noise."

"Officer Yancy isn't dead. That means a witness."

"Why don't you ask him then?"

Oh, for God's sake. Maybe he was as dumb as the kid thought. The Fandors were away. Yancy had heard something suspicious, he went to check. "You went in that yard to paint another garbage can. Officer Yancy caught you and you stabbed him."

Kevin went dead still, bright mind calculating whether he'd admit it or not. He'd know there was no evidence. If he decided to deny it, the cops might believe he was guilty, but they couldn't prove anything.

"Why the artwork? To make your father mad?"

In a split second, Kevin made his decision. Parkhurst caught a glimpse of a seventeen-year-old kid under the smooth exterior. "It drives him nuts. I got an offer for a football scholarship. I want to study art. 'Art is for wimps and queers. You'll never make a name for yourself with art.' " He folded his hands on the table. "Did I make a name for myself?"

He had at that. First the *Hampstead Herald* and then, because it was so odd, it was picked up by a wire service, even mentioned as the final note on network television news. The kid was no coward; when his father found out, he'd beat the hell out of him.

"What'd you see?"

"Nothing. I heard the commotion. And I waited. I figured he'd be after me and I'd have to go over the fence."

"Why didn't you?"

"I don't know exactly. He didn't yell, 'Freeze! Police!' All that. It made me nervous. I waited and when nothing happened I went to take a look. He was on the ground, I thought he was dead. I picked up his flashlight to look and he talked to me. He gave me his keys. Anyway told me to take them. I didn't touch anything in the house but his phone. I did the nine-one-one bit."

"Was his gun missing when you found him?"

"I don't know. I didn't notice anything but that knife. Shoved in his side that way, I've never seen anything like it. I was afraid he'd croak before the ambulance guys got there."

"You could have taken the gun."

"Yeah. But I didn't."

Whether Kevin was lying or not, Yancy's gun was floating around. "What did you do with all the paint paraphernalia?"

"It's under the sink in Yancy's kitchen, with the cleaning supplies."

Parkhurst looked at the kid a long minute, then stepped out to talk with Susan. "We've caught us the mad painter. I don't know what else."

"You think he stabbed Yancy?"

"I could use some breakfast."

23

*F*ood. Susan considered. At five A.M.? Coffee, now there's an idea.

One of the few places open this early was The Best Little Hare House in Kansas out on the Interstate that catered to truckers. Was she strong enough to withstand a jukebox issuing forth country and western philosophy at this hour?

"Let's go," she said.

Breakfast wasn't the only thing he could use, she noted. Sleep was in order, fatigue showed in his face. Unshaven, with dark circles around his eyes, he looked sinister.

A trucker, hunched over the counter, peered into his mug of coffee, either estimating his chances or contemplating the meaning of life. A nasal voice mused musically that the only way to go is past where you've been. At five in the morning even that made sense. She and Parkhurst took a booth. Two men in the next booth were telling jokes.

The waitress, middle-aged and friendly, brought two mugs of steaming coffee and the menus. Rain splattered against the window, washing flickering streams of red and blue down the glass from the neon sign outside. Smells of frying onions fought with frying bacon for first place. Susan's stomach set up a protest. How soft she'd gotten; it used to be, she could snatch anything on the run. Just to prove she still had it, she ordered sausage and eggs.

"You think he did it?" she asked.

"Stabbed Yancy?" Parkhurst ripped open a packet of sugar and dumped it in his coffee. "I don't know."

"The reason being to get the gun?"

"Why else would anybody go after Yancy?"

Yancy was a sweetheart, but that didn't mean somebody couldn't have a reason. "Kevin Murphy stabs Yancy and then calls nine-one-one to get help," she said.

"He didn't want a dead cop, only a live gun."

"For what purpose?"

The waitress slid filled platters in front of them. Susan eyed hers warily. Aha, now there's food. All on an empty stomach. She shouldn't have been so rash. Starting slow, she sipped coffee.

"That's the question." He sprinkled pepper on his eggs. "I think we can rule out target practice."

She forked off a sliver of sausage and nibbled it. Spicy! Oh, yes, hot. Hot hot. Taste buds now awake, eyes watering. Orange juice helped. "What did he do with it?"

"Hid it somewhere."

"You did look."

Parkhurst raised an eyebrow. At the next booth, one of the men said, "There was this eighty-six-year-old man who married this eighty-four-year-old woman. And they were happy and traveling and doing all these things . . ."

"Okay, so why didn't you find it?" Susan said. "He ran across the street, used the phone, ran back. How long was he gone? Two minutes?"

"That's what he says. Yancy concurs."

"Hardly time for anything complicated."

The waitress came by and refilled coffee mugs.

". . . and then one day the woman wasn't feeling well. And she thought it was just the flu. Except she didn't get better and she didn't get better until finally the man told her to go to the doctor and so . . ."

"Yancy wasn't exactly clearheaded," Parkhurst said. "Kevin got rid of the gun, stashed the paints, called nine-one-one, sprinted back. It took longer, five minutes. Yancy maybe didn't know the difference."

She held her mug in both hands. "Why would he want Yancy's gun?"

"To blow away his old man. He hates the bastard with the intensity of tornado winds." Parkhurst's voice was easy, but there was something cold as dry ice underneath.

"That's a lot of hate."

"Murphy Senior is a handy man with his fists."

"You can't know that."

"Trust me, I know. The kid is brave, I'll give him that. Stupid, but brave. That's how he got the bloody nose. I'll lay a year's salary on it. The bastard belted him." Parkhurst laughed without humor. "Picking up Mrs. Yancy had more to do with getting a big dirty dog in his father's shiny new car than with neighborliness."

"Before you jump to conclusions—"

"I'll run a check—emergency rooms, physicians, teachers. I'll find broken bones, bruises, contusions, accidents all over the place."

Victims of abuse commonly explained injuries by saying how clumsy they were; they fell and broke arms, tripped and broke jaws, slipped and got bruises.

". . . and the doctor took all different kinds of tests. X-rays and blood tests and EKGs and EEGs and MRIs and every other initials he could think of. And he couldn't find anything wrong with her. So he said, 'There's just one other test I want to do and the results will be ready on Monday.' "

"You never say the old man beats the shit out of you, and never admit he does the same to your mother, but you think about killing him, and you plan."

"Painting garbage cans ties in with this?"

"Ingenious, this kid. He's dancing on the back of an alligator. I hope Murphy Senior doesn't kill him. I'll have a talk with the navy test pilot, retired. Man to man." Parkhurst's smile was so tight it was nothing more than his top lip flattening against his teeth.

". . . and so on Monday the woman went back to the doctor and he told her. 'I finally figured out what's wrong with you. You're pregnant.' The woman thought about that for a minute and then she called her husband and she said, 'You got me pregnant, you old goat.'

"There was this silence on the other end of the line, and he said . . . 'Who is this?' "

"If you're right, we've exchanged a mad painter for a potential killer. Is he our stalker?"

Parkhurst leaned forward and picked up his coffee mug. Holding it between both hands, he spoke over the rim, "I flat out don't know. The kid is accustomed to lying, he's done it all his life, and he's good at it."

Parkhurst sipped, then sipped again. "He could be. Stalkers grow up in families that are physically and emotionally abusive. Not always, but often enough to throw it into a profile. They're loners. Our boy fits there. Angry. Mentally or emotionally disturbed. Insecure. Unattractive."

"That doesn't fit. Kevin has self-confidence all over the place and he's very good-looking. He's the high school football hero. Much adulation, even from adults."

"Yeah. He is a loner though."

They were into the easy back and forth of an ongoing case, but he was slightly defensive, his shoulders tensed, and she was slightly brittle. Both were pretending there wasn't a big swamp of emotions swimming around underneath them.

"What does any of this have to do with the stabbing of Sheri Lloyd?" she said.

"Yeah."

". . . so there was this guy and for his birthday his wife . . ."

"Hey, Ben." A trucker came up and slapped Parkhurst on the

232

shoulder, in that half challenging, half playful way that passes for friendship in males. "We have a bet going." He nodded at the counter where two beefy males in jeans and checked shirts sat sideways on stools.

"I said you were married to that movie star that's here. The one that's"—he glanced at Susan—"so pretty. Eddie said you wasn't."

"You lose."

"Damn." The trucker went back to pay up.

"*Was* means used to be," Susan pointed out.

"I have also been known to lie. Let's get out of here." He slid from the booth and grabbed the check.

They trotted through rain to the pickup. She started it. "Parkhurst?"

"Yeah?" Impatient. Cautionary.

She wanted to say something like "I'm sorry." For what, she wasn't quite sure. That memories, when they got loose, had thorns, and you got hurt when you tried to pick them up? "Nothing."

Hampstead, just waking up, stirred with people getting off to work.

What would the rain do to Fifer's schedule?

INT. YANCY'S BEDROOM.

Yancy, lying in his own bed, frets because he isn't there.

A mocking smile would go well here. Rain pelted against the skylight, very artistic. Somewhere along the line he'd developed a stake in this movie. It was good to be home anyway, even if he did have Demarco guard-dogging because the chief was protecting him from assassins. Demarco only made one crack about baby cops losing guns, then sat around looking alert.

Dozing took up most of the morning while Demarco sat in the kitchen and read the paper, then Yancy washed as well as he could without getting bandages wet, dressed and shaved and dozed some more. Whatever they'd given him at the hospital had a hell of an afterlife.

In the easy chair, he was dozing over a book on Quantrill's raiders . . . slipping in from the east, hidden by the predawn sky and the seven-foot-high corn in the field, they approached the rural home of John L. Crane. Before sunup Crane was dead, his house burning, and William Quantrill was leading his raiders to Lawrence. The date was August 21, 1863 . . . when a knock brought him up with a start. Demarco let in Stephanie Blakeley, ever-present notebook clutched to her chest, plastic container in her other hand. She came in dripping water. Rain spilled over the wrought iron and ran down through the wooden steps.

"Mother sent this." She thrust the container at him. "Bean soup. It's actually pretty good," she added. Stephanie, at thirteen, didn't always see eye to eye with her mother, but she believed in being fair. She'd been eight, sporting two new permanent front teeth when he had moved in, and had told him astonishing facts about the world as she'd seen it. Now she was a solemn, serious thirteen-year-old who was going to be an author, hence the notebook—to write down important or profound thoughts.

"If you're not busy, I'd like to talk."

Uh-huh. Her questions could get sticky, like Do you believe in God, or What is it like to be in a fistfight. These things were of significance to an author. He shoved the soup in the refrigerator and asked if she'd like a beer.

She gave him a look of withering scorn. "I'm not still eight, you know. That's no longer funny."

Sometimes he didn't remember to respect her thirteen-year-old dignity, which she was quick to point out.

"Coke?"

"Yes, thank you."

Demarco kept himself out of the way at the kitchen table with his paper. Sitting cross-legged on the living-room floor, bony knees poking out of blue shorts, she opened the can and sipped, studying him thoughtfully. "Does it hurt?"

He always answered her questions as well as he could. Not knowing how her mother would feel about these discussions, he tried to walk a fine line between honesty and what his landlady might get upset about if she knew her thirteen-year-old daughter was getting answers from him. "Not a lot."

She tucked a strand of brown hair behind her ear, opened the notebook, and wrote in a tiny, precise hand. "Did it hurt when you got stabbed?"

"Some. But mostly, it was scary."

She thought about that and then nodded as though that made sense. "Did you think you were going to die?"

"I sure thought I might." He hoped she wasn't going to ask his opinions about an afterlife; that was something he didn't feel equipped to handle. He popped the tab on his Coke and took a gulp.

"Some people die and it's a blessing."

"Who told you that?"

"Nobody tells me anything. I'm treated like a child with no intelligence. And I'm neither." Her mouth tightened and she twitched it back and forth. "You, at least, think I have brains."

"Who died going out with a blessing?"

She shrugged. "That's what the women at church were saying about Mrs. Evanosky's husband."

"Did I know Mr. Evanosky?"

She shrugged again. "He's been sick for ages and ages and now he's dead and Mrs. Evanosky doesn't have a penny to live on. That doesn't sound like much of a blessing to me."

Evanosky. The woman in the hospital courtyard keeping a death watch? Her vigil was finally over then.

"Do you know who murdered that actress?" Like a pushy reporter, she had her notebook and pen ready.

"Not yet."

"Why did the murderer try to kill you? Because you were getting too close?"

"Naw."

She made notes. "Maybe you know something you don't know you know."

"That's only on television, Steph."

"Have you been interrogating suspects?"

"Why are you so interested?"

"You're the only one who ever tells me anything. I'm figuring out who did it."

"I'm a flunky who goes where I'm sent to stand around all day and watch other people film a scene."

"Did you ever go anywhere your mother didn't want you to go?"

Uh-oh. "Where'd you go, Steph?"

"Well, the thing is, she doesn't know, and actually she told me not to, but—" She glanced at Demarco.

Narrow face, crew cut, and square chin, he looked like a drill sergeant, which is what he had been before he came to HPD.

"Well, anyway—never mind. I have something important to ask."

She let it sit there until he said, "What do you want to ask?"

"Will you tell me about sex?"

He choked on the cold liquid he'd been tipping down his throat. "Uh—Steph—I don't think your mother—"

She grinned, gotcha. "Well then, will you teach me how to shoot a gun?"

That didn't exactly have an easy answer either, given the way her mother felt about guns. Before he could launch into qualifiers all around a response, there was a knock on the door.

"I'll get it." Stephanie unfolded herself and started for the door.

Demarco beat her to it. Stephanie studied Clem Jones as she came in, glanced at Yancy, and used "Don't forget to eat your soup" as an exit line.

The director's assistant was her usual nightmare vision, only this time her hair was green, but her face was the usual white and her eyes black, she looked like a rakish raccoon. Three painted green teardrops glistened on her left cheek. She wore no coat to keep the rain off; her overalls had rips in knees and the butt, they looked like she'd just shaken out the wino and pulled them on. The sleeveless T-shirt matched her hair. Demarco gave her a hard stare.

"You dead yet?" she asked Yancy.

"No. Would you care to sit down?" He offered her the easy chair.

She ignored the offer and prowled. "You really sick or just malingering?"

"With your great sympathetic manner, you ever think of going into nursing? Can I get you something to drink?"

She shook her head. "We heard you'd been shot."

"I fell and cracked a rib." He took the chair she'd rejected.

"Sure you did." She plucked a book from the shelf, riffled pages, and put it back.

"Small matter of a knife wound. Was it you? A knife in the back seems just your style."

Edging to the couch, she perched. "Is that what happened? Does it hurt? Can I see it?"

"Yes, yes, and no."

"I brought you some magazines, but I left them in the car." As jittery as a prairie dog with a hawk overhead, she reached for the television remote, looked at it front and back, pushed a button, watched the television flicker on, then pushed the off button. "Was it Laura?"

"Laura what?"

"Who stabbed you."

"Why would she do that?"

"I don't know. There have been a lot of weird things that I don't know. I wish I'd never come to work on this movie. What kind of soup?"

"What?"

"The kid"—Clem gestured with her thumb—"she said eat your soup."

"Bean. Would you care for some?"

"I guess not. I'll get the magazines." She darted out, leaving the door open.

The rain had slacked off to a misty drizzle with an occasional fat drop falling from the eaves.

Minutes later, heavy footfalls pounded up the steps. Unless

Clem bought a ton of magazines, this wasn't her returning. Demarco got to the door just as Mac, Yancy's teamster buddy, ducked in with a vaseful of roses in one huge paw.

"Clem said give you these." He dumped an armload of magazines and tossed a small white envelope on the coffee table.

"Sweet of you to bring me flowers," Yancy said.

"Ha. If I cared, I'd bring you a six-pack of Millers. These are from Ms. Laura herself." Mac plunked the vase next to the magazines; jostled roses sprayed rainwater on the table. "I just pick up and deliver. You got any Millers?"

"Budweiser?"

"Bah, bad stuff. If that's all you got." He shrugged off his jacket and handed it over. Yancy passed it on to Demarco.

"Why is Ms. Edwards sending me flowers?" Yancy snatched a beer from the refrigerator.

"To show she's all heart." Mac opened and swallowed. "You don't look all that delicate. Aren't you supposed to have pale skin and shaky breathing, long-faced nurses standing by?"

He drank his beer, told a string of corny jokes, some of which were funny and didn't do Yancy's cracked rib any good, and when he left, gave Yancy a pat on the back that his rib took personally.

Just as Yancy picked up the cans to toss them, there was another knock on the door. And he'd thought making movies was tiring.

Demarco ushered in Serena, still dressed from work in green skirt and print blouse, and said he'd split for a few.

"How are you?" Serena sounded tightly wound and her face was a careful mask.

"Fine."

"I brought Mom."

"Hey, Serena, this is your brother speaking. Did you get dipped in brine on the way over?"

Her face crumpled. "You could have been killed."

"No, Serena, no. I'm fine, going back to work tomorrow. It's just a scratch. Nothing to get uptight about."

"Now look what you did. When Mom sees me, she's going

to be upset." She made quick jabs in her purse for tissues, dabbed at her eyes, and blew her nose. "I wish you'd quit this job."

"I can't."

"It's too dangerous."

He took her hand and threaded his fingers through hers. "It was an accident. Accidents can happen anywhere."

"It wasn't an accident. Somebody tried to kill you. Why do you have Demarco watching over you, if it was just an accident?"

"Serena—" He searched for the right words. All through their childhood they'd depended on each other for survival. If they hadn't stuck together, with their Looney Tunes mother they wouldn't have made it out as normal as they had. They were two halves. If one was gone, the other would be just that—a half.

"You duck out on me by getting yourself killed and I'll never speak to you again. You hear me? Mom's waiting. I wanted to see how bad off you looked before I brought her in." She blew her nose again. "Where'd you get the flowers?"

"The famous and beautiful Ms. Laura Edwards."

"You're kidding. Just a scratch, huh? Why then is she sending flowers?"

"Serena—"

"Yeah, yeah."

His mother rushed in, hugged him—too tight for his rib—and ran her hand down his cheek. "Didn't I tell you not to climb the apple tree?"

Over her shoulder, he sent Serena a look. Serena shrugged.

"Does your arm hurt?" His mother sat on the couch and pulled him down beside her. With a feather touch, she stroked his left arm.

She was back sixteen years to when he'd fallen and broken it. "You're a brave boy." She noticed the flowers. "I knew you'd like the roses. Serena said bring pansies."

Serena smiled sweetly at him and crossed her eyes.

"It's okay." His mother placed a hand on his face and looked puzzled.

"We need to go," Serena said. "Dallas is coming for dinner."

"You might see what's in the locket," his mother said. "That could be the answer."

"I'll do that, Mom."

She kissed his forehead.

As soon as they were out the door, Demarco came back. He was taking this guard dog stuff a little seriously. Yancy picked up the envelope Mac had delivered for Clem and opened it, assuming it would say something like "Get well soon."

Wrong.

Printed in block letters:

What was yours is now mine.
Waiting for the sun to shine.
The Lovely Beauty.
When it's right
This will bring the end of time.

24

Carefully, Susan inserted the poem in a plastic envelope. "When did this come?"

Yancy shifted uncomfortably in the chair. Patrol officers didn't like to be interrogated by the chief when they were sitting down; they preferred to be on their feet, even standing at attention.

"A couple of movie people were here," he said.

"Who?"

"Clem Jones. She's the one who takes care of everything for the director, requests and complaints, whatever he needs or wants. Mac Royce. He's Laura Edwards's driver."

"You must have made a great impression if the megastar sent flowers. Who else was here?"

"My mother and Serena."

"And the kid," Demarco said.

"Right. Stephanie Blakeley, the landlady's daughter."

"Mac Royce brought the note?"

"He dropped it on the table. I didn't open it until after he'd gone."

She sat down on the couch. "Now that you've had time to

think about it, is there anything you can add to what happened last night?"

"Uh—no." He looked embarrassed. "I saw an individual— To be accurate, I saw movement I *thought* was an individual go into the rear of the property at twenty-one twenty-nine Taylor. I knew the residents were away. I thought it was the mad painter at it again."

"You went after him."

"Yes, ma'am."

"You were intent on catching him and didn't watch your back."

"Yeah—yes, ma'am. I felt a push. Like someone was—like somebody had shoved me hard. I went down on one knee, lost my balance or got shoved again, and fell on the damn knife. That's when I knew this was not a good situation. I wasn't thinking about much else for a second or two. Then I realized my gun was missing. I expected to be shot. I heard my heart beat. Loud and clear."

Either the assailant thought Yancy was as good as dead or he was after the gun and didn't care whether he had a dead cop or not. The note indicated the gun was the target. "What else?"

He gave her a half smile. "On that bright and cloudless morning."

"What?"

"It zinged through my mind. 'When the roll is called up yonder, I'll be there.'"

"Anything else?"

"Footsteps."

"Which direction?"

"Retreating."

She closed her notebook and dropped it in her shoulder bag. "Well, you did catch the mad painter."

Yancy gave her a humorless smile. "He more or less caught himself when he crept up to see if I was dead."

"Could he be your assailant?"

"Possibly. He'd have to go through the rear of the property and around to the front to come up at me from behind. If he did, why would he come back and call for help? Oh."

"What?"

"I gave him my house key."

"Parkhurst has it. He checked the place out. As near as he could tell, nothing was missing. Unless you had valuable silver or stamp collections."

"The most valuable thing I own is a T-bone steak in the freezer. Is it still there?"

"I'll ask Parkhurst. He did send someone to collect Kevin's paint stuff. What's the poetry all about?" she said, circling around to where she came in. "Who's the lovely beauty?"

"Laura Edwards, I would guess."

"Why would you guess that?"

He looked at her like this might be some trick question. "I'm aware a nutzoid has been sending her threats. I assumed this was more of the same."

"Anybody come to mind? Always hanging around, getting too close? Someone who just doesn't smell right?"

"Smell," he said.

She waited.

"Why did I think of pumpkin bread?"

"When?"

"Just as I was stabbed."

"What do you associate with pumpkin bread?"

"Thanksgiving. Childhood." He thought. "Sophie the cat lady."

Susan smiled. Sophie baked pumpkin bread and brought it to those in trouble or grieving or feeling low. Or to people she wanted to find out more about. Snooping was almost as big a passion as cats. "Anything else?"

"Only that whoever wrote it is a bad poet."

"You know good poetry from bad?" That sounded surprised and horribly patronizing, which she could see he picked up on.

"Yes, ma'am, I do," he said with no hint of sarcasm. "My mother may be odd in many ways, but she knows poetry and she made me learn."

"If you think of anything else let me know. Otherwise, take it easy. Take a few days sick leave—"

"No, ma'am."

She raised an eyebrow.

"Uh—with your permission, I mean. I'd just as soon go back. If one of those movie people shoved a shiv in me, I'd like to know who. And—" He gave her a cockeyed grin. "This is hard to admit, but I feel a proprietary interest in this movie."

"You're not exactly one hundred percent tiptop."

"Close enough."

"I'll check with Sheffield and let you know."

Officer Demarco, trying to stifle a yawn, swallowed it when she looked at him. "Ma'am," he said.

A body could get used to all this instant respect. She reminded herself, before she got too carried away, that she didn't know what they said behind her back. "You've been here all day?"

"Since oh six hundred."

Overtime. Never did she expect to be concerned about overtime, except her own. "I'll see you get relieved."

"No problem. I'd just as soon see he's taken care of."

"Anything Yancy left out?"

"No, ma'am. I assumed the roses weren't dusted with deadly poison so I let them come in."

Ex-military, Demarco wasn't thrilled by a female superior; by playing single-minded, he got away with snide comments. One day, she was afraid she'd have trouble from Demarco.

Since she passed the hospital on her way to the department, she swung into the parking lot and went inside. At the nurses' station, she asked a young red-haired nurse to page Dr. Sheffield.

Seconds later, the PA system announced, "Dr. Sheffield? Dr. Adam Sheffield."

A man with muscles, dark curly hair, and a day's growth of beard burst through the stairway door. "You wanted to see me?"

"About Officer Yancy," she said. "Is he okay to return to duty?"

"You gonna have him doing sit-ups and fistfights?"

"I didn't have that in mind, no."

"As long as he keeps his ribs taped and doesn't try to run marathons, he should be fine."

Before she even got the pickup out of the hospital parking lot, the radio was chattering at her. "Yes, Hazel?"

"There seems to be a problem with Laura Edwards. She called in hysterics, demanding to see Ben."

"Where is she?"

"In her trailer out there on old Josiah's property."

"I'm on my way."

At base camp, rain soaked into the ground beneath all the trailers, trucks, cars, and vans. California summers didn't include rain; surely, whoever scouted this location had known it rained in Kansas at any time of year. The ground was already soft underfoot when she slid from the pickup.

"Where's Ben?" Laura demanded.

For someone who'd been having hysterics, Laura Edwards looked remarkably unhysterical; what she looked was pissed. Dressed in a tidy little black number that fit like skin, she stalked toward Susan on four-inch heels, a diamond—or what looked like a diamond—pendant hung on her creamy bosom. An exotic sight for a Kansas afternoon. Platinum hair was swept up with wispy tendrils on the sides of her beautiful face, now artfully made-up. She whirled and stalked away, giving them the backless view.

"I'm due on the set," she said.

Directors didn't simply sit around and wait for the sun to shine. Electricians, carpenters, drivers, props, makeup, wardrobe, and everybody else got paid whether they worked or not. After eight hours they got time and a half; after twelve, double time. And that was the least of it; car and van rentals, security guards, hotel rooms, catering. Every day of filming was horrendously expensive. Each day over schedule meant that much over budget, which explained why Fifer couldn't afford to stop shooting for somebody's murder. It cost too much. What little Susan knew about the movie industry came from occasionally working movie detail in San Francisco. She used to have a friend who'd become an entertainment lawyer and defected to Los Angeles.

"Ms. Edwards, could we sit down?"

Laura took in deep breaths, heaving bosom and all. Or tried. The dress was so tight, there wasn't much room for expansion. Susan hoped she wouldn't faint.

Laura debated, seemed about to keep stalking, then went to the couch where she was forced to perch.

"What's the problem?" Susan sat facing her and spoke softly.

"Mac."

The teamster handed Susan a Ziploc bag, inside was a piece of white five-by-seven paper that had been folded in half. Printed in block letters:

MY LOVE, YOUR HEART WILL FEEL NO PAIN
AND YOUR DEVOTION IS MINE TO GAIN.
THERE IS NO WAY TO REST OR SLEEP
UNTIL I COME FOR YOU TO KEEP.
WHEN YOU KNOW YOU LOVE ME BEST
THEN YOU'LL FIND BOTH PEACE AND REST.

A second plastic bag held the envelope it came in with Laura Edwards's name printed on it also in block letters.

And so we learn why the gun was taken. "Where did you get this?"

"Somebody gave it to me."

"Who?"

"Mac." It was more a snapping of her fingers than a question.

"It was handed to me by a kid on a bicycle. Girl. Thirteen, fourteen."

"What did she look like?"

"Skinny. Tan raincoat, hat pulled down. She said a cop asked her to give it to Laura."

"Did she say Laura? Not Ms. Edwards, or Laura Edwards?"

He chewed that over. "I think she said Laura Edwards."

Not that it meant much, but the more formal might mean an individual who didn't know her. "Would you recognize her?"

"Naw. Kids hang around here all the time."

Right. If Laura Edwards didn't draw them in, Nick Logan would.

"I thought it was from Ben," Laura said.

"Why would he send you a note?"

"I didn't give it much thought," Laura snapped. "I was dressing, going through the scene in my mind."

"What does it mean?" Susan tapped the note.

"Isn't that your job?"

It was, indeed. Yancy's gun, the note he received, and now this. Added up, they gave notice of a serious threat to Ms. Edwards's life. Strong indication she was the intended victim and Yancy only a means to that end. Time to circle the wagons. A thought darted across her mind like a bright fish: Delmar Cayliff and his wagon trains. "Who put this in plastic?"

"I did," Mac said. "The kid handled it, I handled it, and Ms. Edwards took it and opened it, but when she—"

Screamed?

". . . I put them in bags, for what it's worth."

Fingerprints needed to be taken for elimination purposes. Susan would send Osey. Taking prints was his idea of fun.

A knock, followed by a damp-looking second assistant saying Laura was wanted on the set, brought an end to the questioning.

"How many notes have you received today?" Susan asked Mac.

"What?"

247

"You claim you received this from a young female with a request to give it to Ms. Edwards. Earlier this afternoon you brought flowers to Officer Yancy with a note."

"Oh, that. Clem gave it to me with a stack of magazines. She said since I was going up, I might as well take them, she had to split."

To be certain she understood correctly, Susan repeated, "Ms. Jones gave you a note and asked that you give it to Officer Yancy."

Susan tracked down Clem Jones inside the mansion where the filming was going on. Distracted, paying close attention to the director and none to Susan, Clem said the kid asked her to bring the note to Yancy. What kid? The one who lives there. Lives where? Where Yancy lives.

And some days you just go round in circles. The *swipe-swipe* of the windshield wiper kept background rhythm as Susan tried to chivvy pieces along so they'd form some shape. Did these recent events clear Laura Edwards of suspicion? Nearly. Susan couldn't see her skulking around in the rain, skewering Yancy to lift his gun and hightailing it back to the hotel. One thing was clear. The intended victim was Laura, not Yancy.

These notes put another plus on the side of Parkhurst's non-involvement; he wasn't silly enough to be writing bad poetry, even on his day off. Where was he when Laura tried to get him? He had a perfect right to go wherever he wanted. Except in the vicinity of Laura Edwards. And that, of course, was the worry; he was out there somewhere, like the Lone Ranger, keeping guard.

The lady had been royally pissed because she couldn't get him. A suspicious person might suspect Laura didn't care, or maybe—for some reason of her own—actually wanted him to lose his job. Stupid of her. He was good at this job, and more than that, it gave him substance.

A leggy female, early teens, but tall for her age with straight brown hair to just past her ears, stepped out on the porch. "You mind talking out here? Mom's giving a lesson."

In the background, Susan could hear the piano being attacked by heavy hands. Lessons were definitely needed. Black clouds and off-and-on drizzle had turned summer daylight gray, drops hit the shrubbery around the porch with a *pit-pat, pit-pat.*

Stephanie, clearly excited by a cop asking questions, wasn't about to let it show. Cool was her stance. She was a typical small-town teenager, lovingly cared for, educated, with a bright future. Her worn shorts and droopy shirt didn't hide glowing health and good grooming. Less worldly, innocent even, in comparison with her big-city counterpart, and how could it be otherwise? In San Francisco, mothers got knifed in front of their kids, friends got mowed down in school yards, baby brothers or sisters asleep in their strollers got shot in the cross fire between drug dealers.

Stephanie was disappointed to be asked only about notes. "Oh, those. I gave one to that chauffeur guy just like the cop told me, and the other to that weird movie person to give to Peter."

"A cop told you to deliver the notes? How do you know he was a cop?"

Stephanie shrugged. "He said he was."

And this child wouldn't ask a cop for identification. "A police officer gave you two notes and asked you to deliver one to Ms. Edwards's driver and one to Officer Yancy," Susan said, making sure she got it straight.

"Yes. Actually, he said one to Laura, but people were all around, security guards and everybody, so I couldn't give it to her. I gave it to her driver."

"He said Laura? Not Laura Edwards or Ms. Edwards?"

"Yes."

"Where was this?"

"At the barn, this morning. They were filming inside. And of course they wouldn't let me in."

"How did you know her driver?"

"I've watched. You know, making the movie. Actually, it's mostly bor-ing. He brings her and takes her and everything."

"This cop. Did you know him? Was he wearing a uniform? What was he wearing?"

"A black raincoat. He was in a hurry, gave me the notes, and rushed off."

I'll bet he did. "Describe him for me."

"Hat. One of those floppy kinds, and he kept ducking his head and looking the other way. I don't even know if he was fat or anything because the raincoat was loose. He had on black shoes, they were getting all wet. He was probably about your height."

Since Susan was five eight and wearing two-inch heels, that made him around five ten. Maybe.

"You didn't take the note to Yancy yourself. Why was that?"

Stephanie stuck a cupped hand over the porch railing and caught drops of rain. "She came—the one with the funny clothes and white makeup—while I was there. And I forgot to give it to him. When I left, she came back down for the magazines in her car, so I thought—as long as she was going back up, she might as well take it."

Ah, Susan thought. Stephanie had a crush on Yancy and felt jealous when Ms. Jones trotted up to see him.

"Let me make sure I've got this right," she said. "A cop gave you two notes. One for Laura Edwards, one for Yancy. You gave Ms. Edwards's note to her driver and Yancy's to Ms. Jones? Is that right?"

Stephanie nodded.

Like the emperor said to Mozart, Susan thought, there are too many notes. She asked Stephanie to come in at some time and have her fingerprints taken.

"Cool."

25

*Y*ancy was thinking he shouldn't have been so eager about telling the chief he was great, rarin' to get back to movie duty. He felt stiff as day-old toast, and trying to shower without getting bandages wet was a joke. A good hard run was what he needed, work the kinks out. No running, no workouts, until the rib knit.

Stepping into uniform pants, he buttoned and zipped, buttoned up his shirt and buckled on his belt with the unfamiliar gun. Nothing better happen to this one or he'd never hear the end of it.

Stephanie, at four P.M., was sitting on the bottom porch step looking woebegone. "Hi," she said. The air was sticky hot with the worst of the day's heat.

"Hi, Steph. Anything wrong?"

She shook her head. "How come you're going to work when you're sick?"

"I'm not sick."

She scowled just like Serena used to when she was a kid. "You should be staying home."

"I can't do that. I'll see you later." From the Cherokee, he gave her a wave as he backed out the driveway. Adolescents, who knew what went on in their minds. Even themselves.

At the department, he picked up a radio, got a squad car, and set out for the mansion. As usual people stood around watching even when they should have been home eating their suppers. He got a call sheet from Clem Jones and ran his eye over SET/DESCR.

EXT. TREES BEHIND BARN

Billy fires at Sara.

Billy, of course, was the hit man hired by the bad guys, and Sara was Laura, the heroine who stumbled across the information that the bad guys had killed her father because he was going to turn them in for using banned pesticides.

COVER SET:

INT. JEFF'S OFFICE

Jeff was the hero cop.

Yancy didn't like this "Billy fires at Sara" stuff. He hied himself over to the prop truck in search of Robin McCormack.

"I told you," Robin said. "All firearms are kept locked in the safe."

"Bullets."

"IN THE SAFE." Robin sighed. "Look, this isn't the first shoot I've been on, no pun intended, and I've got nothing but blanks."

"Let me see them."

"Oh, man, I've got things to do."

"I can shut you down, which will give you lots of time. Now, open up that safe and show me everything you've got in there."

"This is really stupid, man. You think I don't know what I'm doing? You think everything isn't checked and rechecked before it's used? What's got in your soup?"

Robin dialed the safe's combination number, 5-7-3. Yancy, standing beside him, had no trouble seeing what he was doing. If this was how careful Robin was, no telling who had the combination.

"This is what he's going to use." Robin handed him a scope-mounted rifle. "And this is what he's going to be firing." Robin handed over the shells. "If you worried this much about who killed Kay maybe you'd have the bastard by now."

Yancy examined the stock, the trigger, the hand guard, and looked through the scope. He looked at each bullet, definitely blanks.

The Starbucks coffee he'd picked up from the caterer sent fully alerted nerves zinging to attention throughout his body. He moved around and got in everybody's way.

Billy, the villain, was getting some last-minute instructions from the director. Robin handed him the rifle. A black armed condor (metal structure painted black) stood taller than the barn with the light on top blazing. Yancy judged it could be seen four miles in all directions. Probably like the light God had used to shine down on Adam when He asked where the apple came from.

Yancy kept reminding himself Billy had a blank, he probably didn't know shit about rifles, and couldn't hit what he was aiming at in any case.

That went up in smoke when Billy took the rifle and handled it like he'd gone deer hunting all his life. Yancy's adrenaline level kept rising.

Sara/Laura, in a filmy white thing that Yancy assumed was a nightgown, stood by a tree waiting for the director's word. When he gave it, she ran. A path had been semicleared, at least enough so she could run among the trees. If it hadn't been, the chase would have ended about three steps after it began. There was too much in the way, fallen branches, dead leaves, and new growth covering the ground.

Sara/Laura, following the path marked out for her, crept

down a rise, darting from tree to tree. Billy, the villain, stalked. As fetching a sight as the heroine was in her nightgown, or whatever it was—peignoir?—Yancy kept his eyes on the rifle. Occasionally it glinted in the beam of light. Otherwise, it was simply a menacing shadow. Periodically, Billy brought it to his shoulder and looked through the scope.

Jeff/Nick, automatic in hand, was creeping after the bad guy trying to off him before he could put a round smack in the middle of the heroine's beautiful back. Standard movie stuff.

Every time Billy brought the rifle to his shoulder, Yancy's teeth clenched. He'd need a trip to the dentist if this went on much longer. Billy curled a finger around the trigger.

Yancy held his breath.

Billy brought the rifle down and stalked on.

The whole routine again. Stalking, sighting, finger around trigger. Finger tightening.

Yancy discovered it was impossible to take a deep breath with your ribs strapped.

Billy fired.

No recoil on the rifle. Yancy relaxed. Billy had fired a blank. That didn't mean that the rest of them wouldn't be live.

Two more shots. Blanks.

This bit of rifle to shoulder, fire, was repeated over and over. Yancy assumed bullets gouging chunks from trees, boulders, and the very ground beside the heroine would be added at some time, along with close-up views through crosshairs.

Right. They're making a movie here. All make-believe. Nobody's getting shot.

Sara/Laura, face frozen in fear, kept just one step ahead of the bullets. Billy, the villain, expression of a job to be done, relentlessly followed.

Jeff/Nick, the hero, expression of worry, was just a bit too far behind to be of any use. Bit by bit, he was gaining. Finally he fired his automatic. He wasn't close enough to hit anybody and he wasn't aiming, but hey, he was firing like all good heroes.

Fifer kept shooting the scene, even after the pink light of dawn bled into the clouds. Yancy paid close attention to the villain's rifle and the hero's handgun. Sara/Laura shivered realistically with cold and fear, and maybe for real. Early morning chill hung in the air, but wouldn't go on much longer. With yesterday's rain feeding the humidity, it would be humid in spades when the sun got going.

Coffee in hand, Yancy moved around, getting dirty looks from the crew.

"Hey!"

A shot. Two more in rapid succession.

Yancy was a split second slow in responding. He was still in fantasyland.

Oh, Christ!

He tossed the coffee cup and ran.

The spectators scattered. People screamed. Mac, trying to shield Laura Edwards, hustled her toward her town car. People ducked, crouched, darted. Or just looked around in confusion as though they were uninformed of this change in script.

Like a Keystone Kop, Yancy waded into the middle of it, gun in hand. A guy with a handgun was aiming at Laura.

"No!"

The guy fired.

Like a movie scene, Mac looked at his arm in surprise, clapped a hand around it, and watched blood seep through his fingers.

"Put the gun down! NOW!"

Sun, tipping over the rise, spilled golden light into the hollow. Looking directly into it, Yancy saw little more than a silhouette.

"NOW!"

The sniper ran.

Yancy chased. "Police! Stop!"

The gunman ran straight into the sunlight. Yancy stumbled over the rocky, uneven ground.

The guy tried to run uphill, slipped on wet grass, and almost fell. He recovered and dashed left.

With no breath to yell, Yancy kept after him. The sniper ran flat out. Not a smart thing to do on this terrain: holes, rocks, and pockets of rainwater waited to trip up the unsuspecting.

Yancy slowed, fighting for air.

The gunman stumbled, sprawled on the ground.

Yancy sprinted. "Don't move! Stay right where you are!"

One knee on the back of the guy's neck, Yancy grabbed the gun. "One . . . twitch . . ." he panted, "you're . . . dead . . ."

Yancy's lungs felt on fire.

"You're hurting me."

Yancy holstered his gun and fumbled for cuffs, got one wrist cuffed, and thought he'd expire before he got the other. Finally, he managed to bring the other arm around.

Head hanging like a spent horse, Yancy worked on getting air without breathing deeply.

"Could you get off now?"

Wondering how he was going to get himself upright, Yancy eased pressure from the guy's neck.

"How am I going to get up?"

"Well, pal, you're on your own." Yancy could almost breathe again, but fire still locked his chest. "At least till I know whether I'm going to die."

"The grass is wet."

This was true. Yancy could feel it through the knee of his pants. "Roll over and sit up."

"I can't."

"Hold on." Yancy pulled out his radio and spoke to the dispatcher.

"Okay, pal, let's go." Yancy flipped the gunman over. It was the weird history teacher from the hotel. Delmar Cayliff.

With a little help, Cayliff managed to sit. Cracked rib protesting, Yancy got him to his feet.

The gun was his, Yancy was glad to see, but after this, no

telling how long before he'd get it back. They went down the rise a whole lot slower than they'd gone up.

Everybody watched, spectators, crew, actors, directors, and probably the squirrels in the trees.

Fifer said quietly, "Cut."

Everybody clapped. Yancy felt like a complete ass.

26

"Were you trying to be a hero?" What was it about cops? Like teenagers, they thought they were invincible.

Yancy stood more or less at attention in front of her desk. He wasn't ramrod stiff, she thought, only because of pain. At least he wasn't turning pale from hemorrhage caused by a rib puncturing a lung.

"No, ma'am."

She thought he was more embarrassed than anything, but that didn't mean he wouldn't do the same thing again.

"Get yourself over to the hospital and have Dr. Sheffield take a look at you?" She sat down in her chair and made a shooing motion. "And, Yancy—?"

He turned.

"Good work, but if you've done any damage to yourself . . ." She let it hang.

"I don't think I would have been so stupid . . ."

The expression on her face stopped him and he put a lid on it. After she called the hospital to check on Laura Edwards's driver, alerted them Yancy was coming, and went down the hallway.

Delmar Cayliff waited, sitting in a molded plastic chair in the interview room. Parkhurst stood outside looking through the glass. "He hasn't moved."

"He ask for an attorney?"

"He refuses one. He's going to be his own attorney. He's more intelligent, according to him, than any attorney he could hire."

"Oh, boy." Why couldn't the guy just make it easy on everybody and agree to an attorney? He was a lunatic who should be locked away but care had to be taken so they didn't trample on any civil rights. It might be claimed he wasn't able to make this decision for himself. If they didn't get this one put away, he'd kill somebody.

When she opened the door, Delmar Cayliff looked up and smiled. "I've been here two hours, forty-five minutes, and sixteen seconds," he said. Not angry, not threatening, simply matter-of-fact as though she'd asked and he wanted to be accurate.

"Do you know where you are, Mr. Cayliff?" She went around the table and sat down across from him.

Parkhurst, arms loose at his sides, stood behind.

Delmar gave her a superior smile. "The Hampstead Police Department. Hampstead, Kansas. Two miles from the Sante Fe Trail."

She turned on the cassette recorder, stated her name, the date and time, mentioned Parkhurst was in the room, and stated Cayliff's name and read him his constitutional rights. "Do you understand these rights?"

"Yes, I do."

"Do you know why you're here, Mr. Cayliff?"

"I'm not stupid, Ms.—excuse me, *Chief*—Wren. You don't have to talk to me in words of one syllable. I'm educated and I'm intelligent. I have a doctorate in American history. So many people—Americans—don't know anything about their own country. The Sante Fe Trail runs not five miles from where we're sitting. How many people know? How many people even know what it was for? Do you know?"

His eyes stared down at the table or gazed past her shoulder.

"Why did you come to Hampstead?"

"Laura my beloved, of course. The princess of heaven in my heart and the desire of my dreams. Our love in the spring holds enchanting visions of our walking together through the gardens of magnificent palaces."

"You assaulted a police officer."

"The spirits guided me. The most humane way to kill her."

"Kill who?"

"Laura my beloved. We are one. She is mine and I am hers. Hand in hand, we will walk through the flowers of all colors. They helped by telling me where."

"Who helped?"

"The colors." Short, sharp, as though he'd been perfectly clear and she was slow.

"Are you married, Mr. Cayliff?"

"No."

"Ever had a girlfriend?"

"Only Laura my beloved. She is my soulmate."

"How did you know Laura would be working in Hampstead?"

His smile flickered on and off. "*Variety*, of course. Filming on location in Hampstead, Kansas. I had to make sure we'd be together, but I didn't know how until the spirits told me."

"They told you to kill Officer Yancy?"

"To get his gun, so she wouldn't suffer."

"You understand you've been arrested?"

"Yes, yes, read my rights. Mirandized. Isn't that what you call it?"

"You understand what that means?"

"I just said so."

"At any time during this interview, you can stop and ask for an attorney. Do you understand?"

"I don't need an attorney. The plan is finished." Loud, irritated.

Parkhurst, behind him, straightened, alert and ready.

261

"Tell me the plan," she invited.

"I've already confessed," he said. "Freely, with no coercion. I stabbed the police officer to obtain his gun." Delmar wanted to make that clear. He had no animosity toward the police, he simply had to have the gun. "I shot Laura. Now." He looked around. "I need my backpack. It's all in there. It's perfectly clear." He was getting agitated.

"We have it, it's safe. Tell me your plan."

His eyes flicked over her rapidly and found a spot on the wall behind her. "First, I need surgery for correcting nearsightedness. That's very important. Eyes are the mirror to the soul. Glass— or plastic, even polycarbonate—disfigure the soul. Why aren't you taking notes?"

"You said you had it all written down."

He nodded. "I don't know if I can remember every detail."

"You're doing fine."

"This mole must be removed." He rubbed his wrist. "It saps my strength. You see the color? Brown. Brown allows all the inner strength to flow from the body."

"I see."

"I've thought this out very carefully, and the spirits have guided me. I could have committed suicide, but that wasn't right. In court, my plea will be justifiable homicide, and I'll ask for the death penalty. The only stipulation is, I must choose the prison. Our new life has to start correctly. I haven't decided yet. I have a list. It's in my backpack. I really need my backpack."

"You can give me the list later."

"It's very important." He clenched and unclenched his hands. "It's the beginning of phase two."

"What was phase one?"

"Laura's death," he said sharply. "I confirmed my love for her by her death. I have to follow the plan exactly. Arrest . . ." He nodded at Susan. "Prison . . ." He was getting agitated again.

Parkhurst watched closely.

". . . my trial . . ." He calmed down. "I will act as my own attorney, and I will be convicted." He took a breath and his eyes darted around the room.

"I understand," Susan said.

"You don't understand." Voice raised.

Parkhurst took a step nearer.

"That's only the end of phase one. It's all in my notebook. I have to have my notebook."

"Don't worry, Mr. Cayliff. The notebook is being kept in a safe place."

"I have to have it."

"Tell me more of your plan," she said.

"It isn't my plan." He was losing patience with her stupidity. "It's the universe. I had to figure out what the universe wanted. It took a long time and the spirits got angry if I got it wrong. After I'm convicted, I have to be executed by firing squad. One expert marksman with a Springfield 30.06. Facing me, he'll put a bullet just above my right eye, then one above the left eye. He will move to my right side and place one just above the ear. Two in the back of the head, and the final bullet on the left side just above the ear."

"Tell me about Kay Bender," Susan said.

"I don't know anyone by that name."

"She fell from the hayloft and—"

"I killed her." Hands against his face, his fingertips rubbed his temples. "She looked like Laura my beloved. The spirits were confused. I had to remove her."

"How did you kill her?"

"The railing. I cut through it. And put the pitchfork where she could fall on it. It had to be done."

"Why did you kill her?"

"She was trying to be Laura my beloved, invading her soul."

"Where did you get the saw?"

"One of those trucks," he said.

"Who was there while you cut the railing?"

"The spirits wanted me to be alone." He leaned forward and whispered to the table, "I know he's there."

263

"Who?"

"The officer standing right behind me. I can sense him."

That may be the only sane comment Delmar had made since he was brought in. "He's there to listen to this interview. What else can you tell me?"

"The actress who was stabbed."

"You know her name?"

"Of course, I know her name. I told you I'm not stupid."

Susan had deliberately waited to ask about Sheri Lloyd, wondering if he would mention her.

He gave another one of his small superior smiles. "Are you going to ask me if I killed her?"

"Did you?"

"Yes. It had to be done."

"Why did it have to be done?"

"She was making Laura unhappy. That would have messed up the plans. Laura had to be happy when she died."

"Where did you get the knife?"

He thought a long moment. "I don't want to talk anymore. I have a headache. Would you get me some aspirin, please?"

Susan leaned back and let Parkhurst ask questions. Delmar Cayliff refused to say anything more. He refused the help of an attorney. Earlier, he'd been eager to make her understand his plan; now he was through talking. He didn't want to waste any more time. He wanted to join his hand with Laura's in heaven. He wanted his backpack with his notebook.

Susan had Ellis and White take him away. Her mind playing over Cayliff's statement, she wandered along the corridor to the soft drink machine before realizing she had no change with her. Parkhurst stuck a hand in his pocket, brought out a handful of change, and held it out to her.

"You want one?" she asked.

"Sure."

She took enough coins and thumbed them in the slot. One can rumbled down, she gave it to him and collected the second. A few weeks ago, it would have been nothing; now it was awkward. Stupid. There was no emotional significance in taking quarters from his palm. Yeah? Then why did she feel stiff, why did he look stiff?

"Have you seen his backpack?" she asked.

"Not yet."

"Let's take a look."

Five minutes later she dropped Cayliff's backpack on her desk. The front pocket held a topographical map, a hardback, and a paperback both about the Sante Fe Trail. Inside the main section, there was an album with pictures—news photos, glossy studio giveaways, and snapshots, some blurred and grainy, some clear, taken without permission with a zoom lens, clippings, articles about Laura and reviews of the movies she'd been in. There was a bag of trail mix, a roll of clove Life Savers, a pair of white socks, two bottles of water, and a notebook, bluish gray, a three-ring binder like kids used for their homework, filled with ruled paper. In tiny, neat script, he'd written minutiae of his daily existence and the cosmic meaning of it all. On the day he'd gone to the bank, he'd endorsed a check with the bank's pen, it had black ink. Later he'd seen a movie with a character named Black. Black was a murky color meaning the universe wasn't pleased with him, he wasn't trying hard enough. Another movie, a western, had a Wells Fargo stagecoach. His bank was Wells Fargo. The evening news reported a child had fallen into an abandoned well. This meant the spirits were with him and wished him well. Stopping at a red light behind a red car was a double warning; the spirits were angry. A right turn followed by spotting the street sign GOLDEN AVENUE appeased the spirits.

Susan flipped pages until she came to the third of June, the day of the stuntwoman's accident. "She had to die. She looked too much like Laura my beloved. The spirits were confused." Three pages of colors with the descriptions these colors meant for the moods of the spirits, and explanations of why these moods affected the universe. Many pages of detailed plans to kill Yancy and take his gun, all to remove Laura my beloved from this world with the least suffering.

Susan quickly scanned pages and found, "She's stabbed. She can't upset Laura my beloved now."

And June 7. "It's done. The gun's mine. The time is now. I'm coming, Laura my beloved."

"The mayor will be happy," Parkhurst said.

"Yeah," Susan said.

"You can have Osey get on television and tell the world how we captured this guy with diligence and careful police work."

"Yeah."

"He confessed."

"Yeah, he did. Did you think there was anything odd about his confession?"

"The man is a nutcake. Everything about him is odd."

"Yeah."

"You don't sound overjoyed considering you just cleared a very high-profile case."

She wasn't. She was uneasy about Cayliff's confession. Inconsistencies abounded.

"You inform Ms. Edwards," she said. "I'll handle the press."

27

$\mathscr{A}$s Parkhurst shifted the Bronco into gear and pulled out of the lot, he glanced at his watch. Four o'clock. Laura was probably at the hotel. He felt guilty about her and guilty about Susan. Susan had said stay out of it. He'd been as much as lying to her and she knew it. Disobeying a superior hadn't ever been a conscience-heavy matter. Going soft?

Going stupid. Being his superior wasn't the half of it, being Susan got all tangled in there. He could hear his father say, "Hey, chickenshit for brains, you a coward too?" A real sweetheart, his old man. "If you're not man enough to go for it, you're no son of mine."

Aw, Laurie, what are you doing back in my life?

Leaving the Bronco in the hotel parking lot, he weaved through cars and went inside the Sunflower. On the fourth floor, he got off and went to Laura's suite.

Before he could knock, the door opened and Nick Logan stormed out. Seeing Parkhurst, Nick turned and called into the suite, "Your Mountie's here."

Parkhurst thought throwing him against the wall with a forearm across his throat and jabbing one quick punch to the gut was just the thing to let out a shitload of frustration.

"Ben—?" Laura, face shiny clean like she'd just taken a shower, started toward him, arms extended, then hesitated. "What's the matter? You look ready to punch someone. What is it with the male sex? You always want to hit each other."

He half smiled. There was something very clear and pure about rage. You knew what it was and you knew what to do with it. You hit someone. If you were like the old man, you battered your wife and beat up your children. If you were one of the children, you told yourself you were better than he was. You might even have believed it until an ex-wife came along and reminded you you weren't better, simply not a drunk and you had better control.

Laura laughed, a light sweet sound, and walked into his arms, put her hands on his face, and kissed him softly. He was wrong about the control.

"Laura—"

Her arms slipped around his neck, and she breathed into his throat. "I see you haven't forgotten me."

An inner voice ordered: throw her over your shoulder, march into the bedroom, and toss her on the bed. He cupped a hand behind her head and kissed her soft lips. Lightly. Control. Oh, yeah.

"You want to hear the latest from the cop shop?" His voice was hoarse.

Anger flashed up in her blue eyes so quickly, he thought she'd yell at him. She didn't, she slapped him. Not a ladylike tap or a choreographed move, she hauled off and landed a flat palm across his face hard enough to make his teeth clack.

"Hey. What was that for?"

"You know what it was for. For being a prick, for pulling away like you always did, for hiding under your cop shell." Tears filled her eyes.

"Laurie—" He gathered her in his arms again, smoothed back her gold hair, and murmured apologies.

She smiled up at him. Awareness, forgiveness, promise—all in a three-cornered smile. The inner voice again. Throw caution to the winds.

In front of the police department, Susan looked, she hoped, suitably serious and spoke, she hoped, with suitable solemnness. Lights blinded her, mikes bristled in her face.

"Have you arrested the killer?"

"Who is he?"

"What's his name?"

"We have a man in custody," she said.

"Did he kill two people?"

"Does he know Laura Edwards?"

"What do you know about him?"

"Why did he want to kill Laura Edwards?"

"Would you describe him as a stalker?"

"We're not releasing his name at this time," she said.

"Does Laura Edwards know him?"

"Is he a friend?"

"A boyfriend?"

"At this point, we haven't interviewed Ms. Edwards. She is shaken up over the incident. We'll have a great deal more information after we've spoken with her." Susan slipped back inside, as questions were shouted and microphones shaken.

At her desk Delmar Cayliff's notebook waited and she went back to it. By seven o'clock, she was still at it. She squinted, rubbed her eyes, and leaned back, then leaned forward, snapped on the desk lamp, and kept reading. Where was Parkhurst when she needed him? Probably having a jolly little reunion with his ex-wife.

Susan wanted a cigarette. Come on now. No reason he couldn't do anything he wanted, reunite with anyone he pleased. So get your mind where it belongs.

Every entry was dated and the time noted. The first rambled on about Laura Edwards, the movie being filmed in Hampstead,

269

and the many instances that the universe was with him. When he made the decision to come to Hampstead, he wore a blue shirt and saw a blue car with the letter B on the license plate. These were important signs that told him the universe approved his decision. Whatever he did, wherever he went, he made these minute little connections.

In Hampstead, he watched all the outdoor filming; indoor shots, he got as near as he could and watched from there. Getting hired as an extra was big proof the universe applauded his venture.

On Monday, June 3, the day the stuntwoman had died, Delmar had been with other spectators outside old Josiah's barn. Even though he couldn't see any of the filming, it was enough for him to see Laura arriving. He went on for several pages about her love for him and how she looked at him and her plea that he make it possible for them to be together.

The stuntwoman received a brief mention; her attempt to look like Laura upset the spirits.

Susan couldn't define the difference between spirits and universe, except spirits tended toward bad and the universe toward good. The spirits brought fear when the universe wasn't pleased. The entries were hard to read: rambling, convoluted sentences started with one subject, then shot off onto something else. A single sentence was often more than a page in length. Pronouns were used without thought to antecedents, and much of the time only Delmar could possibly know what he was writing about.

In the middle of the next page, she found, "The impostor is dead." That was all, unless "like the sounds of locusts" had reference to sawing through the loft railing. In Delmar's world everything symbolized something. What a very exhausting world he must live in.

She tried to scan pages, but the smallness of the writing and the crowding of words made it impossible. There were a dozen or more pages on the decision that Laura Edwards must be shot, that being "the most humane" death. Pages on the decision to kill Yancy to obtain his gun, and how this would be done.

Pages of despair when he'd not succeeded in killing Yancy in the trees by the river, fear that the universe had turned against him. How in the hell could this man hold down a job? And isn't it grand that someone like him is teaching our college students? Detailed account of Delmar following Yancy, being chased by the dog, pages of the actual stabbing and taking of the gun.

The labyrinthian paths of a psychotic mind were awesome to behold.

On the night of Sheri Lloyd's murder, he wrote about being on the Patio. Yancy's mother, "the quiet woman with knowing eyes," several paragraphs about the "vicious, dangerous dog," pages about Laura and Nick Logan, and Sheri joining them. Imagined looks of love and pledging eternal fidelity from Laura. Her anger at Sheri Lloyd had been twisted into anger at Delmar for taking so long to claim her. No mention of a teenager. The following day, he wrote, "She can no longer upset Laura my beloved."

They could get him for assault, attempted murder, stalking, and a number of other things, and a damn good thing to get him off the street, but—never mind his confession—he hadn't killed the stuntwoman and Sheri Lloyd. Forget the questions about how he could have known where to find the saw and the knife, and forget that he thought he'd killed two people—Laura and Yancy—who were still alive, every tiny detail as mundane as what he ate for breakfast while he was planning to kill them was written about. One line about the stuntwoman and one line about Sheri Lloyd? No way. If he'd killed them, he would have written pages and pages before he did it, and pages and pages afterward.

They still had a killer out there.

Yancy tracked down Dr. Sheffield in the ER. Midmorning on a Sunday, the place was almost deserted. All the bad folks were sleeping it off and all the good folks were in church. The doc was sewing up a little boy who had fallen on some pieces of broken glass. When the boy was handed back to his mother, Sheffield turned to Yancy.

"Does this hurt?"

"No."

"How about this?"

"Yes."

"Any fever?"

"No."

"Bleeding?"

"No."

With a warning to avoid mad sprints until the rib healed, Sheffield scribbled a prescription for pain, told Yancy he was allowed limited duty, and rushed back into the fray.

Yancy was curiously relieved. After seeing this movie through two murders and the stalking of its star, he felt entitled to see it through to the end. He wanted, with his thumbs hooked in his belt, to watch the whole caravan leave town.

After tracking down Mac's room number, he dropped in. Mac, hands behind his head, left biceps bandaged, ankles crossed, was stretched out on the bed watching a soccer game on the television mounted on the wall.

"Well, well," Mac said. "The walking wounded." He clicked off the television. "What? No flowers? No grapes?"

"I thought I'd see how bad off you were before I spent my money."

"Huh. That quack down there in the emergency room claimed the bullet only grazed the skin. Didn't even tear up a muscle. Now, how am I going to get sympathy and workman's comp with that?"

"Isn't it a fine movie tradition that it only hurts when you laugh?"

"As a comedian," Mac said, "you might be a good cop. I keep telling them I'm in terrible pain, but they're going to boot me out of here tomorrow morning anyway."

"As a patient, you'll never get compassion."

"Oh, ha ha. The soccer game was better than this."

Yancy left him to it and headed back to the department to turn in the squad car and pick up his Cherokee. Since the chief's light was on, he went in to relay the news that the doctor had given him a halfway clean bill of health.

Susan threw her pen on the desk and leaned back. "Changed your mind about giving anything to get out of this assignment?"

He smiled, his sweet soft smile. "I think I might miss them when they're gone. I did talk to Howie—uh, he's the assistant manager at the hotel—"

"And?"

"Well, I don't know if it's of any interest at this point, Kevin Murphy—"

"Garbage-can-painting high school football star. What about him?"

"He's been hanging around the hotel. He replaced the battery, like he said. Once he jump-started a van when the lights had been left on all night. But he's been there other times, just to be there."

A seventeen-year-old kid, football star or not, might be interested in the glamorous movie people. Anything more than that? Maybe it was time to go home. She couldn't get her mind interested in picking at ideas.

"Put yourself to bed, Yancy. I can't help wondering if Dr. Sheffield is an idiot, but if he says you can report for duty, who am I to argue?"

She gathered her scattered thoughts and Delmar Cayliff's notebook. The notebook she took to the evidence room, the thoughts she took out to her pickup. The air was velvet and fresh. She rolled down the windows and let the night blow in around her. In San Francisco, darkness could be an enemy, hiding danger. Deep blackness gathered in narrow streets, inside sad houses, and around cluttered corners. Desires and frustrations mingled like explosive chemicals and traces hung in the night air. Given the propensity of fellow cops for twisted humor, Susan had never

admitted to fear, especially fear of the dark, but had used her fa-
cade of cool poise to carry her through. Even more than a year
here didn't let her accept thick darkness as benign.

This damn case. Back to the beginning. God damn it. She
smacked the steering wheel hard with her palm. Someone wanting to kill Laura? Stuntwoman and Ms. Lloyd got in the way.
Laura wanting to kill stuntwoman or Sheri Lloyd?

The kitten was glad to see her when she opened the kitchen
door. Perissa, twisting around her ankles, nattered about neglect.
She dumped fishy-smelling stuff in a clean bowl and set it on the
floor by the refrigerator. As is often the case with love, the kitten left her for something better, food in this instance.

The answering machine blinked about messages; Susan ig-
nored it. She felt two steps behind; this was not a feeling she liked.
We've collared a stalker, she consoled herself. He's confessed.
Yeah, yeah, I've been all through that. I don't think he did it.

So now what? Back to the beginning. Start over. Yeah, I've
been through that too.

Well then, how about a drink? The sharp bite of alcohol to
cool the frustrated brain. A bottle of chardonnay stood in the refrigerator. Naw. In vino, muddled mind. She passed up the tall
cool bottle and moved on to leftover pizza. She never was much
of a drinker; her drug of choice was nicotine, and she'd given that
up. Sometimes, like now, she wondered why. The microwave
beeped a summons and she put steaming pizza next to the *Herald* that she unfolded on the table. The state of the wheat crop
didn't hold her attention, nor did the quilting exhibition or the
proper feeder for purple martens.

Laura Edwards in close proximity to Lieutenant Parkhurst
kept bringing images to mind. Ah yes, well. None of her business. If she ignored famous actresses with cop ex-husbands and
the ties that bind, Kevin Murphy was something to think about.

Sullen, angry young man. Impeccable manners, polite to parody. Complex, filled with hatred for the entire adult world. High
school football hero. Beaten by his father—according to

Parkhurst—retired test pilot. Smart. Poor grades. An extra in *Lethal Promise*. Is any of this interesting? He'd made a name for himself with his garbage-can art and getting dubbed the mad painter. How much more of a name would he make by murdering Laura Edwards? He might have been at the hotel the night Sheri Lloyd was stabbed. Somebody was—a young person, a teenager. It could have been Kevin. Why had Sheri been killed? The answer might shed light.

Yancy's mother had also been there. Raina had left with her dog and started walking home. She'd been picked up by Kevin Murphy. If Kevin had just killed a woman would he stop to pick up Raina and her dog? Unless Parkhurst's instincts were off, Kevin had picked them up to irritate his father—big hairy dog in pristine car.

She scooped up strings of cheese and popped them in her mouth, swallowed and took a swig of orange juice. Her watch said eight-thirty. Too late to drive out and talk with Raina Yancy?

Yes. She was going anyway. Raina probably wouldn't remember the young person/teenager, but Susan intended to ask.

The little brown Fiat, sitting in the garage next to the pickup, could use a wash; it was so covered in dust, the paint didn't even gleam under the light. She drove it barely enough to keep the battery charged and didn't know why she didn't get rid of it; a reminder of another life maybe. She climbed in the pickup.

The just-past-full-moon poured silver light on fields of wheat that rippled in the wind like the sleek muscles of a running predator. The stars blinked in and out of slow drifting clouds. A jackrabbit on the side of the road sat up on its haunches and turned its large ears like antennae, listening for enemies or judging the safety of crossing the road. She slowed and watched it bound past on its powerful hind legs.

Beyond her headlights, moonlight softened the night. The dense darkness out here on moonless nights made her uneasy. A city creature, she felt safer with neon and two-legged animals than with darkness and four-legged ones.

After more than a year here, she was getting better at finding rural places. Having been to the Yancy house before helped, but even so she missed a turn and had to backtrack.

The house, on a rise with a pale glow inside, sat in an island of darkness. Little house on the prairie. The dog barked, and an outside light came on. She cut the engine, but sat where she was as the dog streaked like a demon toward the truck. It danced around, leaping up to stare her in the eye.

Yancy's sister, standing at the kitchen door with the screen open, called to the dog. It gave one last menacing leap and galloped back to the house. Susan slid from the truck, hoping the hound had been fed.

"Chief Wren?" Serena came toward her, dog at her side. "What's wrong?"

"Nothing. I'm sorry, I didn't mean to frighten you. I know it's a little late, but—" The dog came at her. She froze, understanding very well why Delmar Cayliff was afraid of the beast.

"He's very friendly," Serena said.

Right. Elmo shuffled up to her, licked her hand with a soft tongue, and led her into the kitchen. Maybe he was friendly. "I wanted to ask your mother a few questions, if she's still up."

"Oh, sure, she's reading."

"Pretending to read, more like," Raina said. She sat in the overstuffed chair by the window. "Reading isn't what it used to be when you can't remember what you read on the page before." Fear and frustration sat just below the light words.

"You remember Chief Wren," Serena said.

"Please sit down. I'll get some iced tea."

"No. Thank you." Susan sat on the couch and dropped her shoulder bag at her feet. "I'm sorry to disturb you, but I have a couple questions to ask."

With a great sigh Elmo spread himself at Raina's feet; she reached down and smoothed his ears.

"I was here around four days ago."

Raina nodded. "The young actress who got killed."

"You saw her earlier in the evening, before she was stabbed." Raina reached up and turned off the lamp on the end table. "Look," she said.

Out the window, Susan saw a jackrabbit, ears visible over the flowers. She wondered if it was the same one she'd seen on the road. If so it had gotten here almost as quickly as she had.

"They're timid," Raina said. "When they're frightened, they run. They've got long teeth for eating plants—they're—oh, what is that word—"

"Herbivores?"

"Yes. They're not rabbits really, you know, they're hares. Those teeth are made for tackling plants. They've got long claws on their front feet, to pull plants and strip them. They move fast, but if they're trapped, they're not bunnies. Foxes have been known to make that mistake and gotten blinded and gutted. Even a mountain lion has lost its life by trapping one in its lair."

Raina sat in shadow, her profile highlighted by light coming from the kitchen. She looked young and beautiful, her voice soft. She might have been telling a fairy tale to a child, or a witch weaving a spell. "That's what it was, don't you think? Desperation."

Susan shook herself back to her purpose here. "Do you remember being at the hotel?"

Raina blinked, then said, "I've been there many times. Peter says watching the movie being made is boring. Maybe, but it's interesting."

"Do you remember Tuesday evening?"

Raina smiled. "Sometimes I can barely remember my name."

Susan felt a rush of liking and respect for this woman. No wonder Yancy was bent on protecting her. She was charming in what must be to her a devastating situation. "You were on the Patio. Sheri Lloyd was there."

"She was angry, poor little thing. To get her own way, she threatened someone."

"Who?"

"Vengeance was in the air."

"Vengeance?"

"Vengeance is in my heart, death in my hand,
Blood and revenge are hammering in my head."

"Kevin Murphy," Susan said. "Did he have vengefulness in his heart?"

"Oh, yes. Definitely." Raina reached down to stroke the dog's shoulder. "He offered us a ride. Nice of him, even though his purpose wasn't to be nice."

"Was he on the Patio that night?"

"No."

Raina was certain, but how much reliance could be placed on her memory? "Who else was there beside the actors?"

"A very troubled young man. He was afraid of Elmo."

"Anybody else?"

"Not that I can think of."

"Was there a young person there? Maybe teenaged?" Leading the witness, Susan.

Raina thought. "You know I believe there was."

"Who was it?"

"That girl, the one who lives where Peter does. I forget her name."

"Stephanie Blakeley?"

28

$\mathcal{Y}$ancy pulled himself out of bed Monday morning, sat on the edge, and let his hands prop up his head. Why, having been given the opportunity, did he not snap to and take some days off. What? And leave show business?

After an unsatisfactory shower, he pulled on his uniform pants, shrugged into a shirt, buckled on his belt, and went stiffly and creakily down to his Cherokee. At the department, he turned it in for a squad car and set out for . . .

He didn't know where they were filming this morning. That information was on the call sheet, which he'd left at home. He had the feeling this wasn't going to be a great day. He went back to retrieve it. The crew call was six A.M. His watch said 5:45.

Location for shooting was the stable at the Lockett mansion. Fifer had Kevin Murphy, shirtless, mucking out a stall, the muscles showing off nicely in his back and shoulders. He did a good acting job, Yancy thought, didn't look at the camera, didn't ogle the stuntwoman, did exactly what he was told. Sullen expression perfect for a kid who has to work when he'd rather be swimming with his girlfriend. He led a horse from the stall, tied it to a ring, then loaded dirty straw in a wheelbarrow. Howie, however, should stick to the hotel business. He was supposed to drive up and park. That's all. Except he couldn't seem to stop the car at the right spot. After several tries, Fifer dismissed him. Yancy was afraid his friend Howie's movie career was over.

Fifer filmed the new stunt double leading a horse from the stable and tossing on a saddle. As she reached under the horse's belly for the girth, footsteps were heard. She straightened. Guess what? The villain. The stunt double cinched up, leaped on the horse, and galloped away.

That sequence was filmed over and over. Then Fifer did some shots of Laura Edwards standing by the horse, curry brush in hand. It was obvious she wasn't happy to be there. Any actual brushing was done by the stuntwoman, long shots and close-ups of hands and the horse's glossy hide. Even then only the neck and shoulders were touched, the hindquarters were left strictly alone. The horse looked bored.

The morning dragged on with the horse brought out of the stall, taken back in, and brought out repeatedly. No wonder it was bored. It seemed an amiable chestnut who knew his part well, until Laura got near; her tension made the horse uneasy and it continuously stepped away. Either that or the horse had a sense of humor.

When Fifer judged the light was wrong, he called a halt. The predicted twenty percent cloud cover had him in short temper, and he made changes in the schedule and shifted everybody inside the mansion for interior scenes. The crew followed orders without chitchat, praying for the clouds to dissipate. Yancy snagged coffee from the caterer. There was nothing wimpy about California coffee. If it didn't jolt him into serious clear-mindedness, nothing would.

That wasn't cloud cover up there; it was the beginnings of rain clouds. Most likely another thunderstorm was on the way before the skies got brighter. Whether Fifer knew or not Yancy had no idea, but Yancy wasn't going to tell him.

"Gotta talk to you," Robin said to Yancy on one of his trips back and forth to fetch props.

Fifer snapped at Clem because the AD—not Clem's fault—had herded Laura onto her mark instead of the stand-in. Laura threw a fit, went back to her trailer, and wouldn't come out.

Nick, the unflappable professional, flubbed lines over and over on a scene Fifer was trying to shoot without Laura. Robin McCormack forgot a vital prop and had to go back for it. A light blew with a pop that sent everybody six inches off the floor. One take was going along fine, cast and crew just beginning to relax, when a camera jammed.

Fifer went very still, his face hardly moved when he spoke and his voice held the menace of a disturbed rattler. Everybody immediately got so tense a pin dropping would have shattered them like a footstep on thin ice. Yancy, caught up in the tension hanging like low-lying fog, was soaked with sweat, oppressed by the humidity, and limp as a rag. His rib hurt. Fifer called an early lunch break and everybody split like lightning.

In the caterer's tent, Yancy slid next to Mac, who had his left sleeve rolled up above the bandage on his biceps. A plate piled with ravioli, salad, and chunks of bread sat in front of him.

"How's the arm?"

"Hurts," Mac said.

"You couldn't wrangle a few days off?"

"I'd rather keep an eye on things." Mac tore off a chunk of bread and shoved it in his mouth.

Odd, Yancy was under the impression Mac didn't like Laura Edwards. What did he want to keep an eye on? "What's wrong with everybody today?"

After washing down a mouthful of ravioli, Mac said ominously, "Jinx."

"What?"

"Movie people are suckers for superstition. All of them; cast, crew, hired hands, above the line, below the line. They believe this movie is jinxed and they all tiptoe along looking over their shoulders waiting for the crouched beast to spring."

Yancy hadn't known Mac was so poetic. "You too?"

281

"Naw. I do my job, get paid. Don't have my ego nailed to the floor."

"Unless something happens to Laura Edwards while you're driving her somewhere."

"Better me than her." Mac tapped the gauze on his arm. "Fifer, who knows what that one thinks. He's spooky, is what he is."

Yancy circled the tent looking for Clem. He found her in the rear, drinking lemonade and looking miserable.

"You okay?" he asked.

She spun around, face shutting down like a window closing. "Don't creep up on me like that."

"I wondered if you were all right?"

"Why wouldn't I be?"

"Some people get upset," he said mildly, "when they get yelled at for something that wasn't their fault."

"I'm used to it." She stomped off.

Filming in the afternoon was a repeat of the morning—scene after scene went wrong, lines were forgotten, words were garbled, doors wouldn't open, or wouldn't stay closed. Fifer got more and more deadly quiet, which rippled out to cast and crew until everybody was ready to run shrieking into the woods. Yancy included.

There was no chance to talk with Robin, and when Fifer finally called a halt Robin couldn't be found. Yancy decided to try base camp.

Robin was waiting at the prop trailer. "Listen," he said, "there's something you should know. A pair of handcuffs is missing."

"Handcuffs are missing," Yancy repeated.

"Yeah. You deaf or something?"

Yancy looked around at the long, crowded prop trailer. "You're sure?" He found it hard to believe that Robin knew anything was missing.

"It's my job to know," Robin said, a mite irritated.

"Guns missing?"

"Hell, no. All you people ever think about are guns. Guns are locked in the safe. None missing."

"Why would anyone steal a pair of handcuffs?"

"People are nuts. Some actor uses it, they want it. Don't ask me why. We can't even have snapshots developed at the local quick photo place, because some jerk off says, 'Hey, that's Nick Logan' and prints up two dozen extra copies to pass out to his friends."

"What can anybody do with handcuffs?" Yancy was talking more to himself than to Robin.

"Handcuff someone. Hang the cuffs on the wall, put them in a box under the bed. Who the hell knows."

"Where do you keep them?"

Robin opened a chest drawer, five pairs of cuffs lay inside.

"When were they taken?"

"I can't tell you. I had them in a bag with a bunch of other stuff we were using. Sometime this afternoon, I noticed they were gone."

Yancy walked up and back looking at boxes and bins of props, chewing over missing handcuffs.

"I just wanted to let you know. Could you ruminate somewhere else? I'd like to lock up and get out of here?"

"Sure." Yancy clattered down the metal stairs. Nobody was left except the security guys. He nodded to them and wandered around stepping over electrical cables. Something was nagging at him.

"The Blakeley girl's in the interview room," White said.

Susan looked up from her desk. "Her mother with her?"

White smiled. "Stephanie was playing tennis at Broken Arrow Park. I asked her if she'd like to come with me."

White, with his blond hair, round face, and apple cheeks, looked like a Boy Scout. Even his severe crew cut didn't detract from the image. He wouldn't scare anybody.

Susan tucked in her blouse and went down the corridor. "I

need to ask you some questions, Stephanie." She put an edge in her voice.

Stephanie Blakeley turned from the mirrored glass that she'd been studying. At thirteen, she was tall for her age, almost as tall as Susan, and it was easy to see how, in a dimly lit area, she could look in her late teens. A loose T-shirt covered a thin boyish figure. Her brown hair with tawny streaks reached just past her ears, and could be worn by either male or female. Hazel eyes, clear and intelligent, were right now wary and frightened.

"Sit down, please," Susan said.

Stephanie slid onto a chair, and turned wide-eyed when the Miranda rights were read to her.

"Why didn't you tell me you were at the hotel the evening Ms. Lloyd was killed?"

The girl pushed her hands through her hair. "I know I should have." A basically truthful child, this one, and relieved to be clearing her conscience. "I tried to tell Peter. Two days ago. But he looked so—you know, not feeling good and that other cop was there."

Demarco looked like a marine with matters of national security on his mind. No teenage girl would be quick to confide in him.

"Tell me now."

"I was there. Does my mother have to know?"

"You were there without permission?"

Stephanie stared straight ahead like a cadet being disciplined. "Worse. She said I couldn't go."

"Why did you?"

Stephanie sniffed and rubbed a finger under her nose. "There was no reason why I shouldn't. I wouldn't be late, it wasn't a school night. How many times will a movie be made here? I wanted to be around where the actors might be. I wasn't going to talk to anybody, or ask for an autograph or anything. That would be exceptionally gross."

"Then why go?"

"You'll think I'm silly. Childish."

To a teenager, there was nothing worse than being thought childish.

"I'm going to be an author." There, she'd said it. Make ridiculing remarks if you want.

"And?" Susan carefully kept the word neutral.

"I wanted to observe. See what they were like."

Susan put her through questions. When Stephanie accepted that she wasn't being thought childish, she answered easily, but she didn't have anything to add to what Susan already knew. She sketched out the scene with colorful detail. This girl might, indeed, be a writer. Unlike the others, she didn't think Delmar Cayliff was ordinary. She thought he was creepy.

"How did you get to the hotel?"

"I rode my bike. Mom doesn't want me to ride it after dark. It's got lights," she hastened to add.

At that point, Susan would have let her go, except something still sat on her mind, something that wasn't going to be volunteered and Susan wasn't quite sure how to get at it. "What happened on your way home?"

"Well—"

Right question.

"You know that curve on Arbor Street down by the quarry?"

Susan nodded.

"It's sharp, and right there where it sort of bends there's that flat field behind the fence before you come to where it drops off. Anyway, I was riding right at that bend when a car came roaring straight at me. I got pinned in the headlights. All I could think, I'm going to be killed and my mother will know I went out."

"Who was driving?"

Stephanie hesitated.

Susan let her struggle with it.

"I'm sure he just didn't realize how—" She let that trail off, not even believing it herself. "Anyway, when he saw me, he jumped on the brakes, they screamed, and the car fishtailed all over the place."

"Who was it?"

"Kevin," she said after another struggle. "Then he kind of got control and drove off and I came home."

Stephanie sighed. "I figured maybe I'd just stay home next time."

After she let Stephanie go, Susan sent White out to bring in Kevin Murphy.

In the interview room, Kevin slouched in a plastic chair, hands in his pockets. He smelled faintly of horses, having been picked up at the Lockett stables where he'd just finished making his movie debut. He'd pulled on a tank top, tight enough to outline the muscles in his chest. Not nervous, not scared and maintaining his parody of politeness, he looked at her with faint mockery.

"What happened to your eye?" She leaned against the wall, one knee bent.

With fingertips, he touched the fading bruise by his left eye. "I ran into a door."

"Again? First a nosebleed, now a black eye. Clumsy."

"Yes, ma'am, I certainly am."

"On the night Sheri Lloyd was murdered, you were driving your father's car. Tell me again what you did."

"I got off work and went home to shower. Later I started out to see a friend, and then decided not to."

"When you got home from work, you had an argument with your father." She made it a statement, not a question. "He struck you. You took his car. You weren't going to see a friend. Where were you going?"

He raked hair from his eyes. "Just driving."

"With your father's permission?"

Amusement flickered in his eyes. "Not exactly."

She sat down across from him. He drew back and hung an elbow over the chair.

She leaned forward. "He hit you, you got angry and drove away in his car. Weren't you afraid he'd report it stolen? Your emotions were so intense you nearly killed a girl on a bicycle."

"I never got near her."

Due to his young and extraordinary reflexes. "What were you trying to do?"

"See how fast I could take the curve."

"The girl says you weren't trying to make the curve, you were coming head-on."

"She's mistaken."

The kid had been going to kill himself. Susan was at a loss about what to do.

She looked at him. "He would have wept," she said softly. "And everybody would have believed him."

She waited, then went back to it. "You drove around, picked up Raina Yancy and her dog, got blood on the steering wheel and the gearshift." Osey'd also found blood on the door handle and the driver's seat. The shirt Kevin had worn was splattered down the front and there'd been blood on Raina's white skirt—even though it had been washed—as well as on Kevin's handkerchief. It was all his blood. At least, it was all the same type as his. It wasn't Raina Yancy's type and it wasn't Sheri Lloyd's.

He looked at her, no squirming, no blustering. A bright young man with looks, artistic talent, athletic ability.

"You're free to go," she said.

He stood, pushed the chair back up to the table, and walked out.

There might have been time for him to follow Sheri Lloyd to her room and stab her, then go home, get smacked around by his father, and drive off. Except. Except. Why? Sheri might have been snooty to him; she was snooty to everybody she felt beneath her.

And the stuntwoman? A mistake, an attempt at Laura Edwards. Why would he want to kill Ms. Edwards? Well now, let's see here. Perhaps Laura Edwards killed the stuntwoman and Kevin killed Sheri Lloyd. And the stalker stalked.

Sure.

Sitting at her desk, she let her mind drift, coaxing thoughts from the murk on the bottom to float up. She wasn't one fact closer to a solution. One person dead, perhaps by mistaken identity. Another stabbed. Nothing mistaken about that. A stalker who confessed to both deaths. She shuffled papers until she found the autopsy report on Ms. Lloyd. Except for being dead, she was in great shape. Heart and lungs perfect. Kidneys and liver perfect. No diseased tissues anywhere. No traces of drugs beyond a small amount of alcohol in the stomach. The phone rang.

"Yes, Hazel?"

"The mayor is on the line."

"Tell him I'm not in. I'm not available, unless it's important. In which case I'll be at home watching movies."

"Excuse me?"

"Keep it to yourself."

At the video rental place, Susan picked up *When the Rose Blooms* and *Family Style* and *My Sister's Friend*, the movies Raina Yancy had watched on Wednesday. Popcorn? Sure. What's a movie without popcorn. She threw in a box of microwavable popcorn and two Hersheys with almonds.

At home, Perissa, rapidly becoming more cat than kitten, greeted her with loud complaints of neglect and hunger.

"No way," Susan said. "It's not even two o'clock."

She zapped the popcorn, stacked pillows on the couch, slid in *Family Style* starring Laura Edwards and Nick Logan, and settled the bowl on her stomach. Katie/Laura goes home for parents' anniversary. Runs into old boyfriend Greg/Nick. Lots of unfinished family business, snappy dialogue, and touching moments of reality, happy ending.

Where the Rose Blooms, a thriller, also starred Laura Edwards and Nick Logan. Julie/Laura, your normal everyday fabulous beauty, gets threatening messages via her computer. Fast-paced with heart-stopping moments and car chases. Julia/Laura does have long blond hair and somebody does try to stab her. Could this have been the basis for Raina's comment about the woman stabbed?

The third movie had Ms. Edwards but not Nick Logan. Heartwarming with social significance and tear-jerking scenes.

Just as it came to an end, the kitten leaped on her stomach, knocking over the bowl and sending popcorn flying. Susan yelled, the cat got frightened, the remote got lost, and popcorn got all over the carpet.

On hands and knees, Susan gathered kernels and flung them in the bowl. Perissa, thinking this great fun, scooped them out and batted them across the floor.

"That's it, cat. You're an orphan."

The credits were rolling before Susan rescued the remote from under the couch. She watched the names scroll by and told the cat. "Oh, my. Art director."

Perissa approached her sideways, back arched.

"Just kidding," Susan said.

29

Justin Wesley Kiddering the Third. The only person Susan knew down there in Los Angeles living shoulder to shoulder, or maybe acre to acre, with the rich and famous. It had been over ten years since they'd spoken, and in fact, it was entirely possible he wouldn't want to talk with her now.

His father, Justin Wesley Kiddering the Second, was the owner of everything that made money, shipping, land, fishing, stocks. His mother, in pearls and silk blouses, always had her picture in the paper on behalf of every charitable organization worth its name.

The Kidderings lived several blocks up in class, status, and size of residence from Susan's family. He was a rich kid whose father gave him everything the wealthy are entitled to by birthright. Susan was the one who had first started calling him Just Kidding. They were buddies from the time they were eleven. He was tall, blond, and square-jawed, as befitted the heir to the throne.

In high school English class, she wrote his papers. Kiddering the Second wanted him to go to Brown, but he held out for UC Berkeley to be with her.

He went to law school because she did and he didn't have any burning desire to study something else. It wasn't as though he had to earn a living. They studied together, shared notes, and divided topics for research. They hung out in coffee shops that stayed open late, impressing each other with their intelligence, their grasp of humankind, and their free-thinking ability to get to the heart of the problem.

The Big Plan was to open a law firm together and take on causes, raise banners for the underdog and downtrodden. Even at their most committed, she thought they were only playing a fantasy. Shortly before graduation, they had a fight. She told him she was chucking it all to be a cop. A shouting fight followed; he stomped off. She felt he was secretly relieved; he wasn't cut out to take care of the poor. That was the last time she saw him. She signed on with the San Francisco police force and he took his law degree down to southern California and made his name recognized in the entertainment industry.

It was 7:30 here, that meant 5:30 in California. Possibly still in his office. She couldn't believe how shaky her hand was when she picked up the phone. Information gave her an office listing. That number gave her a secretary with a British accent who said Mr. Kiddering was not available, she would be pleased to take a message.

"I'm a police officer investigating a homicide. Tell him I'd greatly appreciate a few moments of his time."

"That's a new approach," she said in her bored, high-toned voice. "I'll pass your message to him."

Even after all these years, Susan recognized his voice with no trouble. "This is Susan Wren," she said.

"Yes?" His voice was cool, approaching Siberian borders. She didn't know if it was because he didn't recognize her or because he did. Oh, hell, why did she use that name? Of course, he didn't recognize it.

Nervously, she cleared her throat. "Susan Donovan."

There was dead silence on the other end of the line. Maybe he didn't want to talk to her, maybe he was still angry.

"The thud you heard," he said, "was my mouth dropping. This is the time for some devastatingly clever remark, but damned if I can think of one. Damned if I can think, actually. How long has it been?"

"Ten years."

"Didn't I stomp out saying something embarrassing like you'll regret this?"

"Something like that."

There was an awkward silence.

"Jesus. Susan. Could you call back tomorrow? Give me time to work up some great lines?"

"Same old Just. Too much class to ask right out, What the hell do you want? You think I called for something deplorable like Mel Gibson's autograph."

He laughed. "You would never be so mundane."

There was another silence.

"To get this conversation rolling, fill me in on the last ten years." He sounded so Hollywood, she would have laughed, except she was afraid it might sound too high-pitched. "Aw, come on," he urged. "To make it easier, pretend like you're giving me a pitch for a new sitcom."

"Well, the night after graduation—"

"Not scene by scene. Just give me the story line."

"I thought you should see motivation to get the essence—"

"Nobody in the Industry talks about essence. We deal strictly in T and A or violence. You got married?"

"You connect violence with marriage?"

"Ex-wife number one did. But not till we got into the divorce."

"How many wives have there been?"

"Only two. The second was very civilized about the divorce."

"Children?"

"Let me think. Yeah. Two, I believe, the first time and one the next time. Does that make three? With a little more thought I could give you their ages. It gets confusing because the ex-

293

wives came with their own. When you jumble them together, you have a hard time remembering which ones are which. You said you were married."

"Yes."

"He died?" Just asked softly.

"How did you know?"

"I still know you. You froze when I asked about marriage. I'm sorry."

"Thank you. Actually, I called for a reason."

He gave a theatrical sigh. "Not just to talk over old times? Are you still one of those"—he lowered his voice and spoke like a broadcaster—"men and women in law enforcement."

"I'm the chief of police."

"No shit? Congratulations. That's terrific. Not San Francisco, or I would have heard."

"Hampstead, Kansas."

"Where?"

She laughed, then told him about *Lethal Promise* being filmed in Hampstead. "I called for information: fact, fiction, conjecture, and gossip. Do you know the director Hayden Fifer?"

"Everybody knows who he is, of course."

"Of course."

He laughed. "Was that a nasty crack?"

"No. Well, maybe a small one." It was difficult talking with a long-ago lover and she suddenly had more sympathy for Parkhurst. You fell right back into the old patterns and then you remembered. What a mess. She shouldn't have called. "Do you know anything about this movie?"

"As a matter of fact, I do. I was involved at the beginning on behalf of some of the moneylenders. Big budget film that keeps getting more and more over the huge budget it started with. A not-very-original script. A thriller–love story about a beautiful sophisticated woman who came from farming stock. Her father, the farmer who has some poetic affinity for the wonderfulness of the land and growing things on it, is killed. Woman finds out an evil agribusiness is destroying local flora and fauna by whatever destroys these things—unsafe and unlawful pesticides probably. Evil agribusiness types have to kill her too. She goes to local law enforcement who say she's nuts. Except for one guy who doesn't really believe her, but falls in love with her. She gets hunted down, chased, shot at, a gratuitous car chase or two. Somewhere she realizes the land, or maybe it's the prairie—I forget—is a sacred trust and must be preserved. The bad guys are about to win. The local cop risks life, limb, and career to save her. End on a romancy shot which suggests happily ever after."

"Romantic walks through the wheat fields?"

"It's probably in there somewhere. I only hit the high spots. Or maybe it's horseback rides through the meadows."

"Is it a good movie?"

"Depends what you mean by good. Will it be intellectually stimulating, full of socially significant questions with or without answers? No. But it should be exciting, funny, moving, and—above all—entertaining. That's the kind of film Fifer does. His last two weren't successes, so he has a lot riding on this. The man himself—"

"What are you thinking? Anything might help."

"For a hotshot director, Fifer has a reputation for being anxious. He's known for his retakes, and not keeping track of dollars. With so much riding on this movie, I'd say he must be *really* anxious and ready to do anything to make it work. Three or four marriages, the usual."

"How did he come to direct this film?"

"Two reasons. Laura Edwards and Nick Logan. Both top of the heap big box office. They have a love affair that's been given much play. Investors were elbowing each other out of the way to get in line."

"Is Laura Edwards good?"

"Have you read a paper in the last five years? Don't they have movies there? Yes, she's good, but she has a tendency to overemote. The director needs to sit on her, make her do what he wants."

"Personal life?"

"Actors—the big ones—don't have a personal life. The public wants to know when she eats, where she frolics on the beach, and who she sleeps with. She's been married a couple of times. Once, come to think of it, to some hometown boy."

She wondered what Parkhurst would think of being referred to as a hometown boy.

". . . childhood sweetheart, or something. Married a pennyweight agent whose name escapes me. I'll bet he drinks himself to sleep every night for letting her get away. He never had or ever will have somebody of her stature. The usual scandals about happily married male throws away wife and family for her. *National Enquirer* stuff."

"Nick Logan?"

"He can act. The viewing public may not know it because he isn't doing Shakespeare or Ibsen."

"Why isn't he, if he's good?"

"Money, darling."

"Rumor, gossip, innuendo?"

"He gives the impression he's an easygoing man, but he's got a temper like a killer bee. He's pushed around a few media people. Smashed cameras. Doesn't like to hear the word *no*. Got a divorce to engage in the romance with Laura."

"His wife upset?"

"It's all very civilized here. We're all still good friends who love each other. She's a model, says the accepted thing, it wasn't working out, she still loves him."

His voice faded and she heard Ms. British Secretary in the background, saying Mr. Anklet was asking how long it would be.

Justin said, "Tell him I'll be right with him."

"You have a client waiting?"

"Naw. I just told Phoebe to say that so you'd be impressed. Are you impressed?"

"Is his name really Anklet?"

"He's changing it from Bracelet. What do you think?"

"I think you haven't changed. Your kids must find you a riot."

"They're great. When can you come meet them?"

"Next time I come to L.A. Right now there's an art director I want to ask you about."

Yancy's rib began to pinch a little as he tromped around base camp. He was telling himself to go home, uneasiness was for movie heroes. *Hear that? I don't hear anything, it's quiet. Yeah, too quiet.*

He was headed over to his squad car before he realized it wasn't quiet. The air conditioning in Laura Edwards's trailer gave out a monotonous hum. She could have neglected to turn it off. If so, it was apt to overload and give out.

Her town car was gone, all the vehicles were gone except the van belonging to security. Yancy knocked on the trailer door. He knocked louder, at the risk of disturbing the female star, if she were inside and busy, like getting it off with a dear friend. Nick Logan's car was also gone, but who knew.

No answer. The air conditioning droned away. He tracked down the security guy. "You know if Laura Edwards is still in her trailer?"

"Not to my knowledge. Far as I know nobody here but me and my partner."

Yancy would have thought it was his job to know these things.

"What're you doing here?" the guard asked.

Wandering around when I should be home. "The air conditioning's on. That happen often?"

"Not to my knowledge."

"You got a key for these trailers?" Yancy asked.

"You think they'd just hand out keys to Laura Edwards's trailer? You been smoking something funny?"

With the guard dogging his heels, Yancy checked every trailer, all quiet and locked.

"You report in at certain times?" Yancy asked.

"Sure. Every two hours. I have an hour and a half to go."

"Call your boss. Let me talk to him."

"I can't do that."

Yancy rubbed a knuckle up and down his forehead. "You see this uniform? See any difference between yours and mine? Right. If it helps you any, you can say I've got you at gun point."

The guard sighed, to show he wasn't doing this willingly, took the cell phone from its holster and punched a number. Yancy was beginning to be a believer in cell phones; they surely were handy.

The security guy handed it over to him. Yancy explained his problem.

"You might have a problem, but I don't. Maybe she wants it cool when she comes in," and hung up.

Maybe he was right. Go home. Yancy went to the Sunflower instead.

"Howie, I'm looking for Ms. Edwards. Is she in her room?"

"I don't know. Why?"

"Put me through to her room."

"We're not supposed to—"

"Just do it, okay?"

Howie started to argue, gave it up and a few seconds later said, "There's no answer."

"Try Nick Logan."

No answer there either. They probably went out together. Oh hell, forget it. He took the elevator to the fourth floor and rapped on the door of Ms. Edwards's suite, then he tried Nick Logan's.

He was overreacting here. There was no reason Ms. Edwards had to be in her suite, or answer phones or knocks even if she was in. He went back down the elevator and hiked along the corridor to the coffee shop.

"One?" The waitress was a college student with an inviting summer smile.

"I'm looking for someone?"

"Who?"

"Famous movie stars."

"They're not here." She waved her arm to indicate the almost empty room.

He could see that. He checked out the Patio; nobody there either. In the lobby, he left a message with Howie to have Mac call him, then headed for the department to turn in the squad car and pick up his Cherokee.

If the Lieutenant or Osey had been in, Yancy might have mentioned it to them. Might have. Even he was beginning to think he was stirring up a bunch of nothing. He took himself home.

Stephanie was sitting on the steps looking morose.

"Hi, Steph." He sat next to her. "What's the matter?"

"I wish I were older."

"Why? Thirteen's a good age."

"Don't patronize me."

"I'm sorry. Tell me what your problem is."

"You wouldn't understand."

"I might. You could give me a try."

She drew up her long legs and rested her chin on one knee. "Do you like living here?"

"Sure," he said, wondering where this was going.

"You think you could like my mother?"

"I do like her."

"You know what I mean."

"It doesn't work that way, Steph."

"How does it work?"

"Poets have been writing about it forever, right?"

"She's older than you are anyway," Stephanie said glumly. "She's overprotective. If she had somebody else to focus on, she wouldn't sit on me so much."

"What is it you want to do that she won't let you?"

"Have you teach me to shoot a gun."

Oh. He wasn't surprised Mrs. Blakely wouldn't allow it. She was totally against firearms.

"Could you ask her for me?" Stephanie asked.

"Oh, Steph, I don't know about that."

"See, I told you you wouldn't understand."

Upstairs, he phoned Mac, who didn't know where Ms. Edwards was. She'd dismissed him earlier this afternoon.

"She told you she didn't need you?"

"That's right. Why?"

"She told you herself? Didn't ask one of her flunkies to tell you?"

"Her assistant. What are you getting at?"

"Probably nothing." Yancy hung up and rubbed the back of his neck. He was getting all worked up over air-conditioning. Ms. Edwards might claim all sorts of concern about the environment, but when it came to her own comfort, she might not give a damn, like the guard said, left it on so the trailer would be cool when she came back.

He sat in the overstuffed chair, untied a shoelace, and slipped off the shoe. He hesitated, blew out a gust of air, and put the shoe back on.

"Got a date?" Stephanie asked as he trotted down the steps.

"Cop stuff."

"Take me along. Maybe I can help."

"You'd be bored. I'm just going to check out the mansion."

Another waste of time, he figured, but he was making sure Ms. Edwards wasn't on a set working with Nick on a scene before he laid this in Osey's lap and listened to Osey laugh.

The place was locked up tight. He walked the outside perimeter, nothing out of the way. Locusts were warming up for the evening. A red-tailed hawk made lazy circles in the blue sky. His rib was beginning to remind him it didn't like all this activity.

Okay, that's it, go home.

He tramped around toward the squad car, then looked over at the stables. Oh, hell, being this far, he might as well give a look there too. Gravel crunched under his feet as he followed the path.

He slid back a door and stared right into the barrel of an old Colt .45.

30

"You couldn't mind your own business."

He couldn't, and that was a fact. Nor was he totally surprised to see who was pointing a revolver at him.

Another thing he couldn't do was draw his eyes from the barrel. It wasn't steady. It downright wavered. Nerves wriggled in his chest like a sackful of garter snakes. Stomach muscles tensed in a futile attempt to deflect a bullet. His rib didn't bother him a bit.

"Help me!" Laura Edwards, hanging with hands cuffed to a metal ring affixed to the wall, twisted and struggled. She still had on the leather pants and vest she'd worn for the filming earlier.

"Come on," Yancy said. "Don't do this. Give me the gun."

"Shut up!"

"Let her go."

"Shut UP!"

"Okay." He held his hands up, palms forward.

"Take out your gun. Slowly! Lay it on the floor." The barrel of the .45 nuzzled up against Laura's neck. "Do it! I'll shoot her."

Laura, face white, eyes wide with fear, froze.

Fancy thoughts tumbled through his mind. Draw and fire.

Movie-style stuff. Laura'd be dead before his finger reached the trigger. "Okay. Stay calm. What are you doing? Tell me what's going on." Gingerly, he laid down his gun. This was the second one he'd given up. If he lived through this, he'd never live it down.

"Step away from it."

He took one step to the side.

The .45 gestured.

He took another. Laura whimpered.

"Now your radio."

He hesitated.

"Do it!"

He unclipped the two-way radio from his shoulder and set it on the floor.

"Take it easy now," he said.

The .45 boomed like a cannon.

$\mathcal{H}e$ left his wife to be with Laura and the wife killed herself in the best movie tradition," Justin said.

"I believe you have cleared up a very puzzling homicide." Susan shifted the phone receiver to her other ear.

"You mean all that was true about murder investigations? It wasn't just a ploy to get me interested?"

The irritating *click-click* of an incoming call broke in, she asked Justin if he could hold a second.

The call was dispatch. "Yancy just requested backup."

"What's going on?"

"I don't know. Too much static interference."

She better send somebody up to check that birds weren't sitting on the communications tower again.

"I couldn't make out more than who was calling before there was a gunshot."

"Where is he?"

"Unknown. Osey's going out to scout."

"Tell him to pick me up. Stat." She got back to Justin. "Thanks," she said. "I have to go, something's come up."

"Hey, you're not going to leave me hanging, are you? The least you could do is let me know what this is all about."

"When it's cleared."

A phone call to Yancy's place got no response. She checked her gun, slid it in the holster, and clipped it to her belt. She was waiting on the curb when Osey pulled up in a squad car.

"Anything?" she asked.

"No. I'd like to hit the overheads and the floorboard, but I don't know where to hare off to."

"Any filming going on at the moment?"

"I don't know."

"Go out to the base camp."

Even without the lights, he zig-zagged through town and churned up mud on country roads. Base camp was quiet, Yancy's Cherokee wasn't around, the security guard came ambling toward them when they slid to a halt.

"Help you?" he said.

Susan asked about Yancy.

"Well, he was here, back maybe an hour. He got a nut in a vise about air-conditioning being on. Used my phone and didn't give it back."

Susan looked around at the trailers. "What air-conditioning?"

"Ms. Edwards's trailer, over there."

Sure enough, the air-conditioning on Ms. Edwards's trailer was humming away, only hers; the rest were silent.

"Is it often left on?" she asked.

"Tell you the truth, I don't know, but your cop didn't think so. He thought there was something fishy about it." He related Yancy's actions.

Like Yancy, she wanted his boss. Unlike Yancy she was insistent, and more clout got the guard's employer chasing out a skinny, worried production assistant with keys to the trailers. Susan tried Ms. Edwards's first. It was cool inside, but otherwise uninteresting. No tables knocked aside or chairs tipped over. No blood spatters.

Much to the disapproval of the PA, she made him open all of

them. While some were messier than others, none had been tossed, nothing indicated a struggle. She thanked him.

"Old Josiah's barn," she told Osey when they got back in the squad. She picked up the mike and told dispatch to send a unit to the Sunflower to ask questions of guests, staff, movie people, hangers-around, ask if anyone had seen Yancy, when they had last seen him, if they knew or had any idea where he had gone. Ditto for Laura Edwards.

The barn stood tall and solid, a monument to the past. Empty, quiet, except for the whisper of ghosts of Josiah's ancestors. Neither Osey, nor she, could find evidence of blood.

"Where now?" Osey said, his face tight with anxiety.

"His apartment. Maybe we can *detect* something."

Mrs. Blakeley refused to unlock the door for them. Osey, with country-boy charm, convinced her, without saying why, that they had a reason. Reluctantly, she agreed. Susan wanted to shake some speed into her as the woman slowly climbed the outside stairs and opened the door. She stood aside to let them in, and watched while they did a quick walk-through and then a closer look.

For all the good it did them. Nothing, not a hint, not a scrap, not a smell of where Yancy was, or the trouble he was in.

"Thank you," Susan told Mrs. Blakeley who carefully locked up behind them.

As they were crossing the sidewalk toward the squad, Stephanie came rolling up on her bicycle.

"Is something wrong?" She propped the bike with one foot on the ground.

"We're looking for Officer Yancy," Susan said.

"Is he hurt again?"

"We just need to talk to him."

"You know where he is?" Osey asked.

"Have you tried the mansion?"

"Why there?"

"That's where he said he was going."

———

To Susan's ears, she sounded like an elephant thrashing through the woods.

Osey had dropped her a mile away, and though she was hardly mountain climbing, the hill was thick with trees, the footing covered with fallen limbs and dead vegetation made slippery by recent rain. New growth covered whatever she might be stepping on. The air was damp and sticky.

From the crest of the hill, she had a partially obscured view of the back of the mansion about fifty yards straight below, and to her left an even more obstructed view of the front of the stables approximately a hundred yards west. She breathed heavily.

A gravel path about a half mile long led from the stables to the road. It was shortly past eight-thirty, and not quite dusk, but soon it would be. Mosquitoes hovered. She stumbled over a hidden root and the crushed plant sent up a pungent odor that cut through the earthy smell of rotting leaves.

Damn Yancy for going off without backup. With Justin's information, she'd finally worked out what was going on and before she could move on it, Yancy had walked right in.

Oh, Christ, don't let him be dead. Not Yancy with his sweet smile and soft voice. Not Yancy, young and idealistic. Smart and quick and sensitive. And inexperienced. If she'd been sharper and faster—what happened to all her experience?—Yancy wouldn't be in trouble.

She was afraid to use time working out a plan. She couldn't get hold of Parkhurst, and none of her officers were experienced in hostage situations. She didn't dare risk radio communication in case the suspect had Yancy's radio.

A stable door slid slowly back. Whoever had opened it was caught in interior shadows and she couldn't see who it was. She eased her gun up, eyes fixed on the door.

Nothing happened. Dusk was creeping in.

A jeans-clad figure with a denim shirt led a chestnut horse with white stockings from the stable. Saddle and halter, no bridle.

Susan squinted, straining to see.

The figure retreated into the stable and the light went on.

The horse stood patiently, ears flicking, looking around as though trying to determine what he was supposed to do. The figure came out again, took the horse by the halter and started walking, then stepped aside and let the horse continued on his own.

Oh, for heaven's sake. Somebody was going through training sessions with the horse. She had come tearing out here, sneaked through a wilderness with lethal mosquitoes, gotten snags in her shirt, twigs in her hair, and mud on her shoes to creep up, gun drawn, on a horse trainer.

And they still didn't know where Yancy was.

In the act of reholstering her gun, she froze.

Oh, dear God.

The horse walked along the gravel path with the trainer walking beside it. A rope, tied to the saddle horn, stretched back to Laura Edwards's neck; a light shone on her face, set with terror. Hands cuffed in front of her, Laura had no choice but to walk along behind the animal.

This was so much a movie scene that Susan simply gaped in disbelief. With a sense of unreality, she watched.

The trainer yelled. Then reality hit. She didn't know what to do. The horse quickened to a trot. Laura, cuffed hands grabbing the rope, staggered after him.

If Susan did the wrong thing, made a wrong decision, Laura would be strangled. Almost anything Susan did would be wrong. Yell, "Freeze! Police!" and the trainer might have the horse tear down the path and hit the road in a flat-out run. How long would Laura survive?

Think. Think.

Shoot the trainer? Unless she hit the target smack on and killed with one bullet—not a sure thing—the trainer could still yell and make the horse move to a gallop.

Oh, Jesus. How long could Laura stay on her feet?

Shoot the horse? A guarantee to spook him unless one bullet dropped him. Where would she have to put a bullet so he would fall in his tracks?

The brain? Horses had large bony skulls, and with the head

in constant motion, she wasn't sure she could hit the exact spot. Even a sharpshooter would have trouble and she wasn't a sharpshooter.

She didn't even consider what the gravel would do to Laura's vulnerable flesh. The pain would be agonizing. The horse trotted sedately. Laura kept on her feet. The trainer jogged alongside.

By going straight down, past the mansion, Susan might reach the road first.

She scrambled, hoping clopping hooves would camouflage any noise she made. She prayed nobody would come streaking up the road, sirens screaming, lights flashing. If the horse took off cross-country, he could bash Laura's head against a tree and split it like a watermelon.

Oh, Jesus.

When she reached the mansion grounds, the trees were thinner and there was no brush to snag her feet, but she had very little cover. If the trainer turned, she'd be seen.

On the path off to the left, the horse trotted along, its white stockings clear in the dusk. So far, Laura had managed to stay on her feet.

Thoughts and rebuttals zinged through Susan's mind. She had no plan. A movie hero would race out, grab the saddle horn, swing astride, and bring the horse to a stop.

The trainer ran up behind the horse, shouted, and clapped. He broke into a gallop. Laura took two or three staggering steps, then fell. The rope tightened around her neck. Her hands clung to it. The galloping horse dragged her.

NO!

Going downhill wasn't easier. Momentum carried Susan too fast to keep her balance. She slid on a pocket of wet leaves, caught herself, took a lurching step, and tripped.

She grabbed at a tree and scraped her hands, but got herself upright.

Oh, Jesus, Laura was being pulled over gravel with a rope around her neck. Hurry!

Susan scurried. The gathering dusk made it hard to see. She pounded along the side of the house, then plunged downhill.

Thick weeds waited to snag her ankles. She fought through them, fell, and tumbled down inside the ditch along the road. Scrambling for the other side, she grabbed at weeds to pull herself up.

On the road, the horse thundered past.

"Cut!" she yelled.

The horse—movie-trained animal that he was—slowed, stopped, looked around, then lowered his head to crop weeds at the edge of the road.

Thank God thank God thank God.

Moving easy, she approached him. He raised his head and eyed her, ears twitching.

"Okay, okay, let's be real careful. You're a good boy."

The horse stepped away.

"Don't do this to me. You don't want to be a killer."

He sidestepped. She stopped. He dropped his head and tore at the weeds. Moving up calmly, she grabbed his halter. He raised his head and chewed placidly.

The trainer had disappeared.

Osey, with White and Ellis right behind him, came running up the road.

"What were you waiting for?" she said. "The credits?"

With a pocketknife, Osey cut through the rope. Susan released the horse and knelt to tug at the section biting into Laura's throat. That famous beautiful face was cyanotic, the leather pants torn and bloody.

Susan pressed fingertips under the corner of Laura's jaw. The pulse was thready and fast, but it was there.

A motor roared. A black pickup with a roll bar jounced toward them, tires spinning in the gravel.

All hands grabbed Laura and dragged her out of the way.

The driver stomped the brakes. The truck fishtailed, the back end slid in the ditch on Susan's side of the road. She grabbed the side rail to keep from getting smashed. Her hands slipped, she struggled to hold on. As the truck bounced back on the road, it made a wide arc. Her legs swung out.

As the truck straightened, she hoisted herself over the rail and fell into the bed. She landed on an elbow; pain shot up her arm. Rolling toward the cab, she drew her gun, grabbed the roll bar with her injured arm.

"Police! Stop!"

The driver cut the steering wheel hard right, throwing Susan back. A left cut tossed her the other direction.

She hooked her arm around the roll bar. "Stop! You're under arrest!"

The driver twisted and fired. Susan crouched. The back window cracked into a weblike maze, a small round hole in the center. The truck swerved erratically back and forth.

Holding on to the roll bar, she smashed at the glass with the butt of her gun. "Stop the truck! Now!"

The truck roared off the road, hit the ditch, faltered, and then bucked and bounced up the other side. It slid sideways out of control down a rise. Susan hugged the roll bar. The truck slammed into a maple tree.

Susan was torn loose. Tree branches spun above as she tumbled over the tailgate. She landed hard on her left side, her gun went flying. Her vision wobbled, had black edges.

Scrambling to hands and knees, she scrabbled through leaves and vines for her gun. Just as she spotted it, two shots made her grab it and scuttle for a tree.

Breathing hard, she sat with her back against the tree trunk and rubbed an arm across her forehead. Jesus, what did she think she was doing? Making a movie?

Her left shoulder felt like sledgehammers had been at it. Served her right if something was broken. You're a cop, not a stuntwoman.

Crouching, she tried to catch a glimpse of movement through branches. Dusk had fallen, and it was too dark to see. Staying low, she eased from pine to ash moving toward the pickup. It sat in a small group of maples with open space all around and directly behind, fifty yards up a rise, the thick trees covered the hill.

She eyed the pickup.

"Get out of the truck!"

Silence. Rustle of tree leaves. Croak of frogs.

Pulling in air, she ran low for the passenger side and pressed her injured shoulder against the door. No sound but the hiss of the radiator and *ping-ping* of cooling metal. Slowly, she raised to look in.

Empty.

Through the driver's window she saw a dark shape streaking up the rise for the woods. Shit. Rounding the pickup, she charged uphill, running at an angle at her suspect, hoping like hell she wasn't going to be picked off like a rookie in a drug bust.

She plunged into the trees, stumbling through brush. A shadow of movement ahead on her right lured her that direction. A bullet bit into a tree at her shoulder. She dropped back, listened, heard thrashing through brush. She caught another glimpse, then the shadow disappeared.

Damn it.

She was making just as much noise, giving away her position. Her leg muscles screamed, her lungs felt on fire. A bullet nicked a tree a foot from her head. Ducking off at an angle, she strained to listen over her own heartbeat. She moved parallel with the shooter using trees to stay out of the way of bullets.

On the crest of the hill, trees stood black against the slate sky. Stars glittered. The moon was bright.

Movement slipped through moonlight. Susan ran, keeping her eyes on her suspect racing toward the mansion.

"Stop! Now!"

She put on a burst of speed. Lowering her shoulder, she rammed into the suspect with an explosive grunt. Her weight brought them both down hard, they skidded a few inches.

Lungs dragging at air that was too thin, she stuck her gun an inch from Clem Jones's throat. "It's a wrap," she said.

32

---

*Y*ou're late again." Susan, breathing hard, stood back and let Osey help a cuffed Clem Jones to her feet.

"Take her in." Susan's leg muscles were beginning to spasm.

"Yes, ma'am." He took Clem's elbow.

"Yancy?" Susan asked.

"Okay. He was locked in a stall with the security guy who was supposed to be taking care of the place."

And very embarrassed about it, she realized when she got back to the stable. The wide sliding door stood open and he waited like a recruit before the drill sergeant, standing in the large rectangle of light reaching out to the gravel path.

"You make a habit of getting yourself in trouble?" she asked.

"I sure hope not," he said fervently, and when he saw her face, added, "ma'am."

EMTs loaded a drugged security guard—a young college student with a summer job—into the ambulance. They pronounced him okay, only sleepy.

"Tell me what happened?" she said to Yancy as she drove them to the department.

He related his vague thoughts about the trailer's air-conditioning and not being able to locate Laura Edwards.

About the time he was talking with Laura's driver, Susan was learning from Justin Kiddering information that had her zeroed in on Clem Jones.

"You gave up another gun," she said.

"Yes, ma'am."

"How did you expect to get out of this one?"

He didn't say he hadn't expected to need getting out of anything, but she could see him thinking it.

"The mansion is kind of far. I figured it might be out of range. I borrowed the security guard's cell phone. It was in my pocket."

"Dispatch heard a gunshot."

"I punched nine-one-one and hoped they could hear what was going on. That was Clem convincing me she'd shoot Ms. Edwards."

"Why couldn't you mind your own business," Clem said sorrowfully to Yancy when he came into the interview room with Susan.

She was so ready to explain, it had taken some doing to stick Miranda in there before she started.

"For my mother," Clem said. Her fingers found the locket hanging on a chain around her neck and opened it. One side held a picture of herself. She indicated the other. "This is her." Blond hair, pretty oval face.

"At her funeral, I promised her Laura wouldn't get away with it."

The Laura Edwards's character in *Lethal Promise* had made a promise to a dead father. Susan wondered if that had affected Clem.

"Laura deserved to die." Bitterness curled the words up at the edges. "Lie in a coffin of dark shiny wood with satin pillows under her head. She killed my mother."

Clem twisted around to see if Yancy understood. "Your mother was at the barn."

He stiffened.

It was him she was explaining to, wanting him to understand. She'd refused to say anything at all unless he was present. Under different circumstances, she'd have been a young woman in love.

"I sawed partway through the railing and somehow I lost this." She touched the locket. "The clasp had broken. I was frantic, but it was right there lying on the straw. I grabbed it and kissed it and slipped it in my pocket. When I looked down your mother was watching. I wouldn't have hurt her."

Yancy gave her a stare of top-grade disbelief.

She blinked furiously as tears pooled in her eyes. Susan thought she was trying desperately to hold on, as though she'd reached the brink of some inner precipice.

"I got it fixed first thing," Clem said. "I wear it always. On the Patio that night before—before Sheri—I kissed it then too." Clem seemed mortified at the tears, and wanting some pride to cling to. Despair settled over her slumped shoulders along with an impotent anger that he was seeing both. "Your mother," Clem said to Yancy, "looked at me with the strangest look."

"What about your father?" Susan said.

"I don't have a father," Clem replied with porcupine reflexes. "He left us. She killed herself." Clem could barely say the words. Her hands clasped and reclasped, meshing her fingers together. "Hanged herself. I was eighteen."

Clem's throat worked. "She couldn't go on without him."

"Why did he leave her?"

Fierce hatred flashed in Clem's eyes. "To be with Laura. He thought she was going to marry him. Would you like to hear something funny? She never wanted to marry him. He was in love." Heavy sarcasm. "Everybody falls in love with Laura. He destroyed my mother and Laura didn't even love him back."

Clem leaned forward across the table. "And would you like

315

to hear something funnier? She didn't even know who I was and I have the very same name as my father."

The look she wore was defiant, tempered with toughness, a look of desperation trying to say, I can nail anybody's ass to the wall.

"What about Kay Bender?" Susan said.

"Kay was an accident. Laura was supposed to be up there. She never pays for what she does, somebody else always pays."

"And Sheri Lloyd?"

"She wouldn't let it alone. I told her and told her, but she was such a flake."

"Is that why you killed her?"

Clem shook her head impatiently. "She saw me come back from the barn. I said I was getting something for Fifer, but she kept threatening me. She wanted me to do things to Laura so Fifer would get mad at her. She babbled on about her astrologer. 'Help will be available from an unlikely source. The color pink is important.' "

Clem rubbed the heels of her palms over her eyes. "The idiot decided I was the help because of my hair color. It didn't even matter when I changed the color, she still—I was afraid she'd say something to somebody with brains and—"

Clem talked to her hands. "And get me caught before—" She looked at Susan. "I wanted Laura to die like my mother."

In her dream, Laura could see Clem's vicious, white face, eyes ringed with black. *You didn't care* . . . The voice was eerie with echoing menace. She wanted to scream, to beg. Hands tied. Rope on her throat squeezing. She trembled, felt herself falling, spinning in black pain. Helpless. Choking.

She jerked awake. The hospital gown felt clammy. She stared up at the tile ceiling, took a breath, working through terror, remembering. She was safe, in a cool white hospital room.

She remembered images, a muscular man with dark curls asking questions and giving orders. Nurses with soft voices. *Take a deep breath. Hold it.* Pain. Needles. Losing consciousness . . . Visions of Ben looking down at her. A dream?

Her mind felt fuzzy. She slept. How long? Hours? Days? Pain made its way through whatever she'd been given. Her head ached, her legs, arms, and stomach felt on fire. Bandages. She worried about her face.

Dr. Sheffield, of the muscles and curls, had been back— when?—and listened to her chest, looked at her throat, peered in her ears, shined lights in her eyes. He'd also checked dressings. Everywhere pain. Pain pain pain.

Resting a hip against the bed, he crossed his arms. "Contusions and abrasions. You're going to feel it for some time. Infection is something that needs to be watched for. But you're going to be fine."

"My face?" She was almost afraid to ask.

He smiled. "Just as beautiful as ever. A scratch or two. Nothing. You're very lucky. If you hadn't grabbed the rope like you did—" She listened in horror at him drop grizzly comments. ". . . dislocate the neck between first and second vertebrae . . . fracture of odontoid process . . . sever spinal chord . . . medulla oblongata . . . outright decapitation.

"The leather helped," he said. "It isn't for show that motorcyclists cover themselves in it."

On those words of information, he strode off and she could imagine him leather-clad and straddling a noisy aggressive machine.

She hadn't been trying to save her life so much as save her face. Pain the length of her body and in her arms had removed even that desire. It had wiped out all thought except how much she hurt.

Tears ran down her face. Everything, it seemed, made her cry. Covered in bandages. *Now Laura May,* she heard her father's voice, *you always do exaggerate.* She reached for a tissue and blew her nose. Why couldn't she cry like she did in films. Tears glistening, a trickle down a cheek. Blah, nose running all over the place.

She was an actress, her face was her biggest asset. With it

damaged permanently, what kind of roles would she get? Her whole life, everyone she knew, everything she did, work, play, revolved around movies. What would happen if she lost it? She wouldn't have a life. She wouldn't get a roomful of flowers; nobody would care she was almost killed.

And balloons, and cards. Nick had sent a bouquet of red roses.

She mopped her face and blew. Mopped and blew. To stop all this, she groped for the remote control, clicked on the wall-mounted television, and surfed through channels. The runaway stagecoach with a cowboy hanging between galloping horses plunged her slipping and tumbling down a long black tunnel. She punched the control.

"... and now our top news story from Bob Randall in Hampstead, Kansas. Bob?"

"It's an incredible story, Jerry. Here in the quiet little town of Hampstead, Kansas, in the middle of wheat fields, actress Laura Edwards came to make a movie. What happened was even more dramatic than the story she was filming. It had everything: suspense, terror, misdirection, a cliff-hanger ending. Even a runaway horse."

Cut to visual of horse looking noble, deigning to accept an equine nugget.

Jerry: "He'll probably be approached with movie offers." Chuckle. "Maybe even a television series. I hope he has a good agent." Serious. "I understand there is a suspect in custody. Can you tell us anything about that, Bob?"

"There is a suspect, Jerry. The police are not releasing any information about him yet."

"Thanks, Bob. And now we take you to the press conference videotaped earlier."

Cut to: conference room. SRO. Chief Wren at a podium, cool and poised. On her right, looking handsome and heroic, Officer Yancy. On her left, looking important, the mayor.

In a dry voice, the chief related the events of Laura's harrowing ordeal. A little expression wouldn't have hurt any, Laura thought irritably. For all the emotion this woman was putting out, Laura might have stumbled stepping off the curb.

Chief Wren fielded questions, refusing to answer most, not even giving out the suspect's name "while the case is still active."

"What about the stalker?"

"Is he involved?"

"I can't comment on that at this time."

"Is it true the suspect you have in custody is a member of the film crew?"

"No comment at this time."

"How badly was Ms. Edwards hurt?"

"I'm not a physician, I can't answer that."

"Will she be able to finish this movie?"

"Is she expected to recover fully?"

Laura thought Fifer must be gloating. He'd see that information and innuendo got spread around, truths and falsehoods and anything else he could throw in. All that free publicity. Star threatened by deranged crew member. There might even be front-page headlines.

"Is it true you personally captured the suspect after a dramatic chase that rivals a movie climax?"

Dry, level voice. "The suspect in custody was brought in through the combined efforts of the officers of the Hampstead police department." Chief Wren stepped down, cameras flashed, motors whirred, mikes were thrust at her. Laura clicked off the TV.

"Terrible performance."

"You could have done better?" Startled, she turned her head. Ben stood in the doorway, looking tight and invulnerable.

"Oh, Ben—" She held out her arms and hugged him awkwardly. Tears started again and for once in her life she didn't want to cry.

"How are you?" he asked.

"Which reply do you want? The one Fifer will give the investors or the real one? 'Ms. Edwards is doing great. A few scratches and a bruise or two. She's shaken up, but she's a great lady and she'll be back at work tomorrow.' "

He sat on the edge of the bed.

"I didn't know I could hurt in so many places at the same time." Damn it, would she ever stop crying.

He lifted her chin with a knuckle and tipped her head to one side, then the other. "You look in good shape for someone who got involved with a runaway horse."

"You wouldn't lie to me, would you, Ben?"

"Have I ever?" He handed her a tissue.

"No, you haven't." She blotted her face. "It's so upsetting to think someone could hate me that much. Clem Jones? I hardly know who she is—" Laura examined his face, trying to see behind his shuttered exterior. "You going to tell me that's why she hated me? I'm so self-centered, I don't see anybody else?"

He smiled.

Tears again. He looked so damn good when he smiled. "You're really arrogant. You know that?"

"So you always told me."

True. He wrapped himself up in so many macho defenses, his armor clanked when he walked. She didn't know that when they were married; she was a lot smarter now. "Do you hate me, Ben?"

"No."

"Did you ever?"

"Maybe. When you left. It's been a long time."

"I was so scared," she said in a small voice. "The rope kept getting tighter and tighter. I couldn't breathe—"

He ran a hand gently down her cheek. "Hey, you came through with barely a scratch."

She pressed her face against his throat and cried. He stroked her hair and murmured, "It's okay, Laurie. It's okay." She heard his heart beat.

He tipped her chin up and she looked into eyes that were softer and, for the first time that she could remember, understanding.

"Are you happy, Ben?"

"Happy?"

"Content, fulfilled, ready to spend the rest of your life here?"

"It's Californians who talk about contentment and fulfillment. In Kansas we talk about humidity and whether it's going to rain."

She put a finger on his mouth to stop him talking. "Twelve more days of filming here. Assuming there are no more interruptions like murder, kidnapping, and—is there anything else?"

"Assault with intent to kill, reckless endangerment—"

She kissed him, sweetly, with promise. "After the filming, do you think you could change your mind and we could go somewhere? You and me? Please?"

3 3

It was just dusk. From the kitchen window, Yancy watched the bats swoop and arc against the gray sky as they left their houses for the evening hunt.

"What is all this?" Serena said warily as he poured coffee into mugs and asked her to sit down.

"Come on. Don't be so suspicious." He cut two pieces of the apple pie he'd bought on the way over, slid them to plates, and pushed one across the table to her.

"You're trying to soften me up for something, Peter. I know you." Her joking tone didn't hide the hint of exasperation underneath. "That stuff may work with Mom, but—" She forked off the end of the pie and stuck it in her mouth. "Uh-huh, good. We better eat before we fight." She took another bite. "We are going to fight, aren't we?"

He sipped coffee. "I have a plan."

She started to say something.

"Wait. Mrs. Evanosky's husband died."

"Who's Mrs. Evanosky?"

"I met her at the hospital. She was trying to survive the vigil of his death."

"So?"

"She has no money."

"Ah."

"You see where I'm going with this?"

"We couldn't afford her."

"We could afford something, and she could live here."

Serena eyed him with her head tilted to one side. "Have you talked with Mom about this?"

"I wanted to run it by you first."

"You think she'll like it?"

"She feels guilty about you, Serena. Like she's depriving you of a life."

Tears came to her eyes. "I know. I love her, Peter, and sometimes I want—and then I'd like—and—"

"Hey—"

"I feel like such a terrible person. And I've been yelling at you and—"

"Serena," he said softly. "Don't get in a knot. You're entitled to a life. It's just that sometimes I forget. This might work."

. . . and all in the name of love.

"Storm's coming," the waitress said as she refilled Susan's coffee mug. "Electricity in the air."

Words of prophecy. She'd barely spoken when the café lights dimmed, then brightened again. Thunder rumbled. In the blink of an eye, rain washed down the windowpane.

A rainy evening for musing over the vagaries of life. Writing to Justin Kiddering had her wondering what might have been. If they had married, if they had opened their own law firm. Two or three children and a divorce? Certainly not a seat in the last booth of a coffee shop in Kansas.

Clem loved her mother who loved her father who loved Laura Edwards who loved . . . And that was the house that Jack built.

They've all returned to Hollywood. Maybe now those of us out here on the prairie can go back to our buckskins and buckboards. Nothing at all pertaining to the subject at hand, but did you know that Daniel Boone never wore a coonskin hat? An entire country believes he did. Just shows the power of Hollywood.

We had it. That power, I mean. It swept through town like the plague. Infected my department. Would you believe even I wasn't immune? True, I'm sorry to say.

All these good solid folks behaving like they were in a movie. I stayed cool until the last reel, then the fever seized me.

I had one officer stabbed. Inexperienced, trusting. He's not as much of either anymore. Although he was on the right track. I called Sophie the cat lady who makes pumpkin bread. Clove is one of the ingredients. No wonder he thought of pumpkin bread when he was stabbed, Delmar constantly ate clove Life Savers.

I think the officer was on the way to being in love with Clem. She loved him, that I do know. He's the hero type. You know, rescue the damsel from the burning tower. One thing, he'd never seen anything like her before.

Another officer—well, I'm not sure what happened to him. Stabbed in the heart maybe. Not literally, of course.

Rumors are rife through the department that he will pack up and take of with Ms. Edwards. His status has never been higher in the eyes of the male officers. If he'll get over it, I have no clue.

Somebody slid into the booth across from her. She felt that electricity in the air and raised her head.

Parkhurst, slightly damp around the edges. Putting down her pen, she leaned back. "Weren't you invited to the promised land?"

He half-smiled. "Sharks stay in familiar waters."